Catherine Cookson was born in Tyne Dock, the illegitimate daughter of a poverty-stricken woman, Kate, whom she believed to be her olde[...] in service but eventually moved sou[...] and married Tom Cookson[...] the age of forty she bega[...] working-class people with wh[...] of her birth as the background [...]

Although originally acclaimed as a regional writer – her novel *The Round Tower* won the Winifred Holtby award for the best regional novel of 1968 – her readership soon began to spread throughout the world. Her novels have been translated into more than a dozen languages and more than 50,000,000 copies of her books have been sold in Corgi alone. Many of her novels have been made into successful television dramas, and more are planned.

Catherine Cookson's many bestselling novels established her as one of the most popular of contemporary women novelists. After receiving an OBE in 1985, Catherine Cookson was created a Dame of the British Empire in 1993. She was appointed an Honorary Fellow of St Hilda's College, Oxford in 1997. For many years she lived near Newcastle-upon-Tyne. She died shortly before her ninety-second birthday in June 1998 having completed 104 works, nine of which are being published posthumously.

'Catherine Cookson's novels are about hardship, the intractability of life and individuals, the struggle first to survive and next to make sense of one's survival. Humour, toughness, resolution and generosity are Cookson virtues, in a world which she often depicts as cold and violent. Her novels are weighted and driven by her own early experiences of illegitimacy and poverty. This is what gives them power. In the specialised world of women's popular fiction, Cookson has created her own territory'
Helen Dunmore, *The Times*

BOOKS BY CATHERINE COOKSON

NOVELS

Kate Hannigan
The Fifteen Streets
Colour Blind
Maggie Rowan
Rooney
The Menagerie
Slinky Jane
Fanny McBride
Fenwick Houses
Heritage of Folly
The Garment
The Fen Tiger
The Blind Miller
House of Men
Hannah Massey
The Long Corridor
The Unbaited Trap
Katie Mulholland
The Round Tower
The Nice Bloke
The Glass Virgin
The Invitation
The Dwelling Place
Feathers in the Fire
Pure as the Lily
The Mallen Streak
The Mallen Girl
The Mallen Litter
The Invisible Cord
The Gambling Man
The Tide of Life
The Slow Awakening
The Iron Façade
The Girl
The Cinder Path
Miss Martha Mary Crawford
The Man Who Cried
Tilly Trotter
Tilly Trotter Wed

Tilly Trotter Widowned
The Whip
Hamilton
The Black Velvet Gown
Goodbye Hamilton
A Dinner of Herbs
Harold
The Moth
Bill Bailey
The Parson's Daughter
Bill Bailey's Lot
The Cultured Handmaiden
Bill Bailey's Daughter
The Harrogate Secret
The Black Candle
The Wingless Bird
The Gillyvors
My Beloved Son
The Rag Nymph
The House of Women
The Maltese Angel
The Year of the Virgins
The Golden Straw
Justice is a Woman
The Tinker's Girl
A Ruthless Need
The Obsession
The Upstart
The Branded Man
The Bonny Dawn
The Bondage of Lowe
The Desert Crop
The Lady on My Left
The Solace of Sin
Riley
The Blind Years
The Thursday Friend
A House Divided
Kate Hannigan's Girl

THE MARY ANN STORIES

A Grand Man
The Lord and Mary Ann
The Devil and Mary Ann
Love and Mary Ann

Life and Mary Ann
Marriage and Mary Ann
Mary Ann's Angels
Mary Ann and Bill

FOR CHILDREN

Matty Doolin
Joe and the Gladiator
The Nipper
Rory's Fortune
Our John Willie

Mrs Flannagan's Trumpet
Go Tell It ot Mrs Golightly
Lanky Jones
Nancy Nutall and the Mongrel
Bill and the Mary Ann Shaughnessy

AUTOBIOGRAPHY

Our Kate
Catherine Cookson Country

Let Me Make Myself Plain
Plainer Still

THE BRANDED MAN

Catherine Cookson

CORGI BOOKS

PUBLISHER'S NOTE

Catherine Cookson has asked us to point out that the composition entitled 'Believe This' in PLAINER STILL, published by Bantam Press in 1995 and by Corgi Books in 1996, has been wrongly attributed to Minnie Aumonier. In fact, the author of 'Believe This' is unknown.

THE BRANDED MAN
A CORGI BOOK : 0 552 14348 0

Originally published in Great Britain by Bantam Press,
a division of Transworld Publishers

PRINTING HISTORY
Bantam Press edition published 1996
Corgi edition published 1997

3 5 7 9 10 8 6 4

Copyright © Catherine Cookson 1996

The right of Catherine Cookson to be identified as the author of this work has been asserted in accordance with section 77 and 78 of the Copyright Designs and Patents Act 1988.

Set in 10pt Garamond Book by
Phoenix Typesetting, Ilkley, West Yorkshire.

Corgi Books are published by Transworld Publishers,
61-63 Uxbridge Road, London W5 5SA,
a division of The Random House Group Ltd,
in Australia by Random House Australia (Pty) Ltd,
20 Alfred Street, Milsons Point, Sydney, NSW 2061, Australia,
in New Zealand by Random House New Zealand Ltd,
18 Poland Road, Glenfield, Auckland 10, New Zealand
and in South Africa by Random House (Pty) Ltd,
Endulini, 5a Jubilee Road, Parktown 2193, South Africa.

Printed and bound in Great Britain by
Cox & Wyman Ltd, Reading, Berkshire.

PART ONE

1

Marie Anne could not believe what her eyes were seeing. From where she stood in the deep shadow of the yew hedge, looking across the narrow sward to where the high summer moon illuminated the two figures leaning against the old willow tree, its ridged bark standing out as if it had been scoured by a penknife, she knew the woman to be her sister Evelyn. She not only knew her, she knew that she disliked her intensely and, too, that Evelyn returned the feeling twofold. And that man with her . . . that man. Oh! no. That was Roger Cranford. He was from The Grange; Mrs Cranford's second cousin, it was said. He had been abroad and was recuperating from a fever and he was so wonderful to look at and to listen to. She had looked at him and had spoken to him and he had been so nice to her. She had thought about him at nights. Oh yes, she had thought about him at nights. More so since last Saturday at the family picnic in The Grange grounds – he had touched her hair and said it was the colour of burnished brass. Evelyn had been there and he had hardly spoken to Evelyn, and yet . . . and yet – the words were ringing loud in her head – they had used her, both of them. Evelyn had told her mother it wasn't safe for her to wander beyond the grounds and by the river because there were gypsies settled in Farmer Harding's field.

On three occasions lately, while out with Evelyn, Roger Cranford had appeared; and once, after she had run to the wall to look over to where the gypsies were encamped, she recalled that when she returned they were standing quite close and laughing.

Her mouth now fell into a gape as she saw her sister's hands go out and cup the man's face. Then her own body jerked as he pulled Evelyn towards him and held her tightly. And when their faces merged she closed her eyes. She couldn't bear it. She couldn't. She couldn't. He had been so nice to her and Evelyn. Oh, how she hated and loathed Evelyn; Evelyn, whom their mother held up to her as a model of decorum.

When she opened her eyes again they were no longer standing against the tree but away from it, and Evelyn's head was strained back as if she were pushing away from him; but she was letting him handle her. Oh Lord! Lord! She couldn't bear it, she couldn't. What should she do? Jump out on them? . . . He . . . he mustn't do that! It was bad, bad: he had his hands inside her summer blouse, which was wide open. She again closed her eyes and now she gripped handfuls of the yew hedge until the crushed leaves stung her palm. She must get away, run back home and tell somebody.

Don't be silly. Don't be silly. This was the feeling that often checked her wild running, especially when she was tired and she still had the urge to rush here and there. Only in The Little Manor, close by, where her grandfather lived, was she allowed uninhibited freedom.

When she next opened her eyes and again made out the pair of them, they were no longer on their feet, and what she witnessed next, but only for a minute or so, was the man without his underclothes and her sister's legs bare up to the thighs, and they were acting like the animals in the fields, like the dogs in the yard.

Picking up the front of her own dress, she turned and ran down the short yew walk into the wood.

She did not, however, make for the house gardens, but cut through a break in the boundary wall and over fields until she came to the river. Here, her first impulse was to plunge in and wash herself clean all over, although without looking at her body. She never wanted to look at her body again, ever, not ever. She stood gasping for air; there was a pain in her chest. Another thing she was certain of, she would never visit the tree-house patch again. At one time there had been a good house up in the branches, that was until Pat fell and broke his arm and Vincent had carried her up the ladder and from there pushed her along a branch. She was six years old then, and he was sixteen, and she always seemed to be wrestling with him. He would start by tickling her, then holding her down on the ground and staring into her face, and always he would call her a brat. But on that particular day she had screamed the wood down and her grandfather had ordered that the tree-house be demolished.

From then on, no-one except herself seemed to visit the small patch of sward and the lone tree. Whenever she went missing it would be assumed she was running wild round the grounds, whereas generally she could have been found sitting with her back against the tree and drawing odd-looking sketches of birds and animals.

Later, when she was sent away to Miss Taggart's school in Hexham, that period too ended with her running away. She hadn't actually run, she had simply caught a train and returned home.

Now they were about to send her away again, but they were still debating as to where. Her mother was for Aunt Martha's in London, there to continue her musical education, because one thing she was good at was playing the piano. From a small child she had picked out tunes without music.

She was about to sit down on the river bank when she was startled by a rustle in the undergrowth somewhere behind her. When she heard actual footsteps, then saw a tall figure slowly loom out of the scrub into a patch of

9

moonlight and move in her direction, she let out a cry that sounded like the squeal of a trapped animal as again she took to her heels and, head down, ran blindly on.

She was not aware that she had tripped, only of being hit on the head by something.

When she came up out of the blackness she did not immediately open her eyes. She was aware only that she was lying on the hard ground. When she attempted to move she groaned aloud from the pain in her foot, but it was when the weird face hung over her that she screamed; and when it spoke to her she sank into the blackness again.

The next thing of which she was conscious was being swung gently from side to side. It would have been a nice sensation, she told herself, if it wasn't for the pain in her head that had moved down to her foot . . .

It was near ten o'clock and the house was still astir when Robert Green, the footman-cum-valet, told Fanny Carter, the second housemaid, that he had been crossing the hall when the knock came on the front door; and that when he opened it there was no-one there. But there was a sheet of paper on the step. The drive seemed to be as bright as day, but he could see no-one; whoever had delivered the note had probably skidded into the bushes. 'Well, there was scribbling on the paper,' he said; 'but . . . well, I couldn't make it out in that light.' He didn't admit that he couldn't read. 'Mr Pickford,' he went on, 'was already in bed, it being his monthly day off, but nevertheless I had to wake him. He wasn't pleased. Well, he wouldn't be, would he? because he'd had a load on. He always does on his day off. Anyway he said he couldn't make out the writing. Well, he would say that, wouldn't he?'

'Yes, of course,' put in Fanny now, and she added pertly, 'I can tell you what you had to do next, Robert, and that was to go out and wake up Peter Crouch to read it. When you think of it, it's funny, you know, isn't it? that there's a yard man, the only one among us who can really read.'

'Well,' said Robert Green, 'that's only because he had it knocked into him in a home which was one step down from the workhouse, if you ask me.'

'Aye, I suppose so; and that's why you all try to take it out of him. But go on, tell me what happened next.'

'Well, he read the note and we couldn't believe it. It said: "Your daughter is lying injured under the wall near the river. She needs help."

Robert was afraid to take it in to the master,' he went on. 'We had to get Mrs Piggott to go quietly upstairs to find out which of the daughters was in. Miss Evelyn was undressing for bed, but Miss Marie Anne's room was empty. I thought the master would have a seizure. I did. I did. As for the mistress, I only heard her speak to him once. "This is final," she said; "something's going to be done this time, d'you hear? Not must be done, but *is* going to be." And I heard him say under his breath, "What about Father?" and her answer to this was, "Father or no Father she's going to be restrained."'

'Poor Miss Mary Anne.'

'You'd better watch out with your *Mary* Anne. You know what the mistress thinks about *Mary* Anne.'

'Yes, I do, and I know what I think about her.'

'Shut your mouth! You know what'll happen one day when it drops open too often.'

'Well, this isn't the end of the world, and if you had any sense you would know it.'

'And if you had any sense, miss, you would realise you won't get better anywhere else: food, togs, leave or anything else.'

'Leave? Talk about leave! One day a month and that starts about one o'clock and you must be back before dark. Don't talk to me about leave.'

He pushed her now, saying, 'Get yourself back into your quarters.'

For answer she snapped at him, 'Don't push me, Robert Green,' before turning and flouncing away.

He stood watching her for a moment the while shaking his head and wondering why he fancied her for, after all, she was only second housemaid and not likely to rise as long as Carrie Jones was about.

Mrs Lena Piggott, the housekeeper, was saying to Carrie Jones, 'Get yourself downstairs quick and tell Bill Winter the doctor wants splints.'

'Splints?' questioned Carrie.

'Yes, I said splints.'

'Well, what size, Mrs Piggot? There's splints of all sizes.'

'Well' – the housekeeper paused, her head bobbing all the while – 'tell him it's for a broken ankle. Get on with you, quick!'

Back in the bedroom, the bustling small body of the housekeeper changed to one of deferential submission as she stood by her mistress and whispered, 'It's being seen to, madam.'

Veronica Lawson made no reply. She was staring at the doctor as he hovered over her troublesome and nerve-aggravating daughter, and she demanded, though quietly now, 'What does she say?'

Doctor John Ridley straightened his back but did not take his eyes off the young girl in the bed as he answered the woman, saying tartly, 'I can't make it out,' yet at the same time he was wondering who it was this young girl thought was filthy, so filthy that she hated her. 'I hate you. You're filthy . . . filthy!' is what she was muttering.

'What is the matter with her . . . I mean, besides her ankle?'

He now turned fully towards the mistress of the house. He didn't like the woman. He was glad she wasn't his

12

patient. This had been an emergency call; he himself usually dealt with the old gentleman at The Little Manor at the far end of the grounds. He got on all right with him, an altogether different person from his son's family who peopled The Manor itself, although he understood the old gentleman was certainly the power behind the throne. 'She has concussion,' he said. 'There is a large lump on the side of her head. She will sleep on and off for the next two or three days, but she'll be in quite a lot of pain from her ankle. It will take some time to heal, and I would advise –' here he paused and looked straight into Mrs Lawson's eyes as he said, 'that she is troubled in no way, I mean that she should be left to rest.'

Veronica Lawson stared back at this young doctor and repeated to herself, Let her rest. Oh yes, she would let her rest. But she herself would be hard at work making arrangements for the bone of contention to be taken out of her life. It was odd, she admitted, that from the day the child was born she had disliked it, and that her dislike had grown with the years. What was more, she could claim that it had been well founded, for if ever there was a changeling in this world it was her daughter . . . her last daughter, her last child, one that was begot through a struggle. She had fought him off before, but never as she had done that night. To give him five live children and two miscarriages was enough payment for being mistress of his house, surely; but then he had to give her the sixth. After the twins went to Canada she had felt that part of the load had been taken from her back, because they too had been a rowdy couple, and if she had been left with only Vincent, Pat and Evelyn, life would have been tolerable. And, indeed, it had been tolerable for a time. Invitations to The Grange had become more frequent, and, of late, to The Hall itself. And these had raised her hopes for Evelyn's future.

Oh, what had gone wrong with Evelyn? It had started

when she was eighteen and had become enamoured of that poverty-stricken young lieutenant. She had put a stop to that. But now, at twenty-five, she was still unmarried. Then there was Vincent. Oh, Vincent was a law unto himself. She wondered if Vincent would ever marry. She hoped he would, because the line should go on. The old man was anxious for it; not that he liked Vincent. No. Only too plainly he showed his feelings with regard to Vincent. Now if it had been Pat . . . everybody seemed to like Pat; he had a way with him. She turned and looked at the white face on the pillow. To her it was a strange face. The features were all too large, the eyes, the mouth, even the nose. But the skin was creamy, yet not of the thick kind that would have made the face look heavy; it was more elfin perhaps, strangely elfin, brought about by the shape of the eye sockets. She would have lived outside, if that had been possible. She was never content in the house except, she must admit, when she was at the piano. And wasn't it strange that she was able to play as she did? Even when she got bad reports from the school, they would nevertheless state that she excelled in music. But then, perhaps the piano could be her own salvation if she could persuade Martha in London to take her, which was more than likely, she knew, because Martha would do anything for money.

What a relief her going would be, because no longer would she have to suffer her temper. Oh, that ferocious temper . . .

The doctor startled both the housekeeper and her mistress by first addressing the housekeeper, saying, 'Did you send for those splints? I only require short pieces of wood, not a tree.' Then to Veronica Lawson, and in much the same tone, he said, 'Will you please fetch your husband? I shall need his assistance!'

Whatever answer Veronica Lawson was about to give was checked by a short fit of coughing caused by the

14

warning inside her, which told her not to bandy words with this man, but to make a complaint to Doctor Sutton-Moore about him. In her opinion he was no fit man to be a doctor: apart from lacking in respect towards her, his voice was coarse. He was coarse altogether, with not a single trait of a gentleman about him . . .

James Lawson and the splints arrived almost simultaneously in the bedroom.

As the young doctor examined the flat pieces of wood he did not seem to be listening to the terse tones of the master of the house as he demanded to know why he was needed, yet the answer came firmly and was accompanied by a straight look into the overfed face of James Lawson, 'I am going to give her a drop of chloroform and I'll need help,' said young John Ridley.

'Chloroform? Why chloroform? I thought these splints were for a sprained ankle.'

'Then if you thought that, sir, you've been misinformed. What your daughter is suffering from is a Pott's fracture.'

'A what?' James Lawson's face was screwed up and he repeated, 'A what?'

'I said it is what is known as a Pott's fracture. To put it plainly, it is a very bad break and, as you can imagine, it will be most painful for her when I try to manipulate the bones into place. And by the way' – he now turned to the housekeeper – 'I haven't enough bandages with me. Tear up some linen into two-inch-wide pieces and do it quickly, please.'

James Lawson stared at this young prig of a doctor: who did he think he was talking to, throwing his orders about? Veronica had been right about him: he didn't know his place; and now when he almost barked at his house-keeper as she was about to leave the room, 'Use fresh linen from the bales in the sewing room,' he decided that it was he who should give orders in this house, and be

15

seen giving them. Then making an obeisance with his head towards John Ridley, he said, 'Well! What are you waiting for? Let's get on with it.'

It was a good half hour later when the young doctor stood washing his hands in a bowl of warm water that stood on the wash-hand stand in the corner of the room.

Patrick Lawson was sitting by the head of the bed and gently stroking the limp white hand of his sister where it lay on the top of the eiderdown, while he stared at what to him was a beautiful face, a child-like angelic face. Even so he knew that her character held little of the suggested qualities, for he was aware she was an imp at heart. And he smiled to himself as he thought, that's all she is, an impish young girl. Why can't they see her like that? He turned to the doctor, who was now putting on his coat, for he was saying, 'I've left some laudanum drops there,' and he pointed to a bottle on the side table. 'She'll be in a great deal of pain when she wakes, which won't be until early in the morning, but nevertheless she will need something. Who will be attending her?'

'Oh' – Pat shook his head – 'I don't know as yet, but one of the maids, probably,' and he looked more intently at the young man, who was now picking up his bag as he said, 'Yes, surely.'

It was as if there were doubt in his words that his sister would be seen to, and so he was quick to reassure the young doctor by adding, 'There are plenty of servants in the house. There'll be someone with her night and day.'

'You'll see to it?'

'No.' Pat's tone was high now and a bit stiff. 'The house-keeper will. She'll take her orders from my parents. What makes you think she'll lack the attendance?'

'Nothing. Nothing. Only I wanted to make sure. Anyway, I'll be round some time in the morning. Good-night to you.'

16

'Good-night.' Pat's tone had been curt, and he now stared towards the closed door as he thought, he was actually intimating that she would be left unattended. What had given him that idea? Oh, well. He again looked towards the face on the pillow. If his mother had been on her high horse and his father not far behind, they certainly wouldn't have given that young man the impression of parental care. Likely that was it.

When the door opened again, there stood his mother, and she did not speak in a lowered voice as she said, 'You're late in getting back. The trap was sent to the station over an hour ago.'

'There was a hold-up on the line, Mother. The train was late getting in.'

She now walked to the foot of the bed, and her hand gripped the brass knob as she looked up the bed towards her daughter, saying, 'Nice kettle of fish. Another escapade. They've got to stop.' Then, without hesitating, she said to her son, 'How did things go in London?'

'Very well, both with business and socially.'

'Socially? What d'you mean, socially?'

'Just what I say, Mother. I was invited to a garden party at Lord Dilly's; then to a house dance at the Admiral's.'

'Oh.'

'Yes, oh, Mother. I thought about you on both occasions: you'd have been very impressed.'

Her momentary relaxed countenance stiffened again as she said, 'Are you trying to be nasty?'

'I had no intention of being nasty, Mother, but I know how you like these affairs, what stock you set by them; if Evelyn had been there you would've been planning wedding bells. As it was—' he smiled now as he added, 'I could hear them for myself, but they came from so many quarters it was difficult to choose.'

His mother turned from the bed, saying, 'You always had a humble opinion of yourself, Patrick,' and she almost added, And you're getting more like your grandfather every day, which, she hoped, did not augur that she would grow to dislike him too.

'Who's going to look after her?' Pat said.

'What d'you mean?'

'Just what I say, Mother. That young doctor challenged me with the same question that I'm putting to you: who's going to look after her?'

'That young man doesn't know his place. I'm going to report him.'

Pat gave a short laugh now as he said, 'From what I gathered of his personality, that'll be like water off a duck's back to him. Anyway, who are you allotting to her?'

He watched her thinking for a moment, and then she said, 'She won't need anyone at nights, she'll be asleep. I'll inform Mrs Piggot to let the second housemaid, Fanny Carter, take over during the day. That's for the time she'll be in bed.'

'Well, that'll be some time, don't you think?'

'What d'you mean, some time?'

'Well, that doctor said it would be a three-month job.'

'What!' The exclamation was so loud he hissed a warning at her, saying, 'Quiet! Mother. You could waken her, and she'll be in a great deal of pain.' He pointed to a table: 'He's left laudanum for her. Didn't you see him before he left?'

'No, I didn't; and I haven't any wish to see him again.'

He now watched her grip the brass rail of the bed with both hands as she repeated, 'Three months! Three months!'

He said sharply, 'How often should she need those drops?' and nodded to the table.

'I don't know, but Mrs Piggot will know. I understand he spoke to her before he left.'

'By the way,' Pat said, 'where's Evelyn in all this? She

18

should be the one sitting with her.'

'Don't be silly, Pat. You know they spark off each other like tinder. The greater the distance between them the better it is for them both. It always has been that way, you know that.'

'I don't know it, not as you mean it; I only know that Evelyn is ten years older than this child here and in a way has brayed her back as much as you have, Mother.'

'Patrick! How dare you! How dare you say that to me!' The words had come out on a hissed whisper, and now making swiftly for the door, she said, 'I'll talk to your father about your attitude.'

'Oh, don't be silly, Mother. You talk as if you were dealing with a boy. I'm a man and twenty-six years old. Don't forget it, Mother.' And now he moved closer to her and his words were low but definite: 'And remember this: Grandfather still rules the roost here. Father may act as the head of the family firm with Vincent playing the great I am, and then comes me, but I'm the one who keeps that business going, because neither of them have ever conducted one business meeting successfully. They don't know how to handle the staff, never mind competitors. I've wanted to say that for a long time, and this is' – he looked towards the bed now – 'a most awful place to come clean, but there you have it. In future, Mother, remember my age. And now you can go and tell Father, and Vincent too, exactly what I have said, and if they deny it, I'll let them go on the next assignment and see what happens. It's happened before, hasn't it? The trouble with this house, Mother, is that its main purpose is prestige. You and Vincent are breaking your necks every minute of the day to keep it up. And for what? . . . One last thing I'll say, and I'm sorry I have to say this to you: remember that Grandfather isn't dead yet and he's a man capable of making changes. Big changes. Changes that would rock this God-appointed house to its foundations.'

When he turned from her and went to the bed again, she did not move. One hand was clutching the front of her dress, the other was across the lower part of her face and gripping her jaw as if to stop it trembling. As she stared at the back of this handsome son she knew that at this moment she hated him much more than she did her father-in-law, because her father-in-law had never spoken openly to her in this manner. He might have indicated what he thought by loud asides, but not even he had ever probed the core of her before. She almost staggered from the room.

At nine o'clock the next morning Emanuel Latvig Lawson actually burst into Marie Anne's bedroom, only to stop short at the sight of her deadly pale face with the tears streaming down it and her breath coming in gasps as she made an effort to speak to him, saying, 'Oh! Grandpa. Grandpa.'

When he put his arms about her shoulders in order to comfort her he was checked when she let out a high scream.

'She's in great pain, sir.'

He looked across the bed at Fanny Carter and said, 'Has the doctor been?'

'Not this morning, but he's coming later, sir. He was here till late. It's in splints.' She pointed to where a stool had been placed in the bed to keep the clothes off the injured leg, and she added, 'That isn't much good, sir. She should have a wire cage.'

'Yes. Yes, girl, yes. It'll be done. But my pet . . . oh! my pet.' He was stroking the wet face now. 'The things that happen to you. What caused this? They should have let me know last night.'

'No, Grandpa; no. I fell. I was running. I was frightened. I saw someone. I thought they were coming at me and I ran and fell.'

'But you were right down near the river against the wall.'

'Yes. Yes. And I was so frightened, Grandpa; I . . . I must have dreamt there was an ogre after me.'

'An ogre?'

'Yes, because when I recovered from bumping my head I saw this face. It was an ogre's face. But I must have imagined it. They say I've got concussion. What is that, Grandpa?'

'Oh, it just means you've got to lie quiet for a day or two. It's caused by having a bump on the head. But you're not bleeding.' He ran his fingers through the back of her hair and gently stroked her scalp, then repeated, 'No, you're not bleeding.'

'Grandpa.'

'Yes, my child? Yes?'

'It's awful – the pain. I . . . I can't help crying and they say it'll make me stay in bed for a long time. I'll die, Grandpa. I'll die.'

'No, you won't, my dear. No, you won't. I'll be with you as much as I can, and this nice girl will be with you too. Won't you, my dear?'

Fanny hesitated for a moment before answering: she had been pleasantly shocked by being addressed as 'my dear' by the old master, who was known to be a tyrant. 'I could look after her, sir; I looked after my mother for years. She had dropsy. And . . . and may I speak, sir?'

'Yes, girl, go on.'

'Well, they were talking about getting a nurse, but I could nurse her, because I nursed my mother and I was very young then and she was in bed with dropsy for a long time, and there was only me to see to her. You see, my father and the two lads were down the pit and they got killed. There was one other boy, but he died at home, and I saw to her for years before I came here, so I could nurse miss quite well, sir. Yes, I could.'

21

Fanny's tragic little story told with lightness had stopped Marie Anne's flow of tears. She said between gasps, 'Oh! you poor thing, Fanny. You poor thing.'

'Oh no, miss' – Fanny was smiling broadly now – 'that's all in the past, anyway. I'm glad to be where I am and –' She glanced at the old man as if about to speak, but simply added, 'I'll look after you.'

'There now. There now, my pet. Isn't that good news? You not only have a nurse, you have a storyteller too, one who can compile her life's tragedies into a story. That is an art.'

Fanny didn't know exactly what the old gentleman meant, but she knew it was a compliment. She smiled at him and, tactfully now, she said, 'I'll leave you, sir, for the present. I'll just be in the next room. You can call me if you need me.'

'I'll do that, girl. I'll do that. Thank you.' He nodded, smiling towards her, and when the door had closed on her he looked down at his grand-daughter and said, 'Now there, my dear, is what I would call a non-servant; a servant who could become a good friend, when one is in need.'

'Yes, Grandpa. I've always liked Fanny. She's always been nice to me. But oh, Grandpa, I feel so bad now, sort of ill, and I'm frightened. They say I've got to be here for weeks. I'll die. Yes, I will.'

'Now, stop that. You won't die, and when you're able and get a bit stronger we'll have you out on the long cane chair and pushed through the grounds. You'd like that, wouldn't you?'

She made an effort to smile as she said, 'No, Grandpa; I'd hate it. You know what I'm like when I get into the grounds; I can't walk; I must run.'

'Yes, my dear; you must run. Now why must you always run? This is when the trouble starts. You must run. Anything that happens and you don't like it you run. Are

22

you running away from something?'

She thought a moment, then sniffed loudly as she said, 'I suppose so, Grandpa. I . . . I run because I want to get away from people, people who don't like me.'

'Oh now, now! That's silly . . . to say people don't like you. Everybody—'

'Please! Grandpa, don't. You know and I know – well, we've talked about it, haven't we? – that everybody can't be liked by everybody, or something like that.'

His hand was again on her hair stroking it from her brow, and he said gently, 'Yes, you are right. I yammer on at you as if you were a silly child, and you're not. You're a very wise young girl. But can you tell me why you were running at that time of night as far away as the river bank and Harding's wall?'

She turned her gaze from him now and looked down the bed to where the bedclothes rose to a peak, and her voice was a low mutter as she said, 'No, Grandpa.'

'No? But something made you run that far. Did something make you run right down there?'

'Yes, Grandpa.' It was another whisper.

'And you can't tell me what it was? Answer me one thing. Does it concern someone in this household?'

She hesitated before she said, 'Yes, Grandpa.'

He wanted to ask: a man? or a woman? but there was only one woman who would be outside at night, perhaps taking a stroll, and that would be Evelyn, and she certainly wasn't a girl for taking strolls, not Evelyn. She would get her feet dirty. Perhaps one of the servants? But she wouldn't be so secretive about what had happened, he was sure, if it had been just one of the servants. Could it have been Vincent? He'd had to put a stop to that young man's horseplay many years ago, when he had detected something in it and behind it that both angered and shocked him. It could have been Vincent. But from what he understood, he'd had his friend Harry Stocksfield here last night and they had played tennis earlier in the evening, then a game of billiards. Well, there was no doubt but that he would get to the bottom of it one day, for he had been her confidant since she could crawl onto his knees, seeking love, perhaps to counteract the hate her mother bore her. He had loved her and petted her for all her young life. But why had he imagined that Veronica hated her own daughter? Perhaps that was too strong a word; 'disliked' would have been more fitting – at least, he hoped so. Yet dislike was a first cousin to hate. The awful thing about it was that the child must have recognised the feeling when her mother first pushed her away from her knee. He himself had witnessed it, and it hadn't been a gentle push, but a thrust that had knocked the three-year-old child on to her bottom and made her cry.

She was crying again now, and he took his large silk handkerchief from his breast pocket and gently dried her tears; while doing so he received the answer to the question that he had imagined would take him a long time to discover. It came when he said, 'Has Evelyn been in to see—?' but did not manage to get out 'you?' before her whole body jerked and she let out a cry of pain, exclaiming loudly, 'No! and I don't want to see her. No!'

'All right, my dear. All right. If you don't want to see her, you won't.'

Ah! Evelyn. Evelyn. And out at night. Now why would she have been out at night, and what could she have done to cause this young sprite to run so fast that she went headlong into a wall? Well, well. Here was something that he would ferret out, but quietly. Yes, very quietly. Who was Evelyn seeing now? Since that business some years ago, when she was breaking her neck to be married and her mother put a stop to it, she'd had one or two men in her sights, but each had come to nothing. She had a very off-putting manner: played the grand dame too much, very like her mother. Oh yes, a strong pattern of her mother. As was Vincent, only more so. The three of them, he would say, formed a close triangle both in personality and ambition. But what about his own son, their father? Oh, he'd had to admit a long time ago that he had bred a man full of pomp and no guts. Yet, through him, Pat had come into existence and Pat was as near himself as you could ever hope any man to be. And then there was this little sprite. The unwanted one, the changeling. She was like himself, in both the values she held and her temper. Her temper, like his own, came in spurts, reached ignition point and set the sparks flying. And her values? Well, she had shown she possessed a few of his: she liked fair play, for both animals and men. This she had shown when she horsewhipped Simon Pinner for beating one of the dogs. The dog's sin had been to rake up a whole row of freshly set seeds and Pinner had brought a whip across its hind quarters, making it yelp. So what had she done? Run into the tack room, got another whip and, as it wouldn't have been much use bringing it across the fellow's legs, because he had gaiters and corduroy trousers on, she aimed for his arms where his sleeves were rolled up to the elbow, and he knew about it. He had complained to the house and she had been put on a meagre diet and kept in her room for three days. She had divided the staff fifty-fifty. Then there was Peter Crouch and the horse trough. The voting that time had been ninety in her favour, for Crouch was known to have a hard hand with the horses, especially when breaking one in. On this day, in the yard, she had seen him use a whip on a horse's hindquarters and bring the animal on to its hind legs in protest. The horse had protested and neighed loudly when pulled past the horse trough and was not allowed to drink, so she had yelled at the man. Unfortunately, he had turned towards her with his back towards the trough, and what was easier than to make a rush at him and topple him

25

backwards into it? They had said in the yard that even the horse laughed, but this time it was a black mark against her and she was sent away to school. That had been when the real trouble started. How many times had she run away? and how many times had he secretly welcomed her back? He supposed that at bottom he was to blame for a lot of her unruliness, because she could always come to him and find understanding and sympathy. He said now, 'Is it paining badly, dear?'

'Awful, Grandpa. Awful. I've never had pains like this before, never.'

'Well, that doctor should be here soon and he will give you some medicine to ease the pain. In the meantime, shall I read to you?'

'No, Grandpa.'

'No?'

'No. Just sit with me and hold my hand.'

'I'll do that gladly, dear. I'll do that.'

'I . . . I still feel sleepy. I . . . I might go off to sleep, mind.'

'Well, that would be the best thing, my dear. I'll hold your hand until you do go off to sleep and I'll tell you a funny story that I read the other day. It's about a kangaroo that lost its jump and it had a baby in its pouch, you know, like we've seen in the picture books. Well, the baby had to teach its mother how to jump again. Now you go to sleep and I'll tell you how it began and how it ended.'

And he did, and she went to sleep. All the while he was making up the story about the kangaroo learning to jump, part of his mind was asking, What would Evelyn be doing outside at that time of night? And what had she done that had frightened this child?

2

Ten days later Marie Anne was sitting propped up in bed. Fanny had just removed her breakfast tray and she remarked, 'By! you look better this morning, miss. More like your old self. Has the pain gone down?'

'Yes, Fanny. Oh yes, it's lessened. That's as long as I don't move my leg.' She smiled at the girl, saying, 'You must have got tired of my screaming, but I couldn't help it.'

'Of course not, miss. I bet I'd have beat you at screaming if I'd been in your place. Oh, I would. Oh' – she straightened the bib of her dress as the door opened – 'here's Master Patrick.'

'Good morning, Fanny.'

'Good morning, sir.'

'How's the patient?' He had purposely not looked at Marie Anne, but went on, 'Has she been behaving herself?'

'Oh yes. She's been very good, very good indeed.'

Pat then turned a laughing face on Marie Anne, saying, 'What d'you think of that? Very good indeed. That's the first time I've ever heard anybody say you were very good indeed. Anyway, how goes it?'

'Oh, I feel better, Pat. My head no longer aches and it's stopped being muzzy, so I'm going to do some drawing today.'

'Good for you.'

'Fanny was going to slip up and get my diary and drawing box from the cupboard in the schoolroom.'

27

'Will I go now, miss?'

'If you would, please, Fanny.'

'Yes. Yes, I'll do that.'

When they had the room to themselves Marie Anne said excitedly, 'Sit down a minute, Pat. Well . . . I mean, have you got time? I want to hear about the new ship leaving.'

'Oh, you mean the new second-hand one.'

'Is she going out today?'

'Yes, on the three o'clock tide.'

'And she's called *Annabella*?'

'Yes, she's called *Annabella*. And between you and me she looks a picture.'

'What cargo are you sending out?'

'Oh, very little cargo this time. Just bales of linen and lace and stuff that she'll drop off at the islands. It's the live cargo she's taking out and, I hope, she'll bring back that is important.'

'Yes' – she nodded at him – 'the guests. It must be wonderful for them.'

'Well, it is as long as the ship's at the quay. What bothers me is if they hit a storm, for three of the couples have never been to sea before. All I can say about them is poor souls, because I myself have experienced seasickness and prayed to die.'

'Grandpa said it was your idea. He was very funny about it. He says it's a cargo you haven't got to shovel in and it pays you for giving it a rough time. Are they coming back with you? I mean, are they going to make the round voyage?'

'I hope so, dear. Yes I hope that they're all alive to do so.' He laughed gently now as he added, 'Oh, they'll be well looked after. Captain Armitage is a fine man and he has two equally good officers under him, and the crew are mostly old hands and have been with our firm for many years. One of them has been made a steward and

28

another an assistant cook-cum-waiter. It's been great fun arranging it all.'

'You like looking after the ships, don't you, Pat?'

'Yes, dear. But between you and me' – he leant close to her now – 'I should hate to have to go to sea.'

'Really?'

'Really. As I said, I'm always seasick; yet' – he wagged his head now – 'there's nothing I don't know about a ship. I seem to have spent the last seven years – and even before that during my holiday breaks from school, climbing perpendicular ladders, iron ones, mostly – checking the bilges; going over the engine room, the holds, the crew's quarters and, of course, not forgetting the Captain's quarters. Oh yes, one must see that the Captain's quarters has the best chairs, the thickest carpets, and a bunk that induces sleep.'

Marie Anne was laughing now as she said, 'What about the sailing ships? You still have one, haven't you? Have you been up the mast?'

'Oh, that isn't fair of you, Marie Anne, to mention the sailing ships and masts, because next you'll be asking if I have ever been in the crow's nest.'

'Yes' – she bounced her head at him and laughed out loud – 'that's just what I was going to ask.'

'Well' – he flapped his hand impatiently at her – 'you've got me there.'

'Not even when the ship was in harbour?'

'Not even when the ship was in harbour could I have attempted that. How those youngsters hang on to those masts when they're in rough seas, God alone knows. And I mean that when I say God alone knows, because it must be a terrible job, and there's some that take pride in it. Yet, I'm forgetting . . . good gracious I'm forgetting that Grandpa has been in the crow's nest, and at sea too. His own father sent him to sea for three years. Hasn't he told you about that?'

She shook her head.

'Well, his father told him – that's our great-grandfather – that if he wanted to make his living by ships then he should know how to sail them. However, three years was enough, but he certainly learned all right, because he doubled the business.' He could have added here, It must be a great disappointment to him now when his own son is being carried by the old hands of the firm.

When Fanny entered the room Marie Anne noticed she wasn't carrying the box and asked quickly, 'You couldn't find it? It was on the top shelf.'

'Yes. Yes, miss, I found it all right and I . . . I was bringing it downstairs when I met the mistress and she asked me what I had there, and I told her it was your diary and drawing-box, and she told me to take it back.'

Pat was on his feet now. 'Don't worry,' he said; 'I'll go and fetch it. Is it locked?'

'Yes, but the key is over there.' She pointed to the dressing-table. 'It's . . . it's in my handkerchief drawer, the little one at the top.'

As Fanny went towards the dressing-table Pat said, 'Don't bother, Fanny; I'll bring it down and she can unlock it herself. Anyway,' he turned and looked at Marie Anne, saying in a loud whisper, 'you wouldn't want me to read all your secrets, would you?' And she answered in an equally loud whisper, 'I wouldn't mind, not in the least, not you; and I'll tell you what: when you bring the box down I'll open it and let you into one of my secrets; in fact, my only secret.'

'You will? A secret in your box?'

'Yes. And it *is* a secret.'

'Something that you have done?'

'Yes, something I have done.'

'Are you proud of this something?'

'Well' – she turned her head away from him – 'in a way; yes, in one way, and in another I . . . I feel it's cruel.'

'Cruel? You're going to show me a cruel secret? I am intrigued, really I am. Here I go, hying for Pandora's box.' He did a side-step that was part of a jig and caused Fanny to giggle, and when the door closed after him she exclaimed to Marie Anne, 'He's a lad and a half is Master Patrick. Well, I mean, miss, he's . . . oh' – she tossed her head – 'I can say it to you, I think he's the best of the bunch.'

'I do too, Fanny. Yes, I do too.'

The best of the bunch was running up the back stairs now and he was still running when he crossed the landing and thrust open the schoolroom door, there to startle his mother, who was standing by the long ink-stained table with the open brown box in front of her and to the side a scattered number of drawings, and in her hand an open diary. This she immediately closed and held tightly to her breast as she demanded, 'What d'you want?'

Pat moved slowly towards her. He looked at the box before bringing down the open lid and fingering the broken lock; then he looked at his mother and said, 'You couldn't wait. You had to force it.'

He glanced along the table now to where the small, worn, sharp-edged poker was lying, and he asked a simple question. 'Why? It held only a child's diary and apparently—' he now flicked the number of drawings to one side, then hesitated and picked one up and stared at it for a moment before looking at her, and she answered his look with, 'Yes. Yes, you might well stare. Did you ever see anything so inhuman?'

He now spread out the rest of the sheets of paper and, after scanning them, he turned to her again, saying, 'Inhuman? D'you realise what these are?'

'Yes, I realise what they are. They're drawings of us, hideous drawings of us.'

'Mother . . . they are caricatures. Really splendid drawings. She has caught us all with a few strokes. An artist

31

would say they're a work of genius for a fourteen-year-old girl.'

'A work of genius!' Her hand went out and grabbed up a sheet, which she thrust at him, saying, 'Look at that! That is supposed to be me!'

The woman depicted was definitely his mother, but she was really grotesque. The body was long and thin; the face was long and thin, but it was the pencilled features that showed the hard ugliness of the woman as he knew Marie Anne must see her: the eyes were like pinpoints; the nose like a snout; the mouth like a snarling dog's. It was really a terrible portrayal. He was silent for a moment before he turned to her again, saying quietly, 'You have only yourself to blame for making her see you in this light.' She made no answer, and he added, 'Why do you feel like you do about her?'

She now fingered the book she was holding in her hands. The action looked as if she wanted to crush it; and then she muttered, 'I can't help it. She . . . she was never like an ordinary child. Not . . . not quite human. Wild. You know she was wild, running here and there. The looks of her.'

'Well, everyone in the family says she resembles the twins, and from what I remember of them they were wild enough. Mad Hatters. But they got on your nerves, didn't they? And you must admit, Mother, you were very glad when they decided they were going to try their luck in Canada. It came as a bombshell to Father, and to Grandfather too; but you took it in your stride, didn't you, because you were glad to be rid of them. Their escapades were too much for you. And of course there were two of them and you had always found them difficult to handle. But she is different; she was a little girl, a baby.'

She rounded on him now and her words came from between her teeth as she cried, 'A baby I never wanted!

32

A baby that came through a physical fight. I had five children growing up fast and I'd had two miscarriages. I was having no more; and Evelyn was ten at the time, remember. Begetting was over and done with as far as I was concerned and he knew this, yet he still came to my bed. That was why I had our rooms moved to the east wing so that you children would not hear the narration that went on from time to time when he couldn't have his way.'

Rather sadly, Pat put in, 'Oh, we heard all right, Mother, at least the shouting, but we couldn't make out what was being said, though Marie Anne did.'

'She couldn't have; she was in the other wing.'

'Not always. Remember the fracas on the night she was found sitting at the top of the lime tree?' He pointed to the window. 'After she was house-bound on your orders for some misdemeanour, she would come up here at all hours, climb through the window and on to a branch and sit in the fork at the top of the trunk. That was until Vincent discovered her escapade and shook a branch so violently that she had to cling on for dear life, and she used her lungs to such an extent that her screams carried to The Little Manor and brought Grandfather post-haste. Then you ordered the windows to be fastened, and as a further punishment she was sent off to school again. But did you do anything to Vincent? No, you didn't; but Grandpa did: he put the fear of God into him. Threatened to send him to sea. Of course, you did something then. You actually pleaded your son's cause. It was only a bit of fun, you said. But all this did not stop Marie Anne, whenever she was home, from coming up here and doing her drawings in secret.

'One night she heard voices coming from there.' He now pointed to the empty fireplace with its high iron grate, and when his mother turned and looked at it she said, 'Coming from where?'

'The fireplace, Mother, the fireplace. You didn't know that this chimney was a branch off the one in your bedroom, did you? All the chimneys in this house branch, you know. The tale of a boy-sweep being stuck up one and dying there is really true. Anyway she heard you and Father going at it quite clearly. I heard you myself.'

He saw that her mouth had dropped into a gape, and he nodded at her, saying, 'I knew of her night visits to the schoolroom, and I also knew that her loving brother Vincent had found out and would do something to get her into trouble. So I came up this night, and there she was sitting on the fender listening. And I sat with her, and I listened too, at least for a minute or so. Then I pulled her away and took her down to my room, where she cried her eyes out. I tried to tell her it was nothing, that fathers and mothers always fought; but that wasn't what had made her cry. It was the fact that you had been talking about her and called her a mad thing and that she was a misery to you. And she repeated practically your own words of a moment ago, that she was born in struggle and bitterness and that she had caused nothing but trouble since she had been born.'

'Oh, dear God.' The words came as a murmur, and because he seemed to recognise a softening, he said quietly, 'Can't you try to love her? At least be affectionate to her in some small way?' And then he was saddened still further with her reply, for, shaking her head slowly, she said, 'I can't. I can't. Because there's something about her. The very look of her repels me. I can't imagine that I gave birth to her. I've tried. Yes, believe me, Pat, I've tried. Years ago I tried. But then I found it was hopeless. She seemed to oppose me at every turn. We were enemies, as it were, from the beginning.'

'Oh, Mother.' He went to her now and put his arm around her shoulders. 'I'm sorry, dead sorry that you feel this way, because if you had got to know the other side of her, and there is another side . . . she's a sweet child really—'

'Oh, Pat!' The words were derisive. 'Sweet, d'you say, and drawing things like that?' She pointed to the papers on the table.

He now picked up another drawing which caused him to laugh and say, 'Well, look at that! That's me. My hair's standing on end because I always run my fingers through it; my eyes are closed, my mouth wide agape, all my teeth showing. That's how I must look when I'm laughing, probably when I'm having a great belly laugh, I should say. Don't you see?'

'No, I don't.' She shrugged. Then opening the book that was still in her hands, she said, 'These writings, they're like her, they're wild. This should be burned. I'll burn it.'

'You'll do nothing of the sort, Mother.' He was actually struggling with her. 'Give me it here!'

They were standing apart now, the book in his hands, and he said, 'If there's anything bad in it, all right, I'll destroy it myself, but meanwhile she must have some pastime, such as her drawing and writing, because she's going to be in that bed for some weeks still.'

She stared at him and there was no softening of her gaze; then she turned and was halfway towards the door when, swinging round, she said, 'Well, the minute she's out of that bed she's for London and Aunt Martha's. I'm arranging it.'

'What!'

'I said, she's for London and Aunt Martha's. She can have a musical career up there. I admit she's good at that. Aunt Martha wants a companion and she's agreed to talk it over. I'm going up there next week.'

He said nothing. What was there to say? Aunt Martha's. That gloomy house in one of the dead areas of London. He had called on Aunt Martha during one of his visits to

London, but only the once. Poor Marie Anne. But yet, if she was going to have a musical career she wouldn't spend much time in that house; she'd be at a school of sorts. And anything would be preferable to the life she had to lead here. Poor Marie Anne.

As he gathered up the drawings he became more amazed at the expertness of the resemblances. It proved one thing to him: she knew people. She could get behind their façade. There was a frightful drawing of Vincent. His face really looked evil but, almost obliterating it, were two hands, the fingers thick and podgy, but all ending in vicious looking claws. He shook his head in amazement. She knew all about Vincent's hands: he was forever pawing her, and not only pawing but punching, all under the guise of playing with her. At times he thought that if anybody's character needed clarifying it was Vincent's.

He paused as he picked up the last drawing. It was a caricature of his grandfather. She had given him a small body with an impish face, but the main feature of the drawing was the two arms outstretched as if to embrace. Oh yes, that child – or young girl as she was now – was, he must admit, as his mother plainly said, possessed of some unusual quality – and it could create love or hate. He imagined that the *Spectator* or *Punch* would jump at sketches like these. There were some prominent caricaturists with whose work these sketches could surely hold their own. They needed only sharp captions. Dear, dear, what was to become of her.

He pressed the drawings gently into the bottom of the box, put the diary on top, then closed the lid; he did not immediately lift up the box, but stood looking at it. How was he going to get over the lock being wrenched open? All he could do was say he found it like that. Of course, she would know immediately who had done it, her mother having stopped Fanny from bringing it downstairs. Well, he had to get to work.

36

He picked up the box and hurried from the room. In the bedroom, he handed it to Marie Anne, saying, 'That's how I found it; but I must go now; the trap's waiting.' Then he added, 'Traps wait but trains don't. Bye-bye dear.' He bent and went to kiss her on the brow, but her hand checked his face and her large dark eyes in their oval sockets stared into his before she said, 'Can't I have anything of my own?'

'It is your own, dear, all your own, and I want to talk to you, particularly about your drawings. They're marvellous.'

'You think so, Pat?'

'Yes. Yes, I do, dear. You have a great talent there. As I said, we'll talk about it when I get back.' He now kissed her brow, then patted her cheek, before hurrying from the room.

Fanny Carter was now standing by the bedside looking at the box lid, and she murmured, 'I couldn't help it, miss; I had to take it back.'

'Of course you had, Fanny. Of course you had.'

'You'll have to have a new lock on it.'

'It won't matter; I won't leave my diary in it again.'

But where would she leave it in the future? because she meant to go on writing in her diary, for it was her only means of working out troubled thoughts.

Had her mother had time to read what she had written about her? Oh, she hoped not, because, as nasty as she was, she didn't want to hurt her, and people could be hurt by words more than blows. She knew that, for she seemed to have been experiencing the pain of words all her life, and the pain of love, withheld love. Her mother had love to give, but she had given it to Evelyn and Vincent and Pat. Never to her. No, never. Nor had her father. Oh no. She couldn't remember receiving a kind word from her father. What she received from him was silence or long strange looks. He rarely spoke to her,

37

although there was one occasion when she had been playing the piano she discovered that he had been listening, and when she had turned to him hoping for praise, his expression and the movement of his head suggested amazement. But he had only smiled at her.

She now turned the pages of her diary until she came to a page headed 'Hands', and beneath it she had written:

Hands can talk, talk in all ways.

Mr Smith in the village, he cannot hear, but he talks with his hands.

Grandpa's hands talk: when they stroke my hair or hold me close they talk loudly. Pat's hands talk. They are smiling hands, they make you laugh. But Vincent's hands are horrible, and Evelyn's are cold; Mother's hands are pushing hands, pushing me in the back, pushing my shoulders, pushing my chest; mostly with two fingers she pushes my chest. Always pushing, pushing me away, pushing and pulling. No, not pulling; she never pulls me towards her. But it doesn't matter. It doesn't matter, for when I run I forget about everything.

She stopped reading and looked down the bed to the wire cage shielding her foot and leg, and – she almost whimpered to herself – will I ever be able to run again? Doctor Sutton-Moore said I will, but . . . but, as Grandpa has said about him, he's a sweet-talk pillow doctor, made to measure for delicate ladies, but he lets the poor cure themselves.

He had made her laugh when he said that the other day. At times he said such funny things. But she knew what he meant in this case; for her grandfather had also pointed out that Doctor Ridley wasn't very popular in certain houses; he was too blunt; but give him Doctor Ridley any time.

Yes, and give her Doctor Ridley too. She liked him, even though he rarely smiled. But he had yesterday when, after straightening her foot, and she had winced without crying out, he had said, 'We're doing fine, fine.' She would have liked to have talked with him, but Mrs Piggott was in the room. Mrs Piggott was a fussy body: she straightened straight counterpanes; she rearranged the already arranged articles on the dressing-table; she dampened her finger and thumb in her mouth and ran them down the straight folds of the curtains. What she didn't do was talk to her. Somehow she felt the little woman was afraid to talk to her. That was another thing her thoughts dwelt on: some of the servants never talked to her except to repeat an order sent by their mistress. Not like Fanny or Carrie or some of the yard men; and the footman, too, was nice. He had once called her a little card. She thought that was a funny name to give her; little card. She didn't ask anyone what it meant but she knew it wasn't nasty, because he had smiled as he said it.

Fanny was speaking to her again, saying, 'I could send the box down to the carpenter, miss. I'm sure he or one of the men could fix the lock.'

She considered a moment, then said, 'Oh, it doesn't matter, Fanny; I'll not be needing it any more.'

'But where will you put your diary, miss?' There was a note of conspiracy in Fanny's voice. 'There's no place here you can hide it.'

She answered quietly, 'It's all right, Fanny; I know what I'm going to do. I'll give it to my grandpa and he'll put it in his safe.' She was sure he wouldn't mind it taking up space in his safe, not after she had explained to him there were lots of things she might forget as she grew older. And she didn't want ever to forget them, because what she had said in this book had been about her life among the people of this house. This house that she should have looked upon as her home but which was, at times, more like a cage. And, as she had already written somewhere in the book, it was indeed a cage filled with different birds, with the big ones mostly cruel.

3

'You must go in and see her; I understand the servants are talking. If Vincent can go in, you can.'

'What did she say to Vincent?'

'She was very civil, very proper. He asked her how she was and she said very well. He asked if her leg was painful, and she answered, "Not any more unless I jerk it." And not even when he said, "It's taken a broken leg to clip your wings," did she round on him as she would have done at one time. And yes, she was indeed civil to him. We must face up to the fact that he has teased her unmercifully for years. I won't have it said that he was rough with her. More likely she was rough with him.'

'Yes, I can well believe that' – Evelyn nodded at her mother – 'because he didn't get the two scratches on his face from the cat, as he made out at the time.'

'Well, yes; but all that has long passed now. None of you are children any more. Not even her, for she'll be fifteen shortly. Well, are you coming? You just need to ask her how she is and it will stop those imbecile tongues wagging below stairs. So come along with you, let's get it over.'

But here Veronica paused and, turning back to her daughter, she said, 'While I'm on, I may as well tell you your father is annoyed at your being late down for breakfast so often now. Three times last week you were late.'

'I had a cold, Mother. You know I had.'

'You hadn't a cold on Sunday when you missed the service, nor the Sunday before. It isn't very much he asks of you; you could please him in this one thing, surely.'

Evelyn Lawson stared at her mother, thinking, as she often did, that she was an incredible woman: she must never see herself as she really was. Asking her to please her father; she should ask herself if she ever did anything to please her husband. She had once heard her grandfather yell at her father, 'Why didn't you keep your mistress, man?' She did not catch her father's reply, only her grandfather's words again: 'Oh, don't give me that, bad for business if it ever came out. Flannagan and Harris have had their women on the side for years and they haven't lost the respect of the office or those on the floor. In fact they're better thought of. You're gutless, man, gutless.'

She had always been sorry for her father. More so as the years had gone on and she had become wise in the way of men and realised that he quenched his appetites through eating, and that he now had to wear a corset to keep his belly in.

Obediently, she followed her mother to Marie Anne's room. And there she was, sitting up in bed, laughing, apparently at something the maid had said.

The sisters stared at each other. From Evelyn's standing position and Marie Anne's sitting upright, their faces were almost on a level.

'Are you feeling better?' Evelyn's voice sounded toneless, and it brought no response from Marie Anne. She wasn't seeing her sister as she appeared at this moment, but lying on the ground with her thighs exposed.

'Oh, we've lost our tongue again, have we?' Evelyn turned and glanced towards her mother, as if to say, what did I tell you?

'Well, you'll likely find it, together with your legs, when you take to your mad-hare running and fighting stone walls.' There was a thin smile on Evelyn's face now as she added, 'It's a wonder you haven't broken your neck before now.'

Marie Anne's arm swung wide and the flat of her hand caught the side of Evelyn's face, causing her to emit a cry as she reeled back.

Now there was pandemonium in the room; Marie Anne's voice was screaming, 'You're filthy! You're dirty! You caused me to break my leg! I saw you—' which was cut off by her mother's even higher scream of, 'Be quiet, girl! Quiet! And *you*, get out! Get out!' This was to Fanny Carter, as she grabbed the girl and thrust her through the doorway. Then banging the door shut she turned to Evelyn, who was leaning heavily on the bottom rail of the bed, her face white, her eyes, showing something akin to terror, fixed on Marie Anne, who now was lying back on her pillows, panting as if she had indeed been running.

Veronica Lawson was also staring at Marie Anne. She had the desire to grip her shoulders and shake the life out of her; but there was something here she must get to the bottom of. Bending slightly towards Marie Anne and her voice a low hiss, she said, 'How dare you strike your sister and say such dreadful things! What did you mean? You're mad, girl, you're mad!'

Marie Anne backed away from the close proximity of the face glaring at her, and although her voice was shaking it held no fear of her mother, for she spat the words back at her: 'I am neither mad nor stupid, Mother. Ask her what I mean and ask her why you've had to force her to come and see me now. I've been in this bed for weeks and she dare not face me, for she wasn't sure whether or not I had found out, because I had kept quiet. Now I know why you hate me, and through that I have grown to hate you. D'you hear? I hate you.' She now beat her doubled fist on the eiderdown and, the tears springing from her eyes, she cried, 'She caused me to break my leg that night, but I would never have spoken of it. No, I never would if she had come in here this morning and spoken to me in a kindly fashion. But no, she

43

spoke to me as she always has done, in that haughty tone, looking down on me as if I didn't belong here. And I don't know how many times over the years she has used your own words to me, telling me that I would end up in a home. Well, I can tell you both now,' her head nodded from one to the other, 'at times, any home would be preferable to this one; and if it hadn't been for Grandpa and Pat I might definitely have gone mad knowing that I wasn't wanted and had never been wanted. I was outside the family, something that had to be put up with, suffered.'

Veronica Lawson stared dumbfounded at her daughter. The girl had never before spoken out like this. Her response to her treatment had been tantrums and running away. Always running away. But now she had to recognise that here was someone who could think for herself, and as such she would become harder to handle in the years ahead, more so than had been the odd wayward child. She'd have to go to Aunt Martha's and get the matter settled there. Oh yes, yes. And then there was this other business with Evelyn. Dear God! what was that about? She had been up to something . . . Oh, not Evelyn, surely.

Without further words, she turned from the bed and, facing Evelyn, she said, 'Come along.'

Evelyn had a hand to her cheek. That slap had been a blow which would leave a mark. Well, what did it matter? When her mother got to the bottom of this, God knows what would happen. There was only one thing certain in her mind. If Roger could find a way to take her with him, she would go; but she hadn't seen him for nearly a week and she was becoming worried.

When her mother's hand gripped her arm, she muttered, 'All right. All right,' but as she followed her to the door she cast a look on Marie Anne, which, had it been possible, would have killed her there and then . . .

44

In Veronica's bedroom, her mother actually thrust her into a chair, exclaiming, 'What's all this about? She saw you with a man, didn't she? Who? Who was it? I . . . I can't believe it. To my knowledge, you haven't been out; it must have been after dark. Look. Tell me. What's it all about?'

Seeming to have recovered herself completely now, Evelyn pushed at her mother and got to her feet, saying, 'Yes, Mother; I was with a man, and it was at night because, tell me, what other time have I to meet anyone whom you would approve of and not frighten away by thrusting marriage at him before he is hardly in the door. So, yes, I have been seeing a man on my own,' and now she stressed, 'of my own choosing, d'you hear? And at night. And I am no longer a girl, Mother; I am nearly twenty-five years old and should have been married these last five years and had a family now, so don't come heavy-handed with me any more. I dislike that girl. I've never considered her to be my sister, and who's to blame for that?'

Veronica Lawson was amazed and appalled by this onslaught for, if she had shown love and affection to any of her children, it was to this daughter whom she saw as being so like herself in many ways. It did not strike her that, in fact, her daughter was taking a course of action similar to that which she herself would have taken under the circumstances, yet she came back with, 'How dare you speak to me like that, Evelyn! You, above all people. Even your father has never—'

'Oh, please! don't bring in Father, or I might say something I'll be really sorry for. Anyway, now you know. I am seeing a man—'

She got no further, for her mother came at her again, her voice a hoarse whisper now, 'To judge by what your sister spewed at you, you weren't only seeing him but lying with him.'

45

When this brought no response whatever from Evelyn and she had to watch her turn away disdainfully and stare out of the window, she almost whimpered, 'My God! My God! girl' – she put her hand to her head – 'that maid, she heard every word. She . . . she'll have to be stopped. Look at me. D'you hear what I said? That maid heard—'

'Yes, Mother, I heard every word you said, and the maid heard too, as well as every word that Marie Anne said and what she did, and likely she is downstairs now spreading the news.'

'Well, don't you realise what that could mean?'

'If you use your usual tactics, Mother, you will now speak to the girl, and should she repeat anything she saw or heard she'll be made out to be a liar. But not dismissed. Oh no; you won't be foolish enough to do that.'

Veronica Lawson could not believe her ears, nor could she take in the fact that this woman, because she *was* a woman, standing by the window looking at her with almost dislike, was her daughter. But she was right about the maid. My God! Yes. She must see to that. She almost ran from the room. The next minute she was pulling the cord in her own room to summon the housekeeper . . .

At that moment, Fanny Carter was standing in the butler's pantry nodding at Robert Green, as she finished, 'I tell you, those were the words she actually said, "You're filthy! You're dirty! You caused me to break my leg. I saw you." And then she took her hand and she gave her a wallop across the face that sent Miss Evelyn flying. Eeh! you should have heard them, the noise and the shouting. I knew that the mistress was terrified I should hear more, and she practically threw me out of the room. I'm telling you. Marie Anne must have seen something that shocked her and made her run, gallop, even, for her to go into a stone wall. Poor girl. I've always been sorry for that one.'

Now bending towards her, Robert Green said, 'Well, look. You'd better keep this to yourself, because if you

46

make your mouth go you could lose your job. They're capable of doing anything to hush up a scandal. And I'll tell you this, Fanny . . . you know Katie Roberts along at The Little Manor? Well, I understand that Maggie Makepeace told her if she didn't keep her mouth shut she would be sent packing, because she had said that she saw Miss Evelyn running towards the wood twice in one week. You know, she's courting Bobby Talbot, the river man. Well, she must have been out on the sly and old Maggie Makepeace got wind of it and scudded her ears, supposedly not for being out but for saying that she had seen Miss Evelyn in the wood, and Katie came back at the old girl and dared to say she hadn't only seen her once, she had seen her twice, the second time with a man. Although she couldn't tell who it was, she said if *she* saw them, Bobby Talbot must have, an' all. Anyway, keep your mouth shut. If there's any bad news to break here, let it be from The Little Manor, not this house.'

'Don't be silly.' Fanny pushed him. 'What have I been telling you? Miss Marie Anne yelled it out.'

'Yes. Aye, well. But go on, get yourself away. I'll see you later tonight, if I can. You'd better not let the boss lady find you round here.'

Fanny had just reached the end of the staff quarters when the boss lady herself appeared, saying, 'What're you doing? You're supposed to be upstairs.'

'I . . . I was looking for . . . I was looking for Carrie, Mrs Piggott.'

'Well, you won't find Carrie down here at this time in the morning, girl. Anyway, the mistress wants to see you immediately. Not back in the bedroom, but in her office. What have you been up to?'

'Nothing, Mrs Piggott. It was the mistress who sent me out of the bedroom.'

'Why? Why did she send you out of the bedroom? You're supposed to be looking after Miss Marie Anne.'

'I . . . I think they wanted a private conversation.'

The housekeeper stared at her, then said, 'Well, get yourself away.' Then as Fanny made to go, Mrs Piggott caught hold of her apron strings and, pulling her back towards her, she said, 'And report to me before you go back to the bedroom. You understand?'

'Yes, Mrs Piggott. Yes.'

Fanny found her mistress sitting behind the long, leather-topped desk. She was in the process of writing a letter, but she stopped immediately and said, 'Since you left the bedroom, have you spoken to anyone else?'

Fanny appeared to think a minute; then she said, 'Yes, ma'am. I spoke to Mrs Piggott.'

'No-one else?'

Again she paused; then looking her mistress straight in the face, she said, 'No, ma'am.'

'Well, girl, listen to me carefully. What you heard Miss Marie Anne say in the bedroom this morning was the result of hysteria. You know what hysteria means?'

'No, ma'am.'

'Well,' Veronica Lawson wetted her lips and groped in her mind for a moment. How to explain hysteria to this simple girl? She could not say it's next to madness, because that would set the tongues wagging more than ever. What she did say was, 'It happens when people lose their tempers and they say all kinds of things. The first thing that comes into their head. But never anything true. All fancies and make-up and lies. You understand what I'm saying, girl?'

'Yes, ma'am. Yes. What you're saying is that Miss Marie Anne was telling lies; it was all fancy due to her temper.'

'Yes. Yes, that's right. And she has a temper.'

'Yes, ma'am, she has a temper.'

'So you will say nothing about what transpired in the bedroom this morning. Nothing whatever. Not to anyone on the staff. You understand what I'm saying?'

'Yes, ma'am. I haven't got to talk about what Miss Marie Anne said.'

'That's right.' She stared at the girl. Was she simple or wily? She couldn't make out. You could never get to the bottom of the mentality of servants, not really.

'You may go now.'

'Thank you, ma'am.' Fanny bent her knee, walked back a step, then turned and left the room.

The housekeeper was waiting for her round the bend of the corridor, and she greeted her with, 'Well?' And Fanny, her voice low, said, 'Oh, it was nothing; just that I haven't got to talk about Miss Marie Anne having hysterics and losing her temper.'

Mrs Piggott narrowed her gaze at the girl; then she asked quickly, 'Well, what did she have hysterics about?'

'I don't know, Mrs Piggott. She was just shouting and yelling and crying like people do with hysterics. I've got to go now; I must get back, and I think the mistress is leaving her office.'

She didn't know whether this was true or not, but it caused the housekeeper to turn quickly away and make for the hall, leaving Fanny to go up to Marie Anne's bedroom, the while thinking, Well, well! Well, well! The mistress has the skitters.

4

Marie Anne had had toothache for two days and just an hour or so ago Doctor Ridley had given her a tincture, which had made her feel sleepy, but, although her eyes were closed and she was feeling more relaxed since the lessening of the pain as her toothache had eased, she wasn't asleep, and so she heard Carrie Jones come into the room saying hurriedly, 'They're all in the dining-room eating their heads off. I wanted to tell you the latest — it comes from Bill Winter. You know there were gypsies in the field the night Miss—' She looked towards the bed, then said, 'You're sure she's asleep?'

'Yes. Yes, she has been this while. Go on, about the gypsies?'

'Well, they went off the next day. He thinks they were frightened at being brought into this affair of her being knocked out. Anyway they've come back again. It's now seven weeks and one of the gypsy fellows told him it was the branded man who found her and wrote the note.'

'The branded man? I thought he had left this part.'

'No; not for good. Bill Winter says he leaves his cottage for London now and again. Anyway, it was him who found her. But that's over and done with; what d'you think about the latest? You know, Katie Brooks had a sister working up at The Grange. She's a year younger than Katie, and bonny. Oh aye, I've only seen her but once. Tall she was, with lovely skin, big blue eyes. Anyway she's got the push.'

'Katie's sister's got the push?'

'Yes; aye. And I'll give you three guesses what lasses like her get the push for.'

'No!'

'Yes; aye. And who d'you think she's named?'

'The butler?'

'Ooooh! no. She didn't stoop as low as the butler. Only the missis's cousin, Mr Roger Cranford.'

'Never! Mr Cranford? Well, he came here. He came with a party of them one day.'

'Yes; since you mention it, I remember too. He wasn't very tall but still good-looking. Oh aye, good-looking. He had been ill or something, been out in India, I remember. Yes, I remember. Well' – she laughed now – ' he's scooted back to India or some place and like a shot. Apparently, the master there had him up about it and he denied it flatly, but the master didn't believe him, although his wife did. Well, he was her cousin, you see. And the outcome was he packs up and leaves, all within twenty-four hours, and there was a screaming match with Winnie. That's the girl, Katie's sister. Apparently he had promised to take her away. She must have been stupid, or up the pole, because it's a joke that the lord of the manor will marry the kitchen maid. Some hope.'

'Where is the girl now? Is she with Katie?'

'Oh no, no; she'll be for the workhouse. There's no other place. They were orphans, you know, and they lived with their grannie in Gateshead until she died. And so it's said she must be for the workhouse . . . Eeh! Miss Marie Anne's stirring.'

'It's all right,' Fanny reassured her; 'the dose the doctor gave her would knock her out. She's always very restless in bed. It's her leg, you know.'

'D'you think she'll ever walk again?'

'Oh yes, yes. Doctor Ridley's sure of it. If it hadn't been for the toothache he'd have had her up today and sitting on the long chair. I've got to keep massaging her legs and hips – he told me how – because he says her muscles will have stiffened and it'll all help her to walk.'

Carrie now asked softly, 'Is it a fact that she's for London?'

'Yes; so I hear. As soon as she can walk she'll be sent there. Anyway it'll likely be a better life for her than this, 'cos she has no life in this house, you know.'

'Look! she's stirred again. I'll go, but I thought you'd like to know, especially on top of the other rumours that have been floating around under the surface like. Bye-bye.'

'Bye-bye, Carrie, and thanks for coming up.'

'You're welcome. I miss you on the floor; I'll be glad when you're back again.'

They smiled at each other; then the door closed on Carrie, and Marie Anne, turning as far on to her right side as her left leg would allow, and under cover of the bed sheet she brought her hand up to her mouth and there held it tightly, her mind repeating Evelyn . . . Evelyn. He hadn't taken her with him, and . . . and she had given herself to him. Oh yes, she had, and that other girl, too, who is going to have a baby. Perhaps he had taken Evelyn . . . Don't be silly. Don't be silly. She moved restlessly. She had heard Pat say only this morning that he was to have shown Evelyn over one of the ships today, but that she was in bed, feeling rather unwell. But being Evelyn, he said, she wouldn't see the doctor. It was just a cold, she said.

Just a cold. Did one take to bed with a broken heart? because that's what happened when a lover deserted you. At least, the stories all said this; and she, too, could believe it. Oh yes, she could believe it. She felt a wave of remorse sweep over her. She shouldn't have said the things she had to her, she shouldn't have struck her because she must have loved him very much. You didn't do the things she had done that night if you didn't love

52

somebody very much. Yet, immediately, there sprang to her mind the voices coming out of the chimney piece, accompanied by the sounds of struggle and fighting. Once upon a time she had imagined you had only to be married to somebody to love them, to love them for ever. She was silly. Many of her thoughts were silly. There was a part of her so childish that she disliked it, the while still clinging to it.

For the first time in her life her thoughts went out tenderly towards her sister, yet she knew she would never be able to put them into words that would bring Evelyn any comfort; even if she were to try, she would be rebuffed. Oh yes. Evelyn would always hate her for having witnessed her degradation.

She wished the weeks would fly until she could walk again and go to London, for she knew that no matter what she met with there, it could only be better than the life she led in this house. Her only regret was that she would have to leave her grandpa and Pat. Oh, she would miss them, miss them both. Yet Pat did sometimes go to London, and perhaps he'd be able to see her. It was a hope, anyway. Of course, there was always letters: she could write every day to her grandfather . . . well, not every day but every week. Oh yes, every week.

London. London. The very name was becoming like a star in the enclosed world of her bedroom.

Her thoughts were about to drop her into sleep when in her half state she suddenly saw a face hanging over her. The moon seemed to be shining on it and it was frightening. It was black with an eye in it. Then the next minute, she recalled, an ordinary face had taken its place, a kind face, and the voice that went with it was kind: 'You'll be all right. You'll be all right.' One of them had been the branded man. She had heard about him. He didn't go into the village. She remembered her grandpa saying they were ignorant clodhoppers and that the man was a sculptor and was accepted in London, and that his work was beautiful. She had a vague memory of him saying the man had been brought up by monks or someone, or something, and that his cottage had been left to him by a relative.

Every now and again she would be startled by the vision of the changing face; in fact, she had come to believe there must have been two people there that night, the branded man and another.

But what did it matter? That was all in the past; London was looming up. And on this thought, sleep finally overcame her.

PART TWO

1

To Marie Anne, it was as though she had been living in the train for years. She was made tired by the rhythm of the wheels ever turning, ever grinding, and by the not infrequent waves of sooty smoke that enveloped her should she open the window.

She was seated in a first-class carriage and she'd had this to herself as far as York.

The guard, to whom Pat had talked quite a lot, had assured him that he would take care of her. And he had been as good as his word: twice he had brought her a cup of tea and a biscuit, and when at York an elderly couple had entered the compartment, he had been quick to explain to them that she was in his care. They, too, had been very pleasant and showed interest in the fact that she was going to London to take up a musical career. However, for most of the journey she had lain back in her corner of the carriage with closed eyes and had mentally gone over the parting with her grandpa. She had cried, and in his eyes, too, there had been tears which had spilled down his lined cheeks, and these had caused him to hold her close and to comfort her, assuring her that if she did not like it up there, she was to return home, no matter what anyone said. But in the meantime she should not worry about him because, on Pat's suggestion, he was going to return to his old apartments in The Manor, for they said he was in need of a little care now and then — Maggie Makepeace was getting on. But nevertheless he meant to keep The Little Manor aired with Maggie and

Barney and Katie still in place there. So she hadn't to worry about returning, if she should want to.

She knew that he had had words with her mother, telling her that she herself should accompany her daughter to London and see her settled into this new life. It was also unfortunate that Pat was unable to leave the business. Some trouble had erupted among the crew, which included a number of lascars, and neither her father nor Vincent was capable of handling such an affair.

So, on 19 October 1899, Marie Anne was assisted from the carriage on to the gaslit platform of King's Cross station and into the mêlée of passengers. The guard, carrying out his instructions to the letter, led her to the barrier, and there held up a board on which was chalked in large letters: Miss Sarah Foggerty.

This brought a movement on the other side of the iron gate, and what appeared to be a woman in her early thirties thrust herself forward, saying, 'I am Miss Foggerty.'

And to this the guard said, 'Well, here is your charge, Miss Foggerty; and she's been a very, very good girl.'

After glancing at the woman who was now standing by her side, Marie Anne held out her hand to the guard, saying, 'Thank you very much, mister guard. You have been very kind. I shall write and tell my grandfather.'

'Oh, that would be kind indeed of you, miss. It's been a pleasure to look after you. Good-day to you now. Good-day.'

She was walking through the crowded station now beside this strange woman, at whom she had, as yet, not looked fully. Nor was she able to see her plainly until they were standing under a street lamp on the pavement outside, when Sarah Foggerty, bending her thin shape towards her, said, 'Everything will be very strange at first, me dear. But I hope you'll get used to it. Were you sick in the train?'

'No. No, I wasn't sick. But I . . . I feel very tired. It was a long journey, and . . . and my first.'

'Well, we will soon be home. Oh, here's the porter with your cases. You only have two of them?'

'Yes, only two.'

After the porter had lifted the cases from his barrow he looked meaningfully at the woman and she, after a moment, fumbled in her pocket, brought out a purse and, picking out a copper, she handed it to him, at which he stared, then turned away without saying a word.

As if undecided, Sarah Foggerty stood looking down at the two cases before she said, 'Yes, we'll take a cab. We'll take a cab.'

Into the first available cab she ushered Marie Anne with her hand on her bottom and a gentle push; then, one after the other, she hoisted the cases along the floor, before calling to the cabbie, 'Seventeen Blake Terrace, please.' Then after lifting herself up the high step, she pulled the door closed before flopping down beside Marie Anne, and saying enigmatically, 'There, that's it; no horse-bus today.'

Marie Anne smiled wanly at this plain-faced and cheaply dressed but, obviously, very competent woman. As yet, she knew little about her, only that she appeared kind and had a nice lilting voice. And when, more enigmatically still, she said, 'From now on, dear, take no notice of what I say, only of what I do. No doubt this'll puzzle you, but as it says in the Bible, all things will be made clear to you in time.'

A moment or so after the cab stopped, the cabbie pulled open the door, and having taken the cases from Miss Foggerty's hands, he helped first her, then Marie Anne to step down on to the street.

'How much is that I owe you?' Sarah Foggerty asked.

'One and a penny, miss.'

'Oh.'

Marie Anne watched the woman take from her purse, first, a silver shilling and a penny, then another penny, and pause before laying this beside the fare. And when the cabbie, looking at it, said, 'Well, thank you, miss, for small mercies; I've always been glad of small mercies,' she replied, 'So have I. So have I. Good-day to you. Come along, dear.' She now lifted up the two cases and walked towards an iron gate which she thrust open with a flick of her buttoned boot, then walked up the short path to an unpretentious front door; and here, nodding towards the wall, she said, 'Ring that bell there, dear.'

Marie Anne did as she was bidden, and after a minute or so the door was pulled open by a maid, who said, 'Here you are then, miss.' And for answer Sarah Foggerty replied, 'Yes, Clara, here we are, in the flesh.'

She dropped the two cases down, then turned to Marie Anne, saying, 'This here is Clara Emery, our one and only –' there was a pause before she added, 'maid.' Then, her voice changing to a low whisper, she leant towards the girl, saying, 'Where is she . . . the missis?'

The answer, too, came in a whisper: 'In the sitting-room, waiting. But she's only been down a little while.'

As if she had momentarily forgotten the new member of the household, Sarah Foggerty turned to Marie Anne while still addressing the maid, saying, 'This is Miss - Marie Anne Lawson, the mistress's new ward,' and the little maid bobbed her knee as she said, 'Welcome, miss.'

All Marie Anne could say at this moment was, 'Thank you,' for the new word 'ward' was probing her mind. So that's what she was to be, a ward. What exactly was a ward? She would have to find out.

She was slightly startled when Miss Foggerty stopped her as she went to take off her hat, saying, 'Don't take it off, nor your coat; she'll likely want to see you in the whole. Come, let's get it over.'

They had been standing in a narrow hall, more like a

long passage, Marie Anne thought. At the end of it was a flight of stairs, but she seemed to be viewing it through a mist, for the place was what she would have termed not exactly dark but dusky.

After first knocking on the sitting-room door, Sarah Foggerty pushed it open with one hand while drawing Marie Anne into the room with the other, and immediately Marie Anne saw that this room was much lighter, yet still devoid of colour. Everything looked as if it was made of heavy dark wood, but there was a long window at the far end through which she glimpsed a bit of green beyond. Between the window and herself sat a woman in a straight-backed chair. She had grey hair pulled tightly back from her round plump face, and she was dressed in unrelieved black.

The woman did not speak until Marie Anne was standing in front of her, and then only after scrutinising her closely through narrowed lids. 'You've got here then,' she said. 'You are much bigger than I thought you would be. How old are you now?'

'I was fifteen on the second of August, ma'am.'

'I am your aunt. Address me as such, girl.'

Marie Anne had wondered about this woman being her aunt, when, in fact, she was only her mother's half-sister, and definitely much older than her mother. Her face wasn't wrinkled, but it was old-looking and tight-skinned. Yes, it was what she would call a tight face. She heard herself obediently saying, 'Yes, Aunt.'

'You know why you're here, don't you?'

'Yes, Aunt. To take up a musical career.'

'Well, let's hope so. We all have to earn a living.'

When Marie Anne heard Miss Foggerty cough she was about to turn and look at her, when her aunt said, 'I'd better warn you. There's no space for your flights of fancy here: if you start running it'll be into the street and under a horse's hooves before you know where you are, or

61

taken up by the police. You understand?'

Yes. Yes, she understood but she said no word, and when Sarah Foggerty coughed again, her mistress turned to her, saying, 'Take her up and tell her the rules.' Then bringing her gaze back to Marie Anne, she added, 'And rules have to be adhered to in this house. You understand?'

Again Marie Anne understood only too well about two things: that she didn't like this woman, and she didn't like this house.

When Sarah Foggerty's hand came on her elbow it had to give her a slight tug before she turned away; then, after they had entered the hall and Sarah Foggerty was about to close the door, Martha Culmill's voice, louder now, came at them, calling, 'Foggerty!'

Sarah Foggerty stepped back into the room, and at the same time Marie Anne went further into the hall, but still within earshot of what was being said, to hear her aunt say, 'You came by cab. Why not the horse-bus?'

'We had missed it, ma'am, and we would have had another hour to wait.'

'What did he charge . . . the cabbie?'

'One and threepence, ma'am.'

Marie Anne's eyes widened. He had charged only one and a penny.

Her aunt's voice came again, saying. 'One and threepence! They never charge more than a shilling. You didn't tip him?'

'Of course not, ma'am.'

'Well, let there be no more cabs.'

'No, ma'am.'

Sarah Foggerty closed the door of the sitting-room, then turned and looked at Marie Anne; and Marie Anne stared back at her, her active mind summing up the means by which this woman had managed to tip the porter a penny and the cabbie a similar sum. She was quick to admire Sarah's ingenuity, and so she smiled at the woman. And as Sarah smiled back she nodded her head once as if acknowledging her co-operation, before she turned and marched briskly to where the cases still stood near the doorway.

Picking up one she pointed to the other, saying, 'You take that one, miss. Share and share alike.'

The stairs were unusually wide but the landing upstairs was narrow, like the hall, with four doors going off it. It was the furthest one that Sarah Foggerty pushed open to show a small bedroom holding a single bed, a wash-hand stand, a wardrobe, and a single wooden chair. Dropping the case on to the bed, Sarah Foggerty stated, 'The only good thing about this room is it looks on to the garden, but I must tell you there's no manner or means whereby you can get out of this window or slide down the drainpipe; it's too far down.'

It was now that, with open mouth, Marie Anne stared at Miss Foggerty, and Sarah Foggerty smiled widely while nodding at her as she said, 'Oh, I know all about you and your capers, oh, every one of them, because it's this way: I have to read her letters to her; I have to read everything to her. She can't see print but she can see everything else. Oh aye, yes. There's something happening to her eyes; the doctor says it's age. So there's nothing for it but she's got to have me read her letters out and oh, girl! I could've split me sides many a time, for you were meself over again when I was young back there, running like a hare across the moor. My running got me somewhere an' all: sent over to England here, and into place. But I had been to the penny school, and I was fortunate, and I was quick to learn. But you, where's it landed you? In this dull house, it has; and this you've noticed already, I can see by your face; and you haven't taken to her, have you? Well, who would? But anyway, you've got two choices: you either put up with it and do some laughing behind her back, or you skedaddle back home, where, by the sound of it, you would be as welcome as an Orangeman in the Falls Road, if you get what I mean. To my mind, girl,' Sarah was bending towards Marie Anne, who was now seated on the end of the bed, 'and I'm going to say it, and I'm sure it won't alter your opinion very much, but I think your mother's a hard nut.'

That Marie Anne was bewildered was evident, but it was a kind of revealing bewilderment, for it was telling her that she not only liked this woman, but also that she would make a friend of her. She was very like Maggie Makepeace, except that Maggie wasn't Irish. Impulsively, she put out her hands and gripped those of the plain-faced little woman, and almost tearfully, she said, 'Thank you for being so kind to me. I'm . . . I'm glad I'm with you.'

It was some seconds before Sarah Foggerty answered, when she said, 'Well, that's nice to know, miss, and they'll be relieved in the kitchen an' all. I can speak for Agnes and Clara. You met her, little Clara, and Agnes is the cook. Cook-general, she's called. We're all generals here. I'm general night nurse, day nurse, secretary, and for what? I come cheap. I'm known as her companion, but I'm no lady born and bred, as you might have guessed, but the ladies who applied for the job wanted twice as much as she was willing to pay, so she picked me, sale price, goods not returnable. That's it, smile, girl. You're a bonny piece, but unusually so: your eyes are too big for your body, I would say, but when you smile you come into your own. Well now, as she said, to rules.

'Cook and Clara get up at half-past six, although it's supposed to be six. I rise at seven. I have to, as I sleep next door to her. You'll get up at half-past seven. Breakfast is at eight. It's usually porridge. Twice a week we have bacon . . . streaky, and once a week we have an egg. At twelve o'clock we have mid-day dinner, whatever

64

cook can devise out of the cheese-paring orders from above. Five o'clock we have tea; bread and butter, jam, plum and apple mostly. Once a week, Cook is allowed to bake a cake, which we have at the week-end. A cup of cocoa at eight. And that's the menu. At least, as is written down on orders from above.' She now raised her eyes heavenwards. 'I have the job of weighing all ingredients, and' – again she was leaning towards Marie Anne – 'you wouldn't believe it, miss, how wrong those scales are at times; so you needn't worry, there'll be a bit of cake out of the secret tin whenever you feel like it, and should you feel hungry at any time, cold sausage on buttered toast is a good filling.'

'Oh! Miss Foggerty.' Marie Anne had her fingers across her lips now. She had a great desire to laugh, but she also knew this might turn into hysterical crying, because she was still very churned up inside.

'Call me Sarah. I'd like that.'

'I will. I will, Sarah.'

'Now for your duties. You are to clean your own room. You are to read to your aunt an hour every morning while I am attending to her mail; she gets quite a bit of this, nearly all concerned with business. She has her fingers in several pies, many of them connected with the chapel. Oh, that's another thing. Sunday morning and evening, it's chapel for Agnes and Clara. They're fortunate to get out like that. But now for the main reason why you are here. Immediately after dinner I will take you to Professor Carlos Alvarez's Academy — so called,' she added with a bounce of her head. 'It's only a house, not unlike this one, but much lighter, I can tell you, although it's at the end of the short row where the three other houses have been turned into hat factories. Just as well, I suppose, so people don't complain about the ding-ding-dinging of the piano. Anyway, what I've seen of it, it's nicely furnished; but then again, I understand there's only him and his wife.

She lives upstairs. I met her the last time I took a message along, which was on Thursday gone. She doesn't sound like a professor's wife; but what's in a voice? Bit of a cockney I would say. I heard her going for him when I was waiting down in the hall. But when he came downstairs to me he was all smiles. He's a nice enough fellow. Kindly, I would say. Anyway he takes you Mondays, Wednesdays and Fridays for two hours. That's from half-past one to half-past three; and on Tuesday and Thursday he can only fit you in for an hour at a time. Then all your spare time she'll expect you to practise.'

Sarah was leaning towards her in that confidential manner that Marie Anne was to discover she used when she wanted to impart something out of the ordinary, and she now did impart, for she said, 'Your mother, in one of her letters, made it plain that you had to be kept at it, and she implied that she wasn't going to pay good money for you wasting your time and going round sightseeing.'

'Good money?'

'Yes, that's what was said.'

'Mother is paying for me to be here?'

'Well, she's to send the cash. I don't know where it's coming from; likely your father, but she's paying for you. O!' Sarah made a round 'O' with her lips and repeated again, 'O!, now you couldn't expect the lady of this house to take anyone in, be it out of relationship, pity, or poverty, now could you? Oh, but you've got a lot to learn yet, dear. Anyway, I know one thing. You can't be sitting at the piano all day long, but if I were you I would sit there as long as possible, that's if you enjoy it. I know we will, the others and me. It would be as good as a brass band. One passes here every Sunday morning, but it's a drum and fife, on its way to the Catholic Church. It's lovely. And oh, how I always wish I was marching with them. And another thing: you've got to be prepared to read the good book to her, or magazines that are almost as holy; but I'll

66

give you a tip: if you get too much of it put your foot down, because if I know anything, she's not going to lose your money, besides the bit she'll be cribbing from the music teacher. Half-a-crown an hour, he was asking. That's one pound a week. But she got him down to sixteen shillings. As she said, you'd be a long-term pupil.'

The sound of a bell ringing in the distance caused Sarah Foggerty to jump towards the door, saying, 'That's for me! Hurry up and have a wash and do your unpacking, then come down, because, if I know anything, she'll be staying downstairs for her tea. It isn't often she makes the stairs.'

After the door had closed with a soft bang, Marie Anne sat down on the edge of the bed again. Her mind was in a whirl. It was inconceivable to her that her aunt would bargain with the music teacher, and to her own gain, over his fees. It only went to show the type of mean woman she was and what she might further expect. And added to this, that her mother was paying for her to be kept here. Her grandfather, she knew, had been under the impression she was to be a sort of companion; she had even heard her grandfather refer to her aunt as being quite warm where money was concerned.

As she sat quietly musing on her present situation she knew that it was such that had she come into it without being accompanied and enlightened by Miss Foggerty, Sarah, as she wanted to be called, she would never have stayed in this house. The dark dreariness of the place alone would have made her start running again; but where to? Under horses hooves or to the police, as that black-garbed woman had said? No; she would have sent a telegram to her grandfather to say that she was coming back and she would have risked the reception she would have received from her mother, Evelyn and Vincent . . .

She had finished her unpacking and washed her face and hands in the cold water from the wash-hand stand jug and had combed her hair back into double plaits when there came a tap on the door, and Clara stood there saying, 'Tea's in the sitting-room, miss, and she . . . ma'am is waiting for you.'

'Clara, there's no mirror in this room. Is there one next door?'

'Oh no, miss. Ma'am doesn't hold with mirrors: they breed vanity, like.' She smiled; then the whisper came confidentially, 'But the cook has one in her bag; she'll let you have a look into it if you ask her. Anyway, you'd better come down, for she doesn't like being kept waitin'; it's her bell that'll be going, else.'

Marie Anne wanted to laugh at the quaint way this little maid talked, and as they went out of the room together she said, 'Where do you come from?'

'Wales, miss; and I wish I was back there because 'tis not much different in this house from the village. As my dad would say, all chapel and hard tack. He used to go to sea, you know, when he was young, my dad, and I'll never get used to the way they talk here.'

Marie Anne had a great desire to laugh loudly, and she was still smiling when the young girl knocked on the sitting-room door before straight away pushing it open; and she entered the room.

Her aunt, as she had to think of her, was still in the same chair and Sarah Foggerty was standing at a side table pouring out tea. She had her back to her and Marie Anne, hesitating on what to do, went to Sarah's side, thinking that she would hand the tea round; but the voice from the chair said, 'Sit down! girl.'

Marie Anne sat down, in the chair pointed out to her. It was near another small table on which was a plate of bread and butter, three buttered half slices on one side, the same on the other, and next to it was a smaller plate holding two pieces of ginger cake.

Sarah Foggerty placed a cup of tea on the side of the

table within reach of her mistress's hand, and one by Marie Anne. Then she returned to the table, picked up the third cup and sat down a short distance away.

'Well, start your tea, girl.'

Marie Anne watched the black-sleeved arm come out, then the fingers scooping the three pieces of bread and butter on to the side plate. So she slowly followed suit, and straight away began to eat the bread and butter, because she was feeling hungry. Only once did she look towards Sarah Foggerty, because she felt embarrassed by the fact that she wasn't eating at all. There had been no plate set for her.

The tea was strong and had little milk in it, but she drained her cup quickly; then, looking towards Sarah, she asked politely, 'May I have another cup, please?'

On Sarah's part there was a slight hesitation to rise from her chair, for she was looking at her mistress and when, after what seemed a pause, her mistress nodded, Sarah poured out another cup and brought it to Marie Anne.

Marie Anne then picked up a piece of ginger cake from the plate, and as she ate it she was made to feel somewhat uneasy by her aunt's eyes being fixed tightly on her; and so she said, 'It's very nice ginger cake,' and added by way of making conversation, 'It's better than Cook used to make. Hers was much too treacly.'

'Have you finished your tea?'

'Yes, thank you.'

'Then go and play the piano. I want to hear what all this fuss is about.'

Even eagerly now, Marie Anne made her way to the piano, which stood in the far corner of the room. It had a fretwork screen front with a green cloth behind it. Before lifting the lid, she looked into the box seat for some music, but found only two hymn books and an album entitled *Favourite Drawing-Room Ballads*. And as she stood looking at it, the voice came at her, saying quite loudly, 'You can play something without music, surely!'

'Yes. Yes. Of course I can,' Marie Anne rapped back and abruptly sat down and lifted the piano lid, to see a set of yellowing keys.

After attempting a scale to test the tone, she stopped, turned on her seat and said, 'I couldn't play on this. It's out of tune.'

'What d'you mean, it's out of tune?'

Marie Anne was now on her feet, walking towards the indignant figure in the chair, and she found, quite suddenly, that she had no fear of this person. And again she said, 'It's so out of tune it can't have been played on for years.'

'Don't be silly, girl.'

'I am not being silly, Aunt. The piano needs to be tuned before I can practise on it. Why haven't you had a tuner in to see about it?'

It was evident that Martha Culmill was stunned into silence, for Marie Anne was able to continue: 'Pianos need attention twice a year at least if you are going to practise anything worthwhile.'

Her voice trailed away now as Sarah Foggerty was coughing, and this brought her mistress's attention momentarily on to her and she cried, 'Clear away! Foggerty, and get the things out . . . Get out!'

Sarah hurriedly collected up the tea things; but it wasn't until the door had closed on her and the wooden trolley that Martha Culmill found her voice again when she said, 'And who, may I ask, is going to pay for a piano tuner?'

It seemed that Marie Anne had to think about this for a moment, or perhaps she was telling herself she would have to live with this woman for some time ahead, so was she going to be mealy-mouthed, as her grandpa would say, or speak her mind? She decided on the latter, and said briefly, 'You could send the bill to my mother and she would add it to the rest.' Then she felt she could have cut her tongue out, because how could she have known her mother paid for her and that she wasn't the guest of this woman? of which she was immediately made aware by Martha Culmill's saying, 'What d'you mean?'

'Well, from what I understood at home, although Mother didn't tell me, she is paying you for having me.' She heaved a big sigh. She had almost got Sarah into trouble there, big trouble.

'You know something, miss.'

This wasn't a question, but a statement, recognised as such by Marie Anne and so she waited. 'Your tongue's too ready for your own good. D'you understand that? And what if I write and tell your mother about your attitude towards me?'

'You're at liberty to do so. My mother and I understand each other very well and she will say it is what she expected.'

Martha Culmill was indeed lost for a reply now, but she just managed to say, 'Leave me, girl! I will talk to you in the morning.'

Marie Anne was not quite sure if, as she opened the door, Sarah Foggerty jumped back; she was certainly standing not far from it, and the tea trolley was just an arm's length away; but when Sarah pulled her into the kitchen, saying, 'Splendid! Splendid! You're a match for her. Oh, by aye, you're a match for her; and keep it like that, me dear,' she knew she had been right in her surmise.

Gently, Sarah touched Marie Anne's cheek, saying, 'Oh, you're not going to cry, are you? Look; this is Cook,' and now the big woman smiled at Marie Anne and said, 'Welcome, miss.'

'Have you a spare bun in that tin, Cook? I know this young lady wouldn't say no to one. You're still hungry,

71

aren't you, me dear? Now don't let the tears come. Come on; you've made a stand.'

Wrapping some eatables in a napkin, Cook said, 'Up to your room with you and finish these off. And if you're eating alone downstairs, I'll see you have a good plate. We're havin' spotted-dick puddin' and that's a filler. And may I say we're glad to have you, miss. We understand, too, you're going to play the piano. That'll be a change for us.'

'I'll never be able to play on that piano.'

'Don't you worry your head, me dear,' put in Sarah. 'I won't be through the door but she'll be asking me where I'll find a piano tuner.'

'Could you get a piano tuner right away?'

'Aye, I suppose I could. I've seen them in the papers; in the adverts, you know. Piano teachers, piano tuners, pianos, every musical instrument you can think of, all second-hand.'

Then a piping giggle came from little Clara, who quipped, 'Not the piano tuners and the teachers, they don't come second-hand,' only to be pushed by the cook, who said, 'There she goes again with her Welsh wit. She'll cut herself one of these days, she's so sharp.'

'She will that, if somebody doesn't cut her Welsh whistle out,' said Sarah. 'But anyway, talking of papers: what did you do with the last one?'

'I used it to get the fire going this morning.'

'All of it?'

'Aye, all of it; but the milkman will be here in the mornin'.'

Sarah Foggerty turned to Marie Anne, saying, 'You may well look bewildered, miss, but we never have a paper in this house unless we fork out for it ourselves; but the milkman's very good that way; he drops in the previous day's or night's. You see, he knows all about her' – her head jerked up – 'I mean, the mistress, for he's been

72

serving her milk since the old cow served the bull who was pawing the ground with a gleam in its eye.'

'He couldn't wait until the cows came home!'

As the Welsh giggle trailed away and the three heads came together, Marie Anne did not know how she then became enfolded with them, but there she was, one arm around the shoulders of the little Welsh girl, the other around the waist of Sarah Foggerty, as, like them, she aimed to stifle her laughter.

But the bell did it for them. It sprang them apart, still shaking with their laughter and Sarah Foggerty making for the door. Here, she stroked her hair back; then pulling the collar of her dark brown uniform dress into place, she walked smartly towards the sitting-room.

As Marie Anne, too, made for the door Cook said, 'Enjoy your bits, dear,' and Marie Anne answered, 'I'm sure I shall, Cook. Thank you.'

In her room, the cold struck her forcibly. She lit the single candle standing in its tin holder; then taking the eiderdown from the bed she pulled it about her before opening the napkin and eating the currant bun and the two pieces of dry coconut cake therein.

Afterwards, she took her writing-case out of the top drawer and arranged herself as comfortably as she could on the wooden chair.

Her heels tucked in behind the wooden rod that spanned between the two front legs, and her knees arranged to form a table for the writing pad, she began to write her first letter to her grandfather:

Dearest, dearest Grandpa,

Oh, how I miss you and Pat . . . yes, and Pat. And you know something? I have been in this house only a few hours and already I would be on my way back to you if it weren't for the three maids here. There is a lovely Irish woman, a sort of maid of all kinds to Aunt

73

Martha. Her name is Sarah Foggerty. Doesn't that sound warm? Then there is Cook, a Londoner, and a little Welsh girl, Clara, who is the housemaid. They are all lovely and have taken me to their hearts, or else I would surely, surely have made for the station again. And I'm thankful for the pound notes you got Maggie to sew into my petticoat pocket.

I don't know what the days ahead are going to be like, but what I do know is, I dislike this house, but more so I dislike the woman I have to call aunt. To my mind she is a hard narrow-minded creature and a penny-pincher. Oh yes Grandpa, a penny-pincher. And thank you so much for the diary with its secret lock. No-one would ever think of finding the key there, would they, in its cosy little pocket in the spine? It's a work of genius, isn't it?

Oh! Grandpa, I am sad inside, deeply, deeply sad. I have laughed with the maids in the kitchen until I cried; but even there I had to be careful for a little less control and I would have howled aloud. Like that poor whippet dog we found on the fell one day. Remember, Grandpa? It howled at night and it died. And if it wasn't for you and Pat I wouldn't mind dying . . .

I don't know whether I will send you this letter or not; it is so sad and may upset you. But I feel that once I get down to my music I will forget about the house and my aunt and everything else, like I used to. If my music could close out my home and all who were in it with the exception of Pat, then I'm sure it'll have the power to shut out Miss Martha Culmill.

2

Three days later Marie Anne added a second page to her letter:

Dearest, dearest Grandpa,

It is three days now since I arrived and I've learned what utter boredom means. Although I have been given duties, reading to my aunt for an hour in the morning, which to me is purgatory, for it's all from the Bible. That's funny, isn't it? purgatory all from the Bible. I feel I am becoming like the little Welsh maid here. She's always turning words and making quips with them. But she has her work to do, as has the cook; and poor Miss Foggerty, she's running hither and thither like a hare all day. The only thing about my duties with my aunt is that I can relieve Sarah a little. And I'm glad Aunt stays in bed most of the time. She was downstairs to greet me when I arrived. Did I say greet! Anyway, all that is over, I hope, because the piano tuner came this afternoon. He said that the piano hadn't been tuned since it was delivered. He took a long time over it, and when he had finished, I played a piece of Beethoven, a loud section, what you used to call the German band, and you know what the piano tuner said when I finished? MY! MY! Just like that Grandpa, MY! MY! But his eyes were telling me that he was surprised and had enjoyed it, and he asked me to play some more. And the maids . . . at least Cook and the little Welsh maid, stopped work and came to the sitting-room door. But after a short while Miss Foggerty, that is Sarah, came running downstairs. She'd been ordered to leave the bedroom door open and that I should continue. No requests made here, Grandpa, they're orders. But I played and I played. I played Chopin and Bach; pieces that I had memorised, of course. I must get some music. Oh, how handy your money will come in, Grandpa. What would I do without it? And again that deep sadness says, what would I have ever done without you?

Good-night, my dearest, dearest Grandpa.
Your Marie Anne

PS. Tomorrow I am to meet my musical professor, Carlos Alvarez. As his name suggests, he is Spanish, and to give you Sarah's description of him, he is a nice gentleman of middle years with very good English and lives in a tall house, with his studios on the bottom and a wife upstairs. But I shall see this all for myself tomorrow. Good-night again, dear Grandpa.

Marie Anne and Sarah Foggerty both stood before Martha Culmill. She was looking at Marie Anne's feet, and said, 'That skirt of yours is too short.'

Marie Anne looked down at the hem of her brown dress and said, 'I don't think so.'

'It's not what you think, miss, it's a matter of decorum. It is too short.'

'It is above my ankles, and that's the way I want it.'

Sarah Foggerty was coughing again. It seemed to be a warning cough, but Marie Anne took no notice of it. She was raring to go for her first lesson with Professor Alvarez. She had listened to this woman's advice for a solid hour that morning on what she had to do and what she hadn't to do; and one thing she hadn't to do was to chatter to the professor; she was there to learn music and nothing else. Nor could she allow her companion to spend two hours doing nothing as she waited for her three times a week, and so she was to be careful with whom she made friends, such as other musicians, because musicians in the main were mostly of low character. And at home she must practise more hymns, with not so much banging and rattling of the keys, but quiet and soothing religious works.

When Sarah Foggerty's coughing seemed to be troubling her again, Marie Anne, glancing at her fob watch and addressing her aunt, said, 'If I'm not at the studio on time, it will be good money wasted; and that would never do, would it, Aunt, so may we go now?'

'You are meaning to be insolent, girl, aren't you? I understand now why you were dismissed from two schools.'

'I wasn't dismissed from two schools, Aunt, I left of my own accord; and I'm not meaning to be insolent; it's just that I'm tired already of petty rules.'

'Then let me tell you, girl,' and now Martha Culmill almost barked at her, 'you'll be more tired in the future, for as long as you stay in my house and under my care you'll obey my rules, or I'll write to your mother and hear what she has to say about it.'

Marie Anne's voice was low and trembling as she responded, 'I think you already know what my mother thinks about me; after all, that's why I'm here.'

'Foggerty, take her away out of my sight. I . . . I never thought that at my age and in my own house I'd have to put up with such insolence.'

So they went out of her sight, not exchanging a word until they were in the street, and then it was Sarah who made a simple statement: 'You've got spunk, I'll say that for you. Even if you have nothing else you've got spunk. And I can see it getting you through life.' Then on a little giggle she added, 'That is, if somebody doesn't shoot you first.'

'Oh, Sarah. She . . . she upsets me. She's awful . . . awful.'

'I agree with every word you say about her, but you're here and you've got to put up with it, and so let's put our best foot forward: we don't want to arrive at the Academy late, do we? And I'd better tell you before you get there, you're going to be disappointed in it. I don't know so much about the man who runs it – although he seemed a nice enough fellow – but it struck me as odd that he let himself be beaten down by your aunt over his charges. I wouldn't have thought he would have done that unless he was short of money.'

'You said it was a house, but did you mean that it was the professor's house and that there was a school attached?'

'Girl, in ten minutes time you'll see for yourself. There's no school, as such, but there are places that are called schools, even academies, all with fancy names, but they're really nothing more than ordinary houses.'

'Oh Sarah, don't say I'm not going to like it.'

'Well, that's up to you, miss. Anyway, it's exactly a fifteen-minute walk from door to door, and as time goes by I can get you there by three different routes and let you see a bit of London, because I think that's the only way you'll manage it; there'll be no Sunday jaunts for you. All your Sundays will be taken up with chapel and prayer.'

'Oh no, they won't. I won't go.'

'Well, that'll be *your* battle. We all have our battles to fight; I'm fighting one inside me every day with that woman, and I can tell you if I could find a decent job tomorrow, I'd be out of this one like a shot.'

'Oh, Sarah. Please . . . please don't think of leaving. I can't see how I would bear that house without you.'

'It might come that you'll have to, dear. But never mind

about the future; it's the present; so come on, step out;' only to ask almost immediately, 'is that foot hurting you?'

'It is a bit when I hurry. It's the one that was broken.'

'Oh, I'm sorry, me dear. I'm sorry. Well, we'll take it easy. What matter if you're a minute or so late.' . . .

They weren't late. They reached the house and walked into a hallway, then into a waiting-room. Here they sat on bentwood chairs and waited. Neither of them spoke; but now and again they would turn and look at each other.

When the door opened abruptly and an elderly woman entered, saying, 'Ah! there you are,' they both rose to their feet.

'I am Mrs Liza Alvarez and you' – she looked at Marie Anne – 'must be Miss Lawson . . . right?'

'Right,' put in Sarah Foggerty, which seemed to surprise the lady, who raised her eyebrows and for no reason said, 'Yes,' then added, 'Come this way; the professor is ready for you.'

Marie Anne did not immediately follow the well-dressed woman. She was surprised to discover that she, a professor's wife, was a common woman.

She now turned to Sarah and said, 'I will see you at three o'clock then, Sarah.'

'Yes, miss. Three o'clock I'll be here.'

At the doorway, two little girls, each carrying music and laughing, squeezed past her into the waiting-room and sat on the two chairs she and Sarah had just vacated.

The woman ushered Marie Anne into a room, saying, 'In here. He will be with you in a moment.'

Marie Anne looked around her. It was a large, some-what bare room. In the middle was a table on which stood small piles of music, and against the wall, opposite the fireplace, was an upright piano. It was a beautiful-looking instrument, very like the one back home, and was made of rosewood.

She walked towards it and as her fingers touched the

inside of the lid a voice startled her, saying, 'It is a nice-looking piano, you think, yes?'

'Oh.' She turned smiling towards the man, who had entered from another room. 'Yes. Yes, it is.'

They stood surveying each other. She saw a man of medium height, who looked well built but wasn't fat. He, too, had black hair, but unlike his wife's, his looked natural. The skin of his face was tanned and his eyes were round and dark and merry-looking. He had what she would call a kind face. When he held out his hand to her, she noticed that his fingers were short and rather plump, but his handshake was firm and warm. That, she was to recall, was her first impression of him: he was warm, a nice man, and warm. And she saw immediately, too, that he looked younger than his wife. She guessed that he was not yet forty years old, but she knew she was no real judge of men's ages. What she did recognise immediately was that he had a lovely voice: he was saying, 'Well, shall we get started? I understand that you already play well, but we shall see, won't we? We shall see.'

On these last words, he bent his body slightly towards her, and when he smiled his teeth looked very white against the tan of his skin.

After adjusting the round music stool to her height and noticing that she seemed nervous, he said, 'Now, forget about me and play; something you know, have memorised, yes?'

She looked down and placed her hands on the keys; then she started to play. All the while she was conscious that he was walking about the room, and only once did he stop by her side, to remark, 'Beethoven's Sonatina in G. That was an easy piece, wasn't it?'

'Yes, but . . . but I like it.'

'I like it, yes, too. Yes, I like it. But tell me, who do you enjoy playing? It's apparent that you like Beethoven, but what about Bach, Mozart, Liszt?'

'Oh' – she smiled up at him now – 'Oh, I like Liszt, but his music is very hard to play. His timing, too . . .'

'You think so?'

'Yes. Although I know I play many pieces too quickly, I don't feel I can ever play his fast enough.'

'Oh well, then, we'll have to see that you practise his pieces. What about Bach?'

'I'm . . . I'm not very fond of churchy music.'

He laughed outright now. 'You call his work churchy? Well, maybe, because he loved the organ.'

Apologetically now, she said, 'It's probably because I don't like hymns.'

Again he was laughing; then bending towards her he whispered, 'I'll let you into our first secret, I don't neither. No, I don't neither.'

She was smiling at him, but she wanted to laugh outright at his mixing up of the language, for it sounded quaint. He had a lovely voice, though. But now the voice changed and became quite businesslike when he said, 'Well, shall we leave all the composers sleeping for today, and concentrate on scales? Shall we? Scales, scales, scales.'

When she looked somewhat surprised, he said, 'Scales can be very musical if they are played correctly, eh?'

She hadn't thought she would be made to practise scales again, but that's how the two hours were spent; and it was not until ten minutes before the end of the session that he stopped his pacing up and down and his shouted corrections and said, 'Please cease now. It has been very tiring for you, I know. Yes?'

'No,' she lied; 'not really, but it's a long time since I . . . well, I played scales.'

'That is evident. Oh evident, evident.' He was smiling now. 'Would you like to play something for me; another one that you like?'

She drew in a long breath, looked down on the

81

keyboard, then said quietly, 'I would rather listen to you, if I may.'

'Oh. Oh.' His face beamed now. 'That is very nice of you, and I will certainly oblige. What would you like to hear?'

She hunched her shoulders just slightly, and there was an impish look on her face as she said, 'Liszt.'

His laugh rang out as he repeated, 'Liszt it shall be, just a little. Here we go.'

As she slid off the stool he sat down, and for the next five minutes or so she stood by his side and became enthralled at his playing. This was real piano playing. She had only once before heard Liszt played and that was at a concert that Pat had taken her to. When he had finished he said, 'What was I playing?'

She shook her head; all she knew was, she would never be able to play like that, and so she said to him, 'That was beautiful, what . . . what was it?'

And he answered, 'Just a part of Liszt's concerto in E flat.'

She repeated again, 'It was beautiful.'

'Well, in a very short time I should be able to return the compliment and say, That was beautiful, Miss Lawson, beautifully played.'

They were staring at each other without speaking; then he said, 'It only needs practise, practise, practise; and I understand you will have time of plenty –' he now took the palm of his hand and beat his brow with it and he laughed as she said, 'plenty of time, Professor Alvarez.'

They were both smiling as he opened the door for her, saying, 'Tomorrow, bring what music you have with you.'

'I haven't any.'

Then, his head bobbing, he said, 'You will have to pur-chase some, eh?'

'Yes;' and she repeated, 'I shall have to pur-chase some.'

In the waiting-room there was a boy of about ten waiting, and he was on crutches. She wanted to stop and speak to him, for she knew what it was like to be on crutches. But there was the Professor's wife at one door and Sarah Foggerty at the other.

'Well! How did it go?' asked Sarah, as they went out into the street.

'Very well. He's very good, at least I think he's going to be, but he put me on scales all the time. I'm to bring my own music tomorrow and I haven't any.'

'In that case, me dear, you'll just have to tell her you need money to buy some.'

'Oh, I know what she would say, and I'd have to get more hymns I suppose. No; I have some money of my own that my—'

'You have money of your own? Where? because I know she's been through your things.'

'She hasn't!'

'Oh, yes, she has. It's amazing how quickly her rheumaticky legs can go when she wants them to. She only found three shillings in your purse, so where's your money?'

'In my petticoat.'

Sarah let out a high laugh as she said, 'Good for you, good for you. Then keep it there. Is it much?'

'A few pounds.'

'Ha! Ha! She would never think of looking there. Anyway, there's a music shop in the High Street; you'll get anything you want there. We'll call on our way here tomorrow. Now, as soon as we get back you'll have to go upstairs and give her the run-down on what's happened; and I'd like to bet she's none too pleased by the fact that four shillings has been spent on practising scales, even when it isn't out of her pocket. And by the way, what did you think of his wife?'

It was a moment or so before Marie Anne answered,

and then truthfully, 'I haven't thought of her at all.' And it was to be the same for months to come: Liza Alvarez was to remain apart from the music room, except when she ushered her in for her lessons.

But months pass and time changes.

3

Dearest Grandpa,

The Christmas holidays are over and I am so thankful. I start school again tomorrow. Each day I am more grateful for your lovely fleece-lined coat and Pat's hood and gloves, because the cold here is different from that at home. It eats into you, and the fog is terrible, oh dreadful. But something nice happened the other day. It helped me to get over not seeing Pat — I cannot imagine Pat falling into a ship's hold; he's so used to inspecting them; but I am so happy to know he is up and about now and walking again, even if it is with the aid of a stick. I wrote him a long letter yesterday and told him about the nice thing that happened to me through Sarah and all the funny things she says. He will likely have already told you, but, anyway, the professor had a cold and so, as it was Sarah's half-day off, which seemed a great piece of luck, she took me on a quick tour of the sights. I saw Buckingham Palace, Grandpa.

We stood looking through the iron railings. There were many other people doing the same thing and all talking about the Queen although, as Sarah put it, there was no hope in . . . you know where, of seeing the old girl, and that was no loss. I don't think she likes the Queen, because she said there's more than one old tyrant in the world. She likes the Prince, although there's a lot of scandal talked about him.

The highlight of our gallivanting was that we went

on a boat on the river, and the sun was shining and a man played a melodeon. Oh, it was magical, Grandpa. And lastly, what d'you think? We had a real tea in The Corner House — Lyons. Then we were ten minutes late in returning to the house, but it didn't matter; we both told the same lie. I'll never be able to thank Sarah Foggerty for all she has done for me. I wish you could see her; or, at least, hear her, Grandpa; she makes you laugh even when you don't want to.

My music is coming on. I feel I'm progressing, and the professor is such a good teacher, so patient. He is a very nice man; you, too, would like him, Grandpa.

I must close now, Grandpa; but having said all this, I am very lonely inside for you and Pat . . . and the dogs and the garden and the open country. Oh, how I long to run, Grandpa; but I wonder, even if I were back home, if I would ever run again as I used to, as my foot still hurts at times.

As Clara is apt to say, we are all miserable belly-fuls. One thing I am sure you have noticed, Grandpa, and it is that my English will not have improved; but the girls' talk here is the only light thing in this house. I refer to them as girls, for I don't think of them as servants or maids; they are my friends. And lastly, to answer one of your questions: no, I have made no new friends here because no-one ever visits, and the pupils at the school all seem to be very young. Except for a lady pupil, I must be the oldest there.

Good night, my dearest, dearest Grandpa.

'We are sad today, my little Infanta; what is it?'

'Nothing. I think I have a cold coming on.'

'You are in the fashion then; everyone in this country has to have a spring cold. Here we have April: the flowers are blooming, the birds are singing, and bumble bees were heard buzzing in the park yesterday; it is the time of coming alive; so, my little Infanta, shall we bring the keys alive?' He put his arm around her shoulders and drew her to the revolving stool, and after she had sat down he gently pulled her around to face him and, bending his face close to hers, he said, 'Is something deep troubling you, Infanta?'

He had lovely eyes, she thought, and his mouth looked so kind. At times, when he came close to her like this, she wanted to put her head on his shoulder, because he was so like her grandpa. No, he was so much younger; he was more like Pat and he had a lovely face and he smelt nice. Yes, he always smelt nice. It was a warm smell. She likened it to the smell that came up from the garden in the evening; one that you couldn't put a name to because it didn't come from any particular flower.

She said to him, 'I long to be able to move' – she impulsively flung her arms wide – 'face space, run and run, to my grandpa and my brother. I have told you of them; they are lovely men.'

'And your mama?'

She turned her head away from him as she muttered, 'My mother doesn't want me at home; I've always been a nuisance.'

'Never!'

'Yes. Yes.' She was looking at him again. 'You see, I know I am impulsive; I do things, and when I'm upset . . . well, when I was back home and upset I just used to run, run out of the house, run for miles.' She smiled now, a wan smile, saying, 'I could, you know, Professor, I could run for great distances and not feel tired, but there's nowhere here to run, is there?'

'Oh yes; yes. On your way back home, your maid could take you through the park. It will only be five minutes further on. You could run from one gate to the other.'

She was smiling broadly now, saying, 'That's an idea.

It's a wonder Sarah didn't think of it. But there, it would make me late, which would get Sarah into trouble . . . there's my aunt, you see.'

He straightened up now and, his face solemn, he said, 'I imagine it. I imagine it. Your aunt is a for-midable woman. Oh, yes. So, what you must do,' he leaned towards her again, 'is outwit her. Eh? Outwit her.'

She smiled back at him as she said, 'I'm always trying to do that, but my tactics are not subtle enough.'

He cocked his head to one side and repeated, 'Subtle?'

'Yes, subtle, deep.'

'Ah. Ah yes, subtle, deep. There are some words I don't often hear, but subtle I shall remember. Now, let us turn to Chopin. What shall we attack first? A mazurka, eh? And I can assure you we shall both feel better in an hour's time because – I will let you into a deep secret –' and now his lips were quite close to her ear as he murmured, 'the man behind the professor, too, is sad, and also for his home.'

As she said, 'Oh I'm sorry,' she felt a great warmth arise in her for this man. He was different from everyone she had ever met and she was liking him more every day, and the desire to put her arms around him as she did with her grandpa and Pat, was very strong in her; but this she knew she must not do, because he wasn't a relation.

His hand came out towards her, then suddenly dropped away, and he turned from her, saying in a quite different tone, 'Another day gone. Tomorrow we shall continue to arrest your hands from racing off the keys.'

Although his tone had ended on a lighter note, she did not smile at his gentle chastising, for she knew that she had long since complied strictly to the time the music demanded.

She did not say goodbye to him in the usual way, nor did he say anything to her, but he opened the door for her to pass into the corridor, and, walking slowly to the little waiting-room, she knew that in an odd way something had happened between them, but what, she couldn't put a name to; she only knew it was in the way he had withdrawn his hand and how he had then spoken to her.

She hadn't been with Sarah Foggerty a few minutes before that very intuitive woman asked, 'Something wrong?'

'No. No, nothing.'

'Well, you do surprise me. You generally come out of there with your face full of stars; but if you had today, they would soon have been wiped off when I tell you that a letter came in the second post. Your mother's refusing to have you back there for a holiday, although, by the sound of things, she and your sister are going off to Scotland; and reading between the lines, they are chuffed that these people who are inviting them are very Dublin.'

Marie Anne hesitated in her step, her expression slightly puzzled, and she said, 'What d'you mean, very Dublin?'

'Well . . . well, as they say over there, talk like a Dubliner and you could be invited to Buckingham Palace. Very top drawer, you know, or up country, as them that come back home from America say. My cousin Shane came back from there. He said it was a place where only money talked and he couldn't learn the language.'

Sarah laughed outright now, as did Marie Anne. Then keeping to the subject, Sarah said, 'I don't see why their going on a holiday should stop you from having a trip home, and why the woman is so determined about it puzzles me. You didn't murder anybody, did you, during your wild days there?'

'No, Sarah, I didn't, although I often felt inclined to at times. No; it's just that I am not wanted in the family. But I can tell you that it no longer hurts me, because *that* family consists of Father, Mother, Vincent and Evelyn only. My family is made up of just two: Grandpa and my brother Pat.'

'Aye well, that's as may be, but your mother seems to have the upper hand.'

Marie Anne was quick to turn now and say, 'No, she hasn't, not really. Grandpa is still master of both houses.'

'Both of them? You have two then?'

'Well, there is The Manor and The Little Manor.'

'My God! Two houses, and your own mother won't let you stay in one. Well it's like they say, the English are the queerest breed on earth, and you can never bottom an Englishman: scrape away as you like, he'll come up with a different face. Now us lot, in the main we are classed as common and ignorant and not over clean. They scorn us because we like pigs. Well, let me tell you, Miss Marie, that a pig is a very clean animal. It picks a place to leave what it doesn't want, and that's more than some English folk can do if you look at some of the streets we pass through. What d'you say?'

Marie Anne could say nothing to this, because yes, some of the streets were really filthy: men spat a lot, and, as little Clara had said, the cleanest places in London were the pubs, because the floors were sawdusted and they kept spittoons there.

As Marie Anne was about to step off the pavement and on to the rough road, Sarah pulled her to a halt, saying, 'I wouldn't die that way; it'd be very painful.' Then as the two great feather-footed dray horses pulling the long flat cart full of barrels of beer rumbled past, she pointed to them, saying, 'My! my! If I only had the money it cost just to make those barrels, I'd be up and away the morrer.'

They had crossed the road weaving through hand carts, cabs and numerous boys pushing barrows, before Marie Anne spoke again, and what she said was, 'Oh, I wish you wouldn't talk like that, Sarah, because, you know, if you did I would be unable to stand that house, even . . . even if I still had the professor and the music, I just couldn't stand it.'

'Oh, my! miss. Don't take any notice of my jabber. I've been going on like that for years. I'm always saying if I had this and if I had that, what I would do, when what I would likely do would be damn all, for if I had a few bob to throw away, it would go along to my sister Annie and her tribe. If anyone needs a windfall it's her. You know, the only time I wish I were male is when I come across her man, Arthur Pollock, then I'd be wearing a pair of hobnailed boots and I'd kick him up the arse from here to blazes. Oh! Oh! Oh!' Quickly now she covered her eyes with her hands, saying, 'Sorry I am, miss, it is, it is. The things I come out with. Now I never use that word, not really . . . well, not in your presence anyway.'

Marie Anne was spluttering now, 'Oh, don't worry about that, Sarah. It isn't the first time I've heard that word. I've heard my grandpa use it when going for some of the men in the yard . . . well, let me put it politely, sitting on that part of their body when they should have been about their work.'

They were walking very close together now, their bodies shaking with laughter. As they drew near to the house, Sarah Foggerty suddenly stopped and remarked, 'D'you know what I'd like to do, miss?'

'Yes,' said Marie Anne on a laugh, 'kick a certain person—'

'No! no! not at this minute. I'd like to go into the house singing. Just fancy if we both went in singing, what d'you think would happen?'

'Oh!' Marie Anne's body was now shaking and she leaned against this lovable woman, saying, 'I dare you to go in singing.'

'I'll do it, that's if you promise when I get the sack, you'll come away with me.'

Their laughter subsiding, they looked at each other; then Sarah said, 'Wipe the smile off your face, miss; it looks as if it's glued there. Remember, you're very miserable. Come on, let's face the meanest woman in this benighted country.'

4

It was a stifling day. A haze of heat was pressing down on the city, and Sarah Foggerty, defying all orders, was walking in the street without a coat; as she said, exposing herself to the whole world in her uniform dress.

As for Marie Anne, she was wearing a very soft print dress. It was of a white background dotted with tiny blue forget-me-nots. It had elbow-length sleeves and a square neck, a low square neck that should have been hidden by the small matching jacket swinging from her hand.

At the door of the house, Sarah left her, saying, 'Well, go on, sweat it out; me, I'm going to jump into the Serpentine, boots, hat an' all.'

'That wouldn't surprise me, Sarah.'

They parted on a laugh.

There was no-one in the waiting room, but the door leading into the passage opened immediately and there stood the professor, saying, 'I thought you would have joined all the rest of my pupils and gone to the seaside. All London must be hanging on to railway carriages today . . . Even Liza. She is attending some woman's group she has joined. I think they are going to put the world to rights. That means getting rid of all men.'

He was laughing loudly as he ushered her into the music room. Then looking into her face, he said, 'Give me your hat; you look very hot,' and instead of waiting for her to put down her music and take off her hat he bent swiftly towards her and pulled the long pin from the back of the straw hat, took off the hat and thrust the pin back into the straw, saying, 'Dangerous things, hat pins. They would have a man up to the law if he carried such a weapon.' Then after a pause and looking at her closely again, he said, 'Do you want to practise?'

'Please.'

'Oh well, it is *your* lesson.'

So she sat down, and first, as was usual, she ran through a series of scales. Following this, she opened her music at the piece she had been practising over the weekend. But when her fingers faltered on the keys he stopped her, saying, 'Oh my dear, you are spiring . . . I mean, perspiring so much. Come; no more for the time being. Let us go into the next room; it is cooler there. The long window, it funnels the air from our narrow passage of a garden lying between its brick walls, and you like the piano there better, I think.'

The room, as she had often thought, must have been used as a sitting-room, for there was a suite in it, both the couch and the two chairs being upholstered in a soft leather, and the seats were very low.

'Sit down on the couch,' he said, 'and I will go and make us a cooling drink, eh?' He smiled down on her now, and she lay back and closed her eyes.

She was so hot and sad inside, and that's what the voice said to her and brought her eyes wide: 'In repose your face looks very sad. Are you sad today?'

She pulled herself up straight on the couch and took the glass of lemonade from his hand, saying, 'Yes, I suppose I am.'

He sat down beside her. He too was holding a glass, and he said practically, 'Well, don't hold the glass with two hands like that, it'll be warm before you drink it. Drink it up; it is made from fresh lemons.'

The drink was cool, and certainly refreshing, and she turned to him and smiled and said, 'It's lovely. We rarely have fruit back at the house, and never lemons. I don't

94

remember seeing a lemon since I came here, except of course in the shops.'

When her drink was half finished, he took it from her, and with his own placed it on the floor to the side of them. Then pushing her gently back on the couch, he too leaned back, though he remained a little distance from her, and asked, 'What has made you sad?'

'Well, the letter I got this morning told me that my brother Pat was taken into hospital last week. His back has worsened. And he was getting on so well. He was going to make one of his journeys down here next week: he does so at least twice a year on business, something to do with the ships, you know. He was going to stay at a hotel. The rooms had been booked, mine also, and my aunt could do nothing about it. I was so excited. But apparently his back has become very painful. I understand they're going to put him into a jacket of some sort, like a brace, so that he'll be able to walk about. He was going to stay here a week.'

Her voice suddenly broke, and she bit on her lip, and at this he moved along the couch and put his arm around her shoulder, saying, 'There, there! my dear. Don't cry, please. Please do not cry; I couldn't bear to see you cry, you who are like bright daylight to me.'

She blinked her eyes and looked into the face that was close to hers and she smiled softly as she said, 'You do say the quaintest things, Professor.'

'My name is Carlos.'

'Carlos,' she repeated.

'Yes, Carlos; and you have said it and it sounded good. Carlos Alvarez, a Spaniard in a foreign country. Although I have been here a number of years it is still a foreign country to me, and it was so dull, so very dull and dreary until one day a dragon comes to me and says, "I have a niece who I want teached . . . taught to learn the piano, but your charge is too large. I will not pay you two and

95

sixpence an hour; two shillings, that is all;" and . . . and so because I have to live I agreed. And then . . . and then . . .' he lifted up his index finger as if he were commanding silence and his voice was very low as he went on, 'the pupil came and from the minute I looked at her I knew I would have been very, very happy to teach her all I knew for nothing, no money whatever, because she is so beautiful . . . so strangely, strangely beautiful.' The finger moved to her cheek, then down to her chin, and up to the other cheek-bone, and she didn't move. The finger then became part of a doubled fist placed close to his skin within the opened neck of his white shirt, and his deep voice was trembling as he went on, 'She was the Infanta of dreams. Dreams such as a man has at night to blot out the drabness of his days and I thought, if I can make this Infanta my friend, that will be enough. Are you my friend, Marie Anne?'

She was unable to speak, for she knew that if he had thoughts of her in the night, she too had had thoughts of him, for she had imagined him touching her face as he had just done. She imagined her head lying on his shoulder. She had even dared to imagine him kissing her lips. But he was a professor and he was married and it was wrong to hold such thoughts about him. But she could be his friend. Yes, yes; she could be his friend, and she said so now, her voice breaking into a whimper as she said, 'I would love to be your friend, someone I can talk to about . . . about everything, especially the music. You . . . you know so much.' An inner voice was telling her, yes that's the best thing to do. Talk about your music. Ask him about the exams. 'In fact,' she now said, 'I wanted to talk to you particularly about the examinations.'

She watched his eyes close tightly, then blink once before, taking a handkerchief from a back pocket and rubbing it round his moist face, he spoke, saying one word: 'Examinations.'

'Yes. I . . . I will have to take examinations and practise for them, won't I?'

He moved slightly back from her now, saying. 'Yes. Yes of course; but . . . but not for a time.'

'I . . . I will soon have been with you a year and I understand I have a number of exams to get through before I can be qualified to teach.'

Leaning forward, he put his elbows on his knees and his joined hands moved between them for a time before, businesslike, he said, 'Yes; yes, you must have examinations before you are qualified; but when you are ready for examinations you will go to an academy.'

'Why? Why?' She was leaning towards him now, her hand on his arm. 'Can't you put me through examinations?'

He straightened his back and looked at her as he said, 'No, my dear. I am sorry I must tell you, and I would ask you to keep it to yourself, but I cannot put you through an examination. I can prepare you as far as any teacher could, but . . . but I cannot arrange for you to have an examination in music.'

She drew her head back from him as if to get him into focus, and then she said, 'Why on earth not? You are a marvellous teacher. I know I have improved to a far greater extent than I ever thought possible.'

He turned towards her again. Their knees were touching and there was a great sadness in his voice as he said, 'This is not a proper academy. I am just like many another in this trade. I . . . I can confess this to you: I am not a professor of music. I have myself never taken an examination, although I know that I am better qualified than the thousands who have. I know I have great ability, but I am of a . . . what you would call a' – he seemed to be hunting for a word, then said, – 'facile nature. Perhaps I am hard on myself in saying that, for I was never given the opportunity. Some day I will tell you my

97

story, then you will understand. In the meantime, my dearest, dearest Infanta' – now his hand was cupping her cheek – 'the day we have to part my life will change, but part we shall have to. When the year is up, I myself will write to your grandfather and put the story before him, and your uncle or someone else responsible will see that you are settled in a good home and as a member of a real academy. Yes; oh yes, you could because, my dear, dear Marie Anne—' he was now holding her face in both hands and his voice was breaking as he said, 'you have a remarkable talent. But you should have been trained from when you were a child. You need discipline. You agree?'

She couldn't say yes or nay: she only knew at this moment that she too would be desolate when she had to part from him, and she was near to tears now as she said, 'I won't . . . I won't bother with exams; it doesn't matter. But I don't want anyone else to teach me but you, only you, ever.'

'Oh, my dear one. My dear one.'

Even before his hands touched her shoulders she was lying against him, and when his lips touched her neck, just above the top of her dress, she shivered from head to foot; but when they reached her mouth, she let herself fall into his arms. And now they were lying side by side on the floor and his hands were moving over her. She found herself being lulled into an ecstatic state by his voice, speaking in Spanish now but murmuring words of love, she knew.

Then, when his weight came on to her, she experienced something that brought her eyes wide, for she was seeing a picture, and it was of her sister's bare thighs, and at this a wave of fear and sanity swept through her, and when she cried out, 'No! No! please, no!' his voice came at her thick, almost fuddled.

'It's all right, my darling. It's all right, my Infanta. I

would never hurt you, never, never, never. It's all right, my love.'

His mouth was on hers again. Even so, she tried to rise. She recalled pressing her hands against his chest and her body heaving to rise. Then in the next moment she was appalled to realise that he was almost fighting with her; and there came a time when she could struggle no more, and it was done.

'What is it, me dear? You've been crying?'

Marie Anne made no reply but kept walking on until she was pulled roughly to a halt, and there was Sarah Foggerty staring into her face and saying, 'What's he done? Has he been at you? Now tell me!' It was a demand.

'No, no.' Her words came rushing out now. 'It was . . . it was just that I was feeling sad about . . . well, about Pat and . . . and him not being able to come. And I was looking . . . well, I was looking forward to it, as you know and I told—' She hung her head, and Sarah, her voice now full of understanding, said, 'And he sympathised with you and that made you bubble.'

Marie Anne's head was still bowed as she nodded.

'Ah well; he's a nice man, thoughtful, and he would feel sorry for you. In fact, anybody would feel sorry for you after meeting your aunt. Come on. Come on. Cook's made a cake for your birthday tomorrow. It's a surprise and I shouldn't be telling you, but it's lovely. She's pinched and scraped and spent quite a few of her own coppers on it, so I know you'll show your appreciation.'

'Oh yes; yes.' Marie Anne's head was bobbing as they walked on. Yes, she would show her appreciation. And he *was* a nice man, understanding . . . except . . . except for . . . That part had been terrible . . . awful, at least for a while. And oh dear me, she wished she was back in her bedroom and had a dish of cold water to wash her body. That was what had happened to Evelyn that night. That was what had made her run, and had resulted in her now being here in London under the guardianship of that awful woman, only . . . only to do the same thing that she had been so shocked by. But she had tried. Oh yes, she had tried to stop him. And afterwards he had been so contrite and worried because she couldn't stop crying. She didn't know if she'd be able to face him tomorrow. Yet she must. Did she still like him? That question she couldn't answer . . . not yet; no, she couldn't. She'd have to get washed; then later tonight, when in bed and she could think, perhaps the answer would come . . .

The answer did come when she was in bed: it said, yes she still liked him, but she didn't know if she still loved him as she had done last night when she had thought about him. One thing was certain: he must never do that to her again. Never. But she didn't blame him entirely: she knew that she had leaned against him; she admitted to herself that she had wanted him to hold her close, even wanted to feel his kisses, but not that. NO! No, not really, because she hadn't thought that far. If Evelyn had come into her mind earlier it might have reminded her.

She knew now that if she had to leave at the end of the year to go to a proper academy, then the parting wouldn't be so hard. She also knew in this dark moment that she should never have slapped Evelyn's face, nor said she was dirty and filthy, for what had happened to Evelyn had happened to her today. Part of it had been beautiful, but another part had been ugly.

'What is wrong with you, girl? You are not practising like you used to, and when you do practise you only play music that murders the keys. Bang! bang! bang! bang!'

'I've told you, Aunt; I have a cold.'

'That's weeks ago you had a cold, girl. You've spent a day in bed twice since then. One doesn't go to bed with a cold.'

'Well, if it isn't a cold, Aunt, it's something that is making me feel unwell.'

'Don't use that tone to me, girl. I've told you before. And let me tell you, the way you're playing now doesn't show any advancement. That man is getting his money easy. Does he oversee your practice at all?'

'Yes, he oversees my practice, Aunt. Every minute of the time I am there I am playing the piano. Non-stop, non-stop.'

Martha Culmill stared at the girl who, during the past months, under her very eyes had seemed to put on years. Listening to her, she couldn't imagine she was but a girl of sixteen and one who, until she had come into this house, had spent her life in the country, in the back-woods, you could say, running wild. Now she spoke and acted like any city woman. Yes, like a young woman, not a girl. Was Foggerty to blame? No, no. She must remember that this girl had been impertinent since the first day she came; it was in her nature. If she didn't know her own half-sister well she could have imagined she might have slipped up here, because this girl had an odd look about her. Beautiful, some people would call her, but to her and to anyone taking her features apart they were odd.

As Marie Anne turned towards the door she called to her, 'Go downstairs and tell Emery I need more coal for the fire; and if Foggerty hasn't yet returned from her leave, and I don't suppose she has, you will bring my dinner tray up.'

No please, or, will you kindly? Marie Anne turned from the door and looked towards the bed. Well, she shouldn't expect that, because she herself was never courteous to the woman.

However, before going downstairs she went into her own room and did a strange thing. After closing the door she stood with her brow pressed tight against the panel, her arms spread wide, and from the depths of her she cried, Dear God! what am I going to do? It was nine weeks now. When she missed her first period she had thought nothing of it, but when the second passed too and she began to be sick and Sarah had found her in the slush room, as the closet was called, vomiting into the pan, she had stood well back from her and with her face held tightly between her hands until her mouth was out of shape, she had muttered, 'God almighty! No! girl.' Then she had grabbed up the flannel that lay near a bowl of water, wetted it, and while wiping Marie Anne's face, she had continued to say, 'No, no! girl, not you.' Then she had pulled the lid of the lavatory seat down, thrust her on to it, and demanded, 'How long?'

When she had stared back at Sarah and shaken her head, Sarah had taken her by the shoulders and shaken her, and she had stammered, 'N-n-nine weeks . . . over.'

Sarah Foggerty had again stood apart from her, as if she were tracing back the time, and had suddenly cried, 'That hot day, the day you came out with your eyes all red; you had been crying. That was it, wasn't it?'

She had hung her head and thought, Yes; yes, that was it. The beautiful and the ugly experience. That was it.

Later, when she went into the kitchen she knew that Sarah had already broken the news, for they looked at her in utter amazement. They couldn't believe it; no, not of her: she was so young in her ways, so gullible. Well, it always happened to the gullible ones; that's what Clara said, and went on to quote her mother: 'If you don't wear bloomers, more than wind gets up your skirt.'

It raised no laugh on this occasion. This was a terrible business, and it had only just begun.

When the professor's wife entered the waiting-room, Sarah Foggerty said, 'Miss Lawson is in bed; she's not well; she won't be in this week. But I want a word with the professor about that. I've also come to settle the monthly bill, and I want a receipt. Will you take it?'

'Yes. I'll leave the receipt on the table here. You can pick it up as you leave. That door there,' the woman pointed.

Sarah tapped on the door, then unceremoniously entered the room to confront a very surprised man.

For a moment or so they stared at each other; then she said, 'You'll be wonderin' why I'm here and not your pupil.'

'Yes; perhaps I am.'

'Well, you won't see her this week; she's in bed.'

'Oh. Oh, I'm sorry. Is she ill?'

'Yes, you could say that. Yes, she is ill. But she'll be worse before she's better.'

It appeared as if he didn't quite understand her; then he said, 'She hasn't been herself this last week or so; she has looked rather pale.'

As her doubled fist caught him none too gently on the shoulder, he sprang back from her and she cried at him, 'Pale! Pale! Of course she's pale. You saw to it, didn't you?'

'What is wrong with you, woman?'

'It's not what is wrong with me, sir, it's what's wrong with you and her. You've given her a baby, and now you stand there and say she looked pale!'

His mouth fell slowly into a gape and he questioned, 'Baby?'

'Yes, a baby . . . a baby, a child.'

'No! Oh! no. I never imagined . . .'

'Well, what did you expect when you had your way with her, and her just a bit of a girl? You're a married man.'

Again he was shaking his head. Then he put his hand out towards a chair and was about to sit down when, addressing her again, he said, 'Please. Please be seated.'

'I don't want to be seated. I'm going to ask you what you're going to do about it.'

'Please! I beg you, allow me to sit. Please take a chair and listen.'

She sat on the piano stool and, glaring at him, she said, 'She trusted you. She thought a lot about you, and of your tin-pot, so-called music school. As far as I can guess, she's the oldest one you teach, the rest are but youngsters. Well, I say to you again, what are you going to do about her?'

He was sitting now with his elbows on his knees and his head in his hands. It was an abject pose; but suddenly he straightened up and growled at her, 'What can I do for her?' He flung one arm wide as if taking in, not only the school, but his life, and added, 'I what you call exist, and that is all at this time. But I will tell you this. I love that girl. Age does not measure out the love one can give.'

'Love! Huh! See what your love has brought her to.'

Pityingly now, he said, 'What am I to do? What's *she* going to do?'

'You've done enough; you can do no more. And she won't be back here again; I also know she certainly won't be going back home to her mother, because she won't have her. That's one thing I know. But her grandfather and brother will do something about it, so I think you should be prepared for a visit from them.'

She watched him draw in a deep breath and straighten his shoulders as if he were already facing an attack. Then half apologetically, she said, 'Well, they'll want to get to the bottom of it.'

'When are you going to tell her aunt?'

'For me, I would say it's best to let her find out for herself, and that won't be long now.'

She watched him screw up his eyes, in fact, his whole face, as if in an effort to be rid of the picture she presented to him.

As she rose to her feet she surprised herself by saying,

'You mightn't believe it, but at this minute I feel sorry for you. I didn't when I first came in, mind.' To this he made no reply, he just shook his head as if in bewilderment.

Nor did he speak as he opened the door for her, although his head jerked at the sight of the woman hurrying away down the passage.

In the street, she stood for a moment breathing deeply, before saying to herself, Now to Annie's to see what further pickle she and her tribe are in.

5

For the next fortnight or so Marie Anne and Sarah left the house as if they were going for the daily music lesson; but each time they would double down the lane and through the back door. For a time they would remain in the kitchen, until the requisite time for Sarah's return brought her to the front door again. Sometimes Marie Anne would lie on Cook's bed in her cubby-hole of a room, and that kind woman would make her tea and provide her with a slice of bread and butter or a bun, or whatever was going, for Marie Anne was finding that she was very hungry these days.

It was fortunate for them all that Martha Culmill kept to her bedroom in the winter, but how long things would have continued in this way is only to be guessed at, because as yet Marie Anne was able to wear a slack pinafore dress with no waistline. However, on this particular day they had a visitor. Little Clara Emery opened the front door to her, and when the woman said, 'I want to see your missis,' Clara, putting on what she assumed was a dignified front, said, 'May I have your name, ma'am?'

'Yes, miss; you may have my name. It's Liza Alvarez, and I don't intend to stand out here in the cold and wait to be announced.'

A voice from along the corridor called, 'What is it, Clara? Who is it?'

When Sarah Foggerty came to the door and recognised the visitor, her mind immediately said, Oh my God! This is the showdown. But she kept her voice steady as she said, 'You wanted to see someone?'

'You know damn fine well I want to see someone, and that someone is this aunt of hers, the little bitch!'

'Don't you dare use that tone here, madam . . . missis.'

'I am neither madam nor missis and I will use what tone I like; and you get to your mistress and tell her I want to speak to her, and speak I will, or here I stay banging on your front door for all to hear.'

Sarah Foggerty pushed the open-mouthed Clara aside, and with a motion of her hand, she let the woman into the hall. Then in a voice as stiff as her expression she commanded the woman, 'Sit there! and I will inform Miss Culmill that you wish to see her. And it will all depend upon whether she wants to see you. Understand?'

She did not wait to hear the woman's reply but hurried up the stairs.

Before opening the bedroom door, she stood for a moment with her hand to her brow, asking herself what might be the best way to go about this; and the answer came: there was no best way. She just had to stand by and let events take their course.

She thrust open the door and in a tone that caused Miss Culmill to widen her eyes, she said, 'There's a woman downstairs wants to speak to you, and speak to you she will, because she's got some bad news to impart. D'you want to see her?'

'A woman wants to see me? What woman?'

'The music teacher's wife, if she is his wife, which now I'm havin' me doubts about.'

'What are you talking about, Foggerty? Why would she want to see me?'

'She has news for you, miss.'

Martha Culmill's eyes narrowed as she looked at her handmaiden; then quite suddenly she said, 'Show the woman up. And when she arrives you will stay here in this room. Whatever she says I shall want a witness.'

'Oh, you'll have a witness without me being here, miss, but nevertheless I'll stay.'

After the door had closed on Sarah, Martha Culmill stared at it in bewilderment. What was this now? What had that girl been up to that the music teacher's wife should want to speak to her?

After being ushered into the room the woman stood staring at the occupant of the bed. Then her glance swept the comfortably furnished room before the invalid almost barked at her, 'May I ask, madam, what you want?'

'You may well ask, and I'm going to tell you. That niece of yours has ruined my life. Everything was going smoothly; then she had to come and set her cap for him, the blazing little hussy. But I wouldn't have minded that; I was used to lasses and women falling for him. But this one, she's driven him away; he's gone.'

'Gone, the professor? Please explain yourself. What has his departure to do with my niece?'

The woman turned now and looked at Sarah Foggerty; she looked straight into her face as if asking her if this woman on the bed was dim or just purposely blind. Then she actually startled Sarah by demanding, 'You haven't told her then?'

'Told me what?'

Martha Culmill was sitting bolt upright in bed now. 'Make yourself plain, woman, and at once.'

'All right, madam; I'll put it into plain words for you. He's skedaddled, and back to Spain, I bet, because he's put your niece in the family way and was likely scared of what would happen to him.'

The woman and Sarah watched Martha Culmill slowly lower herself back into her pillows. Then her mouth opened wide as if she were gasping for air and one hand clutched her throat as if she were about to choke. And at this, Sarah Foggerty sprang to the dressing-table,

108

grabbed a bottle and returned to the bedside to wave the contents under her mistress's nose and she muttered, 'That was nearly a real one, not a make-believe to keep me waiting on her.' She now pulled on the bell-rope to the side of the bed and in answer Clara came hurrying into the room. 'Stay with her for a minute, Clara,' Sarah said. 'If she looks like going off again, waft that once or twice under her nose.' Then turning to the woman, she said, 'I think you've had your say, haven't you? So come on, out of it!'

Without a word the woman followed Sarah on to the landing and down into the hall; but when Sarah went to open the door, she said, 'Hold your hand a minute. D'you think I could sit down? I could do with some smelling salts meself; I feel all come over. This has been a shock to me too.'

She had sat down on the hall chair and she was breathing heavily as she looked up at Sarah and said, 'I wouldn't have cared a damn if he hadn't gone off. I was fond of him.'

'You weren't married to him?'

'No, no; I wasn't married to him, but I put him on his feet. Yes; I did. I made him so he could earn a living. It might have been of sorts, but nevertheless it was a living instead of his playing for drinks and coppers in the bars, as he had been doing. But you see' – she nodded up at Sarah – 'I knew a bit about music. Me mother played the piano and me dad the fiddle and I had been to concerts in me younger days, lots of them, but I'd never heard anybody play like he did. Oh, not all the time, no; only when the place was almost empty and there was nobody to listen to real good stuff; not "Won't You Come Home, Bill Bailey" and "Down at The Old Bull and Bush" and such. No. And I've met a lot of fake music teachers, and so I felt I knew what he could do if he had a home and was looked after properly. And that's what I did six years ago:

I took him in hand, and this is what I've got for it.'

Her voice suddenly sank to a mere whisper and again she said, 'But I wouldn't have minded about the last if only he had stayed. You see, he was a genius. Oh yes, he was a natural genius. He told me, from the time he started to work in a big house in Spain when he was eight years old, he had spent every minute he could dinging away on an old spinet they had moved into the servants' quarters. Then later, when the family would go away for months on end and the place was looked after by the caretaker, he would let him play on the piano in the big hall. Apparently he was fourteen when the master of the house first heard him play, and he sent him to music lessons, which was fine until the man died, when the place was sold and everyone was scattered. He had risen from a boot-boy, he told me, to the equivalent, I should imagine, of a footman in England, but he couldn't get another place. It was a bad time there for everybody. And for some reason he decided to come to England. But he found things worse here. That's when I met him. It took me to point out to him that there were thousands of fake music teachers and language teachers and all kinds of blooming teachers making a living on their little bits of talent. He did get a job for a time in a big house, but he couldn't stand the ways of the staff.'

She now pulled herself to her feet, straightened her hat, buttoned the collar of her quite smart velour coat and ended, 'But even if he didn't earn a penny he knew he was all right with me, because I'm not without a bit and that's my own house, bought and paid for. I've been in the clothes business for years and made a bit.'

Sarah had opened the front door for her, and as the woman went to step out she turned and had the last word, saying, and bitterly now, 'I could kill that young bitch, I could that' . . .

Back in the bedroom, Martha Culmill seemed to have

recovered somewhat for her words came in the form of an attack: 'You . . . you knew about this!'

'Not until a day or so ago, ma'am, and I was for breaking it to you then, but didn't know quite how.'

Sarah watched her mistress thumping her breast with her doubled fist as she repeated, 'Didn't know quite how!' Then she started again: 'She can't stay here, no matter what Veronica says. Bring the writing pad. No; wait. How far has this—' she had to gulp before she could force herself to mention the matter in any form, then she said, 'this . . . this business gone?'

'You mean, ma'am, how far is she with the child? I would say near on, as far as I can guess, three months.'

'Three!' she choked, 'And . . . and you tell me you didn't know?'

'Well,' Sarah's voice sounded quite casual now as she replied, 'Well, you didn't notice yourself, ma'am, did you?'

'I don't have dealings with her as much as you have. Surely she . . . she showed some distress.'

There was a quick glance between Clara and Sarah; then Sarah lied in her usual fashion: 'Not so you'd notice, ma'am. A bit down in the mouth perhaps, but then she nearly always is, for she would like to be at home.'

'Home! Yes, home; and that's where she's going. Definitely, she's going home, for I'm not having this. No; not in my house.' She now looked at Clara and ordered, 'Get yourself away about your work, girl.'

Clara went swiftly from the room and made straight for the kitchen, where Marie Anne was waiting. She was sitting by the side of the table, the fingers of one hand moving as if over the piano keys, and Clara said immediately, 'She nearly passed out. I had to keep wafting the salts. But she's come round now, because she went for Sarah, and she's having to write a letter. And that woman, I heard her say she wasn't his wife. Well, from what she

111

said that's how I took it. What happened when she came downstairs?'

Marie Anne made no answer, but Cook said, 'Enough for me to hear, and anyone in the front street, I would say, the way she went on. It was an eye-opener and I think to Miss Sarah an' all.' Then addressing Marie Anne pointedly she said, 'Was it to you, miss?'

Marie Anne stopped her drumming fingers, and her voice was very low as she answered, 'Yes, Cook. Yes, it was.'

A few minutes later Sarah came bustling into the kitchen. She had a letter in her hand and she spoke straightaway to Marie Anne: 'She's for sending you home right away. I've got to go to the main office with this.'

Marie Anne was on her feet. 'I'm not going! I'm *not* going home! I . . . I couldn't.'

'Girl. Girl. We've got to talk about this. Look; put on your hat and coat, wrap up and come along with me; the walk'll do you good.'

It wasn't until they were in the street that Marie Anne spoke again, when she said, 'I'm not going home, I couldn't, I just couldn't. Don't you see?'

'Yes, I see all right; but where d'you think you're going, me dear, if you don't go home, 'cos she won't have you back there, that's certain, not if your mother were to offer her a mint. So we've got to talk this over, girl.'

They continued to talk it over until late in the night, although it was merely a repetition from both sides. Sarah could see no other way out but that Marie Anne should go home; and Marie Anne was determined that no matter what happened she couldn't go home. Not even to the wonderful grandfather would she hear of presenting herself in her present condition, for she kept saying, 'I would die, and he would too, at the sight of me. I'm not going home.'

112

One strange thing on that day of revelation was that Martha Culmill had not demanded to see her . . .

It was late in the afternoon of the following day that a telegram arrived at the house. Sarah took it upstairs, and when she went to hand it to her mistress that woman barked at her, 'Open it and read it, woman!'

The message, being a wire, was brief, and so she read;

ON NO ACCOUNT MUST SHE RETURN STOP
DEFINITE STOP LETTER AND ADDITIONAL
SUPPORT FOLLOWING.

Martha Culmill would have welcomed the extra support to put up with her half-sister's daughter, but not with her sinful daughter. Never! Never! And she said those last two words of her thoughts aloud; in fact, she yelled them at Sarah, 'Never! Never!' and then she added, 'Never! will I tolerate that girl in my home a moment longer than can be helped. She must be found a place somewhere else. If her mother won't have her I certainly shouldn't be expected to take on the responsibility. Dear Lord! No. Not that kind of responsibility. Wickedness, unclean. Never, never will I tolerate such. She must go.

'Foggerty!' She called Sarah from the other side of the room, where she was attending to the fire.

'Yes, ma'am?'

'Go this minute to the Chapel House and tell the Reverend Trackman that I wish to see him as soon as possible. Stress that, will you? as soon as possible. Tell him the matter is very urgent and important.'

'Yes, ma'am.'

'Well! don't just stand there, woman!'

Sarah Foggerty did not hurry from the room; she left quietly. As she passed through the kitchen on the way to Cook's bedroom, where she had left Marie Anne a short while before, Cook spoke one word:

'Bad?'

And Sarah answered with another, 'Worse.'

In the bedroom, Marie Anne was sitting in an old basket chair. She was wearing her winter coat. It wasn't buttoned, but one side was pulled over the other and her arms were about it as if she were hugging herself.

'Why didn't you light the gas?' Sarah asked her. 'Sitting in the dark's not going to help.' She put a match to the gas bracket on the wall, and the shabby room became softly illuminated and cosy-looking, even though there was no mantle. Neither was there one in her own bedroom, nor in Clara's; in fact, there hadn't been one in Cook's room until she herself had seen to it. Sarah then pulled the curtains across the window before sitting down on the foot of the bed, and pointing at Marie Anne, she said, 'Now listen to me. Things are bad; they couldn't be worse. Your mother has sent a telegram. I'll give it to you plain: on no account is she having you back there. She's even sending your aunt more money so as to keep you here. But even the thought of more money is not going to soften that one's feelings towards you. She's going to have you out of this house and as soon as possible. I'm on my way now, at least so she thinks, but it'll have to be pretty soon, to the Reverend James Trackman. Well, you know what he's like, but most of all you know what his dear wife Delia sounds and looks like. There's not a penny to choose between her and that one upstairs. Now that is the situation facing you. You've got to get out of here, and soon. Likely they'll put you in some home.'

'Oh no! they won't. Oh no! they won't.'

'Then if you don't propose going back to your people, and you said you wouldn't, where do you think you can go?'

Marie Anne was on her feet now but her voice was a whimper as she said, 'I don't know, Sarah. I don't know.

But I'm not going into any home to be locked in at night, like Clara said.'

'Clara says more than her prayers and she whistles them: there's homes and homes, and you're in a pregnant state, you're going to have a child. It'll be some place likely where you'll be taken care of.'

'But you won't be with me.'

'No, I won't be with you. You've got to get that into your head an' all, I won't be with you. How can I be? Oh, me dear.' She now flung her arms about Marie Anne's shivering body and pulled her close, saying, 'I only wish I could be. There's nobody I'd like to serve better than yourself, and if I had a place to go to I would take you with me; I would this minute. There's me sister's, of course, but with her tribe, you couldn't exist there, not in that quarter anyway . . . Yet there's worse. Oh aye, there's worse; and she does her best, I'll give her her due. But for choice, I wouldn't be found dead in the place. So I say to you, me dear, I'm stuck here and you're for a home of some kind, unless, that is, unless you swallow your pride and walk in on that grandpa of yours.'

Marie Anne pulled herself away from Sarah's hold and, shaking her head, she said, 'I . . . I could more readily face my mother than I could him as I am now, because he thinks so much of me and I fear the shock would kill him.'

'It takes a lot of shocks to kill men, old or young; and that brother of yours, the one with the bad back, he sounds a decent enough sort. Couldn't you write to him?'

'Oh no. Oh no. He is the same as my grandpa. But whatever I have to do or wherever I go, I will write to them first.'

'You'll write to them and tell them about it?'

'Oh no, no!' Marie Anne tossed her body from side to side. 'No; how could I? I will just say that I can't live with my aunt any longer and that I'm going into lodgings or some such. I'll think of something; I'll have to. Anyway, if I was going to go into The Little Manor it would all come out about what my mother has done, and my grandfather would dislike her more than he does already.'

Sarah Foggerty sighed deeply; then she said, 'Well, I'll leave you to think over what you intend to do, because I'm past thinking; but I'll have to go to this damn parson now. I won't sin me soul away by entering his chapel, though: if he's in there, he'll have to come into the street to talk to me because, as you know, that's one thing I've stuck out about here. I'm a Catholic, maybe a wooden one, but so I'll remain. Well, do as I said, do some thinking. I'm off now.'

Within an hour of delivering her message to the chapel house the Reverend James Trackman and his wife Delia were at the house. Clara showed them up to her mistress's room and, as she said to Cook on her return downstairs, they were like two black spiders.

Sarah was in the room when the visitors entered, but before her mistress spoke to either of them she was ordered out.

Downstairs again, Sarah went into the kitchen, where Marie Anne was now slowly finishing a meal, and Cook greeted her with a short laugh as she pointed to Clara, saying, 'That one says they're like two spiders, and she's not far wrong, is she? I've often wondered where I could place them meself, but she, as usual, has put her finger on it.'

Marie Anne had now stopped eating and was looking at Sarah, who said to her, 'I was ordered out. Before she said a word to them she ordered me out.'

'Sarah, I am not going with them. I've told you.'

'Me dear, I don't suppose you'll be asked to go with them: if that one up there is going to throw you out they're not the kind that are going to catch you with open arms. Anyway, while they're plotting, let me have a bite

116

because I'm sick of this day; in fact, I'm sick of life in this house, I really am.'

Cook went to the oven and took out a covered plate, saying. 'It'll be dried up now.'

'No matter; at the moment I could eat a horse between two mats,' at which Clara let out a giggle of a laugh as she said, 'With or without mustard?'

Sarah smiled at her. 'There's one thing I know, Clara,' she said, 'life will never smack you in the face, for you won't give it a chance. If your people gave you nothing else to get you through life but a sense of humour, then they made you rich.'

This unusual compliment caused Clara to lower her head and give way to a blush, and Marie Anne, looking at her from across the table, knew a feeling of envy rising in her for the little-maid-of-all-work, for she was aware there was respect for the girl in Sarah's compliment, whereas she now had none for her, no more than she had for herself.

Of a sudden she sprang to her feet and her voice was a cry of anguish as she said, 'I won't be put in a home, Sarah. I've told you I won't be put in a home, no matter what she said or what that parson does. I won't, I won't. I know what I'm going to do; I've made up my mind. I still have my Christmas money left from what Grandpa . . . and Pat sent me. I'll get a room and I'll write or I'll draw. You've seen my sketches. You said they were funny. I'll . . . I'll take them to a newspaper. They'll buy them. *Punch* and such.'

'Don't be silly, girl!' Sarah got up from the table and went to Marie Anne and, placing her hands on her shoulders, she said, 'Sit yourself down, calm yourself.'

'No, I won't. I won't, Sarah. The time has passed for telling me what I must do.'

'Yes, all right, all right,' said Sarah soothingly now. 'I'll not tell you any more, or give you any more advice. Once

117

you know what she intends to do,' she jerked her hand upwards, 'you can make your own way. Nobody's going to stop you.'

When the bell rang three times Sarah hastened out and up to the bedroom, there to be told to see the visitors out . . .

It was as the minister pulled on his black felt hat that he looked down on Sarah saying, 'You will bring the girl tomorrow; your mistress will give you the details. It could be the saving of her; God is good.'

It was Sarah Foggerty, the whole woman, who retorted and loudly, 'And the Devil is not bad to his own.'

'What did you say?' asked the minister's wife.

'You heard me, missis. I said, And the Devil's not bad to his own. And I know which side I'm on in this business.'

The man peered at her as he said, 'You are a Catholic?'

'Yes, that I am.'

'Dear, dear! Dear, dear! Come.'

He now almost lifted his wife through the open doorway as if from contamination with evil, but she'd hardly put her foot on the pavement before the door was slammed hard.

God is good! She was stumping up the stairs now: Priests, popes, parsons, and ministers, they're all alike at bottom.

As soon as she entered the bedroom she was greeted with, 'You will tell that girl to have her things packed ready for tomorrow morning; it has been arranged that she goes into a home. She's very lucky to get there. The minister's wife has influence or she wouldn't have got a place otherwise.'

'May I ask where the home is and what it's called?'

'Yes you may ask, because you're the one who will take her there. It is Mary Ping's Home for Distressed Women.'

'For the what?'

'You heard what I said, Foggerty, distressed women, and that girl is in a distressed state, isn't she?'

'What if she decides not to go into your home for the distressed; what about that, then?'

'She has no other option. Her mother on no account will tolerate her return, you know that. Haven't you taken in what you have read to me?'

'Yes, ma'am, very much have I taken in what I have read to you; and I'll tell you this much, I wouldn't wipe me feet on a woman like her mother.'

'Be quiet! and don't give me any of your Irish slang in this room please. Now go and inform her of what is in store for her.'

'Wouldn't you like to tell her yourself?'

Martha Culmill began to breathe heavily and she put her hand to her throat before she said, 'I will see her before she goes, and that is all the contact I need to have with her.'

The mistress and her maid exchanged a long glance, before Sarah turned and went out, closing the door none too gently behind her.

In the kitchen, she said to Marie Anne, who was sitting close to the oven door, 'You'd better get upstairs and start packing your things, for you're for the road tomorrow. Which road, I don't know. That'll depend mostly on you.'

Marie Anne was standing up now and again she started, 'I'm not going into—'

'All right. All right,' put in Sarah, flapping her hand almost in Marie Anne's face, 'I've heard that 'till I'm tired: you're not going into a home. Well, from now 'till tomorrow morning you can mull over it and tell me where you want to go, either to the station, or . . . well, where else I don't know. Only go on now.'

Marie Anne went out almost at a run and Cook asked quietly of Sarah, 'She's picked on a home then?'

'Yes. Yes. I've never heard of it before, but I've got to

find it tomorrow and take her there. The minister's wife
has a hand in it.'

'What do they call it?'

'Well, it's a fancy name all right, and I suppose it suits
the condition that she's in, I mean Marie Anne. It's called
Mary Ping's Home for Distressed Women.'

'What!' The word came high from Cook's throat. 'Mary
Ping's? Oh my God, no!'

'What is it? Where is it?'

'You might well ask, but haven't you heard of Mary
Ping's? You've been in this end of London long enough.'

'No, I haven't heard of Mary Ping's.'

'It's a noted house for fallen women, and from what
I've always been able to gather they're mostly off the
streets with their bellies so full no back-street old girl
could get rid of it for them. Whores, the majority of them.
Oh, here and there will be a decent enough lass who finds
it's a choice of there or the workhouse. Well, believe me,
from what I hear about it, give me the workhouse. Mary
Ping's! And you've never heard of it? It's a joke: You'll end
up in Mary Ping's.'

Sarah flopped down on to a chair and her voice was
very low now and tired sounding as she said, 'She
wouldn't do that if she knew what it really was;
she wouldn't do that, I mean, her up there.'

'Well, apparently she's done it, and through religious
quarters an' all. Oh, Mrs Delia is noted for her good
works. She has collections every now and again in the
chapel for the bare-footed lot, but whether the money
ever sees boots I don't know, nor does anybody else,
except at Christmas when they bring in some urchins off
the streets and dress them in somebody's cut-me-downs.'
Cook now leaned across the table and touched Sarah's
arm, and with almost a plea in her voice, she said, 'You
can't let her go there.'

When Sarah said nothing, Cook went on, 'Go early in

the morning and see for yourself. It's a big house behind iron gates and a high fence. They would let you in, likely, if you were to say you had come to make arrangements about the girl.'

Sarah turned her gaze up to Cook as she said, flatly now, 'I'm worried sick about her. If only she'd go back home and brave her mother. But that's the last thing she'll do, and she thinks her grandfather and brother will die of shame when they know what's happened to her. Yet they both sound lovely men, and I'm sure they would take it in their stride. But she won't have it. She's strong-willed, you know. Oh aye, she's headstrong in some ways, and she's just as likely to go out of here tomorrow on her own and end up in some cheap hotel, and from there what? Only God knows.'

'She couldn't go on without you, Sarah; and she knows it. She thinks the world of you, and rightly so, because you've been more than a friend to her. So she'll do what you say in the end.'

'Oh no, she won't, at least about going back home. No, I can't bend her that way.'

Both Sarah and Cook turned to where Clara was washing up dishes in a bowl set in a shallow stone sink, for she was saying, 'Wouldn't your sister take her in in the meanwhile?'

'Oh.' Sarah smiled at the young girl as she said, 'Me sister, Clara, has ten bairns and the oldest is eleven. They live in a tenement, and the tenement is part of a court, and there's courts and courts, and this one is a court! It's four-storeyed, and Annie lives on the third floor. Mind, she's lucky, she has four rooms, although two of them are just like boxes; but every drop of water has to be carried up stairs from the tap in the yard. And there's four water-closets down there too, and they have to serve the whole of that court. So that's the picture of where me sister lives, Clara; but it was nice of you to think along those lines.'

'I'll miss her.' Clara had turned from the sink, and Sarah and Cook exchanged a warm glance as they said almost simultaneously, 'So will we, lass. So will we.'

'She has no side, not like some, and she was learning me words.'

Again there was the exchanged glance; then Sarah rose quickly from her chair, saying, 'I'll be away up to her.'

As she made for the door Cook said, 'Bring her down for a bit of supper. I got four fresh herrin' today from the fish-woman.' . . .

As Sarah opened the door and went into the room, Marie Anne turned from lifting a case from the bed and, putting it on the floor, she said quietly, 'I'm all packed.' Then going to Sarah, she looked into her face, saying, 'I have been thinking, Sarah: if you would help me to get a room, a furnished place, I . . . I could find work of some kind; with the money I have I'd manage somehow.'

'Come and sit down.' Sarah pulled her onto the edge of the bed and put her arm around her shoulder, and said very quietly, 'That's a good idea, a very good idea, but it will take money. How much have you got?'

'Altogether, eighteen pounds five shillings.'

'What!' Sarah's arm dropped from Marie Anne's shoulder. 'Eighteen pounds five shillings? I thought the last you had was about five pounds or so.'

'Yes; but Grandpa put some paper money in his last letter, and so did Pat; and I didn't tell you because I was keeping it a secret. Well,' her head bowed, 'I . . . I wanted to buy you a present, but I wanted to find out first what you wanted most.'

'Oh! love. Oh! me dear.' The arm was about her again, hugging her close now. 'Oh! God bless you for the thought. But eighteen pounds five shillings! That's a lot of money. Next door, she knows nothing about it?'

'Oh no, no. She informed me when I first came that if my grandfather sent me money it must be put into her

122

keeping, because, she inferred, most servants were thieves.'

'She did, did she? Well! well! I can only say it would be a clever thief that could pick her pocket. Anyway, leave everything until tomorrow. Now, I might have to go out early on me own, but I'll be back; and from there . . . well, we'll work it out. Come on now downstairs for your last real meal in this house. Cook has got some fresh herring. Let me tell you something.' She nodded into Marie Anne's face. 'They're goin' to miss you down there, especially Clara, 'cos you are the only other young thing in this house. Yes, Clara's goin' to miss you, as we all will.'

'Oh Sarah, please.'

'Now stop it. No more tonight; leave it till tomorrow morning. Come on.'

Mary Ping's Home for Distressed Women was situated at the end of a long street that had once housed well-to-do merchants. It was a flat, grey-stone, barrack-looking establishment without the relief of tree or grass.

The woman porter who had let her in through the iron gate now led the way into a large hall. The floor was tiled, and at each end two women were scrubbing it. When they glanced up at Sarah their expressions were similar and portrayed total weariness.

The woman, who was walking ahead of her along a passage, now turned to her and said, 'You wanted to see who?'

'The mistress of the house, the matron . . . whoever.'

'The matron?' The woman laughed. 'Don't you know her name?'

'No; I only know that she's expecting somebody in this morning.'

'Oh, another of 'em. You her mother?'

'No, I'm not her mother.' It was almost a bark and the woman turned on her and said, 'Don't you use that tone on me, missis, unless you want a smack in the gob.'

They stared at each other, before the woman moved on again, and at the end of the passage she thrust open a door and cried, 'Betty! Take this woman to the waitin' room; she's for Miss Frank,' and without more ado she turned on her heel and walked back up the passage. And there was the said Betty standing in front of Sarah, a wide grin on her face and her stomach so large that it seemed as if it would overbalance her.

'Why, hello!' she said. 'So you're for Miss Frank, are you? Come in. Come in an' join the club.'

Sarah passed the grinning girl to enter a room where at least ten women were at work, and her entry immediately stopped their chatter and it was obvious to Sarah that they were all in different stages of pregnancy. Four of them were sitting at a table busily sticking something together. She couldn't make out what it was except that it was flat and to do with paper. One was sitting at a treadle machine. Another was sewing what looked like hessian aprons. Others were hemming babies' napkins, while yet more were seated in the far corner of the room, although she couldn't take in what they were doing, only that most of them were grinning at her.

'How's the world outside, missis?' one called to her. And another heavily laden girl laughed as she said, 'You're new, aren't you? Which Holy Joe's group do you belong to?' while a woman at the table addressed the other saying, 'Have you ever seen anybody as flat as that in your life? Not even a little bun in her oven.'

Sarah had been about to follow the laughing Betty when one of the women came out with a mouthful of blasphemous curses that absolutely shook her, for the girl was probably no more than eighteen years old.

Being Sarah Foggerty and having been brought up with a houseful of male Foggertys, she had been used to damns, bloodys and buggers. Such words punctuated

124

their daily speech. But when the name of Jesus and the Cross and his Mother all rolled into one came flooding from those young lips, bringing giggles and laughter from the other occupants of the room, Sarah could stand no more. She turned on the girl who was not more than a yard or so away from her and she cried, 'Shut your filthy mouth! you young whore, you!' Then casting her infuriated glance over the rest of those present in the room, she cried, 'When I came in here, I expected to be sorry for you. But I can see you're all where you belong and you deserve no better;' and now she rounded on Betty who, surprisingly, was no longer laughing and she said, 'I don't want to go to your waiting-room; I'm leaving.'

'Well and good, missis.' Betty now led her back to the door, and standing there for a moment she looked into Sarah's face and said, 'You've made one mistake, missis: we are not all where we belong; we're just making the best of a bad job. Phyllis has a dirty mouth – it's a pity – but it's the only way she can vent her feelings. It compensates, like, for being kicked from dog to devil.'

Sarah had the uneasy feeling that this young girl was putting her in her place and her voice was now low as she apologised. 'I'm sorry. This set-up has come as a bit of a shock. You see, I was to bring a young girl here whose people won't have her, but . . . but now I can't do it, even if she would come.'

The young woman looked at her intently for a moment, then said, 'Aye, well, I understand. Has . . . has she been dropped? Oh, what a damn silly thing to say? Why would you be here if she hadn't? Anyway' – the smile returned to her face – 'I wish her luck, wherever she lands. In any case, she'd have been one too many here: it's only supposed to take thirty, and we're thirty-two so far.'

'Goodbye,' said Sarah now, and the girl answered, 'Goodbye, missis.'

Missis. It was nice to be called missis; but she'd never be a missis.

As if she had known that this particular visitor would be leaving very soon, the woman who had shown her in was standing by the front door, and she preceded Sarah down the gravel drive, unlocked the gate and let her through without either of them speaking a word, not even of farewell . . .

Sarah did not return to the house straight away. Instead, she boarded a horse-bus which would take her further into the East End, and when the conductor shouted 'The Priory' she alighted.

Some distance along the street she passed a set of iron gates which led to the House of The Brothers of St Peter the Rock, and further on she passed The Church of The Blue Virgin. She was always amused by the nickname given to this street – The Holy Walk – because at the far end was the Convent.

A narrow cut led into a densely built-up area and to a quarter known as The Courts.

As she crossed the yard of Ramsay Court a man was shovelling ash, piled up in the corner of the yard, into a high-sided cart, and a woman was on her hands and knees scrubbing the brick floor of the second in the row of closets. She turned and glanced at the newcomer, then sat back on her haunches and called, 'Hello there! You're early.'

'Yes, Mrs Barnes,' Sarah called back; 'I'm up before me clothes was on.'

They laughed together before Sarah entered the second door of the block of flats and immediately side-stepped two small children playing in the small dim hallway, and bending over them, she said, 'You shouldn't play behind the door.'

The second flight of fifteen stairs took her to her sister's flat. She was puffing as she pushed open the door marked

'3', and brought a cry from numerous children and a loud 'Good gracious! This time in the mornin'?' from her sister Annie.

'Oh! those stairs.'

'Something the matter?'

'Aye; you could say that, Annie, something's the matter. Have you got a drop of tea on the hob?'

'Yes; it'll be as black as the ace of spades, though. But you like it that way, don't you? Help yourself and tell me why you are here at ten in the morning. Has she died?'

'No; but I wish she had. Have you ever heard of Mary Ping's Home for Distressed Women?'

'Huh! who hasn't? It's a street-woman's house, infamous it is. Don't tell me you're goin' in. It used to be a laugh, because when Father Weir tried to go in there and drag out the Catholic young 'uns I'm told they nearly stripped the clothes off him. Well, what about it?'

'Just that's where that old faggot of mine was having Miss sent. Got her minister and his wife there last night and it was settled between them. Well, after Cook said as much about the place as you've just done, I went to see for meself. I only saw one room full of the lasses but that was enough. Dear God, it was. Yet, as one young lass put it, they weren't all alike, luck and upbringing had something to do with it. But the thought of Miss Marie Anne going into that place nearly caused me hair to stand on end. I needn't have worried, because she proposes going into a furnished room and getting a job. But Annie, girl, she'll be eaten alive, because she's beautiful, strangely beautiful. There's something about her face that's fetching, and her nature too: she's a lovely lass. Headstrong, oh aye, and with a temper, but who hasn't? Anyway, I've been thinking. Are those two rooms in the attic up there still empty?'

'Yes; they're still empty, and I've got the key. He knocks sixpence a week off the rent for me showing people round. It's been empty this last month and there's only one bloke came and looked at it, but when he knew the water had to be carried up that far he said no way was he payin' half a dollar a week for those two shanties.'

'Could I go up and have a look?'

'Help yourself to the key; it's on the mantelpiece there. But in the name of God! woman, that lass would never exist up there. Every drop of water has to be humped up, and every shovel of coal.'

'Well, she wouldn't be alone, Annie, for I'd be with her. I'm heartily, heartily fed up with that woman and her meanness. I really do think the lass would shovel coal in hell as long as I was with her, for she has come to rely on me; more's the pity, really, for I feel responsible for her and the feeling's becoming a burden, I can tell you that.'

'You mean you'd come and live up above us?' Annie's voice sounded eager.

'Just for the time being, anyway. But the place would have to be furnished.'

'Oh, that won't cost you all that much if you're not going to be too particular. As you know, you can buy anything from a grand piano to a sculler boat in Paddy's Emporium. Go and have a look.' . . .

Sarah stood in the middle of the large room with the ceiling sloping at both ends. The floor was covered with linoleum that still bore its pattern. The fireplace was an open range with an oven at one side and a hob at the other, but there wasn't a stick of furniture in the room. She walked down its long length and pushed open the door at the far end and here immediately she saw furniture of a kind. There was a double brass bed, but without a mattress; yet the springs were firm enough. This floor, too, was covered with linoleum, and on the far wall there was a decent-sized window, as large as that in the main room. Before leaving the room she felt the brass knobs on the ends of the bed. They, too, were firm. It was a good bed.

Downstairs once more, Sarah said, 'Tell him we'll have it.'

'No! Just like that? Have you taken into account the lugging up of everything, coals, water and doing the washin' in the poss-tub downstairs? An' think of your legs at the end of the day. Mine are burstin' gettin' up just this far.'

'Yes; you've pumped that into me over the years, but all we can do is try. I can't let her go out into this city on her own; I'd have to live with meself after.'

'But Sarah,' Annie said, 'for another sixpence or a shilling you could get a decent flat on the level and not have all the humpin' to do.'

'Well, don't think I haven't thought of that, Annie, but she's only got so much money, and so have I. It won't last us all that long, and I'll soon have to go out on a job of sorts myself, and I'd like to think she was near someone safe when I left her, for she's on four months gone now and there's little chance of her gettin' a pianist's job, although she could carry that off, she plays so lovely.'

'I can understand all you've said, Sarah, but let's face it: how's she going to make the other flight past this door?'

'Oh, she's young; she'll make it better than I will.'

'You're talking like an old woman.'

'I'm feeling like an old woman, Annie. Anyway, I must get back now. Time's going on, if we want somewhere to sleep tonight. By the way, where is he?'

'Oh, he's as far as Brighton now with the gang. They are demolishing a big hotel. It'll take them another week, I should think.'

'Thank God for that.'

'Oh, he can't help what he is, Sarah.'

Sarah shook her head slowly now as she said, 'You

puzzle me, our Annie. He's not worth livin' with and still you're for him.'

When a little voice piped up now, saying, 'You goin' away so soon, Auntie Sarah?' Sarah, bending down to the four-year-old, said, 'I'll be back, love; and you Callum' – she ruffled the curls of the three-year-old boy, adding, 'you get bigger every week.' Then turning to her sister, she asked, 'Where are Kathleen and Joseph?'

'Oh, they started at the new school, both in the sixes. I know I should've kept them with the nuns, but they weren't learnin' anything. Hymns and Irish songs and Catechism and the rosary and a bit of drawin' and playing with plasticine. Billy's been there for a year and he's streets ahead. He can read and write and count. But then there's Michael. He hates going all day; he wants to play the nick like Shane. Still, many a day I'm glad of that boy playing the nick for he can earn up to two shillings bagging coal dust. Of course, I've got to put him in the wash tub at night to get the muck off him; that is when his dad's at home, other nights he sluices under the tap in the yard. There's going to be hell to pay when Father Weir gets wind of the two youngsters going Protestant. It's no use me reminding him they're all Protestants, because their father's a Protestant. Oh, but he says I'm a Catholic and as their mother I've got to go as far as fighting hell fire with lamp oil to save their souls.'

'I'm away, Annie. I'm away.' Sarah went out laughing. Fight hell fire with lamp oil . . . did you ever hear any such thing? In a way she'd be glad to be living near to Annie again. It would be just as they were before they came across the water to make their fortunes, God help them.

They both stood some distance from the bed and staring at its occupant, who was addressing Marie Anne, saying, 'Girl! I cannot bear to look at you. You are dirty! filthy! vile!'

Marie Anne's jaws were gripped tightly together, yet as she listened to these words she heard herself yelling them at Evelyn: dirty, vile, filthy: and once more she was sorry that she had ever said them.

'You are going into a home which will be no better than a house of correction, and you will be made to see and face up to the wickedness of your ways, because you are a wicked girl at heart. Even before you sinned you were of an unruly mind and temper.'

When Martha Culmill paused for breath, Marie Anne said quietly, 'Are you finished, Aunt?' a question which seemed to stagger the woman, for she said, 'What d'you mean, am I finished?'

'Just that; are you finished telling me how wicked I am, because I want to begin telling you how wicked *you* are. You are a mean, nasty, intolerant woman and, I've got to say it, you are from the same side of the family as my mother and you are similar in many ways.'

'How dare you! How dare you! Get her out this minute, Foggerty. I never want to lay eyes on her again.'

'I'll do that, ma'am, in just a tick. Now, as you know, you pay me every Saturday. Well, that's four days gone and I'm wonderin' if I could sub half the week's pay that will be due to me come this Saturday. I'm really due to four shillings, but I'll take three.'

'You'll what! What are you talking about, woman? Why do you want the money in the middle of the week?'

'It's to go towards something, ma'am.'

'Go towards something? What?'

'You wouldn't understand, ma'am, but I'm going to need every penny. If you could oblige me by—'

'Really! This is the latest. Fetch the box.'

Sarah brought the box, and her mistress opened it with a key she took from a vanity bag that was lying on the bedside table. After she had extracted three shillings from it and thrust them at Sarah, the shrewd, even sagacious,

Irish woman, put them in her pocket, saying, 'Thank you, ma'am. Now we are straight. I've stolen nothing from you, I've just taken me due.'

The woman was sitting straight up in bed now and looking from one to the other, for her servant and her niece were both dressed for outdoors, and she said, 'What is the matter with you this morning, Foggerty? Get about your business now. You know what you've got to do with her. Then get back here, because today I intend going downstairs.'

'Ma'am, I think you'd better steel yourself. Yes, I'm goin' about me business, and her business, too' – she motioned with her head towards Marie Anne – 'but she's goin' into no home.' Her bantering tone changed now as she went on. 'Home? House full of street whores! I have been there this morning, and if I had one wish, it would be that I could transport you into the middle of them and leave you in the place you were goin' to put her. They were all young whores. D'you hear me? ma'am, young whores. They were the dregs of the street, vile-mouthed and brazen. Now, for your further information, I'll tell you this: I'm leaving with her.'

'You're not. How dare you! You're employed here. I will have the police on you both. I will wire her mother . . . her grandfather.'

'I wouldn't waste your money, ma'am, for she's already written to them both, and she's told her grandfather that she is leaving here because she can't stand you any longer.'

It would appear that Miss Martha Culmill had been struck dumb or had had a seizure, for she was lying back on her pillows, her mouth agape; that is, until they both moved towards the door, when she screamed, 'Foggerty! Foggerty! You will come back here! I need you, I'm a sick woman!'

'Then you must pay for a proper nurse, ma'am.'

'I will have you found and fined if you—'

'You can do what you like, ma'am. Come along, dear.' She put out a hand towards Marie Anne, who seemed to be taking one last look at the woman in the bed, and they went out, followed by high screams of, 'Foggerty! Foggerty! Come back here!'

Agnes and Clara were waiting for them. Clara was crying and the cook was biting hard down on her lip and visibly trembling as she said, 'It'll never be the same again. It's been bearable with you being here, Sarah, but now, Clara and me, we'll try to get a place together. You see, she's like you miss' – she nodded towards the young girl – 'or even worse, she's got nobody at all who wants her. And so I've promised I'll not move without her, even though I know it'll be difficult to get a situation together.'

The little maid now made a rush at Marie Anne and put her arms around her neck, and they clung together for a moment until Cook said, 'Your sister, Sarah . . . I know you're goin' to your sister's, but where does she live?'

Sarah turned to look at Marie Anne, who was now crying, and as if making a decision she said, ''Tis better you don't know, Cook, because if you did and anybody came here, I mean her people lookin' for her, out of pity alone you would likely give the show away. So just leave it at that. But, I can tell you, we'll pop in the back door now and again to see if you're still here, and say hello.'

'You would do that, Sarah?'

'Yes, we would, we would, wouldn't we, miss?'

'Oh yes. Oh yes, Cook.' Marie Anne was now enfolded in Cook's embrace. Then, taking charge of the emotional situation, Sarah said, 'Well, come on; let's get our luggage out of the hall and into the front street. And there we must take a cab, because if we want to sleep tonight, there's a lot still to be done.'

*   *   *

Ten minutes later they were in a cab and waving goodbye to the big woman and the small maid standing on the step . . .

One mile and fifteen minutes later, after a detour so as to bring his cab to the opening of Ramsay Court, the cabbie helped Sarah to put the cases just inside the yard. Having been told his fare was ten pence, she proferred him a shilling, saying, 'There you are, then; and thanks.'

She had never before had the pleasure of tipping a cabbie tuppence, but like most ungrateful cabbies he showed little pleasure at her generosity.

When Marie Anne now went to pick up two of the cases Sarah said quickly, 'Leave them be! I'll take two up now, and you stay there with the rest of the clutter, because we can't carry all that stuff upstairs at once. Don't leave them for a minute, mind, or let anyone near them, you understand?'

Marie Anne did not nod in reply but watched the trim figure hurrying across the yard, a suitcase in one hand, a bulging holdall in the other, leaving her standing in some amazement at the sight before her. The strangeness of it had opened her eyes wide: there was a woman emptying a bucket of hot ash onto a sizzling heap in the corner of the yard; and outside a small building another was wielding a poss stick up and down in a poss tub. She had seen women possing before. There were two poss tubs in the ash-house at home. One was used for the staff clothes and one for the house clothes, so she understood what the woman was doing, but she was further amazed when a man, adjusting the front of his trousers emerged from what she took to be a water-closet.

She stiffened as the man, pushing the tail of his shirt into his trousers, turned towards her.

'Want a hand, lass?'

'N-n-no thank you,' she stammered.

'Waitin' for somebody?'

'Yes. Yes, I am.'

He looked behind him and around before he said, 'You comin' to live here, then?'

She did not answer, for beyond the man she could see Sarah approaching. The man himself turned and, seeing Sarah, called to her, 'Oh, hello, Sarah. It's you!'

'Yes, Mr Barnes, it's me.'

'You not at work?'

'No. Had the skitters for days; weakens you, like.'

Pointing to the luggage, he said, 'Don't say you're coming to live here, Sarah.'

'Yes. Yes, we are, for the present.'

'Top flat?'

'Aye, top flat.'

'My God! that's a haul.'

'Aye, it is.'

'Come on, pick them up,' Sarah was addressing Marie Anne now, and at this the man said, 'Oh, give me the big case; I'm still strong enough for that. Take it up as far as our landing anyway.'

'Oh. Oh, thanks, Frank.'

When they reached the first floor Sarah said, 'We'll manage all right from here, Frank, let's have it.'

The man smiled and said, 'Good enough.' Then he stared at Marie Anne and asked, 'You stayin' here an' all?'

Before Marie Anne could answer, Sarah put in, 'Yes, she's stayin' here an' all, Frank. We'll be seein' you,' and straight away picked up the two cases, leaving Marie Anne to follow with the rest of their belongings up the second flight and into Annie's flat, and there Sarah, dropping her cases, said, 'My God! I'll be dead before I start. Well, Annie, this is Miss Marie Anne Lawson. This is my sister, miss.'

The return to formalities caused Marie Anne to respond with, 'How do you do?' only then to thrust out a hand and say, as Clara might, 'Pleased to meet you.'

'Aye, and you, miss.'

It was evident that Annie was staggered by her sister's charge, this tall girl who seemed to be much older than sixteen. Well, that's what Sarah had said she was; and she'd said she was beautiful. To her mind she wasn't beautiful – but odd-looking, foreign-like.

As for Marie Anne, she couldn't yet take in the fact that this was where she was to live. She had never imagined Sarah living or being associated with anyone who existed under these conditions. Ten children, Sarah said, lived here. Then there was that yard and people doing different things as if they were everyday occurrences. Of course they *were* everyday occurrences. What was the matter with her? And if she was to live here some of the things they were doing would become everyday occurrences for her, she supposed.

Sarah was saying, 'Well, if we want a mattress and something to cover us for the night, we'd better be off to Paddy's. I'll move our stuff as soon as I get back, Annie.'

'Oh, it can stay in the corner for as long as it needs. Anyway, I wouldn't be surprised but the two of you'll be sleepin' on the mat here in front of the fire tonight; you're not givin' much time for gettin' beddin' up there. But there'll be a meal for you when you get back, even if it's only mutton broth and suet balls.'

Marie Anne would always remember the two hours she spent in Paddy's Emporium. If she had been amazed by Ramsay Court and the conditions under which Sarah's sister lived, she was utterly dumbfounded by the conglomeration of articles that she walked over, pushed through, squeezed through from the ground floor to the fourth. The ground floor was a mass of machinery in disordered heaps, seeming to be the result of an explosion; the first floor displayed chairs, couches, beds et cetera; the second, everything needed in a gigantic kitchen; the next, the remnants of linen of all kinds, from dishcloths to curtains; and on the top floor, odds and ends of china and crockery.

It was the third floor to which Sarah made her way. Here was linen of all kinds; that is to say, remnants of it: sheets, blankets, bed covers, pillowcases, towels, curtains.

Paddy O'Connell had followed them upstairs. It was a Wednesday, and it was strange that Wednesdays should be such quiet days. It was the middle of the week, he supposed, and people didn't know if they were coming or going. He studied the woman and the young girl and he summed them up as different types from his usual customers.

'Can I help you, ladies?' he asked.

'Yes, you can, Paddy. It's like this.' Sarah faced him squarely. 'I've got a sister livin' in the Court. It must be twelve years ago since you furnished her four rooms for next to nothing. Well, we're in the same boat as regards money: we have only so much and we want to furnish a kitchen-cum-living room and a bedroom, but we want some of your decent stuff. Have you any planted on the side?'

'Oh, miss. Miss. Me plant anything on the side? For God's sake! look about you: everything's open to the eye.'

'Aye, so I've heard.' And Sarah turned to a bundle of sheets now, saying, 'Look at them! They're made up of patches, and even those you could read the paper through.'

'Well, look down the barrel; you might find something better. People never get to the bottom.'

Sarah now turned to Marie Anne, saying, 'Do as he says and get to the bottom of that, and see what you can find. Look out for pillowcases. We want everything: sheets, blankets, pillowcases, towels; we want a bed. Well, we've got a bed, it's a big brass one. That's the only thing in the room. But we want a decent mattress for it, and I'm not havin' any of yours, because it wouldn't have to go on the handcart, it would walk there itself.'

'Now, now! that is not kind, miss. But perhaps I can find you something decent down in the huts. First of all, tell me how much you've got to spend.'

Sarah eyed him, then said, 'First of all I'll tell you again what I want. I want two pairs of sheets and pillows and pillowcases and three blankets; I want half a dozen towels, large ones; a table cover or two. Two pairs of curtains. None of your flimsy stuff. I don't care how badly they're faded as long as they're thick; like tapestry, you know.'

He was nodding at her, punctuating her demands with, 'Just as you say. Just as you say.'

'And I want some mats, decent rugs. I want a couple of easy chairs – I can do without a couch.'

'Oh, we must have a couch.' There was a touch of sarcasm in his voice, and she came back, imitating him, saying, 'Just as you say,' and this caused him to laugh.

'How much have you got to spend?'

Marie Anne cast a quick glance at Sarah, and as if learning quickly, she looked at the assortment of sheets and pillowcases she had pulled from the barrel and said, 'There's nothing here really worth having.'

As Sarah stifled a laugh the man said, 'Well, well! and that said to your face and in your own shop; but just as you say, there's nothing there worth having.'

He turned back to Sarah, saying, 'Well, I asked the question, how much money are you going to fork out to furnish two rooms completely? It's like setting up a house for life, mind.'

'Two-ten to three pounds. That's between us.'

Again Paddy O'Connell looked from one to the other and he summed them up correctly as being from different classes and he wondered why they were going into such a place as Ramsay Court. One looked like a well rigged-out servant, and she talked like one, too; but the other, he couldn't place her, middle-drawer type, he would say. He seemed to reach a decision, and said, 'How soon are you wantin' to get set up?'

'Now . . . today. You still have your flat cart?'

'We not only have our flat cart, miss, we've got a van.'

'Oh, that's even better.'

'And you want a full house geared for two-ten to three pounds? You're not expecting much, are you? Well, as far as I can see, as the young miss there is so particular about bedwear, she's goin' to turn her nose up here and there, more often here than there. So, I could strike a bargain with you. I could turn your two rooms into a comfortable little palace say for' – he looked from one to the other – 'three quid each.'

'Three pounds each! Mother of God!' Sarah turned her full gaze on Marie Anne, and to her surprise found she was aiming to smile, and she said, 'Did you hear him?'

'Yes,' said Marie Anne, 'and we could likely stretch to it.'

'Oh, I don't know.' Sarah shook her head.

Then briskly now, he said, 'Mattress, bedding, furniture, the lot and the best of stuff. Oh aye, not meant for the shop, just private deals.'

'Well, let's see it.'

'As you say, miss. As you say.'

He led the way down to the ground floor where a young man was helping another to extract a complete iron-framed fireplace from among the jumble and he called to him, 'I'll be in the far store, Barney,' and the man called back, 'Right, Mr O'Connell.'

Paddy O'Connell unlocked the double gates of the storehouse. He then ushered them along a narrow passage, put a key into another door, stood aside and let them enter a very large room. Within a few steps they both stood still and looked about them in amazement. The room wasn't packed like the storehouse next door: all the articles were arranged as if for inspection, and they all looked new or newish. Without a word Paddy O'Connell passed them to go to a cupboard and, pulling open the double doors, pointed to shelves full of linen.

6

The two sisters stood side by side in the middle of the room and Sarah said, 'Well?' And Annie said, 'God in heaven! it's all new.'

'Well, nearly.'

'And it's beautiful stuff; it's transformed this place. I'd never have believed it. And look! Look at your mats. But they're not mats, they're rugs. You've even got your fire alight; but you'll have to get some black lead on that stove, mind. I'll come up and do it for you one day, for you're past dirtying your hands like that, aren't you?' She dug her elbow into Sarah's side, then looked towards Marie Anne, who was standing near the bedroom door. She was wearing a blue woollen dress and her brown hair was hanging about her shoulders, and she was smiling as she called to Annie, 'Isn't it lovely, Mrs Annie? Come and see the bedroom.'

As Marie Anne turned, Annie whispered to Sarah, 'Well, well! She looks a different lass. By! I can see why you think her bonny.'

'Aye, she is a bonny piece, Annie. Go on; look at the bedroom.'

In the bedroom, Annie again exclaimed, 'Well, you couldn't get much more in here, and such stuff, a wardrobe, a chest of drawers, and a dressing-table, and all to match. Saints alive! I've never clapped eyes on such furniture since I was in service years ago.'

'But you've seen nothing yet; look at the sheets,' said Marie Anne excitedly as she pulled down a blue, quilted

141

eiderdown with its matching undercover; then two fleecy blankets and exposed the sheets. They were lawn sheets, and as Marie Anne fingered them she said, 'They're not worn and there's not a patch on them, except that someone has burnt a hole in the hem. We got three pairs; and they're all alike, aren't they, Sarah?'

'Yes, dear, yes; they're all alike.'

'And the same with the towels. Some of the towels have pieces cut out of the ends. Now don't you think that's strange, Mrs Annie?'

Annie turned and looked at her sister and one eye seemed to wink; and after a moment, she confirmed, 'Strange indeed. Somebody must have been smoking in bed.'

'But why should they cut pieces out of the towels?'

'Oh girl! there's some funny people in the world. But my! you've got it splendid up here. If only there was taps in the flats. We can manage lugging the coal up and taking the ashes down but it's the bloomin' water.' She now walked back into the living-room, saying, 'A kitchen dresser an' all! Oh, I've always wanted one of them.' Then when she knew she was out of earshot of Marie Anne, she looked at Sarah and whispered, 'Am I thinkin' the same as you about the bedding and such?'

'Aye, I shouldn't wonder, Annie. Exactly. Every damn thing in that store I bet had been pinched. Paddy said at first there wasn't any cutlery, but he threw some in. He said it wasn't silver, but the next best thing. Anyway,' – she poked her face against her sister's and said, 'I'm not going to confession about this or anything else he's likely to offer me,' a statement which caused them both to laugh.

'But how much did he rip you for it?'

'Six pounds.'

'Oh my God! that was a price. He's charged, hasn't he?'

'Oh, Annie, what's six pounds for this lot. No, Annie;

142

whoever he's rooked before, I don't think he's rooked us. And you were talkin' about the water and the coals. Well, I've thought about it. Now look; I'll give each of the lads sixpence, one for bringing the coal up and taking the ashes down every day, the other for bringing up the water and taking down the ordinary slops. The other kind I'll see to meself. How about it?'

'Oh, they'd be glad to do it. Michael's dying to make a copper. Oh yes; they'll be glad to do it.'

While they talked, Marie Anne had seated herself in the small basket chair that was wedged between the head of the bed and the wash-hand stand, and was gazing at the bare window. Tomorrow they'd have the curtains up and they'd go back to Paddy O'Connell's and see if he had a lamp or two. They had forgotten about the lamps. There were gas lamps in the streets, but Annie had said they wouldn't put gas up here, because some day and in the near future the whole block was to be pulled down; and yet, as she had added, they had been saying that for ten years, to her knowledge.

She felt happy and she shouldn't be feeling happy: she was still carrying a baby, and there was still the shock that her grandfather and Pat would experience when they read her letter. She'd tried to reassure them that she was all right and was working hard at her drawings. But she must be careful never to let slip the address, or within hours they would be here, only to be completely shocked by her condition.

Within a week the occupants of the garret had fallen into a daily routine. Of course, there had been a few obstacles to surmount. As Sarah put it to herself, some things were bad now, but they would get worse for Marie Anne as time went on. However, at the moment, with her easy chair to one side of the fire, looking at Marie Anne at the other, her feet resting on a lately acquired steel fender, her knee supporting a drawing board, she wouldn't call the Queen her aunt.

She stopped scanning the situations vacant columns on the back of the newspaper for a moment and, looking across to Marie Anne, she said, 'Are you nearly finished with that lot? Why can't you let me have a look at them?'

Marie Anne did not raise her head as she answered, 'Another few minutes or so,' to which she added, 'Have you found anything?'

'Nothing that I could take: housekeepers, cook-generals, parlour maids –' she laughed now, saying, 'Cook and Clara should go after such. And there's plenty for night work. That means washing up from ten 'til two in the mornin'. Annie once had to take a job like that for three ha'pence an hour. She said it was hell. But I'll have to find something soon; we can't live on air.'

This statement stopped Marie Anne's hand, and she said, 'We've still got seventeen pounds left. The rent's paid for a month, and so it's only the shilling a week to the boys and—'

'And it'll cost six shillings a week to feed us at the least,' Sarah put in now; 'more, I should imagine, the way you're eating, miss. And then have you thought about a doctor and clothes for the coming child? By the time it is due, if we both sit on our backsides here doing nothing, you'll have said goodbye to that seventeen pounds.'

'I mean to get work, and soon. Look!' She thrust the drawing-board towards Sarah, who could only gasp, 'My goodness me!' and begin to chuckle, before saying, 'Good lord! Well, I never! They wouldn't know themselves. How can you remember their faces? And what's this you have written at the bottom . . . huh! . . . TABLE MANNERS.'

Marie Anne had drawn Annie's children, nine of them sitting round a table, all eating in a guzzling fashion. Shane was recognisable, with a mutton bone held in his mouth as if he were playing a mouth organ; Michael, whose mouth was stuffed with a suet dumpling, was slapping Joseph's back and Mary was wiping her fingers in Callum's hair. The one-year-old baby was in the wash-basket under the table with what looked like the black stew-pan between its knees.

Sarah was laughing heartily now, saying, 'Eeh! that's funny, that really is. But surely they didn't really look like that to you, now did they? Annie makes them behave themselves as much as she can. True there was a bit of an uproar last night. Maureen started it. She's a starter. She's always pulling the lads up, and they do things to aggravate her. But oh my! that is funny. Yet it's a good job Annie will never see it, 'cos she would recognise them, even with the funny faces you've given them.' She stepped back now and, shaking her head, said, 'You have a gift, you know, Marie Anne, not only on the piano but with a pencil; you have indeed.'

'And I'm going to use it,' Marie Anne emphasised, nodding her head. 'I'm going to sell these.'

'Ah now, now! hold your hand. Where d'you think you're goin' to sell stuff like that?'

'To the newspapers . . . I told you: *Punch* and *The Illustrated London News,* and the daily newspapers, *The Times* and the *Daily Telegraph* and papers like that.'

'And will you tell me, me dear, how you're goin' to get in touch with anybody who works in those newspapers?'

'By going there. By going to the offices. And I *am* going. Well, I mean *we're* going; you're going with me.'

'Yes?'

'Yes.' Marie Anne's voice was not so definite now. 'Well, Sarah, I . . . I've got to do something. Don't you see? Like you, I, too, have to earn a living.'

'You, like me, me dear, have not got to make a living. If you'd only be sensible . . . but it's no good talking along that line again I suppose; yet I'll keep on.'

'Well, you'll be wasting your time.' Marie Anne's voice

was flat now, and it was a minute or so before she picked up another drawing, only for Sarah to exclaim again, 'My! my! That's Paddy O'Connell standing among his junk; and you show the four floors above his head and all his junk spillin' out of it. Eeh! girl, how d'you do it, and with just a couple of strokes of a pencil? Eeh my! that is good. Well, after seeing that I take back all I've said. And what have you written underneath? LIFE'S LITTER. That is wise, it is indeed; because everything he's got is what's left of somebody else's life.'

Sarah looked down into the deep brown eyes gazing up into hers and, putting her hand out, she touched Marie Anne's cheek gently, saying, 'There's much more in you, miss, than meets the eye. I've thought that from the beginnin' of our acquaintance.'

Now Marie Anne, quick to take advantage of Sarah's appreciation, said, 'And you'll come with me if I go to the newspaper offices?'

Sarah straightened up and in her usual terse tone, she said, 'Now would I be lettin' you go on your own? Will you be takin' all your stuff with you?'

'No; just a few samples.'

'And, of course, those two,' Sarah pointed to the last two drawings, and Marie Anne said, 'Oh yes; they're my *pièces de résistance.*'

Sarah stared at her for a moment but didn't ask her to translate the saying, for she had got the gist of it.

The November day was dull, cold and damp. Everyone prophesied there'd be a bad fog that night. Marie Anne – in fact, both of them – were experiencing the same feelings as the atmosphere was giving off: they felt dull, very cold and very damp. They'd had short shrift from the clerks in the offices of *Punch* and *The Illustrated London News.* They had been asked if they had an appointment. When Sarah said no, but this young lady had something to sell, that they were marvellous drawings, they were told they had a number of artists already on the staff who did marvellous drawings. Good-day.

In *The Times* office they had enquired if she was from an agency and when Marie Anne said no, that she worked for herself, she was told they weren't taking on any more freelance people at the moment.

At the *Daily Telegraph*, Sarah took charge and asked if they could see the editor.

Had they an appointment?

No. But her companion had some splendid drawings she would like him to see.

She was informed that the editor didn't see anyone without an appointment, and then never artists. That was a special department.

Then could they see someone from the special department?

No, they couldn't; they must write in.

Write in to whom, asked Sarah.

'The head of the Art Department,' the man emphasised; 'that's if you want to sell drawings. I'll make an appointment.'

Sarah came to the conclusion that she hated Fleet Street and that they had better go home; they were both getting wet.

It was as they turned down a side street and saw the offices of the *Daily Reporter* that Marie Anne now almost beseechingly said, 'Just let's try one more place; let's try here.'

The door led into a small square hall which led into a larger hall. Behind a counter were a number of desks at which men were working, and no-one took notice of their entry until they moved to a counter at the end of the room, where a man rose from his desk, asking, 'Yes? Well, what can I do for you?'

It was a case of who was the more surprised, the man

147

or Sarah Foggerty, when Marie Anne, whipping out the drawing pad from her bag, placed it on the counter, flipped back the cover and, pointing to the top sketch, said, 'I want to sell these.'

The man did not immediately look down at the drawing but kept his gaze on Marie Anne. The dampness outside had brought colour to her alabaster skin and for a moment it seemed he could only stare into the strange pair of eyes that were staring hard at him. When he did lower his gaze it was to see a conglomeration of children sitting around a table. He looked at it for some time, moving it first one way, then another. Presently he let out a short laugh and smiled from the young woman to the older one, saying one word, 'Funny.'

Marie Anne and Sarah glanced at each other and managed to suppress a smile. The next drawing was of Paddy O'Connell and his emporium, and this elicited another single word: 'Clever,' the man said.

'Worked long in this line?' he asked Marie Anne, and she swallowed as she answered, 'Some time.'

'Sold anything else?'

'No.'

'Well, 'tis a pity, but we never do anything like this.' He lifted another page to show a woman possing at a tub. She was standing in a littered yard and the caption was 'CLEANLINESS IS NEXT TO . . .'

The man made a noise in his throat and said, 'Hang on a minute.' He picked up the three drawings and was about to move away when Sarah put in quickly, 'Where are you going with them?'

He took a step backwards and, leaning on the counter, he pushed his face towards her, saying, 'I'm going to reproduce them and sell them for a mint. All right, missis?'

As he left, Sarah muttered, 'Cheeky monkey,' and she grinned at Marie Anne, although she was watching the man disappear into another office.

After five minutes or so he reappeared, accompanied by another man. Ignoring Sarah and Marie Anne he went through a doorway at the far end of the office. Soon afterwards he beckoned to them and raised a hinged part of the counter and ushered them into a large office. The man to whom they were introduced as the editor was elderly, with white hair around the temples and he had bushy eyebrows. Almost peremptorily, he said to Marie Anne, 'You did this work?'

'Yes, of course.' And her own tone surprised the first man for it was so different from that of the older woman.

'Are you a freelance?' the elderly man continued.

Marie Anne blinked rapidly. 'You could say so,' she said.

The man now moved his head as if to get a better view of her, and he then asked, 'How old are you?'

Without hesitation she said, 'Eighteen.'

He nodded. 'How long have you been at this kind of work?'

'Since I first recall holding a pencil.'

'Really!' His tone was an imitation of her own now. 'What's your name?'

She gulped and glanced towards Sarah, who was amazed to hear her say, 'Marie Anne Foggerty.'

When the second man turned to his companion, saying, 'Now what d'you think? Would that be an Irish name,' and the latter replied, 'Surely, surely,' their supposed senior muttered, 'Quiet!' Then addressing Marie Anne again, he said, 'This paper doesn't do anything in this line; at least, it hasn't done up till now. But we're not against trying something new. You know what I mean?'

The man now peered at her, saying, 'It'll be a try-out. We won't be able to pay much; say, four shillings each.'

'Five.'

The three men turned as one to look at Sarah, and she stared back at them, 'They're worth more than that. They're brilliant drawings.'

'Well, if they're so brilliant, why haven't you sold them before?'

'We haven't tried,' Sarah lied. 'You're the first we've visited.'

Again there was an exchange of glances between the men, and now Marie Anne put in quickly. 'I would have liked five shillings each, but I'd be willing to take four.'

The elderly man and Marie Anne exchanged a long glance. Then by way of introduction, he said, 'I'm the editor. My name is Stokes, John Stokes, and this is my assistant, Mr Mulberry.' Then nodding towards the man they had first encountered, he added, 'Doulton, my clerk,' and went on, 'Now I'll take these first three drawings you have shown me. You have more in your portfolio, I guess, but I don't want to see them at present, because I have an idea about these three and if it works out I shall let you know. Where do you live?'

When Marie Anne hesitated, Sarah put in, 'Top Floor, Ramsay Court, off Bing Road.'

The editor and his assistant again exchanged glances and when he said, 'You're in the deep East End there,' it was Sarah again who answered, saying, 'I suppose you could say that, sir, but only for the present.'

John Stokes looked hard at Sarah as if he found it difficult to make out her position. Then with a little shake of his head he turned his attention back to Marie Anne, saying, 'You accepted four shillings apiece but you could do with five, you say. Well, what's a shilling here and there in a new enterprise, eh? We'll say five shillings each, Miss Foggerty. How about that?'

'Thank you, sir. I'm grateful.'

The man now turned to Doulton and said, 'Give me the ledger and the form,' and the clerk went to a filing cabinet that stood against the wall and brought from one of the drawers a sheet of paper and a ledger.

After the editor had written something on the paper, he passed it to Marie Anne, saying, 'That is the receipt for your drawings. Doulton will give you the fifteen shillings as you leave, but first I would like you to sign this book.' He now opened the ledger, found a clear page, wrote in it; then, turning it round towards Marie Anne, he said, 'Read what I have written.'

And Marie Anne, taking up the book, read aloud, 'Deposited this day, the twenty-sixth of November, nineteen hundred, three drawings to be printed as drawn, but allowing for the captions to be changed if necessary. Signed—' She now placed the book on the table, took the pen that he was offering her and signed her name as Marie Anne Foggerty. She smiled as she turned the book round towards him again and handed back his pen, and he smiled at her before rising to his feet, saying, 'Who knows, that might be the beginning of a long-term deal; but you won't likely be hearing from us until at least the middle of December; very likely later. It all depends if they catch the public interest. You understand?'

She didn't quite, but she nodded, saying, 'Yes, I understand; and thank you, sir.'

'Thank you, Miss Foggerty.'

As they were making for the door that was being held open by the clerk, the editor said, 'I didn't get your name, missis.'

And at this Sarah turned and, looking him full in the face, she said, 'It's Foggerty, too, sir,' and on that they went out, leaving the editor and his assistant both biting on their lips to still their laughter. Then John Stokes said, 'Well, what d'you make of it?'

'She's pregnant.'

'What?'

'She's pregnant, the young 'un.'

'How on earth d'you know? She looks as flat as a pancake.'

'Not from the side she doesn't; and don't forget I've got three. I would say she's in her fourth month, or a bit more.'

'Well, well! But one thing I do know, her name is no more Foggerty than mine is Windsor.'

'You're right there; but tell me, why did you want her name put down in the ledger. I mean it was an ordinary deal, no different from buying an article.'

'It'll be different if they catch on. She's a born carica-turist and although she's not from any ordinary folk she's got an eye for them, and she'll certainly have plenty of material in the East End. Send Doulton along there tomorrow to see what Ramsay Court looks like; I'm inter-ested. And you say she's pregnant? Well, well. I would like to bet that her family are either looking for her or they've thrown her out. But whichever, she has a good champion in the woman she had with her, and I'd make a guess that one's stays are laced with barbed wire.' . . .

The woman whose corsets were surmised to be laced with barbed wire was at that moment walking smartly by the side of Marie Anne towards a horse-bus. Although cold and wet they were both in a high state of excitement, for they kept glancing at each other and laughing, appar-ently at nothing at all; but once seated in the horse-bus, Sarah said, 'My! I am hungry; I could eat a horse.' And when Marie Anne, to use Clara's quip, put in, 'With or without mustard?' their heads came together with their hands over their mouths to still their laughter.

'I tell you what we'll do,' said Sarah. 'We'll celebrate. We can afford it today. We'll go to Ernie Everton's for a bite.'

'Ernie Everton's? Where's that?'

'Oh, it's only two stops before we get to the priory. It's a well-known eatin' house, good staple food, an' you can have a drink an' all if you want it. At night-time it's full because they have a singer an' such entertainment. Their pies and peas are grand, so is the sausage and mash; or you can have brawn or pigs' trotters and brown bread. It's a kind of family bar. They're crowded out after weddings and things . . . and funerals an' all. Very rarely any fighting there. Nobody would dare; Ernie's about twenty stone. Nice man.'

When Marie Anne said, 'Well, I'll have pie and peas, sausage and mash and a couple of trotters,' they were again laughing with their heads close together . . .

Ernie Everton's Eating House, as the board above the main door proclaimed, consisted of two large rooms, with the bar counter running the length of them both. They were separated by a partition, the right-hand one being accessible only through a door in the partition just inside the main door. It was a men's room, more like a club where they could drink, play billiards or cards and if they didn't keep strictly to the notice which warned, 'No Gambling Allowed', who was to know? But the main room, the restaurant, was taken up with tables to seat two, four or six people, with enough space left to form a freeway to the side of the partition, where, on a small platform, were set a piano and a music stool. There was also space in front of the counter for customers, those waiting to be served or taking a drink.

As it was now two o'clock and the dinner-time rush was over, there were only about six people seated at the tables, although quite a number were still waiting to be served.

After telling Marie Anne to take a seat at a table for two, Sarah took her place at the end of the queue. A man of gigantic proportions was standing at the far end of the counter. He was measuring out a small whisky; but nearer to Sarah, the woman, much smaller than the man and whom Sarah knew to be his wife, was ladling out peas onto two plates but seemed not to be paying attention to what she was doing, for she called along to her husband, 'When she comes in, I'll tell her to keep her hat and coat on, I will that!'

And the answer came back in a very small voice for such a big man, 'You'll do nothing of the kind, or else we'll be stuck.'

'She's done this too often,' the woman snapped back.

The man ahead of Sarah was now facing the woman behind the counter and he said, 'I'll have a pint of mild, missis,' and at this the woman said, 'Oh dear! Can you wait a minute?' Then looking towards her husband, she called, 'Ernie! a pint of mild,' and he called back briefly, 'Presently.'

The man now politely moved along the counter to make room for Sarah, and as she took his place she cast a glance behind her at the queue that was forming there, when what she later called a bolt from the blue, like a nudge from heaven, made her lean towards the woman and ask, 'Could I be of help, missis, temporary like? I did two years bar work some time ago. My friend and I just came in for a bite' – she motioned with a nod towards Marie Anne – 'but I've got an hour to spare if it would help.'

The woman looked along the counter to her husband, then said, 'Can you pull a pint?'

'Oh aye, missis. It's a few years since I was at the pumps, but you don't forget.'

As if making a quick decision, the woman said, 'Go through that door there' – she pointed to the far end of the counter – 'it'll bring you round to the back.'

'Right,' said Sarah. 'I'll tell me friend,' and at this she hurried to where Marie Anne was seated and gabbled at her, 'Go to the counter and get something to eat; I'm going behind to help them.'

'What . . . ?'

'Never mind what, do as I say,' and with some surprise Marie Anne joined the queue at the counter.

A few minutes later she was amazed to see Sarah standing behind the beer pumps and heard her saying, 'Will I give it a try? The first one will likely be over-full.'

'Well, have a shot,' the woman said as she put a pie on a plate of peas and handed it to a customer, saying, 'That'll be fourpence.'

Behind the counter Sarah looked at the two pumps, one for mild, one for bitter, and gripping the top of one of them just below the highly polished brass cap, she slowly drew it towards her while holding a pint pot under its tap. But when she managed to shut it off, the beer was running over the side of the pot and she glanced back at the woman saying, 'First try.' Then when a man asked for a pint of bitter, she took in a deep breath, gripped the other pump, drew it slowly towards her until the pint mug was half full, then she slowly let it return to its base, leaving a good head of froth on the mug.

She was grinning widely as she placed the pint pot before the man, and he pushed fourpence towards her and without any adverse comment, said, 'Thanks, missis,' and took his drink over to a table.

Mr Ernie Everton now shuffled up to her side, saying, 'Twasn't bad that, not at all, so can I leave you this end? Flatten out so I can get past you, missis;' and as if Sarah had followed the command every day, she moved from in front of the pump sink and pressed herself against the inside of the counter, and Mr Ernie Everton slithered past her, to stop by his wife and say, 'She'll do for a fill-in any time.'

His wife did not answer him, and he disappeared beyond the partition that cut off the piano platform from the next room, while Mrs Everton hurried along to Sarah and, pointing to the overflowing pint pot of beer still standing on the tray, said quietly, 'Divide that out between a few mugs, then fill up on top; can't waste any – that's if they ask for pints. But if they're just half, pull them straight, you understand?'

'Yes, yes; I understand.'

Mrs Everton now turned to the laden rack of bottles that were interspersed here and there with pewter mugs and Toby heads and, picking up a tube that was attached to the plate lift in the wall, she blew into it, then said, 'Send up another dish of peas, Daisy, and don't start the sausage and mash till four, but I could do with some more brown buns.' . . .

Some half hour later, there were only two customers at the counter finishing their pints and Sarah, dropping into an old routine, was wiping down the wet counter when Mrs Everton said, 'You came in for a bite, lass, didn't you?'

'Yes; yes, I did, missis.'

'Well, we'll be slack for a time now, I should think, and all we have still hot are the pies and peas, but there's good brawn there.'

'I'll go for the pie and peas, if you don't mind.'

As Mrs Everton ladled out a generous quantity of peas beside two pies on a plate, she said, 'You've been a godsend today. She who should be here's goin' to get my toe in her backside. I took her on when she was hard up, but I don't know what's come over her. I think she's on the game' – she nodded – 'you know, or some such. Anyway she can't be in need of money, and we pay well here: threepence an hour and all the tips you can get and as much grub as you can put into you. You don't get that everywhere today.'

'No, I'm sure you don't.'

'So go and have your bite, and I'll settle up with you later. You might have to do another little stint for us before you go. Do you live about here?'

'Oh, ten minutes away.'

'Are you in work?'

156

'Not at the moment.'

'Would . . . would you mind doing something like this?'

Sarah thought for a moment, then said, 'No, I wouldn't, but it could only be so many hours a day.'

'Well, that's all we want of anybody, so many hours a day. Usually starts at twelve 'til two. Sometimes it goes on a bit longer. In the evening we're always very busy; that's from five till ten.'

The plate in her hand, Sarah picked up a pie and took a bite from it before she said, 'Well, thank you very much, missis. Daytime would be all right, but I don't know about the evening. You see, that young' – she had been about to say 'lady' – 'I mean, girl down there, well, I sort of look after her, and I couldn't leave her all hours at night.'

'You could bring her with you.' The woman laughed now. 'It might get a bit rowdy, but there's no rough stuff here. Ernie sees to that.'

'Oh well, thank you very much. We'll talk about it. By the way' – she looked towards the platform and the piano – 'she's a grand piano player; plays lovely.'

'You don't say.'

'Yes; yes. I bet she'd give her eye teeth if you'd let her play while I'm eating.'

'Oh, definitely. Only too pleased to hear her. We've got a fellow comes in at night. He's no great shakes, but he knows all the popular tunes. Plays by ear, I think.'

'I'll tell her.'

Sarah almost skipped round the counter and into the restaurant, and there, dropping her plate on the table, she said to Marie Anne, 'Would you like to play for a bit?'

Marie Anne stared at her. 'Play for a bit? What d'you mean?'

'What's the matter with you? Have you turned daft all of a sudden? Play the piano.' She pointed.

'They'd let me?'

'Well, I've just got permission for you.'

'Oh, Sarah. Sarah. Oh that would be lovely.'

'Well, go on.'

First, Marie Anne went to the counter and said to the little woman, 'Oh, thank you very much. Thank you.' Then she stepped up on to the low platform, lifted the lid of the piano and saw it was of a very good make. Before sitting down on the stool, she ran her fingers over the keys, and with real delight she noted that this piano didn't need tuning.

Sitting down now, she paused a minute before her hands fell on the keys and softly she started to play the adagio section of a Mozart sonata.

When it ended, she cast a glance over the tables. There were four people seated now, but they were giving her their full attention and Mrs Everton was beaming at her, and, as if the looks were giving her encouragement, Marie Anne plunged into Beethoven's Appassionata, and so lost did she become in her playing that she wasn't aware that Mr Everton had appeared and the two men standing drinking at the counter had moved towards the platform.

When she finished with a flourish, there was silence for a moment, and she heard a woman say, 'My! My!' which seemed to prompt one of the men to remark ''Tis a while since I heard anything like that. It's a pianist you are, miss, a pianist.'

She turned towards the man. She didn't know that there was sweat on her brow. Then Mr Everton's small voice came from his large body, saying, 'The surprise of the day! Do you play in an orchestra, miss?'

'No, sir; no.'

'A band then?'

'No; nor a band either.'

'Well,' said the woman, 'wherever you play I would say you've been well taught.'

Somewhat embarrassed now, Marie Anne turned to the

158

keys again and her fingers were light on them now as she played a Brahms lullaby.

By now Sarah had finished her pie and peas, and, taking her plate to the counter, she said, 'I'll stay if you want me, Mrs Everton, but I can see you're very slack at the moment.'

'Yes, we are; but I'm very obliged for your help.' And pulling open the till she took from it a sixpence and handed it to Sarah, saying, 'You haven't been here even an hour, but that's for two and for being so obligin' and lettin' us hear your friend's music.'

She looked along to where her husband was still standing listening and she said, ''Tis different. What d'you say?'

'Oh, aye' – he nodded at her – 'chalk and cheese. She can play for me any time, this one. But with her quality, I doubt if she could play the rag-a-tag, Marie Lloyd stuff that he knocks out. Still, you never know.'

'I'll get my coat and hat now, and thank you very much for the money. It is kind of you,' Sarah said.

'Works both ways, miss. It works both ways. But I tell you what you can do. You can leave an address where we could get in touch with you if we were in a fix, that's if you hadn't any work on.'

For a moment Sarah hesitated, but then she said, 'Well, it's top flat, Ramsay Court.'

The woman couldn't hide her surprise as she repeated, 'Ramsay Court. Oh, yes; yes I know that area. I can get you there if I want you?'

'Yes, that's where you'll find me.'

'What were you doing before this, may I ask?'

'You well may ask, Mrs Everton, and you can believe it when I say that I was a lady's maid to an invalid; a lady's companion I was called.'

'Really?'

'Yes, really.'

159

'Well, all I can say is it's a long way from there to pulling pints.'

'It may be, but I know which I would prefer to do from now on.'

'Aye? You mean that?'

'I mean that, Mrs Everton.'

At this, Sarah left the amazed little woman, collected her coat and hat from the peg, and slowly put them on, thinking: it never rains but it pours; and thank God for it. She was still pondering when she tapped Marie Anne on the shoulder, saying, 'Come on; you've had enough, we're ready for the road.'

'Oh. I was lost in thought.'

'I could see that.'

As Marie Anne stepped down from the platform, one man was still standing holding his empty pint mug and, looking at her, he said, 'Thank you, girl. Thank you.'

'You're welcome.' They smiled at each other. Then Marie Anne went to the counter and to Mrs Everton she said, 'Thank you so much for letting me play. I haven't a piano now and I miss it. Would . . . would you allow me to call in occasionally in the daytime and play, just for a short while?'

Mr and Mrs Everton exchanged glances; then it was he who, nodding, said, 'Any time you're passing, miss, and there's nobody on the seat' – he nodded towards the piano stool – 'and there never is during the day, you'd be welcome. I can't say I'll engage you, but you could have your fill of food for the both of you. Can't be fairer than that.'

'Thank you very much, very much indeed,' and Marie Anne backed away from the counter, nodding first at one and then the other; then she almost skipped round to join Sarah, and like a pair of youngsters, they ran out of the restaurant and into the street. There, turning and looking

160

at each other, Marie Anne said, 'A magic day, don't you think, Sarah? a magic day. I must write and tell Grandpa and put his mind at rest.'

And in answer to this, Sarah said, 'Aye, do that: write and tell him that I'm pulling beer behind a bar and you're playing the piano to the men sloshing it down.'

7

The magic of that day was soon to evaporate. After running joyfully through the rain, Sarah, being the hardier of the two, avoided suffering from being soaked to the skin, but Marie Anne developed such a cold as to cause her to stay in bed; and on the advice of Annie a doctor was called. But she warned Sarah that he'd likely charge them two shillings: he would recognise straightaway Marie Anne would be in a position to pay more than he normally charged his Ramsay Court patients.

It was as Annie foretold: the doctor did charge two shillings; but he was also very kind, and only slightly curious about her condition and why she was living in such a place.

It was a week before Christmas. Marie Anne was up and about; she hadn't dared risk going out into the murky days and foggy nights, for she was still coughing. Nearly two months had passed since the *Daily Reporter* had taken her drawings and she had had no word from them, and although she still relieved the monotony of her days with drawing, she was becoming very bored and somewhat irritable, her only light relief being Annie's children, particularly the older ones. They would bring up their coloured paper from which they would make chains to decorate the house. And at such times Marie Anne would sketch them, much to their delight. When she gave them funny faces, Maureen would tease the boys, saying, 'Oh! that's you,' and they would come back at her, 'Aye well,

162

our Maureen, we haven't got buck teeth.' And such repartee lightened the dark days in the garret flat, for dark they were, until one morning Sarah sat bolt upright in the bed and, pointing to a chink in the curtains, she cried, 'I think the sun's out.' Jumping up, she pulled the curtains back and, turning a bright face to Marie Anne, who was now rubbing the sleep out of her eyes, she said, 'Look! the sun. Isn't it marvellous! It's days and days since we've seen it. Come on, get yourself up; you can go out today all right. And we'll give ourselves a treat: we'll have a bite at Ernie's and you can play the piano again. You never took up their offer and I'm sure they've been wondering why. Come on now, get a move on.'

Marie Anne got up; but she was finding it rather difficult in the mornings to put a move on, she wasn't feeling too good, sort of weak, such as she had never felt in her life before and she was finding this difficult to handle. She was having to do what she called push herself.

But this morning she gladly pushed herself. After breakfast and the beastly chores done, they stood in the room ready to go out. Sarah had pulled the collar of Marie Anne's coat well up at the back and under her hat, and when she tucked the scarf into the front of her coat Marie Anne exclaimed, 'That's it! Go on, choke me. Why are we going to Paddy's first? We've got everything.'

'We haven't got everything. Have we got a cradle?'

'Oh . . . no, but—'

'Yes, but. Well, there's little chance of us getting a cradle but we can get a decent sized wash-basket and a couple of flat pillows, and instead of using your pencil during the next few weeks you could cover them into nice little bed ticks, and the basket an' all with a frill or two. And don't hang your head like that, girl, every time it's mentioned. It's more than half there' – she tapped Marie Anne's stomach – 'and it'll come; and he or she will be lovely and we'll be a family.'

Even as she was saying this, she could hear her mother's voice crying, 'One more mouth to be fed and Dailey won't keep me scrubbin' job open, not him, the ungrateful bugger, and all the work I've done for him,' and she thought, Poor Ma; but she got through, and so will we. Then cryptically added, But how, in the name of God! as yet I don't know.

'What are you thinking, Sarah?'

'I wasn't thinking.'

'Yes, you were. I always know.'

'You know too much, but come on: let us to the Emporium go, not by a chariot that is too slow, but on wings of love.'

At this and on a laugh Marie Anne pushed Sarah against the door, saying, 'I didn't read it like that; you would mangle it, wouldn't you? Anyway you shouldn't pick up second-hand poetry books, for you've always told me you can't stand poetry.'

'Nor can I. Come on!'

Mr O'Connell greeted them as if they were old friends and at once supplied them with a large, clean wash-basket, two pillows, and even extra linen cases for them. But the bargain of the morning was nearly half a bale of printed cotton, all of fifteen yards left on it, he said, and all for two shillings, which meant that the bale had cost him one and six. But as he pointed out to them, he had been getting tuppence ha'penny a yard for it, and when Sarah came back, saying, 'That must have been in the year dot,' he retorted as he usually did when stuck for words, 'Just as you say, miss. Just as you say.' And when Sarah asked if he would look after their purchases until they returned as they were going to Ernie Everton's for a bite, he sent them both away laughing with the words: 'Paddy's Emporium at your service, missis; and have a pie and peas for me.'

It being just after eleven o'clock there were very few

people seated at the tables and a couple of men and a woman at the bar counter. But besides Mrs Everton, there was a very smartly dressed but peevish-looking young woman serving.

Immediately she saw them, Mrs Everton called, 'Well, well! now. We haven't seen you for some time. We thought—'

'She's been ill in bed, Mrs Everton. She's had a very bad chest cold.'

Mrs Everton looked at Marie Anne and, shaking her head, she said, 'Oh I'm sorry, I'm sorry to hear that; but we did wonder. I suppose you would like a ding-dong?' She had poked her head across the counter towards Marie Anne, and Marie Anne said, 'I would indeed, Mrs Everton, if it's all right with you.'

'It's more than all right, dear. We'd all be very pleased to hear you again. We've talked about you a lot. But are you going to eat first?'

Marie Anne and Sarah exchanged glances, and it was Sarah who replied, 'She would rather play first, but I'll eat now.'

'Good enough. Good enough.'

As Marie Anne made for the piano, Sarah said, 'I'll have sausage and mash today.'

'And what about a bit of liver with it?'

'Oh yes, thank you.'

At the piano Marie Anne flexed her fingers before she ran them lovingly over the keys. Softly the scales went up and down, forming themselves into what sounded like a composition. Then quite softly she began to play . . .

As Mrs Everton blew down the order, a man came up to the counter and was greeted straightaway by her: 'Oh, hello; you're back then?' she said.

'Yes, Mrs Everton, I'm back.'

'Well, well; nice to see you. The usual?'

'Yes, the usual, all of half a mild.'

165

'Shippin' order comin' up,' and she laughed as she drew the half pint of ale; then as she pushed it across the counter to him, she enquired, 'For how long this time?'

'Oh, I go back in the New Year.'

'Been workin' hard in the meantime?'

'Yes. Yes, indeed: the Brothers are hard taskmasters.'

'They always were, and they know how many beans make five. Is old Brother Percival still wielding his hammer and chisel?'

'As much as ever, Mrs Everton. Yes, as much as ever.'

She watched the man drink half the glass of ale before she said, 'By! they don't half know how to charge for those pieces, which must be nearly all yours, you know, 'cos I should imagine he's beyond it now, ninety if he's a day.'

'Oh no, no, no. He's working on some quite big stuff in the back. It's only the little odds and ends that are mine.'

'Huh! I wish I had enough money to buy just a couple of your odds and ends.'

'Oh now, now, Mrs Everton, they don't charge that much.'

'Oh, they do at that. As it is said, it's because of the dealers. They come there and would buy up the lot if the Brothers let them. They've got wily heads, those Brothers in there. I was always surprised when you didn't become one of them.'

'I was myself, Mrs Everton. They tried hard enough, but I haven't the qualities to make a good Brother, I'm too worldly.'

She laughed at him now, saying, 'Go on with you. You? worldly? D'you like where you're livin' now?'

'Very much, very much indeed.'

'You've got a workshop?'

'Everything. Everything to hand.'

'I heard they tried to stop you going, and that it was

only because you promised to bring your odds and ends, as you call them, twice a year that you got free.'

'Nonsense; nonsense, Mrs Everton. The Brothers were only too pleased to be rid of me. But seriously, I've a lot to thank the Brothers for. They were all fathers and mothers to me. As you know I was brought up by them and thankful that I was.'

There was a sound of a whistle blowing and the food lift behind Mrs Everton came into view bearing Sarah's meal. And when Mrs Everton placed it on the counter the man said, 'Oh that does look nice; I wouldn't mind one of those myself, Mrs Everton.'

'Well, you shall have it, sir, you shall have it,' and she turned to order it, and the man, now turning towards the piano called over his shoulder to Mrs Everton, 'Who's that playing? You're going up in the music world, aren't you, Mrs Everton?'

As she turned back to the counter Mrs Everton answered, 'Oh, it's just now and again we have the pleasure of that one's talents. She's a friend of Miss Foggerty here.'

Sarah and the man looked at each other, she straight into his face. He said, 'She plays beautifully.'

'Yes, she does,' Sarah responded as she walked to a near table to eat her meal. She recognised this man – she had heard of him from Annie – the Brother with half a face. He was wearing a kind of mask. It was as if half his head was strapped in a dark brown cotton scarf with a white lining. His large slouch hat could only, of course, cover up one side of his face from the corner of the right eye, just visible under the hat, past his high cheekbone, and slant-wise across the cheek, just missing his mouth, then to his chin, disappearing into the top of his white shirt.

Annie had said he must have been scalded when he was a child; others that it was a birthmark. However, this was

167

discredited, for surely you could never have a birthmark as large as that. But he had wonderful hands, Annie said; she had seen some of the things he had made on sale at the bazaar the Brothers held twice a year. It was a strange kind of bazaar. Most of it was given over to second-hand clothes, second-hand books, second-hand boots and hand-made items that the parishioners had donated and which were very rarely sold, because who was going to pay one and six a pair for hand-knitted socks when you could knit a pair yourself for sixpence. But then there was what was called the sculpture stall. Old Brother Percival had been a noted sculptor in his day, and since he had come into the Brotherhood they had profited by it. The Brothers also ran a small private school.

It was said that the tall fellow standing at the counter had been handed a chisel when he was three years old, by Brother Percival, and he had never been allowed to drop it since, and how old was he now? She gave a guess. Thirty, she imagined.

He was walking towards the platform when the whistle blew again and he returned to the counter, and after paying for his meal took it to Sarah's table and asked her, 'Would you mind if I sat with you?'

'Not at all. Not at all. You're welcome.'

After seating himself, he looked towards the platform again, saying, 'Your friend plays beautifully. Indeed she does.'

From where he was sitting he could see only her back, and he further remarked, 'She's young. Is she training at a music academy?'

'Er, no; not now. She was, but . . . but she had to leave.'

'Oh, that *is* a pity.'

He started to eat his meal and was halfway through a sausage when he stopped and, again looking towards the platform, he said, 'That's Liszt, and very difficult to play.'

'D'you play the piano?'

'No, I'm afraid not. I used to try the organ when I was in the priory. You heard what Mrs Everton said' – he nodded towards the counter – 'I was brought up by the Brothers.'

'I know that.' She smiled at him.

'Yes?'

'I'm Annie Pollock's sister. She lives in Ramsay Court.' She watched his eyes widen and his eyebrows rise under the rim of his soft felt hat; and now his mouth went into a wide smile, and in so doing crinkled the cloth mask here and there into ridges as he said, 'The Pollocks of Ramsay Court, the bane of Father Broadside. Your sister committed the unforgivable sin of marrying a Protestant, didn't she? one Arthur Pollock. Oh, how I remember the time.'

Sarah was now laughing openly. 'So do I,' she said. 'He was never off the doorstep. But he always managed to get there when Arthur was out and heap coals of hell fire on Annie's head; worse than Father Weir. At first, she was scared of him, but she toughened up as time went on.' Then, the smile leaving her face, she said, 'And you know – or perhaps you don't, not being a Brother or a priest yourself – they can cause just one hell of a lot of trouble in a marriage. Naturally, Arthur insisted on the children going to a Protestant school; he wasn't going to pay a penny or tuppence a week at the nuns' place along the street.'

'Yes, yes, I know. In his case I can understand that. I argued against it once and was told I was a renegade and was given a stiff penance. Not by the Brothers, oh no; they are moderate men, all of them. No; it was our good Father Broadside.'

He made her smile again when he said, 'You know, in a naval battle the big guns shoot broadsides through the side of the ship, and Brother Percival used to swear that Father Broadside was never born in the ordinary way but

169

through such a broadside. Oh yes, he is a hard man; and yes, so very bigoted.' And they smiled and nodded at each other in agreement. And now turning his attention to his meal, he said, 'There's always good food to be got here, isn't there?'

'I've only come to know it lately,' Sarah answered.

The sound of applause made them both turn to look towards the platform. Marie Anne had stopped playing and the other customers were showing their appreciation.

It was as Marie Anne made her way to the counter, where Mrs Everton was waiting to take her order, that the man almost sprang to his feet, and for a moment it seemed as if he was going to step forward, but he remained staring at the young girl at the counter.

It was evident that she was carrying a child, the bulge, as yet not very large, being nevertheless noticeable. Then, as Marie Anne, with her plate of pie and peas, turned from the counter the man's bottom jaw dropped just the slightest. As for Marie Anne, she did not look fully at him until she reached the table, when he held out his chair to her, saying, 'Take this; I can get another,' and for a moment she was startled. She did not know why. Although the man was wearing that big hat and with half his face muffled up, he looked odd; and there was definitely something else making her feel uneasy. Then there was his voice. He did not speak like a Londoner, or anyone she knew of. It was obviously an educated voice, a distinct voice, one she seemed to remember.

'You've chosen pie and peas,' Sarah was saying; 'you should've tried the sausage and mash today, with some liver thrown in; it was lovely.'

The man drew up a chair for himself, the uncovered side of his face visible to Marie Anne, and she was very conscious that his gaze was centred on her. Sarah, too, was aware of this, and so, leaning across to Marie Anne,

170

she said, 'What d'you think? This gentleman and I have something in common: we both know Father Broadside, the priest I told you about who used to chase Annie and raise the house on a Monday morning if she hadn't been to Mass. If he couldn't save the souls of her children he was determined to save hers. Well, this gentleman, here, was brought up by the Brothers in the priory, just along the street here, and he had heard all about Annie and her brood and the two priests trying to save her soul.'

Marie Anne now turned and smiled at the man and, merely out of politeness, asked, 'Are you a Brother at the priory?'

'No, no. As I have to tell people, I have none of the virtues that go to make a good Brother, so they threw me out. But I return twice a year to visit them and bring odds and ends for them to sell.'

'He's a sculptor—' Sarah was leaning across the table again towards Marie Anne, and she added, 'and he's noted all about for his work. There's going to be a show of it tomorrow; we'll go and see.'

He turned to her, smiling again, saying, 'I haven't your name, miss.'

'Foggerty.'

'Well, Miss Foggerty, the Brothers wouldn't thank you for aiming to make me vain about my small talents.' Then he laughed outright as he added, 'But go on, for I can tell you on the quiet you get very little of it in a priory, at least openly. Behind your back they'll say kind words, but to your face they'll remind you that your talent is only loaned from God, and that in a way it's got nothing to do with you, that you're only working to instructions.'

His laughter was light and merry, and both Sarah and Marie Anne joined in. Then rising from his chair, he asked, 'Will I be seeing you at the bazaar tomorrow, then?'

'Yes, yes, we'll drop in,' Sarah said, 'but not, let me tell you, to buy your expensive animals and such.'

'What a shame! What a shame! We are very much in need of money.' He was laughing as he spoke; then touching his hat to both of them he went to the counter and had a word with Mrs Everton before walking smartly out.

'God's slipped up many a time,' Sarah remarked, 'but in putting a mark on that fellow He did a bad day's work, even if He did give him a clever pair of hands.'

The next morning the sun wasn't shining and the sky appeared so low it could have been resting on the chimney pots, and as Marie Anne and Sarah emerged from the cut which would bring them to the priory Marie Anne shivered and pulled her coat tighter about her, which caused Sarah to say, 'I've told you, you'll have to buy a bigger coat than that. That single breasted's no good to you now and the second-hand shop I told you about isn't a rag stall; it sells very good pieces.'

'All right, all right,' said Marie Anne rather sharply; 'we'll do as you say some time later, but at the moment we're going to the bazaar and we'll be expected to buy something there.'

'We will not, and just you remember that, miss, unless it's a book that's going for a copper. That statement of his yesterday that they were in need of money is all my eye. Those Brothers must be rolling in it, and it's mostly made, I'm sure, from his and Brother Percival's work. You heard what Annie said last night, that come Christmas and June, thereabouts, his bag's loaded with stuff. Apparently he comes by train from wherever he lives and loads his bag into a cab. Shane used to do odd jobs for the Brothers. No pay; oh no, everything must be voluntary. Anyway, as Annie said, the other day Shane saw a number of bags and wooden boxes being unloaded from the cab.'

172

'It seems to prove one thing,' said Marie Anne; 'he must have been quite happy being brought up among them and so his two trips a year are a form of repaying them in some way, I suppose.' . . .

Inside the gardens of the priory a number of stalls were set out under a canvas awning and at the back, near the wall, was a long table upon which was arrayed a large assortment, in marble, of animals, birds and reptiles and, in wood, of ornamental candlesticks, cigar boxes and ladies' vanity trays. At each end of the table was the carving of a figure, holding a lamp aloft. One was of a beautifully formed young woman, the other of a young man with the body of an athlete. Each was mounted on a plinth carved out of stone, of the colour of bleached rock.

When Marie Anne stopped in front of the female figure, the Brother behind the table approached her and remarked, 'It's very beautiful, isn't it?'

Marie Anne smiled into the round red face and replied, 'Yes, very beautiful. They're a beautiful pair.' She turned to look towards the other end of the table. 'Were they carved here?'

The Brother recognised the tone of her voice and, sensing he might have a customer, he said, 'No; our dear friend Don McAlister' – he pointed towards the bookstall where the man she had met yesterday was obviously discussing a book with a customer – 'he made them in his workshop, and he'll tell you all about them and why, himself. I'll bring him across.'

'Oh no, please don't bother. I . . . I have met Mr' – she paused – 'McAlister.'

'Oh! then you know of his work?'

'Not really. I made his acquaintance only yesterday.'

'Only yesterday?'

She nodded.

'Ah, then,' he poked his finger at her chest now as he

173

went on in a high and excited voice, 'are you the young lady who played the piano so beautifully in Ernie Everton's Eating House?'

'Yes; yes, I am. Well, I played the piano, but I don't know about beautifully.'

'He said you did, and he has an ear for music. Oh' – he slapped the side of his head – 'that is an exaggeration, if not a lie. He had an ear for the organ and used to deafen us.' He looked over her head now, saying, 'Oh! here you are then. I'm just speaking the truth about you for once. You met this young lady yesterday, I believe.'

Marie Anne turned and faced the odd man, as she thought of him.

He was smiling at her and saying, 'Good day, Miss Foggerty.'

She could never get used to being called Foggerty, but she answered him with a smile as she said, 'I was admiring the beautiful lamp.'

'And Brother John here has persuaded you to buy it? He's only asking twenty pounds.'

'We haven't mentioned money yet, and it's twenty-two pounds. It's only twenty each if you take the pair.'

'Well, what's forty pounds? Would you like them wrapped up now or shall I send them by horse-bus?'

She laughed outright while wondering how he could joke, situated as he was with seemingly only part of a face.

'Ah, and here's Miss Sarah coming. I bet she's bought the other one.'

'What's all this I heard about buying?' asked Sarah.

'Well, Miss Foggerty, Father John here has persuaded your sister to buy a lamp. It's only twenty-two pounds, but if you'd like the other one as well, he'd let you have them for forty.'

'Now that is kind of him,' said Sarah, her voice serious. 'But we'll take them only on the condition that you send them to my sister Annie's flat in Ramsay Court and have

174

Father Broadside go and bless them.'

The deep laughter of the two men mingled with Sarah's, but Marie Anne only smiled. There was something about this big man that was making her feel uneasy. It wasn't that she felt afraid of him – well, not really – but he reminded her of someone, or something. She moved away from them to further along the table, the while shaking her head at the wonder of the scales on a crocodile's back and at an elephant not more than two inches high with a young one by its side and which looked to have been carved in ivory. There were blue tits, too, and an eagle, the latter with its wings half spread, as though about to take off from the table. Then there was the rearing horse. It was about five inches high and carved from a dark wood.

Her fingers were touching it when Don McAlister's voice at her side said, 'I like him too.'

She was slightly startled and when he picked up the piece and held it towards her, he said, 'It's bog oak. It's beautiful stuff to work with, but difficult at times, because just as you're finishing it, your fingers seem to tremble. It's as if something from the earth is saying, Why can't you leave me alone; that knife of yours is sharp, you know.

Marie Anne stared at him unsmilingly. She felt a wave of irritation for him sweep over her. Yes, that was the feeling he aroused in her; irritation. It was his manner; his constant manner of making light of things. He was either quipping or quoting someone. It was as if he felt he had to be entertaining, but why? Why? looking as he did. Perhaps the reason *was* because he looked as he did.

With a sudden swift but careful movement he placed the rearing horse back onto its small stand; then turning to her again, he said, 'If you will excuse me,' and quickly disappeared through a flap at the end of the awning.

Sarah approached, saying, 'Seen anything you like?'

After a moment Marie Anne pointed to the rearing horse. 'Yes, I like that,' she said. 'I would like to have it and send it to my grandpa for Christmas.'

Sarah picked up the rearing horse, read the tag on the back, and replaced it on its stand, saying, 'Come on. You can forget it; it's five pounds.'

And with this she gripped Marie Anne's arm and turned her about, only to find her hand thrust away and to hear Marie Anne, in a low commanding tone, saying, 'Don't pull at me!'

Surprised and feeling repulsed by this attitude, Sarah moved quietly ahead and out of the gardens. Marie Anne followed her, and they were going through the passage again when she caught up with her and said, 'I'm sorry, Sarah. I'm sorry. I don't know why I acted like that. Oh yes, I do; it was that man. He irritates me.'

Sarah stopped and turned and looked hard at Marie Anne: 'Mr Don McAlister irritates you?' she said. 'Why? How? You've only met him the twice and he's been a most pleasant and agreeable person. If you ask me, we could do with more of his company. Irritates you? How does he irritate you?'

'Sarah –' Marie Anne's voice was low and her words came slowly, 'I don't know, but he gives me a most strange feeling. I can't explain it. I . . . I can only tell you that when I first looked at him I was startled. Why I should have been, I don't know.'

'Just because his face is scarred in some way?'

'No; not really. I tell you, I don't know.'

Sarah sighed; then her voice changing, she said, 'Oh, come on with you. They say when a woman's pregnant she doesn't know which end of her's up. I tell you what: we'll call in on Annie. She'll likely have a pot of mutton broth on. *He's* expected home tonight. I hope he's as sober as when he came last time. Then he was so sober

176

and civil I thought he must have joined the Band of Hope.' . . .

As soon as they entered Annie's room, she greeted them with, 'A letter came for you, miss.'

'For me, a letter?' Marie Anne turned on Sarah a sharp look which said, Who knows I'm here?

Annie took the envelope from the mantelpiece and handed it to Marie Anne.

Again she exchanged a look with Sarah; but, even as she did so Sarah exclaimed loudly, 'I know! I know who it's from. Open it, woman!'

Marie Anne slit open the envelope, took out a sheet of paper, and read:

Dear Miss Foggerty,

If you would care to call at this office on the third of January we could discuss using more of your work. Perhaps a series of the family of children. We did not have an immediate response to the cartoons, but just lately there have been some requests for more of the 'manners' type of cartoon, depicting the children at the table.

Hoping that this suggestion meets favourably with you.

Yours truly
John Stokes, Editor.

Marie Anne now turned and threw her arms around Sarah, saying, 'I've got it! I mean, I've got the work. There, read that.' And turning to Annie, she said, 'I took some of my drawings to a newspaper. They want more for next year.'

'Oh, I'm glad, miss. Oh, I am. Now you'll feel more settled and at ease, with something coming in. Oh, and it'll fill your time.'

'As for me,' put in Sarah, 'I can now go and pull pints at Ernie's, knowing that you're not sittin' up there moping.'

'Sarah' – Marie Anne turned to her appealingly now – 'I could get that horse now, couldn't I, to send my grandpa? I . . . I know it's five pounds, but we'll soon be earning.'

'Yes, I know that, me dear, but five pounds is a lot of money. Anyway, you can have your horse, but you're not going round there to get it; I'll get it and for less than five pounds.'

'Oh no! Don't bargain with them.'

'Don't bargain with them?' Sarah turned to Annie now. 'Did you hear her? Don't bargain with the Brothers! Jews are nothing in it, are they? The Holy Catholic Church puts them in the shade every day when it comes to rakin' money in. They'd skin a louse for its hide. Don't bargain with them, she said. Have you any soup goin', Annie?'

'Don't I always have soup goin' on a Saturday?'

'Well, give her a basinful, will you, and I'll be back in a few minutes.' And at this Sarah went out; but her lightness of manner had changed even before she reached the bottom of the last flight. Five pounds! If she got it for four that would bring her stock down from ten pounds to six, and she had another good four months to go yet. She seemed to think that her drawings were going to make a fortune; if she were to sell two a week that would bring her in only ten shillings. And then there was the child. How did she expect to manage with a baby up on that top floor? Of course, Annie had managed her brood just on the floor below, but she was a different kettle of fish. She and Annie had been brought up in a different school altogether from that girl. Then there would be the doctor and the midwife to be paid.

Oh, let her have her damned horse and send it off to her grandfather, if that would make her feel happy. Well,

178

perhaps as happy as she could be under the circumstances . . .

Quite a number of people were still in the garden.

She made her way to the long table and immediately saw the tall man talking to two others. She didn't want to be served by one of the Brothers; she could talk to Mr McAlister, for she felt he had taken an interest in Marie Anne, perhaps recognising her to be of a different class from herself. She could hear him saying, 'Not a penny less, for you know, and I know, that the price will be doubled once it reaches Regent Street or somewhere like it.'

'You're a difficult man to deal with.'

'These are difficult things to make.'

'Brother Percival said he would meet us halfway.'

'That was because Brother Percival knows as much about business as I do about ballet dancing. Anyway, there it is, take it or leave it. The five pieces you have chosen are forty pounds, no more, no less, and if you don't want them it doesn't matter, because Stevens will be in before the day is over and he has the same taste as yourselves.'

'You needn't keep on; we get your point. Pack them up.'

Sarah watched each piece being carefully wrapped and laid in a cardboard box, and while one man placed the boxes in a flat basket the other grinned as he handed over the money, saying, 'Happy Christmas, and we'll see you again in the summer, or thereabouts.'

'Yes; if God designs.'

The men went away laughing as they repeated, 'Aye, if God designs.'

Don McAlister had noted that Sarah was waiting as if she wanted to speak to him, and so, approaching her, he said, 'You back again? You're going to buy the lamps?'

Sarah smiled as she said, 'That'll be the day. No; she has her heart set on that horse' – she pointed along the table –

'but at five pounds, oh my! no, we could never run to that. So I wondered if you had another like it; what they call seconds.' Up till then she hadn't thought any such thing, but now she went on, 'Just a bit faulted or something. You used to sell pieces like that at one time, if I remember; a little chip off that could hardly be seen.'

He bent down to her now and in a low voice he said, 'Miss Foggerty, Ireland has lost a fine diplomat by not using you before this.'

'Away with you!' She flapped her hand at him. 'Diplomacy bunkum. I'm just statin' a fact. You did used to sell marred ones, didn't you?'

'That was a long time ago.' He chuckled as he stretched out his arm and picked up the horse. 'Who does she want it for; some child?' He had his back to her.

'No, no; she's got a very fond grandfather and she wants to give him a present.'

He turned quickly towards her. 'You say she's got a grandfather? Then why . . . ?'

'Oh, I can't go into it; it's a long story; I can only say that if I had my way she'd be back with her grandfather this minute, because she doesn't realise what's ahead of her. You know the Courts don't you? Well, we're on the top floor. But we've got it comfortable, mind. Paddy's Emporium's been a godsend.'

'Oooh! Paddy's Emporium. What would this district have done all these years without Paddy's Emporium? But tell me, does the grandfather know where she is?'

'My! no; of course not.'

'Has he never known her address?'

'Yes, at one time . . . Look! it's a long story, Mr McAlister, and it's her business and I'm not goin' into it. I'll only say this. Most of the English rich are cruel, heartless buggers, and I hope they burn in hell.'

He was grinning at her again as he said, 'What about the Irish rich?'

'Oh, there's not enough of them to matter. Anybody that owns anything in Ireland is English.'

His laugh was ringing out again and, pointing to a Brother at the end of the table, he said, 'As Brother John is apt to say, you do me heart good, Miss Foggerty; and as for this animal here' – he was now stroking the rearing back of the little horse – 'it does have a fault. You see that hoof, the higher one? Well, look closely, it's much bigger than the other one. They don't match, do they?'

Sarah stared at the prancing hooves; then, her eyes twinkling, she looked up at him, saying, 'You're right. You're right, Mr McAlister. It's what you would call half an inch less.' Then she added on a low giggle, 'How long is half an inch?'

Don McAlister rubbed his eyes with one hand as he said, 'How about two pounds long, Miss Foggerty?'

'Oh! thank you. Thanks. That's good of you.'

He now stretched out his other hand and, picking up a small carving from the table, he handed it to her, saying, 'This isn't a Christmas box; it's just a little gift from me to you for being a very good friend to one in need.'

For a moment Sarah stood speechless as she looked down on the piece lying in the palm of her hand, and she thought: It's a black beetle. She hated black beetles. Somewhat choked, she now asked, 'What kind of beetle is it?'

'It's what they call a scarab. The ancient Egyptians prized it very highly. They thought it would help them to come back after death. It's . . . it's considered to be very lucky.'

Her fingers now closed gently over the beetle as she said, 'Well, we're badly in need of that at the moment – luck, I mean – so thank you very much indeed. And it could be lucky at that, because this is the second good thing that has happened to us in an hour. You see, when we got back to the Courts she found a letter. It was from a newspaper. They're going to take her on; well, take one or two of her drawings each week, I think. She draws what you would call caricatures. They're marvellous and very funny.'

'Really! She draws caricatures? How old is she?'

Sarah turned her head away; then with a shrug of her shoulders she said, 'She's eighteen to everybody who asks, but she's really only sixteen.'

He made no response, but continued to stare at her enquiringly until she spoke as if he had accused her of something, saying, 'I can't help it. I've talked to her till me mouth's dry and told her what would be best for her.'

His voice sounded flat as he muttered, 'And what d'you think would be best for her?'

'That she should go home, of course! But she's got a mother who, if I had my way, would be locked up for cruelty. Oh' – she tossed her head – 'it's her business. Believe me, Mr McAlister, I've done my best.'

'I haven't the slightest doubt about that, Miss Foggerty, not the slightest.' His face and tone were serious now. 'And I can only repeat what I've already said: she's lucky to have a friend such as you. I must go now, but who knows, we may be seeing each other again. Anyway, take care of the scarab.'

'I will, and thank you. Goodbye.'

'Goodbye.'

It was three o'clock in the afternoon. The Brothers had closed the gates of the garden, for they had learned that as soon as night set in all the oil lanterns they could muster would not stop articles disappearing from the stalls. And having been fearful for the precious pieces remaining on the long table, these had been cleared a good hour previously. Today, three dealers had helped to thin out the stock, but there were quite a few pieces still to be packed away, and Don McAlister saw to this himself, for tomorrow he would have to unpack them again to join with some special pieces for a private showing.

The other articles not yet sold were being packed by the Brothers in the storeroom ready for the next day, when Paddy O'Connell would surely be round to offer them a pittance to take them off their hands.

One of the Brothers, passing Don, said, 'Not a bad day, Don. Eight pounds tuppence ha'penny for books and rig-outs.'

'Good. Good, Peter.'

'Aye, it may be, Don; but I'd rather dig the plot or shovel coal any day in the week. Outside, people are odd you know, Don, very odd. Half of them frighten me to death.'

'Go on with you.' Don pushed the Brother in the shoulder. 'You're an old fraud; you like being with people,' and bending towards him, he whispered, 'and if the prior knew about the stuff you give away, he'd have you on the carpet. He already wonders why there's not more coal roundies on his fire at night.'

The elderly monk's face became full of concern, and his voice was very low as he said, 'I only put a few bits in the lad's bag when he leaves at night, and there's a squad of them. I bet you got that from Brother David or Brother Malcolm, 'cos they're up there in the schoolroom with the pampered children. Not that they do much teaching, for they're forever looking out of the windows spying. Anyway, God knows what I do, and that's all that matters.' And at this the elderly man shuffled off, and Don shook his head. Dear Brother Peter. And if there was such a thing as a holy man, he was a holy man. He was the only one of the Brothers who could neither read nor write, yet he could count money up to a pound. He also took on the most menial and distasteful tasks that could befall a man, with never a murmur. But he could never accept he was being teased in all good faith about his cribbing of coal and any loose pieces he could lay his hands on in the kitchen, even from the food store, if he wasn't watched, and all to give to some deserving child.

He called to him now, saying, 'Peter, if anyone should ask for me I'll be in the chapel.'

'Oh, you're going into the chapel?' The old man's face lit up: 'Good. Good; I'll tell them.'

As Don made his way to the private chapel, he told himself that hope never dies in a good heart, for he knew that Peter hoped, as they all did, that one day he would tire of his liberty and the wickedness of the outside world and return to the order and peace that lay within these old walls, this priory that had been conceived on a rise amid fields that stretched to the river, but which was now so surrounded by habitations of all kinds that the inhabitants wondered how it was that peace still reigned within its precincts.

The chapel was small, as was its altar. At one side there stood a statue of the Virgin with the child in her arms, and at the other, the statue of a robed youth, St. Aloysius, the Italian Jesuit monk who, at the age of twenty-three, willed himself to die following a life of scourging, prayer, fasting, and self-denigration.

He himself always felt guilty about this statue because he found it impossible to honour this saint: to his mind he had wasted his young life. Also, he found it odd that the patron saint of the Jesuits should be standing on a Benedictine altar. The story went that, years ago a man of wealth entered the Brotherhood with one condition: that he could bring with him the family statue; and, as money always talks, his unusual demand was permitted.

After genuflecting towards the altar, Don McAlister entered the first pew. He did not kneel, but sat staring at the large wooden cross attached to the wall and from which limply hung the body of Christ, the head hanging well forward, the face grey.

After staring at it for a moment he closed his eyes, then muttered, 'Tell me what I should do. It's like this . . .'

After he had finished speaking he sat silent, waiting.

When the inner voice came to him, saying, 'Why come to me when you've already made up your mind,' he answered, 'But I want to know if I'm right to interfere.'

'Well, you know for a fact,' said the voice, 'if you don't interfere you'll go back there and your days will be plagued with the question of why you didn't do something about it when you had the chance. And if I remember rightly, you are apt to use the phrase "Chance never repeats itself"; and also, "There's no time like the present".'

Don McAlister lifted his hand, opened his eyes and looked up into the face that seemed as if it were looking down into his, and he said low but audibly, 'Father Prior won't like it when I leave tomorrow; he'll be disappointed.'

Did he hear the voice utter a laughing 'Huh!'?

A gentle smile came on his lips, because he knew exactly what Father Prior would say. Don McAlister now did a strange thing: he got to his feet, put both hands together as if in prayer, then pressed them against the face of Christ before bringing them to his own bandaged cheek, murmuring reverently, 'Thy will be done. I believe; help Thou my unbelief.'

Father Prior said, 'Oh no! Don; not tomorrow. It's the day before Christmas Eve. You know how the Brothers love you here at this time. And Christmas Day, so full of jollity, is the only time in the year I can listen to Brother John playing that dreadful mouth organ of his, and then only because your voice guides him. And don't forget there's a special showing of the pieces. But tomorrow, why tomorrow? You always stay till the New Year.'

'Well, Father Prior, suddenly I have some business I must attend to.'

'Suddenly?'

'Yes, Father Prior, suddenly. So suddenly that I . . . I went in' – he jerked his head towards the chapel – 'and asked His advice.'

Father Prior looked down at his hands resting on his desk and thought, Dear! dear! that again. He recalled the fuss there had been about it when the three-year-old Don said that Jesus had spoken to him and told him why his face was stained. Dear! dear! that had been a time. He himself had still been only a Brother then, and he had been put in charge of the maimed child. He had done his best to rid the boy of the idea that Christ was able to talk to him from the cross; but he had succeeded only by keeping him out of the chapel. Unfortunately this had brought on nightmares, bedwetting, and bouts when he was so defiant that nothing could be done with him. And so, eventually, he had been allowed to go his own way, which was towards Brother Percival and sculpting. From then on he developed into a normal boy, then a normal young man, except that an obstinate nature developed with him, which was to manifest itself when Father Broadside requested – no not requested but demanded – that he be sent to a famous Catholic Seminary to be trained as a priest. It would be enough, the Father Prior of that time had decided, if he became a Brother, for he considered Don to be a Brother in all but name. But here they ran into another obstacle, for Donald McAlister, the child they had reared and who should, through gratitude alone, have pleased them by joining their Benedictine Community, had told them flatly that he did not consider himself to be a Brother or cut out to continue that form of life.

When asked if he was aware that he could not go out and face the world in his condition, he answered plainly that he was well aware of the drawback, and so he would work for them with Brother Percival and in this way repay them for their kindness.

Finally, Father Prior remembered the day the Abbot had called and asked Don why he was so obstinate, and he had replied that he didn't know; and that he had asked the Lord about it but hadn't received a straight answer from Him, but just the words 'wait and see.'

The Abbot and Father Prior had talked late into the night about this statement and both agreed that it was just as well that the young man remained under the care of the Brothers, because, let it get about that Jesus was speaking from the Cross to one of them, then half the population would be outside the gates wanting another miracle. No; the best thing was to keep him, as it were, under guard. They would know where they had him then.

Jesus talking from the Cross. Dear! dear! What next.

Then came the day the solicitor arrived and informed Don of his inheritance. Was that only eight years ago? And what a difference it had made in him. He had gone out into the world and accepted it gladly, as if he had been waiting for it to happen. Of course, he had had to find out that the world did not always accept oddities gladly. But he knew that, in spite of this, he had left them for good.

Father Prior now looked up at the tall figure of a man who would have been very handsome had he been able to reveal a normal face, and he said, 'You know, Don, you are always disappointing people. When I had the care of you as a boy you were forever disappointing me. Then you disappointed our good' – it seemed he was having difficulty in controlling his features as he said – 'Father Broadside, when all he wanted to do was to put you into the hands of God. And then there was that do with our dear Abbot. Oh, you are a disappointment to so many people, Don. Do you know that?'

'Yes, Father Prior; and I've heard it all before: *He* said

your very words to me not five minutes gone.'

Father Prior swiftly raised his hands from his desk and rose to his feet, and his voice took on a stern tone as he said, 'You're not still keeping up that game, are you, Don?'

Don McAlister, his face straight and his voice as serious as the Prior's, said, 'It is *His* game, Father; it has never stopped. And while we're on the subject, Father Prior, and I have never brought this up before, I ask you: haven't we all got a small, still voice inside us that keeps telling us what is right and what is wrong?'

The Prior's head moved from side to side before he agreed, 'Yes; yes, I suppose so, Don.'

'Well, I don't know how others react to their small, still voice, but mine has never been still. Small, yes; when I was young it spoke to me as one child speaks to another, but as I grew, it grew with me. There was only one difference: as a child we seemed to agree about most things, but in my youth it acted as a parent might; then when I became a man it left the decisions to me, the while being critical of them. I suppose one of your modern writers on psychology who deal with the duality in human nature would say I was just talking to myself, asking questions and giving myself the answers I had already prepared. Of late, I've read quite a bit about that kind of thing. Still, what d'you say, Father Prior?'

The Prior cleared his throat, then coughed before he said, 'What can I say that you don't already know, Don? I have never liked this attitude of yours; it . . . it is not natural.'

'Talking to God is not natural, Father Prior? May I ask how you talk to God?'

'You know quite well, Don, how we talk to God. God the omnipotent has to be approached with reverence, as has his only begotten son, Jesus Christ.' He bowed his head as he spoke the name.

188

They stared at each other until Don said, 'I know that, Father Prior, and I'm never irreverent, but the difference between us is that I cannot see Him away up there in the never-ending sky. I suppose a part of the child is still in me. Remember that awful hymn, Father Prior, that the nuns used to make the little ones sing? There was one line in it that stuck with me, "Christ is nearer than my skin; I make him cry when I sin," and that's how I feel, Father Prior, when I get in touch with Him.'

At this, the Prior smiled knowingly, saying, 'Well, your psychologist could be right after all; it's a developed childish imagination, a fantasy. No matter; but you'd better go now and tell the Brothers that you mean to leave us tomorrow, otherwise there'll be questions thrown at me from all sides to which I cannot give any answers, can I, Don?'

'No, Father, not yet. But I promise I will explain everything to you when I return, and that will be as soon as possible.'

'Well,' said the Prior, practically now, 'don't come back empty-handed; bring a few more pieces with you.'

'I'll do that, I'll do that, Father Prior; and thank you.'

After Don had gone, the Prior sat back in his chair and stared towards the closed door for some minutes, his thoughts a mixture of sadness and impatience. He and that voice. In some ways he was so ordinary and in others so complex, even worldly. He must admit that, when he'd had charge of him, he often looked upon him as a son. At such times he would quote to himself the words of God that he read every day: 'Thou art my beloved son in whom I am well pleased.' And again he recalled the day the little boy came to him and placed his hands in prayer but in a strange manner, for he put them against his maimed cheek as he said, 'Why is God vexed with me? Sister Matilda says he has made me different because of the sins of my father.' And he himself had groaned. Sister Matilda and her theories: 'For I the Lord thy God am a jealous God, and visit the sins of the fathers upon the children unto the third and fourth generation.' It had taken Brother Percival a long time to remedy that, by suggesting to the child that he was meant for great things and that he had to forget about his face and concentrate on his hands, because the Lord had blessed him with wonderful hands.

The Prior sighed again, for he didn't think Don had ever and would ever come to believe that he had been a difficult boy and that he was still a difficult man.

8

It had been a long and tiresome journey. Being Christmas Eve it seemed that all London was moving north, for the Scottish Express was packed to capacity.

When travelling, he usually gave himself the privilege of booking a window seat in a first-class compartment, and often he would have the carriage to himself for the whole journey. On these trips he had become well-known to the porters and it was wonderful what a silver sixpence could do to secure privacy. But should there be passengers in the compartment who seemingly became put off by the odd man who kept his hat on, and it such an unusual shape, too, once he spoke they would be re-assured, and probably accepted that the man had had a facial accident.

On this particular journey, however, the compartment had been packed, so that he felt relief when he alighted at Durham and took the local train to Chester-le-Street.

It was dark now and Don, after walking some way along the main road, turned into a bridle path that ran quite steeply downhill, before turning to the left to zig-zag its way towards the river; but at this point he diverted into a field that sloped gently towards the dry-stone wall that bordered the back garden of his cottage. In the dark-ness he couldn't actually see it, but when his hand touched it, it seemed to linger lovingly on the stone. He walked by the side of it until the wall turned, to stop abruptly by the side of the cottage; or, to be more accu-rate, the studio he'd had built at the side. Here, it was pitch dark, made so by the fringe of a wood not two yards away and which ran down to the river. Beyond the cottage was a similar wood separated from this one by a wide green sward, which also ran down to the river.

Taking a key from his pocket, he opened the door to the cottage and paused for a moment within its threshold, and as he stood there he drew two long breaths into his lungs. The smell that he breathed in had never faded during all the eight years he had lived here. He had first smelt it on the day the solicitor had opened the door for him. It was like no other smell he could imagine. It wasn't of roses, which at that time half-filled the back garden; nor of the lavender walk that led to the little rill; nor of the herbs in their patch: mint, rosemary, thyme, wild garlic or the rest. He could think of it only as coming from a wholesome human being. And it wasn't fanciful that he should think it was from her, the aunt he had never seen but the one who had given him freedom to live a life as other men or as near as he would ever get to that state.

The first thing he did now, and in the dark, was to whip off his hat and coat, before groping along the wall to the left of the door to a table on which stood a lamp and a box of matches.

Once the light flared up he let out a long slow breath and looked about the room and saw it afresh, as he always did on his return from a journey. There, at the end of the twenty-foot room, in the open fireplace, lay a mush of silver ashes and half-burnt logs. In front of it was the old couch with its patched chintz cover. There was a deep armchair to the side of the fireplace. This was covered in hide, but the sheen of the skin had disappeared from part of the arms and the seat.

But in contrast to the wear and tear of these two pieces of furniture, an oblong trestle table stood against one wall, a carved back wooden chair at each end of it and two at one side. The set appeared to be so new one couldn't imagine it had ever been used over the years, yet through the inventory of the house, Don knew that the pieces had been carved almost a hundred years before.

At the centre of the table stood another lamp. This one had a rose coloured glass shade, and when he lit it the room took on a warmth, as did the threadbare carpet that covered the whole room and the faded tapestry curtains hanging at the long windows.

Dropping onto his knees, he took some paper and kindling wood from a log box to the side of the hearth and thrust them in between the half-burnt logs. He put a light to them, and as the dry sticks crackled and the half-burnt logs caught the flame, he dropped to one side on the home-made rug that flanked the stone hearth and, staring into the flames, he asked himself what he should do. Should he go along there now? even though it was Christmas Eve, because he wouldn't venture on Christmas Day in case they were having a jollification. Yet from what he could make out from the chatter that came third-hand through Farmer Harding, there was never much jollification in that house. However, he wasn't so much concerned about those in the main house, but was wondering if the old man had yet taken up permanent residence in The Little Manor. There had been talk of that too. But if he didn't go this evening and he didn't go tomorrow it would have to be on Boxing Day. But if the old man was to make the journey he'd need time, and the middle of next week would be the best time to travel, for, as he knew, the trains would be more crowded than ever around New Year. What, however, he would like to do at this minute was to get rid of the damn mask, have a wash down, make a meal, then put his feet up on that old couch there.

There's no time like the present.

But he must have a drink, a hot drink, before he went out again. Even before this, he must get rid of this

193

contraption for a while; thinking which and rising to his feet, he took the lamp off the table and went up the room and into his bedroom.

The shabby comfort of the living-room was certainly not repeated here. The single plank bed with a biscuit mattress had neither a head nor a foot; it had replaced the double feather bed in which his aunt had not only been born but also died. Beyond it, in a corner, stood a battered mahogany chest of drawers, and on it was a polished cabinet, eighteen inches high by twelve inches wide, fronted by two doors.

After putting down the lamp, it was to this he turned. He did not move towards it, but to the small Regency dressing-table. It was quite bare of any trinkets.

He leaned forward and stared at his face in the small mirror, before unloosening the button of the high collar of his jacket, which he took off. Then he unclipped a buckle behind his shoulders, so releasing a framework from which he withdrew his arms, before lifting from his head the apparatus over which the cloth mask was stretched.

After loosening the mask from the frame, he placed them both on the foot of the bed. From the top shelf of a cupboard he now took a clean mask and, laying it beside the used one, he clicked his tongue: London was getting dirtier. And then there were the trains.

He returned to the mirror and peered at himself. He hated doing this, but it was like a self-inflicted penance, and he asked himself what he expected to find, a miracle or that the dark brown tortured skin had faded to a grey instead of beginning to form darker patches? If the skin had only been smooth and like that of the strawberry-coloured blemishes . . . But no! he had to be given the lot. Yet it could have been worse, so he had been informed; it could have been almost dead black. Why, as a child, hadn't they peeled the skin off him? Then there would have been only physical pain; he wouldn't have had to create another self in order to deal with it. He recalled never liking Brother Bernard, because once he had said, 'One must put a face on things,' and of screaming back at him, 'You've got a face to put them on.' He would have been fourteen years old at the time, and his reaction to Brother Bernard's apology was to hit him.

If only it hadn't invaded the corner of his eye.

He pulled himself up abruptly, saying, 'Get on with it! Take a clean shirt in with you.'

He made for the kitchen.

This was a very ordinary room, the only surprising thing about it being the modern open-fire stove with a cooking oven to one side, a hot-water boiler to the other.

He took a pan from the cupboard, half-filled it with water from a lidded bucket and returned to the sitting-room to place it on the hearth at the side of a burning log.

Back in the kitchen, he then emptied half the contents of another pail of water into the quite deep stone sink and gave himself a good wash.

About fifteen minutes later, after having made himself a cup of cocoa, he was in the bedroom fully dressed and ready for outdoors.

As he went to leave the room he again looked towards the cabinet as if about to speak, but turned away sharply.

Before leaving the cottage he performed one more task. Still holding the lamp, he went along a narrow passage, unlocked the door at the end of it and, holding the lamp high, he surveyed his studio.

Everything was as he had left it; although it hadn't always been so. On his return from London, soon after he'd had the studio added, it had been a different picture. The room was fourteen feet long by nine feet wide. Its four windows were placed close to the ceiling line, so that it was impossible for an inquisitive person to discover what was going on within.

On that occasion the glass had been carefully cleared from one frame in order to let someone down into the room. There had been no need to bring any implement of destruction for there was a row of tools to hand on the bench. A wooden mallet had sufficed.

The only blessing about that time was that he had taken the best of six months work up to the priory that Christmas. Nevertheless, there had been twenty or so pieces left on the shelves. Yet when he came to examine the debris he knew that everything hadn't been broken; some pieces must have been taken away whole.

Quite definitely there had been more than one intruder, probably from the nearby village, where the name of The Branded Man had already been stamped on him and as such he was a figure of curiosity. Nothing further had happened since that night, which he knew had come about through Farmer Harding, an understanding kindly man, and Bob Talbot, the river man who saw to the fishing and the banks.

Thinking of Farmer Harding, he closed the door. He must let him know he was back.

In the kitchen he lit a lantern before extinguishing the first of the two house lamps. In the sitting-room, he placed a guard around the open fire and put out the other lamp.

After stepping carefully off the edge of the paved way fronting the length of the cottage, he walked slowly down a rutted pathway bordered by the wood on one side, a hillside on the other.

Where the wood ended, open land ran straight down to the distant gleam of the river. Ten minutes later he came to the field where the gypsies had camped. However, he did not jump the wall that would eventually have brought him into the grounds of the main house, but kept on walking by the foot of the hill until he entered the gardens of The Little Manor. The lights from the house showed it to be anything but little.

The whole of the front came within the light given off by the lanterns attached to the wall on each side of the studded oak door. There was no balcony to the long low stone house and, but for a shallow step, it lay flush with the gravelled drive.

Don hesitated for a moment before lifting his hand and taking hold of the iron bell-pull.

The echo of the bell ringing came to him but he had to wait a full minute before he heard footsteps on the other side of the door; and when it was opened by the small, bright-faced maid and she saw standing there none other than the weird man about whom she had heard so many tales, the man with only half a face, the rest covered by a great slouching hat, the masked man himself, the man who frightened the wits out of people, she opened her mouth wide and let out a high scream.

When his foot stopped her banging the door closed, she turned and fled, crying, 'Mrs Makepeace! Mrs Makepeace! It's him! It's him!'

The girl's cries brought Maggie Makepeace from the kitchen, and she too was yelling now: 'What in the name of God's gone wrong with you, girl? What's the matter? Who is it?'

'It's him! Mrs Makepeace,' Katie Brooks was gasping. 'He's there! he's at the door. I couldn't close it.'

'Who's there? Before I shake the life out of you, girl, who's at the door?'

'I'm not going back; I'm not going back.'

Maggie Makepeace thrust the girl to one side and made for the door, and there, she too saw the tall figure, but her reaction was simply, 'Oh. Good evening. She's a silly girl.'

'Yes, I understand that, Mrs Makepeace. Can you tell me if your master is with you? I mean Mr Emanuel Lawson.'

'No; no, sir; he's along at the house. He's had a cold, so

197

he stayed there for a few days. Was it something special like you wanted him for?'

'Yes, Mrs Makepeace, very special.'

'Oh. Well, will you come in for a minute, please.' She pulled the door further open and Don stepped into the hall. 'And if you'll be seated, I'll send for Mr Makepeace; he'll know better what to do.'

'Thank you, Mrs Makepeace.'

Don waited in the hall, seated in a carved chair with arms depicting snakes. They had been beautifully carved, so much so that he thought one could imagine they were fashioned out of skin. The chair was one of a pair, and, looking around, he noticed there were other pieces of Indian-worked furniture, a cabinet and small tables. On the walls there were a number of large oil paintings, all seascapes. That would be, of course, because this family was in shipping. To the left of him he glimpsed the beginning of a beautiful spiral staircase, the banister and supports in wrought iron, and it was carpeted in a deep rose pile.

Matching it was the same coloured carpet in the middle of the hall, and, flanking each side, what he took to be two Persian rugs.

He was brought from further examination of the hall by Barney's voice saying, 'Oh, hello, Mr McAlister. Can I help you?'

Don rose to his feet. 'Yes, Mr Makepeace, you can. You see, I . . . I have some important news for Mr Lawson . . . the elder, and . . . well, I thought he might be living here.'

'He does on and off, Mr McAlister, but there's more folk to see to him down at that end when he's not very well, and Mr Pat gets worried about him, and he can't keep an eye on him up here.'

'Is he in bed at present?'

'Oh no; no, he's not in bed, not by any means. You can't keep him in bed. Excuse me, sir, for saying that, but he's

198

got a will of his own, has the master. You wouldn't like to go down and speak to him there?'

'I wouldn't mind in the least, only I'm afraid I might get the same reception as I got from your little maid.'

'Oh, Mr McAlister, don't take any notice of her; she's an ignorant little snipe. I'll give her the length of me tongue later.'

'Oh, I wouldn't do that. Her reaction was understandable.' He did not add, It is my fault; I forget at times that I do not look like other men, but went on, 'Do you think you could have a private word with your master if you went up to The Manor?'

'Oh yes; yes, sir. He sees me at any time.'

'Well, then, would you do me a favour and tell him I have very special news for him and that I have told you to stress the word special?'

'I'll do that, Mr McAlister, right away; I'll do that. Now would you like to sit in the drawing-room and wait? There's a fire on in there; we always keep it on in case the master pops up, which he does at times. You never know with him. He likes this house much more than the other one. His good lady and he were very happy here. Or would you rather sit in the kitchen and talk with my missis? I'm sure she'd be very pleased to have your company.'

'You are sure?'

'Oh yes, Mr McAlister, I am sure. She's no idiot, not like the rest of them.'

When Barney Makepeace led the tall fellow into the kitchen, where the maid was in the process of slicing sugared cherries and handing them to Mrs Makepeace to put the finishing touches to a cake, Katie's mouth fell into a gape.

Pulling a chair out from under the table, Barney said, 'Sit down, Mr McAlister. I won't be ten minutes or so.'

'Thank you, Mr Makepeace,' Don said; then, leaning

across the table, he said in a low voice, 'Would you mind, Mrs Makepeace, reassuring your assistant that I only eat maids on a Saturday and never before twelve o'clock?'

In answer, Maggie Makepeace threw back her head and let out a high laugh; and then she asked, 'Who do you eat on a Sunday then, Mr McAlister?'

'Cooks, Mrs Makepeace, always cooks.'

There was a muffled giggle from the end of the table, but neither Maggie Makepeace nor Don seemed to take any heed of it, and when Mrs Makepeace, carrying on the farce, said, 'D'you prefer cooks for lunch or dinner?'

'Oh, lunch, Mrs Makepeace. Something light you see; I leave the heavy stuff for dinner.'

'And who, may I ask, do you choose for that?' Mrs Makepeace was now wiping her eyes.

'Definitely a priest or a parson.'

'Oh, Mr McAlister, Mr McAlister! you'll get hung.'

'Yes, I know; and I shouldn't eat them because they both give me indigestion, dreadful indigestion,' and added, 'just listening to them.'

It seemed now that Maggie Makepeace was enjoying herself, for she asked, 'D'you change your menu for the weekday, Mr McAlister?'

'Yes; during the week I go through the servants' hall.'

'You do?'

'Oh yes; and I start with the butler. I can never stand snooty butlers.'

Now the giggle from the end of the table was a gulp and very audible; and Don, keeping the good side of his face towards her, smiled at the girl, and she, looking up at him under her eyebrows, half fearfully still, smiled back.

Mrs Makepeace, after wiping her eyes, resumed her work of sticking the half cherries into the soft icing topping the cake, explaining, 'This isn't a Christmas cake, you know, but it's a kind of cream sponge that the master likes with a cup of coffee in the mornings. We've got all the Christmas fare ready in the larder there' – she nodded towards a white-painted door across the room – 'just in case something makes him change his mind and he doesn't stay up there for the meal. And it could happen. As I say to Makepeace, times are changing all over, but particularly here and I wouldn't be surprised at what takes place next, not me, never.'

'Nor would I, Mrs Makepeace, nor would I; but let's hope that Christmas brings some nice surprises.'

He watched Maggie, now unsmiling, sigh as she said, 'Things are not like they used to be. We used to feel settled at one time, but not any more, and the world's in an awful state. The old Queen's not well, and there's been riots in London.'

'Riots in London! I've just come from there, Mrs Makepeace, and I never heard of any riots.'

'You didn't?'

'No. Well, not where I was; and I didn't see it in any of the papers.'

'Well, that's funny. Robert Green, he's a footman over there, and I know he can't read, but he told Fanny Carter that he got it from the butler, Frank, that the Irish were rioting in London for home rule or something, and I said, why don't they give it to them and send them back home?'

Don closed his eyes tightly for a moment, coughed, then said, 'That would be a good idea. Yes, it would be a good idea. Give it to them and send them back home.'

'But there, you can't believe a word anybody says, these days; the bits that Fanny Carter tells Katie about goings-on over there, you wouldn't believe. Well, as I said, you can't. I only wish the master would make up his mind to stay here. He is always happy when he is here. When the weather's clement he goes out for long walks or spends most of the day here in the library. And it's odd,

201

you know, Mr McAlister, he can be so funny. When he was here last week it was one of those dreadful days, thick mist, you could hardly see a finger before you, and there he was, muffled up to the eyes. He had come up from The Manor, and I said to him, "Why must you be out a day like this, sir?" and you know what he said? "I'm going out this minute to look for a bridge high enough to jump from."' She choked now, saying, 'That's what he said, Mr McAlister. Can you imagine him going to look for a bridge high enough to jump off, the master? But then he's always had a joke for us. The mistress used to say to him very firmly, "Emanuel Lawson, they've heard that one before, it's got fungi growing on it." Yes, she used to say that to him. She was a lovely person, wasn't she, Katie?' She had turned to the girl, and Katie, daring to look at the man, said, 'Aye, she was lovely. She took me on when I was nine, on condition that I would go half a day to school. I hated school but I wanted to work here, so I did that, went half a day.'

'And you learnt to read and write?' asked Don.

'Aye, somewhat. I was never very swift at it.'

'Oh,' put in Mrs Makepeace, 'she can write her name and address and print out a note if she has to. She can print better than she can write; but the teacher at the school wouldn't have that, would she? Didn't like printing, you had to do copy-book writing, didn't you?'

They nodded at each other as friends might, and Don thought of the strange companions people chose out of close proximity forced on them through circumstance, because this middle-aged woman and this very young girl were friends at heart. From time to time, doubtless, the older woman would box the younger one's ears, but in the long run it made no difference.

A commotion in the hall disturbed them, and Mrs Makepeace, quickly wiping her hands, straightened her apron and said to Don, 'This'll be them. Come on;' and she opened the door and went out, followed by Don.

Barney was taking his master's coat, and Don, inclining his head towards the old man, greeted him saying, 'Evening, Mr Lawson,' then turned to Pat to greet him similarly: 'Good evening, sir.'

'Good evening, Mr McAlister. I understand you have news for us.'

'Well, don't let us stand here; let us sit some place where it's warm,' and now Emanuel Lawson made for the drawing-room, saying, 'Is there a good fire on, Barney?'

'There was when I left, sir.'

Barney Makepeace pushed open the drawing-room door to allow his master to enter, whilst Pat Lawson stood to one side and motioned Don to follow his grandfather.

When they were seated around the large open fire, Emanuel Lawson said, 'I hope this is something I dearly want to hear.' He was looking straight at Don, who said, 'I'm sure it is, sir.'

'But . . . but before we start,' Emanuel Lawson said, 'and I don't mean to be rude, please believe me, but I can hardly see your face for the large brim of that ridiculous hat. Must you always wear it indoors, sir?'

'No, sir; I don't always wear it indoors, because I am rarely invited indoors, except at the priory where I was brought up. I wear it outside because it keeps my cover in place, but I suppose, really, I wear it to focus people's attention away from my face. It helps to mask my disfigurement which, I have found, is distasteful to some and embarrasses others.'

'I am very sorry, sir, that I spoke as I did.'

'Please, don't be sorry, sir; I'll do as you ask, and willingly,' and for the first time in his adult life in any company except that of the Brothers, Don took his hat from his head and laid it on the floor to the side of his chair.

The two men stared at him. They were seeing hair, and,

lying in it, a crown-like metal ring supporting a number of narrow straps.

The cover on his face now appeared to be much broader than when he had worn the hat.

Emanuel Lawson coughed hard in his throat now; then briskly he said, 'Well now, make yourself at ease and give us your news. You have seen and spoken with my grand-daughter?'

'Yes; twice, sir.'

'Where? Where was she?'

Don paused before answering, 'The first time, playing the piano in an eating bar in the East End of London.'

'*What*?'

The old man looked as if he was about to spring to his feet, when his grandson thrust an arm out quickly, saying, 'Careful! Grandpa.'

'But in a bar, playing a piano?'

'Just that, sir. Oh, she wasn't engaged there. But her friend, a Miss Foggerty, was serving behind the bar as a temporary help.'

Emanuel Lawson seemed to sink lower into the cush-ions of the couch and his thin lips champed each other for a moment before they muttered, 'Dear God!'

'Yesterday, sir, I saw her again. She and her friend, Miss Foggerty, had come to the priory sale where my work was on display. As I think you know, I am a sculptor and I live at Rill Cottage. Mr Lawson here' – he turned to Pat – 'and I have met on the river bank at times; we are both fish-ermen.'

'But my grand-daughter, sir, how is she?'

'Well, healthwise, sir, I should say she is all right, but I fear I must tell you' – he paused here – 'she's . . . she is in a certain condition.'

'Condition? What're you talking about? She is ill? T.B., consumption?'

'No, no.' Now Don and Pat exchanged glances; then

Don said quietly, 'I think she's in about the fifth month of carrying a child, sir.'

'God almighty! What? What did you say?' The old man fell back among the cushions, his hands to his head, and emitting one word over and over again: 'No! No! No! No!'

Pat had moved up close to his grandfather and, with an arm round him, he cried, 'Now don't excite yourself. It doesn't matter about that as long as she's all right and safe. And she is safe?' He turned to Don, who answered slowly, 'Yes, I suppose you could say she is safe, but she is living under very poor conditions. As far as I can gather, she and her friend occupy the top two rooms in a block of flats at Ramsay Court, and I may add here that the word "Court" in this case is very misleading. It is in a very poor and low quarter of the city. Oh, there are much worse and the people there, the working people in the building, try their best to live decently, but the conditions under which they live have to be seen to be believed. It is some years since I myself went through The Courts; it was bad enough then, and I understand it hasn't changed. To put it plainly, sir, the sanitation is very primitive; all water and coal must be carried up from the yard and the stairs are very steep, and this, I know, is one of the things that worries Miss Foggerty.'

The old man was sitting with his eyes closed and he muttered, 'Foggerty. She's always talking about Miss Foggerty. Sarah, she calls her, the greatest friend of her life.'

'Well, she's speaking the truth there, sir, for without Sarah Foggerty I wouldn't like to think what would have happened to your grand-daughter in that city. I enquired of Miss Foggerty why your grand-daughter wouldn't come home. From the little information Sarah gave me I understand that her mother was very much against her return.'

The old man was sitting up straight and, turning to his

grandson, he said, 'Did you hear that? She must have known . . . she's known all along.'

Pat nodded and he repeated quietly, 'Yes, she must have known all along. Good God!'

'Pat . . . there are going to be changes here. Oh yes. They've been asking for it for a long time; but now that time has come.' He now turned to Don, saying, 'Could . . . could you persuade her to come home?'

'Me? Oh no!' The answer was definite. 'She is, I'm sure, slightly afraid of me because, you see, sir, I was the one who found her the night she knocked herself unconscious against the wall. But she recovered somewhat and saw me, and without this.' He patted the side of his face. 'I take advantage of the dark by walking without it. She must have glimpsed me and the sight must have frightened her and I'm sure it's in the back of her mind and that she's trying to recall it. I saw that in the look she gave me when we first met.'

'She doesn't know who you are, then?'

'Oh no, sir. Neither of them does. Why should they? This is Northumberland, where she had the frightening experience, as she would think of it, but, there, we were in London.'

'Well, what d'you think we must do?'

'You must go and see her yourself, sir.'

'Oh no!' Pat put in quickly. 'Grandpa hasn't been very well of late; he could never make that journey.'

'Shut up! Pat. What're you talking about? I'm not in my dotage yet, and let me tell you I'm better on my legs than you are since you had your trouble. Of course I can make the journey to London; and I mean to, and as soon as possible. Damned holidays! There'll be no trains running tomorrow or on Boxing Day. The following day would be all right, though, wouldn't it?'

Don nodded: 'Yes, that would be much better for travelling.'

'Well, then' – the old man now turned to Pat – 'book us a compartment on an early train.' He now turned back to Don, adding, 'The carriage will pick you up from the top road at an appropriate time.'

'Sir, it's very kind of you, but I always travel—'

'Yes, yes; I know, second-class.'

'No; not at all sir.' Don's voice was stiff now. 'I always travel first-class, in the hope of travelling alone.'

'Oh, I'm sorry; no offence meant. But you're coming with us, so you're travelling with us. Anyway we can do nothing without you. If there's three flights of stairs to their rooms, I could certainly never make it, nor could Pat here. He's having a job to climb from one deck to another. Is there a hotel nearby where we could talk or where you could bring her?'

'I couldn't bring her anywhere, sir; it would have to be Miss Foggerty, and there's no hotel nearby that I know of. However there would be no need for that: you could stay with the Brothers; they are used to visitors. There's a section of the priory set out for guests on retreats. You would be quite comfortable there, I'm sure, and welcome too.'

The old man nodded; then awkwardly drawing himself to the edge of the couch and turning to his grandson, he said quietly, 'And she has known all along and not given a damn. Your mother, Pat, is not a woman, she is a heartless bitch of a female. Damn and blast her to hell!'

'Grandpa, now don't get excited. Look! what about a drink . . . a toast to the good news.'

'Now you're talking sense, Pat.'

The old man now turned to Don. 'Do you drink?'

'Yes, sir; I like a glass of wine or such.'

'What is your favourite?'

Don smiled. 'Port sir, a nice port.'

Now, for the first time, Pat saw a glimmer of a smile on his grandfather's face as he said, 'A nice port. Go and tell Barney to bring up an eighty-two.'

'An eighty-two? My! my!'

'Yes, do as I say, and when I want your opinion on my preference I'll ask for it.'

'Of course you will, Grandpa. You always have done, and you always will,' and Pat went out laughing.

Now speaking in a very quiet and controlled voice, Emanuel Lawson said, 'When I have time to work this all out, sir, I will then realise how much I am indebted to you for what you have done this night, for I can say to you that my grand-daughter has always been the only dear thing left in my life since I lost my beloved wife. I am, as you might have noticed, very fond of the grandson who has just left us, but Pat has had no battle to fight. He's of a pleasant nature, and most people like him, but with my Mary Anne – I've always called her Mary Anne, I don't like the fancy "Marie" – she's had to fight all her young existence. But she's had my support since she was a child, and so we grew very close, and when she went away I was lonely indeed, but when I received her letter to say that she was . . . well, apparently disappearing, and for why I didn't know, I was devastated. Strangely, I had never felt old and helpless before, but for the past few months I've felt my resistance to life slowly slipping away from me. When she is back I shall live again. Although I shall welcome her child as I shall welcome her, I cannot but say it is a great shock to me to know she is in this condition at all. Do you know how it began?'

'No, sir; I know nothing further than what I have told you, but I think, whatever happens, you can be thankful that she has such a friend as Miss Sarah Foggerty.'

'Rely on me, sir: I shall never forget anyone who has befriended her during this time of trouble. But when I think of that mean old dry stick of a woman under whose care my daughter-in-law thrust her, I feel inclined to murder.'

As he entered the room carrying a tray on which stood a bottle and three glasses, Pat looked towards his grandfather, saying, 'I didn't decant it. I thought I'd better leave that to you with your expert hand.'

When Don was handed a glass of the port he sipped at it, and when his eyes blinked and he smacked his lips the old man said, 'It has that effect on me too.'

'It is a very fine wine,' Don said. 'Unlike some of the Brothers, I am no connoisseur of wines, but I can recognise this as a beautiful port.'

From then on the conversation became general, at least a matter of question and answer: Was he a Brother of the society? How did he come to be there at all? Where were his people from, the answer to which was that he unfortunately did not know. Did he like the new kind of life he was living now? Oh yes, yes. This was freedom, for no matter what position one might hold in the priory, life there was restricting. And yet, Don admitted, he owed the Brothers a great deal, all of them, especially his tutor, Brother Percival, a great artist who was at one time very well known in Rome.

There followed a pause in the conversation, when Don sensed that this was the time to take his leave. Getting to his feet, he took up his hat from the floor. He did not immediately put it on but held out his hand to the old man, saying, 'Apart from everything else, it's been a pleasure to meet you and talk with you, sir.'

'Pleasure? That's all on the other foot, sir, definitely all on the other foot. I'll be indebted to you, I am sure, all my life. Anyway, we'll be meeting again soon; Pat here will make the arrangements. Good-night to you.'

'Good-night, sir.'

At the front door, Pat said, 'You've done us a very good turn this Christmas Eve . . . What is your Christian name?'

'Donald . . . Don.'

'Don?'

'Donald I can't abide.'

'Well, Don, speaking for myself, I can't wait until we're on the train, because, like Grandpa, I'm very fond of Marie Anne, and it would be wonderful to have her back, although the circumstances are going to be awkward all round.'

'I can understand that, but it will likely work out in the long run; these things do.' . . .

Walking back to the drawing-room, Pat repeated the cliché: things will work out in the long run; they usually do. Not in this house, they didn't; or, rather, in the one further down, and this was confirmed when he re-entered the drawing-room and his grandfather immediately said, 'Get down there, Pat, and tell them not to expect me, not tonight, nor tomorrow, nor the next day.'

'Oh, Grandpa, you can't do that, I mean it's—'

'Boy, don't say to me that it's Christmas. It's Christmas for that girl up in London at that place where they've got to carry water up three flights of stairs and she now heavy with a child.'

'Well, I don't suppose, Grandpa, that she does the carrying of the water.'

'Why do you not suppose that? She's living in the slums, isn't she? Are her neighbours going to wait on her hand and foot? Now look, do as I say, go down to them and say that . . . well, I'll tell you what to say. Tell your mother that your grandfather is not coming back into that house until he brings her daughter with him, and that she is five months gone with child.'

'Grandpa, please!' Pat went close up to the old man and, taking him by the arm, led him back to the couch saying, 'Come on, sit down.'

'I don't need to sit down, Pat. At this moment I feel stronger than I have done for years. Perhaps it's with indignation but, whatever it is, I hope this feeling lasts;

and it will once she is back with me, and when that happens there are going to be great changes made here, Pat, oh yes, great changes. They've been festering in my mind for some time; but then I told myself I couldn't do it to them; but not any more. I'll do that, and more. They'll get the shock of their lives. They should have had it years ago. My son would have been more of a man now had I stood my ground.'

'Grandpa, I am not going into that house to say anything about this matter at all, not tonight nor tomorrow. I will say that you feel very tired and that you've decided to stay here for the next day or two. The matter in question can be left until we bring her home.'

'Do you think they'll swallow that? They'll want to know why.'

'Well, if they persist I'll give them an inkling, but only an inkling, because . . . because I feel that whenever this news breaks, Mother will go out of her mind.'

'That woman's been out of her mind for years or she wouldn't have treated her daughter as she has done, and, whatever happens, she's brought it on herself. Oh, this is going to be retribution, and for the first time in my life I'll see it falling where it should.'

Pat sighed and looked hard at this man whom he loved, this man who, with his indomitable will, had brought the family business to where it stood today. Twice the size it was forty years ago now that it was in steam, and highly respected in the shipping lines. But that same will was at work now, and he shivered to think what the result would be; not to himself but to the rest of his family.

As he reached the door his grandfather called, 'See Maggie on your way out and tell her to put some bottles in my bed, and now, because I won't be long out of it.'

Pat gave no answer to this and as he was crossing the hall he met up with Barney, his arms full of logs, and he

211

said, 'I would ask you, Barney, not to mention to anyone who the visitor was tonight.'

'As you say, Mr Pat. As you say.'

'No-one, mind.'

'I heard, Mr Pat. I heard.'

'Does Maggie know?'

'Yes, and Katie.'

'Well, tell them, will you, not a word to anyone; they'll know soon enough the result of his visit. If anyone from the house should ask you – anyone, mind – the man was a stranger to us. Yes, somebody came to see my grandfather, but he was a stranger to you, and you don't know what it was about.'

'Don't worry, sir; no-one will find out from this end, I can assure you.' With that he humped the logs further up into his arms and went about his business.

Pat got into his overcoat, wrapped a scarf around his neck, pulled his cap on and, finally, picked up a walking-stick from the hall-stand and went out.

The night had become bitterly cold. Already the frost was lying thick on the roofs of the stables and the outhouses and his steps sounded crisp on the pebbles of the broad path that connected the two houses. When walking leisurely, one could cover the distance between them in four minutes, but tonight Pat was not walking leisurely. He had the same feeling which must often have inveigled Marie Anne to take to her heels and run and run, not towards the house but away from it . . . away, away. In this moment he felt he wouldn't mind changing places with Marie Anne down there in London; only for his thoughts to jump to her condition, which made him cry inwardly, Oh, Marie Anne! Marie Anne! Not that! How on earth had it come about? She never made friends with men. Well, there had been no chance while she lived here, had there? She was so young, childish in a way, and had been considered not fit to be in social company. One

212

thing about her was quite true and the coming exposure would show it, at least from his mother's point of view, and that was that, wherever she was, Marie Anne created disaster.

As he emerged from the path on to the end of the main drive and crossed the large open space fronting the balcony, he saw to the right of him one of the yard men leading the horses of the big carriage towards the stables, indicating that the visiting party had returned, and he earnestly hoped that his mother had gathered enough invitations from The Hall and its satellites to keep her happy over the holidays, for when the storm broke, her social status would be washed away, as it were. At least, he knew that's how she would see it.

In the brightly lit and festooned hall, he pulled off his outer things, threw them onto a chair, then approached the drawing-room, where the sound of voices told him the family had gathered.

When he entered, his mother was in the act of carefully removing her large, ostrich-feather-trimmed hat, the feathers being held in place by what appeared to be animal claws attached to the crown. It was her latest acquisition and she was very proud of it.

Turning to Pat, she said, 'Oh, there you are Pat. We've had a lovely time; you should have come. Such interesting people: there was Sir Eustace Dodd and Lord Dean's cousin Clive Parkington – he's an MP, you know – and Mr and Mrs De Fonier – she is a famous French designer. What's the matter?' She was looking at him intently now. 'Something happened?'

'Yes; you could say something's happened.'

She moved a step towards him. 'To Father-in-law?'

'Yes, to your father-in-law.'

His father had moved quickly towards him, saying, 'Where is he, Pat?'

Pat returned his father's look, but did not answer

immediately. As he so often did, he was again feeling sorry for this weak and vacillating man who led such a miserable life because he couldn't stand up to his wife. And so, when he did answer it was in an even and kindly tone: 'Grandpa's decided to stay at The Little Manor, Father.'

'And he's still there?'

'Yes, Father; and he would like to stay there over the holidays –' and now he added more kindly still, 'if you don't mind.'

'Why does he want to stay there over the holidays? This is something new, isn't it?'

Pat turned to look at his brother Vincent and said, 'Yes, I suppose it is.'

Now his mother's voice cut in, saying, 'Look here! Something must have happened. What is it?'

'I can't tell you tonight, Mother. I could, but I'm not going to. It'll keep till after the holidays.'

'Pat!' cut in James, 'there's something not quite right here; if you won't tell me, I'll find out. I'll go along and see for myself.'

Quickly, Pat thrust out his hand and gripped his father's arm. 'I wouldn't if I were you, Father; just leave it till after the festivities,' and with this he turned to make for the door.

But there was Vincent standing four-square against it and he was saying, 'Oh no, smart fellow. You're not going out of here unless we know what this is all about. You have done something that has caused Grandpa to leave here and stay along there. So, out with it!'

'I haven't caused Grandpa to do any such thing. Please allow me to leave the room!'

'No, I damn well will not let you leave the room and leave us all dithering, waiting to know what's got into Grandpa to make him leave the house on such a night as this, and he not well. So come along, stop playing your little game.'

214

'Get out of the way, Vincent!' Pat's voice was commanding but quiet. 'If you don't I'll be forced to move you.'

'Huh! don't be silly; and stop playing heroics and tell us what . . . Oh!'

It had happened so swiftly that the cries from the others did not escape them until Vincent staggered from the door, holding one hand on his chin and the other on his throat, spluttering and coughing.

Facing his family, Pat looked from his father to his mother, and then to Evelyn, who had not yet opened her mouth, and he was about to turn and leave the room when his mother, arms outstretched as if she were about to shake him, cried, 'What's got into you? You could've killed him.'

'Yes, I could, because I felt like it at that moment,' and his voice now changing, he emphasised, 'and not for the first time. He's taunted me once too often, and he'll not do it again.' And turning to Vincent, he added, 'I've learnt a lot while crawling the decks these past years and doing the dirty jobs that you should have been doing but found too distasteful. You don't like mixing with the common herd, do you?'

'Pat! Pat! Pat!' His father had now put a gentle hand on his arm, and he went on, 'Enough. Enough. Remember it's Christmas Eve.'

'Oh, Father!' Pat's voice was almost pitying now. 'Christmas Eve. What does that matter in this house? I've seen more Christianity enacted in the bowels of a ship full of roughnecks than I've ever witnessed in this house, and this I will tell you: your Christianity is going to be tested within the next few days. And yes,' his voice was rising again, 'I'll tell you further what you want to know, and you'll be delighted to hear this, Mother' – he concentrated his gaze on Veronica Lawson's livid countenance – 'your dear daughter is coming home. A gentleman called

215

tonight to tell Grandpa he had found Marie Anne living in the most appalling conditions; but that is not all; she is also in a certain personal condition, being five months pregnant. And there's more to it than this, and which you will all learn about as soon as Grandpa has brought her back and installed her in The Little Manor.'

'No, no!' It was a whimper from his mother now. Veronica Lawson's head was wagging like that of a puppet, and, her body half-turned, she was stepping backwards, her hands groping outwards like those of a blind person feeling for a chair.

It was the couch she found and fell upon; and then she was moaning aloud, 'No, no! I . . . I couldn't bear it. I couldn't bear it. I won't have it! d'you hear? I won't have it! Oh God in heaven!'

Adding to her words and her moans there came a strange sound into the room: It was someone laughing hysterically and it propelled James Lawson to hurry to his daughter and to take her by the shoulders and command, 'Stop that! D'you hear me, Evelyn? Stop that noise this very minute!'

But his daughter could not stop her laughter, nor could she stop herself from saying, between great gusts of mirth, 'It . . . it didn't happen to me. It . . . it couldn't happen to me, could it? She's . . . she's pregnant! Wild and windy Marie Anne is going to have a child. Hurray! Hurray!'

When her father's hand came across her face in a resounding slap, the laughter ceased and Evelyn became quiet; that is until her tears started to roll down her cheeks, and with this, Pat hurried towards her and, taking her from her father's hold he said, 'Come on, dear. Come on upstairs.'

In her room he sat her in a chair. The tears were still flowing down her face, and she whimpered now, 'I'm sorry. I'm sorry.'

'What have you got to be sorry for? You should have done that a long time ago. Your back's been too stiff.'

'She's really going to have a baby?'

'Yes. Yes, she's really going to have a baby.'

'And she's five months gone?'

'Yes, five months.'

When she licked the tears from her face Pat pulled out a handkerchief and gently wiped her cheeks.

'Pat.'

'Yes, dear?'

'I . . . I wanted a baby.'

'Well' – he paused – 'it's only natural to want to have a baby.'

'No . . . No.' She shook her head. 'It was when I went with *him* I wanted to have a baby.'

He straightened up slightly from her. He was puzzled. For a moment, he thought she must be slightly delirious; and guessing this, she said, 'I'm . . . I'm telling you the truth, Pat. That's how . . . why Marie Anne went for me, for she thought I was wicked. She had seen us.'

'Who?'

'It was the night she hit her head against a wall. She was running away.'

He couldn't believe this: he couldn't take it in that the girl, or the young woman as she was now, sitting there was the same Evelyn to whom he had spoken before she had earlier gone out visiting, and had jokingly said to her, 'Mind you beware, because Mother'll have you matched up this afternoon before you know where you are,' and she had turned a haughty glance on him, but made no reply. But here she was, the real girl that had been crushed down into her secret self by her mother.

He took both her hands now, and crouching down on his haunches, he said, 'Don't worry. You'll see, one of these days you'll come across a man and you'll know immediately you're for him and he's for you. It happens like that. It's happened to me.'

'Yes?' She sniffed and swallowed, then brought a perfectly folded handkerchief from her sleeve, shook it out and wiped her eyes before going on and asking, 'Who is she? Do . . . do I know her?'

'No; I've kept her a secret, even from Grandpa. She's a working girl; but when the time is ripe we will get married.'

'You're so lucky, Pat, with your kind nature and everything else. I know I've had a bout of hysteria, but I did want to laugh before that, when you hit Vincent. I've wanted to do that for years.'

They smiled at each other and he said quietly, 'When Marie Anne comes back, try to be nice to her. She's a lovely creature at heart. Wild, yes, I admit, but I do know that throughout her young life she's craved friendship and love.'

'Since she's been away I've felt guilty for having been so horrible to her at times. I realise now that it was Mother's doing, that I was just following her example; but with regards to being nice to her, I doubt if we'll come across each other. I don't suppose I've visited The Little Manor more than twice in the last two years, and doubtless she would feel better if she didn't see me.'

'Oh, wait and see. She too will likely be changed . . . she's bound to be. Anyway, we're going up to London the day after Boxing Day. I've no idea when we'll be back; it'll all depend how soon she can be persuaded to return. From the letters I have occasionally received from her, which were quite different from those she sent to Grandpa, she was emphatic about never coming back here. She has ideas of taking up a profession for herself in London through her drawings.'

'Really?'

He nodded. 'She's already got a small commission, I

understand, from a newspaper; and of all places she's been playing the piano in a sort of pub-cum-eating house.'

'In a pub?'

'Yes, that's what I understand, in a pub; not for money, but just because there was no piano available anywhere else. They let her play there because her close friend and guardian, as I take this Miss Foggerty to be, now and again helps out behind the bar, pulling pints, as she refers to it.'

'You can't believe it really! can you?'

'No, Evelyn; it's very difficult to believe, but she's done it.'

'You know something, Pat? I envy her. Oh, how I envy her!'

To this he could only bend towards her and kiss her cheek, saying softly, 'Don't worry; your chance will come. Sleep well. I'll see you in the morning.'

In the drawing-room, James Lawson stood some distance from the couch, and as he looked at his wife and elder son, he with an arm around his mother's shoulders, he could not prevent a cold shiver from running through his body as he listened to Vincent saying, 'Whatever you did, you did for the best. She was always a dirty, filthy little slut. And I can promise you one thing: I'll make her pay for what she's done this day. I've hated her since she was born, and if it's the last thing I do I'll see my day with her.'

9

Before they entered the cab that was to take them from the station to the priory, Emanuel Lawson turned to Don, saying, 'Is there any possibility that we can view this place where she lives before we go to our destination?'

'Oh, sir, I don't think you would see much, except the yard and—'

'Well, that will be quite sufficient, I suppose,' said the old man impatiently. 'But you have talked of little else but the conditions that prevail in this area, so I'd like to see some of them for myself. Isn't that possible?'

'Yes. Yes.' Don smiled, then said, 'I'll direct the cabbie.' And this he had done, the while thinking of the old man's words, 'Talked of little else,' yet all he had done was answer his questions, and these had come in shoals between his frequent naps.

Now here they were, and he was helping the old gentleman down onto the greasy pavement before the wide opening that led into Ramsey Court yard.

When Pat went to take his grandfather's arm his hand was brusquely pushed away with, 'I don't want holding, boy. Just give me my stick.'

Leaning heavily on it, he walked forward and into the yard, but stopped within a few feet at the sight of a woman coming out of a water-closet. She was adjusting her clothes at the same time as she kicked a small tin out of her path to send it scudding across the yard. And when a man appeared from another door, tucking his shirt into the back of his trousers, the woman called to him as she pointed to a boy tipping a bucket of hot ashes onto the pile in the corner of the yard: 'When are they coming to clear that lot?'

Emanuel Lawson stood wide-eyed, gazing at the scene.

As a youth during his three years at sea he had been in many ports and seen hovels of all kinds, but they had been forgotten memories until now, for he had never encountered a hovel such as this.

His eyes again travelled up to the top of the building and to the row of small windows flanking the roof . . . My god! His Marie Anne lived up there.

He was well aware that the condition of the cottages in the hamlets around his own estate left a lot to be desired. They, too, were without proper sanitation. But this disgusting scene would be one of many, he supposed.

'Come, Grandfather.'

Emanuel's expression was one of distaste and bewilderment, and as he turned to move back to the cab he passed Don without making any remark whatever.

They were settled in easy chairs in a small but very comfortable room. A fire was blazing in the grate and the Father Prior himself had introduced them to Brother Peter who, during their stay, would attend to their needs; and he was sure they would be glad of some refreshment now after their long and tiring journey.

It was Pat who thanked the Father Prior, but Mr Lawson said nothing: he was lying back in the chair, his eyes half closed; but when he became aware that Don was intending to leave the room with the Father Prior he turned to him and said, 'Are you going to see to this business right away?'

And to this Don answered, 'Not right away, sir. First, I have to explain to Father, here, the reason for our visit.' And at this, he followed the Father Prior.

The first question that the Prior asked of Don as they

crossed the hall to his office was, 'Have we a querulous gentleman here, Don?'

And Don's answer was, 'Not really, sir. I think you will understand when I tell you the story, at least what I know of it. But first, thank you so much for wiring your answer to receive us.'

'No need for thanks, Don; it was the outcome of human curiosity: I couldn't wait to hear what all your coming and goings were about.' . . .

Five minutes later the Father Prior had the full story, as far as Don knew it, about the grand-daughter of a Northumbrian gentleman, and his first response was, 'And you say she is with child?'

'Yes; five months, Father.'

'And does he know this, I mean, what to expect?'

'Yes; I put him in the picture.'

'But if the girl's mother rejected her before, she is not likely to welcome her back with open arms, is she?'

'I don't think she'll be given any choice. There are two houses, The Manor and The Little Manor, and it is in the smaller I should imagine he'll have her installed.'

'And at present you say she is living in Ramsay Court?'

'Yes, Father.'

'Dear, dear! Dear, dear! Will she not get a shock when she sees her grandfather?'

'Yes; yes, I thought of that, Father, so I think the news should be broken to her before she comes here.'

'And that'll be left to you?'

'Well, I can't see anyone else doing it, Father, although I'm certainly not looking forward to it.'

The priest had been sitting, but now he got to his feet and, going to Don, he placed a hand on his shoulder and said, 'You know I've always said you're a great disappointment to us all' – he was smiling as he spoke – 'but now I think that God made provision for you to have your freedom, as you call it, to serve a purpose. He knows what's in store for you. So, go on, get about your business; and I want to hear about the happy ending.'

Without further ado Don took his leave of the Prior; although once outside the door he hesitated for a moment while his mind repeated the words, He knows what's in store for you. Well, he wished He would give *him* an inkling, because of late he had become uneasy as to what he was going to do with the rest of his life. During his first few years at the cottage, his work had brought him a modicum of happiness, but of late it hadn't seemed to be enough, especially during the evenings when, after the day's grind, he would sit alone before the fire reading, or stripping off his harness and going out into the dark night, rain, hail or snow, letting the weather blow on his face and lift up his hair. At such times he longed for the comradeship of the Brothers and, deep within him, he admitted to a loneliness; during the last few weeks he had comforted himself by thinking that when Farmer Harding let him have the puppy it would make a difference.

'Oh, hello! Don. Hello! So you're back. Oh, that's lovely. You'll be here for the New Year service? Brother Ralph has composed a new hymn. It's lovely, and I'm trying it on my mouth organ. That is, of course if' – he now poked his head towards Don – 'Father Prior doesn't confiscate it and throw it on the fire. Where are you off to now?'

'I'm off to the kitchen, John, to see if I can scrounge a cup of tea and a bite before I go out again on an errand.'

'Will I see you after prayers?'

'You will; you will, John.'

'Good. Good.'

The night was bitterly cold and murky, so much so that the street lights seemed to find it difficult to spread their light for any distance over the greasy pavements.

When he emerged from the black passage he was

somewhat surprised to find very few people about in the area, until he realised this would be the eating time for most working families.

An oil lamp was hanging outside the entry to the flats, and as he crossed the yard towards it a small group of children came scampering out of the door, to be brought to a halt at sight of the big man in the broad-brimmed hat. Then with little squeals they scattered into the yard.

When he reached the first landing, Don drew in a deep breath; but on the second he stopped, because not only was he out of breath but he had walked into darkness, illuminated only by the faint light coming from the outside lantern.

Having ascended the third flight he was pleased to see a glimmer of light given out by a night-light candle set in a jar.

For a moment, he stood quietly drawing in deep breaths of the fuggy smelly air, before putting out his hand and knocking gently on the door.

He was about to knock a second time when it was pulled open and Sarah stood there, dumbfounded and her mouth agape, before exclaiming on a high note, 'Why! Mr McAlister. What's brought you up to heaven so soon?'

He laughed outright as he answered her bantering greeting: 'The Archangel Gabriel called me up. He said I had to bring you tidings of great joy; to bring a message to a Miss Marie Anne Foggerty.'

'Oh! well, in that case who would dare to defy the Angel Gabriel? Come in.'

As she closed the door behind him he stood for a moment in amazement at the brightness and comfort of the room, so much so that he remarked upon it, before he addressed Marie Anne, saying, 'What a lovely room you have here! Really beautiful. Good evening, Miss . . .'

His voice trailed away for he could not say Foggerty, nor could he say Lawson.

Marie Anne was standing by the side of a chair. There was an enquiring look on her face as she said, 'Good evening, Mr McAlister.'

Sarah now put in, 'Won't you sit down? But not in my chair: with your weight and size you'll go through the bottom of it. Here! this one should suit you,' and she brought from the far wall what he recognised was a Sheraton armchair, but with one very obvious false leg.

When he sat down very gingerly on the proferred seat, she laughed, saying, 'Don't worry; it won't give way, it's been well and truly tested.'

He too laughed as he said, 'I'll take your word for it.'

Seating herself on the edge of her own chair, Sarah said, 'Have you come to tell us you've found work for us both, something refined where she can play the piano and I can waste me time looking after some old lady? But mind you, I' – she now thrust her finger towards him – 'I insist on vetting anyone of that ilk.'

He did not answer her smile with another, but turned towards Marie Anne, whose look was eager, and he said, 'I'm sorry I haven't come to offer you work. I've really come to talk to you, Miss . . .' again he paused; then looking Marie Anne straight in the face, he said, 'Lawson.'

Marie Anne's mouth dropped open just the slightest; then she seemed to close it with a snap, but she didn't speak; nor did Sarah make any remark, but she looked from one to the other and waited.

'I recognised you, Miss Lawson, the day we met in the restaurant. Perhaps you won't remember, but you had encountered me before, and even before that incident I had seen you a number of times from when you were quite young, running like the wind across the fields. I used to think you only needed a slight lift and you could have flown like a bird.' There was a soft smile on his face now, and he waited for a response from her. But when none came, he said, 'I know you were puzzled, too, when

225

we first met here. You felt you had seen me before, and you had, because it was I who found you the night you crashed your head against the wall. You were definitely running away from something or someone, and when you partly recovered and saw me you . . . well, you got a shock and fainted again.'

When the expression on her face hadn't changed, he said, 'You remember?' and she nodded at him, saying slowly, 'Yes; yes, I remember now.' And she did. This is what had bothered her: the moonlight shining on an ordinary face, then a dreadful frightening one taking its place.

As she stared at him now, she knew what the felt hat and the bandage covered. This was the branded man whom she had heard Fanny mention as if he were an ogre. How awful! because she had also heard he was a sculptor and a clever, educated man who lived in a cottage along the river bank back home.

What was she talking about, back home? Well, the place where she had lived. And here he was, come to tell her something about that place. She was sure of it. She said bluntly, 'Why are you here, Mr McAlister?'

After staring at her for a moment he rose to his feet and, looking down at her, he said, 'I am here, Miss Lawson, to tell you that your grandfather and your brother Patrick are at this moment resting in the guest room of the priory.'

As Marie Anne's hand went out and groped for the support of a chair, Sarah got up quickly and, going to her, put her arm around her shoulder, saying, 'There now. There now. It had to come some time.'

They were all silent. Then Marie Anne, looking at Sarah, said, 'You knew all the time?'

'Indeed no! I knew nothing of the sort. I'm hearing it for the first time, like yourself. I could never have kept a thing like that to meself. But having said that, it's the best thing that could have happened to you; I mean, you going back to where you belong.'

'I don't belong there, Sarah. I've told you; and now I'm telling you, Mr McAlister, I can't go back there. You should never have done this: it will break up the family; my mother will not have me.'

'As far as I understand it, Miss Lawson, your mother has had no say in this matter whatever; and you won't be going back to your old home, but to The Little Manor, which is being prepared for you and where your grandfather also intends to live permanently. And I can tell you another thing, Miss Lawson: until you decide to return home he will not leave London. Already, he abhors the place and all that he has seen so far, especially of the yard below and this area.'

'He has been here?' Marie Anne's face was screwed up in disbelief, but Don nodded at her, saying, 'Yes; straight from the train he came, for he demanded to see where you were living. Now, speaking personally, as I view him he's an old man and, this winter, he has already suffered a severe cold. And that was when he was living in clean air. What a few weeks in this atmosphere might do for him, I wouldn't like to say.'

Marie Anne now put her hands across her rising belly and almost pityingly said, 'I can't show myself to him like this. He always took my side and held me in such high esteem. He and Pat were the only ones who saw any good in me, and now—' Her head drooped.

'He still holds you in high esteem, because he loves you. You seem to be the only thing in his life that he cares about; and if there's any blame to be allotted, he blames himself for allowing you to come here in the first place.'

Addressing Sarah, Marie Anne said, 'Oh, what am I to do, Sarah?'

'You know damn fine well what you have to do and what you're going to do. You're going back now with Mr McAlister and you're going to see your grandfather and the brother that you're always yapping about. And tomorrow I'll have all your things packed up and ready for the road.'

'Oh no, you won't!' Marie Anne was on her feet again, all indecision gone. 'Whatever happens, arrangements have to be made and they'll take more than a day or so. And what about Annie and her brood?'

'What about them?' The question came high from Sarah. 'Aye! what about them? They are my concern, not yours.'

'They're the concern of both of us; she's been good to me. And then there are the drawings. I must visit Mr Stokes and tell him I'm leaving here, and . . . and tell him that I want to keep on sending him the drawings. Oh yes, I do. They are something I'm good at; and I could make a career of it. Yes, I could.'

'All right! All right! All right!'

'Well, I'm going to see him and tell him I could send them to him through the post. And don't forget he was good to me: he gave me five shillings a drawing.'

'Only when *I* pushed him up.'

During this exchange Don had been standing on the side, as it were, his head moving from one to the other.

'Then there's Mrs Everton. I must go and see her. She was very good about letting me play the piano.'

Sarah was now standing with her arms akimbo, and she put in sarcastically, 'And you mustn't forget, must you? Mr Paddy O'Connell and his Emporium.'

At this Marie Anne's head drooped and she held her face between her hands as she muttered, 'Well, he did set us up here nicely, didn't he? And yes, I will go and see him. And oh dear me! all this before I meet Grandpa.'

She was sitting down again, the tears running down her face, but this time they brought no sympathetic gesture from Sarah, who went swiftly up the room and into the bedroom, returning within a minute carrying Marie Anne's coat, scarf, hat and boots, and saying brusquely,

'You can stop that now and get into your outdoor clothes, because you're wastin' Mr McAlister's time. And what's more, I think he's had enough of your emotions in the last five minutes or so. Now come on.'

Obediently Marie Anne got to her feet and allowed herself to be helped into her coat, the scarf put around her neck and the hat put into her hands. But there the hat remained and Marie Anne said, 'You're coming with me.'

'Oh no, I'm not.'

'Well, then' – the voice came very firm now – 'You're forever pushing me around, Sarah Foggerty, and telling me what to do or what I haven't got to do. Now this time I'm telling you, if you don't come with me, I don't go.'

Again there was silence between them until, in a throaty voice, Don said, 'Miss Foggerty, I would get into your outdoor clothes if I were you.' . . .

Twenty minutes later they were being greeted by Brother Peter in the hall of the priory; but when he went to lead Marie Anne to the sitting-room door she turned and looked at Sarah, saying, 'You're coming in with me?'

'No.'

'But—' Marie Anne's beseeching tone was cut short by Don saying quite firmly, 'You must do this alone, Miss Lawson; your grandfather would expect it of you.'

Sarah and Don watched the door being opened and then closed, and from then the only sound that came to them was the high cry of, 'Grandpa!' followed by, 'Oh! Pat,' and at that, simultaneously they turned about and in a low voice Don said, 'The Father Prior would like to meet you, I know, and hear more about her background, as only you know it. If you'll take a seat in here I'll go and see if he's available.'

After he had left her in the small waiting-room Sarah sat with her hands pressed tightly between her knees. If she had ever wanted to cry in her life she wanted to cry at this minute: she was asking herself what she was going to do without her, because she had grown to love her as if she were her own daughter, the daughter she'd never had, nor was likely to have. They had been together only about fourteen months, but it could have been fourteen years; it was as if she had taken her out of the cradle. But now, she chastised herself, she must take a back seat in this. It was the best thing, perhaps the only thing that could have happened to the girl, she knew, for she had been secretly worried to death about what they would do when the child came, and they at the top of that house with those crucifying stairs. So, what had happened tonight had happened for the best. God knew what He was doing . . . But did He? Had He given a thought to the bastard child? It would have been accepted in the flats; but what about the class she was going back to? She was a young lady, a very young lady, and she had been with a man: she wouldn't be classed fit to enter into society of any kind, even if she were under the protection of her grandfather and all the weight and power he seemed to carry.

In a way and in this minute, she imagined the girl would have had more happiness in working and bringing up her child in the Courts, if only they'd been able to live on the ground floor and not halfway to heaven.

They had talked half the night. They had gone to sleep arguing. Sarah was adamant that in no way would she fall in with Marie Anne's plans, and Marie Anne was adamant that in no way was she going back to Northumberland without her, Grandpa or no Grandpa . . .

Now it was ten o'clock the following morning and they were both ready for outdoors, and Sarah had been bidden to be at the Brothers' house at half-past ten, because Mr Lawson wished to speak to her.

They were ushered into the sitting-room by Brother Peter, and Sarah stood nervously and stiffly aside while the elderly man embraced Marie Anne; then when the younger man approached her, holding out his hand saying, 'I'm Patrick, Marie Anne's brother,' she said, 'How d'you do, sir?'

'Grandfather,' – Pat was leading Sarah forward towards the old man – 'this is Miss Foggerty, about whom Marie Anne has told you so much.'

When the elderly man peered at Sarah she looked him straight back in the face, saying, 'Good-day, sir.'

'Good-day, Miss Foggerty. Do please take a seat,' and Emanuel Lawson pointed to where Marie Anne was already seated. Then, seating himself before her, he said, 'I have much to thank you for, Miss Foggerty. From what Marie Anne tells me, I gather she doesn't know where she would have been at this moment, had it not been for you; certainly not in comfortable rooms, even if they are very high up, as I understand them to be, and among good friends. And all through your guidance and kindness. She tells me quite firmly and heartlessly' – he now turned a soft glance on Marie Anne – 'that she will not return with me unless you accompany her. Now, now!' He lifted his hand and his voice changed to a firmer note as he went on, 'As you know, for the next few months she'll be in need of a nurse-companion. Now, I am not doing you a favour by asking you to take on this post; we're just being selfish. We are wanting your services; or at least I am; Marie Anne, I think, requires something more from you, something that she has had all along, for she seems to think you are the only woman who has ever shown her any love. And so, Miss Foggerty, let me hear what you have to say.'

There was a long pause before Sarah said, 'What I have to say, sir, is a very deep and sincere thank you for your kindness and your offer, but, as I tried to explain . . . well' – she gave a half smile here – 'your grand-daughter, sir, is very stubborn, I don't know who she gets it from, but she is, and we talked and practically fought half the night about this. But it's this way, sir. To put it plainly, I have a sister who lives in Ramsay Court, on the floor below us, and she has ten children. I have always tried to help her, and at this time she is more in need of my help than ever, because her husband has injured his foot and is unable to work, at least for a time. So I feel responsible for her and for the children. Her eldest son, Shane . . . well, he is very bright but he doesn't attend school as he should, because he works on coal bagging.'

He stopped her here by saying, 'What is coal bagging?'

'Filling sacks with very dusty coal, sir.'

'Oh.' He nodded at her, then said, 'Go on.'

'Well, that's all sir; except that, as I've had a little education – I read well and have a good hand at writing – I should like him to have a chance.'

'Yes. Oh yes, I understand you had to write and read all the letters that passed between my daughter-in-law and her half-sister, and thereby you doubtless learned a lot about Marie Anne's mother.'

'Some, sir.'

'Yes, indeed, some. Well, now.' He turned to Pat and asked brusquely, 'Well, what've you got to say about all this?'

'Nothing more than what we discussed earlier, Grandfather.'

'And you're willing to leave the big house and come and live at The Little Manor?'

'Oh Pat, no.' Marie Anne was on her feet now and moving towards Pat. Taking his hand, she said, 'You can't do that, Pat. Oh no!'

'Why not? I am not happy there; you know I'm not, no more than you were.'

'But she'll . . . she'll hate me more than ever.'

'Putting it bluntly, dear, she couldn't possibly.'

Marie Anne's head sank, and she said, 'No, perhaps you're right there.'

'It's only what she's asked for, and for a long time, and when you get home you will know there's going to be other changes, too; but that we'll leave for the present. Let us finish with Sarah's problem.' And looking towards Sarah, he said, 'Grandfather is thinking of setting up a running household in The Little Manor, a house further along in the grounds and where he used to live at one time with my grandmother. Lately he has been living in The Manor itself and just staying odd days along there, and so he kept on only three servants all told, two old retainers and a young girl. Maggie and Barney Makepeace have looked after him for a long time, Katie is the maid. But since it is now to be an occupied family home, we shall want more staff. Grandfather means to take some from the main house but, as he said, the staff has to be ruled whether it's large or small and we will need a house-keeper, and from what Marie Anne tells me, you know everything about running a house. You had to do it for your mother's sister for a long time; and Marie Anne also tells me' – he smiled now – 'you're very careful about money, even cheese-paring.'

'Oh! miss.' Sarah had turned to look at Marie Anne, and Marie Anne said, 'Well, you are; you're too careful for words.'

'Needs must, miss.'

'Oh yes, that's an old saying,' put in Emanuel Lawson: 'Needs must when the devil drives.'

'Yes, sir.' Sarah was smiling at him. 'And the faster he goes the more he charges.'

That anyone, especially a servant, should dare cap his grandfather's sayings brought a tight smile to Pat's face. It could be seen it had left that particular gentleman a little nonplussed.

He now went on, 'Marie Anne tells me that you have helped to support your sister financially for some time.'

Rounding on Marie Anne now, Sarah said indignantly,

'You haven't left anything out, have you?'

And at this, Marie Anne answered pertly, 'Yes; there are still a few things, but they'll come to mind shortly.'

This exchange brought the two men looking at each other; then Emanuel Lawson said, 'What was your wage when you worked for Martha Culmill?'

'Six shillings a week, sir.'

'Six shillings a week!' he repeated incredulously as he glanced towards Pat. 'Were there any servants?'

'A cook-general and a young maid.'

'No night nurse and such relief?'

'No, sir.'

'And tell me, what did you allow your sister out of that?'

Sarah moved slightly along the couch as if she wanted to evade the question: she didn't like it; it was her own business what she did with her money. But anyway, here was a man who wanted answers and so she said, 'Half; three shillings.'

'So it's a matter of money that's keeping you tied to your sister and her family?'

'No; no, sir, not altogether; I'm very fond of them. They're the only family I've got and if I was hard pushed for a job I could always go back there. And that's where I took Miss Marie Anne when we were up against it.'

'But her main need, at the moment, is money. Isn't that so?'

'Well . . . yes, I suppose so.' Her head was nodding. 'When you come down to rock bottom it's always a matter of money.'

'You're right there. You're right there. So, this is my proposition: I want a housekeeper. I'm willing to pay her a pound a week, added to which will be her keep, her uniform and a comfortable apartment. That's how it's said, isn't it, Pat?'

Pat was laughing outright now, and he knew his grandfather was enjoying this interview as he enjoyed few things, and so he said, 'Yes, Grandfather; something like that.'

'So, Miss Foggerty, that is my proposition.'

Marie Anne had come back to the couch and taken her seat beside Sarah again, and she was now holding her hand, and she saw that this dear friend of hers was unable to speak. Presently, as they sat looking at each other, Sarah muttered, throatily, 'But what about our flat upstairs and all the bits and pieces?'

'I've thought about that,' said Marie Anne. 'I'll continue to pay the rent on that, because I'll definitely be making money out of my drawings, and it will be a place for the older girls to sleep, and perhaps a place for Annie to escape to. And, you know, I feel I owe the tribe something, because the editor wouldn't have taken those other drawings if he hadn't first seen the dinner-table one.'

'Well now' – the old man had risen briskly from his chair – 'what time can we get a train back today?'

'Today, Grandfather?'

'Yes; you heard me, Pat, today.'

'Well, it's nearly eleven now. I think there's a train leaves about one.'

'Oh! we must say goodbye to our friends,' Marie Anne put in.

'Are these friends of yours very far away, Marie Anne?'

'No, Grandpa, ten minutes.'

'And your flat is quite near. So you have an hour or less to be back here, bag and baggage, for I' – his voice trailed off – 'I dearly want to get home and out of this city. The air stifles me.'

'Yes, Grandpa; we'll be back, bag and baggage.' She leant towards him and kissed his cheek, saying, 'Oh, you don't know, Grandpa, how lovely it is to see you again,' and he, putting his hand on her hair, said, 'For me too, my dear, for me too. But there now, go along.' But he pulled her back to him and, in a stage whisper, said, 'And keep a close watch on your friend, because I can see her reneging before we get on to that train.'

Marie Anne laughed, saying, 'No, she won't, Grandpa; she's going to love it, I know. Aren't you, Sarah?'

'That remains to be seen, miss; and if I can't stand things I can always go to Mr McAlister's. He tells me he lives just along the river bank.'

The old man's face was straight now as he said, 'Yes; speaking of Mr McAlister, we have a lot to thank that gentleman for, and we must never forget that.'

'No, Grandpa; as you say, we must never forget that.' . . .

It was Mr McAlister who saw them into their compartments. It was Mr McAlister who had sent a wire to one Barney Makepeace of The Little Manor, Moorstone, near Chester-le-Street, Northumberland, and the message ran:

HAVE MAIN CARRIAGE DURHAM STATION,
SEVEN O'CLOCK TODAY.

And it was Mr McAlister who had surprised the old gentleman by refusing to return with them, because he had promised the Brothers he would spend the New Year at the priory.

And it was Mr McAlister's face, the visible part of it, that had taken on a deep rosy hue when Sarah Foggerty had at the last minute reached up and cupped his maimed cheek with her hand and looked deeply into his eyes.

But the effect on him was not evident when Marie Anne, after offering him her hand, said, 'Thank you for giving me a new lease of life. I don't know what the future holds, but I shall never forget the relief I am feeling at the present moment, and it is all due to you. Thank you.' . . .

He remained standing on the platform until the train disappeared from sight; and then he walked slowly out into the murky thoroughfare to make his way back to the

Brothers' house. Before this he had always enjoyed bringing in the New Year in the company of the Brothers, but during the last few days he had experienced association with women . . . well, a woman and a girl . . . a strangely beautiful girl at that, and their presence had created a new warmth in him. But now a harsh reprimanding voice from within said, 'The quicker that feeling is put in its place the quicker you'll return to your normal way of life.'

As he mounted the horse-bus he imagined he must be feeling like a man whose one desire was to get blind drunk; but knowing he could not take advantage of the suggestion, he decided, if the opportunity should arise this evening to sample Brother Peter's latest brew. He would not refuse it, for whatever harm it might do to the stomach, it would certainly bring oblivion to the mind.

PART THREE

1

The family, with the exception of Patrick, was gathered in the study. This room lay between the library and the billiard-room, and its situation made it possible for a voice to be raised without it being overheard in the main part of the house; and Veronica Lawson's voice was certainly raised now as she addressed her husband, who was sitting in a leather chair to the right of the fireplace.

'Do something! D'you hear? Do something. You must. Go down there and have it out with him. Ask him plainly what more he is going to do to us.'

James Lawson was bent forward, his hands gripped together in front of his protruding stomach, his gaze seeming to be concentrated on the rug at his feet, and when his wife's tirade ended with the words, 'It's not to be borne; and I won't stand any more,' he slowly straightened his position and, looking up at her to where she was standing to the side of his chair, in a dull heavy voice he asked, 'What are you going to do then?'

'What do you mean?'

'Just what I say. If you can't stand any more, what are you going to do about it?'

Veronica Lawson took in a deep breath and shifted her gaze to her son, seated opposite, then to her elder daughter, who was standing looking out of the window and on to the snow-covered garden, and for a moment it would appear that she was lost for a reply; but not so: 'I'll go down there myself and demand,' she said.

'Shut up! Mother.' Vincent had risen to his feet, and he

went on, 'Anyway, I don't think we'll have to wait much longer for the climax. This morning I overheard Billings chattering in the stable. It appears Young took Grandfather into Ferguson's office last week, and Ferguson came with his clerk yesterday.'

'The solicitor?' The word came out high from Veronica Lawson's mouth, and her lips drew back from her teeth for a moment before she repeated, 'The solicitor?'

'That's what I heard, Mother; so we can only await his next move.'

'What more can he do to us?' she now appealed to her husband. 'He has taken our carriage and Young who has been with us for years, as well as two yard men.'

With an impatient movement James Lawson pulled himself to his feet and reached up to grip the mantelpiece, and his voice was certainly not quiet as he corrected his wife, saying, 'He has taken *his* carriage and *his* men, Veronica.' Then swinging about, he looked at her and, almost yelling now, he said, 'Have you asked yourself who is to blame for all this? No; no. It's all put on Marie Anne; but if you had ever played the mother towards that child as you have done to Evelyn there' – he pointed towards the window – 'we wouldn't be in the state we are in today. The trouble with you is, you're an unnatural woman, all through. Do you hear me?'

'Father!' Vincent's voice came like a reprimand, and James turned on him, actually yelling now, 'Don't you use that tone to me, either. I should have dealt with you years ago, for at bottom I've recognised you are a cruel bugger; and you were the means of getting the child into trouble more than once. So don't you come and dictate to me in any shape or form. D'you hear me?'

Evelyn had turned from the window, amazement on her face, for this was the first time she had heard her father speak as he was doing now as master in his own house, or, to be more correct, in his father's house, for this had been made very plain during the last three weeks since Marie Anne had come back. And for the first time she felt respect for him when he turned and marched from the room, banging the door behind him.

Before any of them had regained their breath, the door opened again, and Pat entered, saying, 'I have just told Father we all have to assemble in the library at two o'clock this afternoon. Grandpa will come here.'

'Orders from the palace. I thought you said you weren't going to act as a go-between.'

'Nor am I, but this is a private matter, as I think you will find out.'

'So it's all cut and dried.'

'No; it is not all cut and dried; I know no more than you do about what Grandfather intends to do or say.'

His mother now stepped towards him, saying, 'But I hear that he's seen his solicitor. The man was with him yesterday, and he was at their office last week.'

'Well, if that's what you've heard, Mother, it's likely right.'

'Oh; and you don't know anything about it?' Vincent demanded.

Patrick rounded on Vincent, 'In this case you're right; I don't know anything about it. Nor do I want to know. This is not my battle.'

'No?' It was a question. 'But you jumped at the chance to go and live with him,' in answer to which Pat said, 'Yes; and glad to do so, for with no stretch of the imagination could anyone say this is a happy house, or has ever been so.'

'Oh!' It was an agonised cry now from his mother. 'I can't bear any more. I can't. I can't,' and at this she made a rush for the door; and Vincent, about to follow her, turned and hissed at Patrick, 'One of these days, boy, I'll settle with you. You wait and see.'

Left alone, the brother and sister looked at each other,

before Evelyn walked slowly towards him and asked quietly, 'You don't really know what's afoot?'

Shaking his head, Pat answered her: 'Honest, Evelyn, I don't. I know he's making changes, for he wanted to discuss it with me; but I said no, it was better that he kept it to himself.'

'Do you think it's something drastic?'

'I couldn't say. I only know that changes are going to be made. How and where, I don't know; but why, I do know, and that why is Mother. Apparently Grandfather never wanted her as a daughter-in-law; however, once she was established he did his best to meet her halfway. But her ambitions for recognition in the county got under his skin. He and Grandma were highly respected and all doors were open to them. But he was never a man for visiting. His life was given over to the business, and the first clash between Mother and him, I understand, was when she was for sending out invitations to a ball, and two-thirds of the guests he had never heard of, never mind met. This was during the second year of the marriage, and he put his foot down, and there it remained until Grandma died, from which time Mother took on her string-pulling again. Well, you've had a taste of it, Evelyn, and from what I gathered a few weeks ago she's still at it. This man she has lined up for you; how d'you feel about him?'

'I don't know, Pat. He is more than twice my age and has been married before. Quite honestly, the prospect makes me shudder, yet it seems it has to be him, or Mother and this house for the rest of my life. I am twenty-six years old, Pat, and I can't see young men flocking to my feet again, can you? But then, they never did.'

'What's twenty-six these days? Opinions are changing. It's talked of in places that when the Queen goes, and she can't last for much longer, there'll be a revolution in thought. For instance, there'll be a man on the throne and he, as you know,' – he smiled here – 'is a very liberal thinker. But seriously, don't do this just to be able to leave home, please! Evelyn, because there's bound to be somebody, bound to be. You are a beautiful woman, girl . . . you're still a girl to me and you don't look your age, not by years, that's when you're smiling and your back bends a little.'

She put out her hand and caught his. 'You know, Pat, it's strange, but ever since the night I gave way and cried I've felt different altogether inside. I wish I could say lighter, but definitely it's different. I seem to be seeing people in a different way. Even Marie Anne. But, oh dear! dear! I thought the other night that if she had been born to royalty, the whole world would have been at war.'

At this he laughed outright, saying, 'Poor Marie Anne, creator of wars now; and if you really knew her, Evelyn, you would find her of a kind and endearing nature. But speaking of wars, I'm dreading this afternoon.'

'Is it true that Grandfather has that branded man up to dinner in the house sometimes?'

'Yes; yes, it is, Evelyn. And the branded man, as you have referred to him, is Don McAlister, and he is an educated and intelligent man, and a clever sculptor into the bargain.'

'Really?'

'Yes, really.'

'What's the matter with his face then?'

'I don't know; I've never asked him.'

'Was he burnt?'

'I really don't know, Evelyn.'

'I heard Fanny Carter and Jones talking one day before they were sent to The Little Manor. It was about the maid, the Makepeace's girl, Katie. She is supposed to have squealed the house down when she first saw the man at the front door. Had he anything to do with Marie Anne's coming back?'

'Yes; everything, Evelyn, everything. It was he who found her. I'll tell you all about it some time.'

She stared at him as she said, 'D'you really mean to stay there; I mean, to live there with Grandfather?'

'Yes; yes, I do. There's a different atmosphere altogether in that house: you hear people laughing and not afraid to do so.'

Her voice had the old tartness to it as she said, 'Well, you should have been here for the last fortnight and you would have heard laughter all right. We've never had so many visitors in years, all expecting to see the errant daughter, and all so solicitous in an underhand way, while laughing up their sleeves at Mother. I can't help it, but at times I have felt sorry for her, having to put on a face when all she wanted to do was slap them. And she's sick at heart; I know now it's because she hasn't had a formal invitation to The Hall Ball, even though during our visit there before Christmas, Lady Knight was discussing it with her as if our presence were a foregone conclusion. What's made things worse, in my opinion, is that a maid was dismissed from there not so long ago. She was in the same condition as Marie Anne . . . but *she* was thrown out, not welcomed back like the prodigal daughter.'

Evelyn turned sharply away and walked from him back to the window.

He looked towards her rather sadly – the old Evelyn was still there. But it was understandable.

And on this, he went out.

It was the butler, Frank Pickford, who opened the door to the old master and Mister Patrick, saying, 'Good afternoon, sir.' He then proceeded to help the old man off with his coat.

'Where are they?'

'The family are in the drawing-room, sir.'

'Well, tell them to come to the library.'

246

Almost five minutes later Veronica Lawson, a step ahead of her husband, entered the room; Evelyn followed, leaving Vincent to close the door none too quietly behind them, and they all stood for a moment looking towards Emanuel, who sat at the far end of the long library table, on which he had set out a number of parchment-looking papers. Returning their gaze, he said, 'Well, since you're here you might as well sit down; it's going to be a long session. But you, James' – his voice seemed to soften a little – 'I'd like you to sit beside me, here, and opposite Patrick.'

'Yes, Father.'

As James obeyed his father's request it would seem that the quick action of Vincent placing a chair for his mother and almost pushing her into it, stopped her from expressing straightaway her opinion of the whole situation. The chair was at the end of the table, and she immediately laid her hands on the inlaid leather top and drummed her fingers quite loudly until Emanuel, looking down the table towards her, said, 'When you've finished with your war signal, Veronica, and Vincent and Evelyn have seated themselves, I shall begin.'

Emanuel waited a further moment before picking up from the table a roll of parchment and wagging it, saying, 'I don't think any of you know the real history of this house and The Little Manor, as it's called, but if you have, it won't hurt you; in fact it is necessary that you should hear it again. The Little Manor was built in 1750 and its name then was The Fallow. Why, I don't know, except that it's like a field at rest, being on flat ground. The owner was one Isaac Wilding, who was in shipping. Eight hundred acres of land went with it, and six hundred more were leased as a little farm, which today is still under lease to Mr Harding. At this time, Mr Wilding's business was prospering at such a rate he decided to live in a bigger and better house. He was an ambitious man, and he also had an ambitious wife.' Emanuel did not raise his eyes and look at his daughter-in-law, but went on, 'He bought another fourteen hundred acres and on it he built this house and collected a stud of horses. He lived well, I understand, and entertained lavishly; and he overspent lavishly and so his business went bust.

'I omitted to state that he had turned over The Fallow to his son, and his family went up with the balloon. It was then that Great-grandfather, my great-grandfather, bought this place in about 1780, and, as did the man before him, he put his son into The Fallow or, as it is now known, The Little Manor. But neither of the heads of the family lived very long to enjoy what they had worked for, and my grandfather took over in about 1800 and moved into this house. He had two surviving sons out of a family of six and, like his predecessors, he put one into The Little Manor to which my grandfather added another wing because of his son's growing family. And by the way, that wing hasn't been used much for years, but it's open again now . . . oh yes, it's open again.' He nodded from one to the other. 'Anyway, my father was born there and twenty-three years later I was born there, and that is why I preferred living there with my wife rather than here, which is why I handed this place over to you, James, on your wedding day.' He now bounced his head towards his son. 'And that was a mistake. Oh yes, it was a mistake. But one thing I didn't do; I put nothing in writing. Instead, I gave you a verbal assurance that the house was yours to live in as long as you required it. Remember?'

James stared back at his father. His face was flushed, his lips were moving one over the other, but he didn't say anything, and the old man now said, 'I'll continue. During all that time, close on thirty years, for the twins must be nearly twenty-nine, I have paid for your staff. Every penny you needed for your indoor and outdoor staff I have seen to, and not only their wages, but also for their uniforms, male and female. However, I've done it with less grace each year, I may tell you, for as your family grew older and fewer in number when the twins went to Canada and Marie Anne was banished—' he turned a deadly glance now towards his daughter-in-law, which she dared to respond to in similar fashion, then he went on, 'more staff seemed to be needed, and for what? To eat their heads off, to laze about the grounds. Two thousand, two hundred acres, and what has been done with it? Apart from the four hundred acres of woodland, it has been given over to pretty lawns and flower beds and vineries and hothouses for exotic plants that you don't even know the names of, and I've stood aside and let it go on, thinking, What odds? I'm getting old, it doesn't matter. But now I know I am not too old to enjoy my last days of life and also to see that others enjoy the years they've been deprived of.'

When he felt an uneasy movement at his side the old man turned to Pat, and said, 'I'm all right. I'm all right Pat. Don't worry, I don't intend to have a seizure, although I've had enough cause. Well now, to finish this part of the business and . . . yes, this is only half of what I've got to say to you all. As there were originally eight hundred acres attached to The Little Manor, not counting Harding's farm, it left one thousand, four hundred acres, so I am passing four hundred of them on to John Harding to give him a decent piece of land to till or for grazing. That'll be cut from the west side of the estate where it is cheek by jowl with his own piece of land. Thus I am creating a boundary of sorts. It might be invisible, except on paper—' he now tapped another piece of parchment saying, 'It's all here, cut and dried. You'll have a thousand acres left' – he nodded towards his son – 'and, as your land has been depleted, so will be the staff who run it; and don't forget you'll have to pay your staff out of your own pocket from now on. In fact, I'm dating it back to the first of January in this new century so, the fewer men you have outdoors and the fewer women in, the easier it will be for you to manage. To that end I have already taken two yard men and Young, together with the carriage. I'm not depriving you of transport, because you've still got the working carriage. If you're wise, you'll cut another two from the gardens. Then there's the indoor staff. I have already taken two maids and because, as far as I can remember, you've never asked to look at the bills that your staff has cost me, I suggest you do without either a footman or a butler. In my opinion, Green could answer for both. Do you know' – he leant towards his son again – 'I have reckoned up and have made it my business to find out the number of staff, indoor and outdoor, of The Hall and of Baintrees. With all the requirements at The Hall, which includes the accommodation of passing royalty and other bigwigs from London, there are only four more on their payroll than I've been paying out for this establishment. So, James, you have a word with your housekeeper and see if she can economise, because if not, you could tell her, or at least hint, that there is a possibility she might lose her position, because great changes are about to take place, and not before time. Oh no, not before time. And lastly, while we're dealing with the staff outside, I'm taking Lady and her foal with me.'

'Oh no, you can't do that!' This came from Vincent. 'Lady's mine! I've always ridden—' He had half risen from his chair, his face suffused with anger, when the old man interrupted him, bellowing, 'Your horse? Since when?' but more quietly he then continued, 'I think I remember buying her ten years ago, and I also remember that I rode her for about two years. I recall too, that about four years ago I forbade you to ride her any more, because you always drove her into a sweat. I told you then that Brindle was more suited to you. She was a heavy goer and could carry weight, and moreover you couldn't get your own way with Brindle. I always considered Lady much too fine for your handling. Well, sir, in future, if you want such a horse as Lady then you'll have to buy one, and before I'm much older I'll find out which yard man disobeyed my orders. But on further thought, it would all have come about through you playing the master. Well, we'll leave this matter for the present.' He could not explain why he wanted the horse and her foal, only that there was a far picture in his mind of a little girl riding a pony. And so he said, 'The second part of this business won't take very long.' He looked straight at his son. 'We are a private business, by the way.' He now turned his gaze on the still scarlet face of Vincent, then on to Pat, who was now standing by his side, and he said, 'They won't believe that you knew nothing about what I have just said, and much less about what I am about to say, but I have never discussed this business with you, have I?'

'No, Grandfather.'

'Well, that's that. Now James, as regards the company. As I said, we are a private company and, as my solicitors have told me, having been into this matter, as the head of it I can do as I like with the shares that I possess, and they are sixty-one per cent of the whole.'

It seemed to take James an effort to bow his head in assent.

'Well, then, take note: you, James, hold twenty per cent of the shares. That is right, isn't it?'

When his son did not answer he practically bawled at him, 'Don't you?'

'Yes, Father. Yes.'

'Well, then, the next ten per cent Vincent holds, and the remaining nine, Pat. I haven't bothered about the twins; they are doing well for themselves and don't need any help from me, alive or dead. Well, now, I propose to add a further ten per cent, taken from my own, to Patrick's holding, bringing him up to nineteen, leaving me still in control. There is another matter about the shares I would like to discuss with you, James, but in private, after you have given your new situation and the demands upon it some thought, because you must ask yourself from where you are going to get the money to keep up this establishment as it is now, for you must admit your salary doesn't warrant it. Does it?'

'No, Father.' It was scarcely a whisper.

'Well, then, we'll talk about that later. But now I must tell you that were I to die tomorrow all my shares, which are the controlling interest of our company, will be passed on to my grand-daughter, Marie Anne Lawson. She will then control the company.'

Before he could utter another word there was a scream from the end of the table, followed first by James jumping to his feet, and then Vincent, the different voices forming a chorus of 'No! No! You can't.' Surprisingly, Veronica remained seated.

Emanuel looked from one to the other, then said, 'What you forget, all of you, is that it is *my* business, and I more than any of my ancestors have worked hard personally to bring it to its present level, and I have done this with only one of you assisting me, and that is Pat here. For years now, Pat has thrown himself wholly into the business: he has actually worked on the ships, looked into every grumble and growl, examined holds and almost broken his back doing it, didn't he? But you, Vincent, have been too big to go down into a dirty bilge or into a stokehole! No, I don't think you've ever been over a ship, even walked its decks; and James, you have hardly left your office for years. No; it's all been left to Pat and, until recently, me, so, as I've said, Marie Anne will own the company, and as such, should you die, James, she will make Pat her managing director. It's all been done legally and signed, and it didn't need any of your names because I am the owner of this family business. I also own this house and The Little Manor. So if you wish to continue here, James, you are very welcome, but, as I have said before, you'll have to find means of maintaining it, because you can no longer rely on me.'

'You are an old beast! a filthy old beast! I hate you!'

Vincent was now restraining his mother's hands, for one was quite close to a heavy glass inkstand, and he wasn't the only one who had thought she was about to grab it and throw it at her father-in-law.

'You're wicked! wicked!'

It was Emanuel who now pulled himself to his feet. He took three steps along by the side of the table until he was almost hovering over her, when he said, slowly, 'You *dare* to call anyone wicked. *You!* who turned your young, innocent daughter over to the care of a woman who happens to be as big a fiend as you are. You even sent wires forbidding your sister to allow your daughter to come back here to me, and insisted that she put her into a home, any home. And the home to which Martha intended sending her was for prostitutes, young whores off the streets; and there she would have landed had it not been for Miss Foggerty. It was she who took matters into her own hands: she left Martha's employ and took Marie Anne to her own sister's, a poor place, but the saving of your daughter, and where she met with more kindness, understanding and help than she had ever received in her own home. And finally, let me tell you, woman, that everything I have said at this table, all the changes I have made today and which will have repercussions for many years to come, have come about through one person and one person only, and that is you. My son made the biggest mistake of his life when he married you – at least, you saw that you married him – because you came from nothing: one little boot shop, your parents had, but you had big ideas, hadn't you? Ideas of grandeur, of mixing with the mighty, the famous, didn't matter if some were notorious, just as long as you could drop their names. Now it's up to you, daughter-in-law, whether you want to go on residing here with a very depleted staff, or move elsewhere.'

Aware that she was so furiously angry that she could not answer him, he moved back to his chair.

Vincent still held on to his mother's hands as he glared towards his grandfather, who was now addressing him, saying, 'You have a very good salary and a share in the profits, so you could help to support the house, as I'm sure Pat would have done if he had decided to stay here;' and now turning to his grand-daughter, he said, 'Well, Evelyn, that leaves only you; and you have not been forgotten. Should you not marry, you will be provided for. In the meantime, I propose to give you a good dress allowance.'

Not a muscle of Evelyn's face moved. This old man had just wrecked the family. It had never been close before, but now it was torn asunder, and the idea that Pat would be senior to Vincent was unthinkable; Vincent would surely do something desperate. More so, he would never be able to stand the fact that one day the company could fall into Marie Anne's control.

As for her mother, she appeared to be a broken woman. But was she? No; she was of the type that would survive if it was only to pray for disaster to strike her father-in-law dead.

Her grandfather, she knew, was waiting for some form of thanks, but she could not bring herself to give it to him. She would rather that he had left her out of it.

James Lawson was sitting at the table again, but his head was bowed over his joined hands, and when his father said quietly, 'James, I would like to see you, say tomorrow afternoon, by which time you will have thought things over; or perhaps that might be too early.'

James lifted his head, and without a shred of emotion he said, 'No, Father; I'll be there tomorrow afternoon.'

As Pat helped his grandfather up from the chair, he looked towards his father and gave a small shake of his head as if in understanding; then he waited as his grandfather gathered up the documents from the table, saying, 'They've never been opened. I intended that they should all see what has been done with regards to the grounds and the rest, but you can see them tomorrow, James, if you wish.'

When the door closed on his grandfather and brother, Vincent helped Veronica to her feet and without a word escorted her from the room, leaving James still seated at the table. Evelyn looked at her father and her gaze was pitying. She saw a man in his early fifties looking at this moment as old as his own father; and beaten, yes that was the word, beaten. She had always known him to be a weak man and without gumption, else he would have stood up to her mother long before now. The only time he had seemed to make a stand was in the privacy of their bedroom; and even before her mother had moved it to the far end of the house, she had known what their almost nightly battle was all about.

As for her mother, she had always seen her as a forceful, social-climbing woman, and knew that she had looked upon her younger daughter as something of an impediment that stood in her way, but to have gone to such lengths as to have her put away, and into such a place as her grandfather had described, was incredible. The word 'wicked' didn't seem to fit her, 'terrifying' was more like it, and she was aware that also applied to her unbreakable determination to see that she herself should be married, not for her happiness but for her own prestige. The man she had chosen to hunt this time was rich. He was half-American and his business was to do with the new-fangled automobiles, one that promised to make him richer still. But was it coincidence that he hadn't called on her in the past week? She knew he was due to go back

255

to America – perhaps he had already gone – but either way it didn't matter, because she had braced herself to face her mother's fury when her answer to him would have been 'no'.

She now walked towards her father and looked down on his bent head, and when she said softly, 'You know what I would like at this moment, Father?' he turned his face up towards her and she saw it had become drained of all colour. He didn't respond but just stared at her, and so she went on, 'What I would like is a large glass of port without lemon,' to which he answered with a nod of his head and saying, 'It's a good idea, but at this time in the day it'll be remarked upon.'

'Not if I go and fetch it myself. There'll be no-one on guard in the dining-room now. I can slip in the side door.'

He put out a hand and patted her arm, and when he went to rise heavily from his chair she said, 'Go and sit by the fire,' and as she hurried out he did just this, after pulling an easy chair closer to the hearth, for he felt chilled to his very core.

It wasn't a chill caused by the atmosphere but by his self-knowledge that he was a failure of a man: fifty-one years old and still in thrall to his father. And because his daughter had recognised this, she had spoken to him as she had never done before, kindly, even lovingly. When she returned with the port they would drink together; but he would have just one, at least now; later he would drink himself into a stupor and blot out the thought that he had to face his father again tomorrow.

2

James Lawson had never before knocked on the door of The Little Manor to gain entry; he had always walked straight in. But now the situation was different, for the houses were no longer as one. He had walked along the crisp, snow-covered ground that lay between them and as he had passed the end of the yard, he had seen two men at work there, one exercising Lady and her foal, two men whom up to a few days ago he had thought of as *his* men, *his* servants, if he had thought about them at all, and he had to admit to himself they represented the cleavage that had taken place.

He stood on the doorstep. It had been cleared of snow, and this fact brought him to clearing his boots on the ornamental iron scraper that lay to the side of the door, the while he wondered at his action, for he couldn't remember ever doing it before. Whatever condition his boots had been in, they were pulled off by his butler or his footman in the hall, and house shoes would be there to replace them, so he did not question further when his hand went up to the iron handle of the bell-pull.

When Carrie Jones opened the door she exclaimed on a high note, 'Oh! Good afternoon, sir,' and he found himself answering, 'Good afternoon,' hesitating on her name before adding, 'Jones.' He could not remember ever exchanging a word with this servant. Her face was familiar, but that was to be expected, because he must have passed her every day for years.

'It's a snifter out there, sir, isn't it?'

She was talking to him and he said, 'Yes; yes it is, it's very cold.'

As she helped him off with his coat she said, 'The master's in the sitting-room, sir.'

The sitting-room. That room had always been called the sitting-room in this house; in The Manor it was the drawing-room.

'Thank you.'

As he left her to cross the hall towards the far door it opened, and into the hall came a young woman. She was wearing a loose woollen-type gown, but it could not hide the mound of her stomach. Her shining brown hair lay in rolls on the back of her head. He stopped dead at the sight of her. He couldn't believe she was Marie Anne, his daughter whom he had last seen almost sixteen months ago. There was no semblance left of the child he had known. Here was a young woman, a pregnant young woman.

She had stopped too, one hand still on the door handle, that is until she saw him slowly lift his arms towards her, and then she was running into them, whimpering, 'Oh, Father! Father!'

As James Lawson clasped his younger daughter in his arms he had a great desire to cry. He knew that for the moment he was unable to speak, even to mention her name, because he was realising that for the first time in his life his arms had enfolded the child who had been conceived out of a battle of wills and reared under hate.

'Oh, Father, it's good to see you' – she had pressed herself from his embrace but, elbows bent, they were still holding hands breast high between them – 'I'm sorry for all the trouble I'm causing. I . . . I don't want it, Father. Believe me, I don't want it.'

'Shh! . . . shh!' The sound of his own voice seemed to give him courage and he said, 'It's all right, I understand.' Then there was a tight smile as he made a moue with his mouth before asking softly, 'Where is he?'

'In the sitting-room; but he's just nodded off, and he generally sleeps for half an hour after lunch. Come . . . come along here.'

She was leading him by the hand now, out of the hall and along a short corridor towards a door which led into the west wing.

He couldn't remember how many years it was since he had been in this wing. It must have been some time before his mother had died. She used it for what she called her retreat, but from that time it hadn't been closed up, but just ignored, because his father wanted only the Makepeaces and a maid to see to him during the odd times he came back here.

They were now in a small hall, with a corridor going off one side and a flight of shallow stairs off the other, and these led to the one-time nursery. Perhaps it was the effect of the snow outside, but every place looked extra bright and shining.

Marie Anne said, 'Come into my little sitting-room; it's warm in there,' and added, 'Oh, it's lovely to see you, Father, and to be able to have a chat with you.'

He did not answer, And with you, Marie Anne, because he was amazed at the change in this girl who was now, to all intents and purposes, a young woman and, strangely, so like his mother used to be, for he recalled now that she, too, had used this room. He noticed at once that the carpet, curtains and covers had been replaced; in fact, the whole place must have been redecorated to suit his father's beloved grand-daughter.

When they were seated on the couch by the open log fire, she repeated, 'I'm sorry, Father. I didn't want all this change; I mean, the things Grandfather's doing, believe me. I think if I had known he was going to be so drastic, I wouldn't have returned.'

'My dear, you had to.'

'Oh no, Father; no, not really. Not after I escaped from Aunt Martha's. Oh! Father,' she said as she shook her head.

He too now shook his in agreement as he said, 'Oh, you have no need to tell me about Martha, Marie Anne. You were on my conscience for a long time, knowing that your mother had sent you to her.'

'Well, when Aunt Martha was for putting me in that home, I don't know what I would have done if it hadn't been for her maid, Miss Foggerty . . . Sarah. She it was who saved me from so many things. I thought I would be able to manage on my own, but now I know I never could have, not in London and' – her voice dropped – 'the way I was placed.' She now put a hand on his knee as she asked quietly, 'Would you meet Sarah? I mean, Miss Foggerty. Grandfather has appointed her his house-keeper, and although she is on the staff now, she will always be my friend.'

'Well, if you would like me to; yes. Yes, of course.'

He watched her rise and with a natural movement pull the bell-rope to the side of the fireplace before sitting down again, and when the door opened and Fanny Carter appeared she said to her, 'Would you tell Miss Foggerty, Fanny, that I would like to see her for a moment if she's not too busy?'

'Yes, miss. Yes, miss.'

When the door closed on the cheery voice James looked hard at this daughter of his. She was acting as mistress of the house and in such a way that would have been an object lesson to his wife.

Leaning towards her father, and her face bright now, Marie Anne said, 'You won't have to mind, Father, what she says. You'll see, or you'll hear immediately that she's Irish, and she comes out with the funniest things. And she has no idea of place. To her, everyone is the same.' Then, her smile fading, she added; 'There were times, Father,

260

when it was only her humour that dragged me up from the depths of misery and saved me from doing something silly. I was so unhappy there. Oh, so unhappy.'

His hand now came on hers and he said, 'If anyone is to blame for that, it's me. Oh yes, yes, it is. I should have made a stand years ago, and it's only recently I have had to face the fact, been forced to face the fact, that I am a weak and self-indulgent man and that all you've gone through since you were a child I could have prevented had I been other than I am.'

When there came a tap on the door Marie Anne took her hand away and rose to her feet to greet Sarah, saying, 'I would like you to meet my father, Sarah.'

As James Lawson attempted to rise to his feet Sarah put out her hand as if pushing him back and in a conciliatory voice she said, 'Don't fash yourself, sir. Don't fash yourself; but I am very pleased to meet you.'

When James took her outstretched hand and it was shaken twice, he said, 'I am very pleased to meet you, too, Miss Foggerty, because I learn you have been very good indeed to my daughter when she needed help and a friend.'

'Oh, it's worked both ways, sir, both ways, because I took her under my wing the first day I saw her; and it isn't often one gets prizes for rescuing lost birds. And haven't I been given one out of all proportion to my deservin'!'

Marie Anne saw that her father was smiling; then she thought he was going to burst out laughing when Sarah said, 'Could I get you something, sir? A cup of tea? It's on three o'clock. Miss usually has a tray about this time.'

James now turned a swift glance on Marie Anne. She too was smiling, and he said to her, 'That would be very nice, wouldn't it?'

'Yes, Father; yes, it would.' Then turning to Sarah, she said, 'That would be nice, Sarah. Yes, please.'

'No sooner said than done; I'll see to it meself, miss.'

The door had hardly closed on her when James covered his eyes with his hand and bit on his bottom lip, and Marie Anne, leaning against his arm, said, 'I know what you're thinking, Father. She is, as she thinks, carrying out the housekeeper's post and she's playing it as she sees it should be done. It's impossible to be dull where she is, Father. Fanny and Carrie like her; although I don't know so much about Mrs Makepeace. She's ruled the roost for so long she can't see any need for a house-keeper. However, Sarah will get round her, never fear. But imagine, Father, if Mrs Piggott heard her. She would collapse with hands in the air, wouldn't she?'

'Oh yes, indeed, indeed.'

'Father' – Marie Anne's face was straight now – 'I learned about life under Sarah, life such as I never imag-ined anyone could live. Her sister lives on the third floor of a tenement. She has ten children and an unhelpful husband, and Sarah has helped to support them for years out of a salary of six shillings a week.'

'Six shillings a week?'

'Yes, Father. That's what Aunt Martha paid her, and she was on duty night and day. It was to this family she took me, the only place she had to take me when Aunt Martha was, as Sarah said, hell-bent on getting me into a house for fallen women. And that's how we came to live in the two attic rooms above her sister. But there were three long flights of stairs, Father, and everything had to be brought up or taken down: coal, water, everything. Oh, I learned a lot about life and kindness and love, and also, Father, and you'll never believe it, I learned how to earn a living with my drawing.'

'Earn a living with your—?'

'You know, my caricatures.'

'Really! You've managed to sell them?'

'Yes' – her head was wagging proudly now – 'and to a daily newspaper. At first, they wanted to give me only four shillings a drawing, but Sarah, being there, demanded five, and we got it. That was . . . oh, in December. Then when I thought they had forgotten me I received a letter, asking me to meet the editor at the beginning of the New Year, and he was going to take me on, I think, permanently. Anyway, I would have to supply one or two drawings a week. He was greatly taken with one of them; and you know where I got the idea for that?'

James shook his head, and she went on, 'From nine of the children sitting round the table guzzling lamb stew, arguing with each other as they ate, gnawing at the bones, and so I did a caricature of them and called it "Table Manners". It's funny; I must show it to you. Anyway, I wrote and told him of my changed circumstances and that my name was not Foggerty, and I got such a nice, a really nice letter back from the editor. He was so enthusiastic about my work, and so we have done a deal and I shall be sending sketches each week.'

'Not really!'

'Yes, Father, really. But Pat says he's a daylight robber.'

'Why?'

'Because, Pat says, I should have had at least a pound a sketch, if not more, and when he's up in London he's going to see him and suggest a contract.'

'Well! well! you do surprise me.'

'Yes, Father' – her voice was flat now – 'I suppose I do in all ways.'

His hand now came on her arm as he said softly, 'Don't be offended at what I'm going to say, my dear, but is the father of your child aware of your position?'

She turned her head away now, saying, 'Yes. Yes; as soon as he knew, I understand he went back to Spain.'

'A Spaniard?'

'Yes, Father.' Then she looked him fully in the face. 'He was the music teacher that Aunt Martha chose for me after she had bargained with him to reduce his price from

263

two and six an hour to two shillings.' And here she shook her head as she added, 'There are many kinds of humiliation one can suffer in life, Father.'

'Yes; yes, my dear. But anyway, I'm glad to know who it was: it has cleared my mind, because some people have got it into their heads that it was . . . well, that man McAlister. Yet I couldn't believe it, because my father thinks so highly of him.'

While her father was speaking Marie Anne had pulled herself slowly from him and up to her feet, and her mouth was in a wide gape now as she exclaimed, 'How . . . how dare they! I mean . . . Mr McAlister? He . . . he's a fine gentleman and I'm here today only because of him. He saw me playing the piano in the eating house and recognised me, and he came back here and told Grandpa and . . . and Pat. That's how it started, I mean my return . . . Mr McAlister. Oh, how could they! And him . . . well, him so disfigured.'

'That's . . . that's what I thought.'

'Who is saying this, Father?'

'It seems to be the rumour among the servants, because your Grandfather has invited the man here to dinner, I understand.'

'Yes; yes, he has, because both he and Pat consider him a very clever man: he's really a sculptor, you know, and all the work he does here he takes to the priory near where The Courts are. That's what they called the slum houses where I lived with Sarah. Grandfather insisted on going to see this place. He was horrified. And it was Mr McAlister who arranged for Grandfather and Pat to stay at the priory, and that's where Mr McAlister took me to meet him. Oh, that man's done everything in his power to help me; and for them to say such a thing!'

'Treat it as servants' gossip, my dear.'

'But servants' gossip gets about, Father; you know it does.' And now she added almost angrily, 'They'll all be waiting for my child to be born to see if it's got a brand on it.'

'Oh no! No, no!' He shook his head. 'Come here and sit down again. I'm sorry I mentioned it, but I'm so glad you've given me your confidence.'

'Well, Father, perhaps if it *had* been him he wouldn't have left me like the other one did.'

'Was he young?'

She sat down now, and her voice was without lightness as she said, 'No, he wasn't; he . . . he was almost forty.'

'Blast him!' came as a muttered growl, and Marie Anne said, 'You must blast us both then, Father, because . . . because I thought I was in love with him. But then, of course, I didn't know what love was, and . . . and still don't.'

Without her usual tap on the door, it swung open and Sarah entered the room pushing a trolley, the top shelf laden with tea things, the lower one holding buttered tea cakes and scones.

'Will I pour out for you?' said Sarah.

'No, thank you, Sarah; I'll manage.'

'Well, try the buttered teacakes first, while they're hot,' and she was about to turn away when the door opened again and Emanuel Lawson stood there, saying, 'Well, well! This is what happens when I drop off for a minute.'

'I was coming in to you, Father, but you were—'

'Sit where you are, James. Sit where you are. I'm going to sit here, and if our Miss Foggerty will bring another cup and saucer, I too will have a cup of tea.'

'At this very minute, sir, this very minute.'

As Sarah hurried out, Emanuel leaned across to his son, saying, 'I had never had so much light entertainment in my life until that one came into my establishment. It isn't what she says, it's the way she says it; that and her voice. You've just got to hear it, and you laugh.'

James nodded with a smile, saying, 'Yes, it's her voice.

You wouldn't have to ask her where she came from.'

'Are those toasted teacakes?'

'Yes, Grandfather,' said Marie Anne, as she held out the plate towards him.

'Strange,' Emanuel said, 'but *I've* never been given toasted teacakes with *my* three o'clock cup of tea? Whose idea was this?'

For answer, Marie Anne said, 'Your housekeeper's, Grandpa.'

'Oh aye! another one of her innovations? The morning porridge has changed, too, James, you know: it has more salt in it and it's made with milk, and believe me, although I wouldn't dare let this come to Maggie's ears, it's a great improvement.'

They were laughing together when the door opened again and Sarah entered with a cup and saucer and small plate, and turning to Marie Anne, she asked, 'Will I not pour for you? It'll save you gettin' to your feet.'

After a quick nip at her bottom lip, Marie Anne said, 'Do that, Sarah, please; yes.'

So Sarah pushed the trolley to one side and deftly poured out the three cups of tea; also, she brought up a small table and placed it at her master's side; then another, a little larger, she put between Marie Anne and her father; and all without a word. But as if she had just accomplished some handiwork, she dusted her hands lightly down the small frilled apron that hung from the waist of her pale blue print uniform dress, and said, 'Well, I'll leave you to it to look after yourselves;' and smiling from one to the other, lastly at Marie Anne, her smile seeming to ask, how am I doing? she turned and went out.

After a moment's silence, Marie Anne handed the plate to her father, saying, in a good imitation of Sarah, 'Would you be for havin' one of these, or are you rather for a scone?'

And James, answering in like fashion, said, 'If it's all the same to you, I'd be after a scone.'

Sitting back in his chair and chewing on a piece of the teacake, Emanuel realised he was watching his son laugh, and he asked himself how long since, if ever, he had seen his son laughing wholeheartedly. He must have forgotten for the moment what his visit portended and, too, that his lightness of manner might not be all due to the Irish woman's chatter but also to the fact that he was talking with his daughter, which he had certainly never seen him do before; in fact, not with either of his daughters. And he knew that James had been here for quite a while, because when one of the maids had come in to make up the fire he had been awake and she had said, 'Mr James has come, sir, but Miss Marie Anne took him along to her sitting-room; she didn't wish to disturb you.'

That must have been all of twenty minutes ago or more and he had sat there waiting until he had become impatient. And so here he was with his son, who appeared to be somewhat different from yesterday, even though he must know that something dire still awaited him . . .

Between them they cleared the plates of teacakes and scones, and after a second cup of tea and perfunctory conversation Marie Anne rose to her feet, saying, 'I'll leave you for a time to have a talk with Maggie and see how the dinner is getting on, because I know she wasn't pleased with Sarah's menu this morning. For a start, she snorted at the Irish broth, saying her Scotch broth had been good enough up to now, and whoever had heard of putting a sauce on lemon sole? Sauces always took the taste of the food away, et cetera, et cetera. So, Grandfather, don't be surprised if you get Welsh broth tonight and tartare sauce so tart you'll never want it again.'

Emanuel was laughing as he, too, bantered, 'It's a wonder your Irish wizard hasn't got round Maggie before now; her powers must be waning.'

'Oh, give her a chance, Grandpa, Maggie is a tough proposition. But don't worry, your housekeeper' – and she stressed the word – 'will succeed in the end; she always does.'

After Marie Anne had left the room an embarrassed silence fell between father and son, until at last the old man said, 'I suppose that's the first time you've seen her in this long while?'

'Yes, Father, it's well over a year.'

'Well, what d'you think?'

James moved uneasily under the question before he said, 'She's so changed. She's no longer even a girl, and you can't imagine her ever being wild and of a fiery temperament. That seems to be all gone.'

'Oh, don't you believe it. Her wildness might be subdued, for she can no longer run like a hare: that ankle of hers is still painful too; but as for the temper, I wouldn't want to be the one to cause her to use it.' Here Emanuel paused and stared into the fire; then sharply turning his head towards his son, he said, 'I'll tell you this much, James, I don't give a damn what anybody says about her giving birth to an illegitimate child. I only know that she has given me a new lease of life, just being with me, near me. In the short while she's been here she's turned this house into the home it once was when your mother was alive. Two years ago, before your daughter left, I was planning for my demise, and my worry then was what would happen to her when I was gone; who would understand her, who would look after her, and now here she is looking after me and bringing joy into my life. I now have a purpose in living. Of course, I have also realised that I have no power to forestall death. It could be tonight, tomorrow, or years ahead; but just in case it is tonight or tomorrow is the reason why I have made all these changes, some of which – in fact, all of them – must seem unfair to you. So this is why I wanted to see you privately and put something to you which will undoubtedly seem even more unfair. However, first I will tell you that The Manor is yours. I have willed it to you. But as I said yesterday, how long you keep it in its present condition will be entirely up to you, providing you cut down and turn it into a home run by a reasonable number of staff. It's not too late to put your foot down, man; I'm telling you it's not too late.' There was no need for him to point out on whom he had to put his foot down, but he went on, 'I will never see you pushed up against the wall; but what help I give you will be done in private, for I don't want anyone in that house thinking that I'm still backing you. You understand?'

James stared at his father, but made no comment, so Emanuel went on, 'Now for the part that isn't going to be so pleasant. You own twenty per cent of the shares of the business, so what I want you to do is sell me ten per cent. On the face of it you would be selling them to me; I would give you three times their worth, but I would not keep them for long before I passed them on to Pat. Why? I see you are asking. Well, be honest, James, has Vincent any quality at all that would entitle him to be managing director of the business? On the other hand, Pat is not only more naturally qualified but he has worked for such a position, whereas Vincent wastes his time in that office. He wasted it when he knew I was just a door or so away from him; so what he does now . . . well, I suppose only you could tell me, James, but you won't. Anyway, you were never very good at giving orders, were you? and over the years, since I retired anyway, you must admit you've left all that side to Pat. So you can understand why I want Pat to be the governing body and adviser to Marie Anne, and he won't be able to act that part unless his shares give him the power. So if you were to sell me half of yours, this would bring his holding up to twenty-nine per cent.'

'He wouldn't stand for it, Father; I mean, Vincent.'

'He need know nothing about it. This could be done quietly by our solicitors and it would not be made evident until you died, when anything Vincent had to say wouldn't hurt you; and then Pat would legally take your place as managing director. In any case, whatever you decide to do, James, I mean to make it impossible for Vincent to assume that position.'

James looked steadily at his father. He had always been slightly afraid of this man, and now he knew why: it was his indomitable spirit; and at this moment he recognised that it was from this man that his wayward, wild and stubborn youngest child had inherited her character. Nothing of himself was in Marie Anne, nor of the woman who bore her. Oh no, there was no vestige of her mother in Marie Anne. He wondered why he hadn't recognised this before, why it hadn't become evident. Likely, because, over the past month and up until yesterday, his father had never shown his hand. Yet, all things being said, his father's present attitude should have engendered a greater fear. Strangely, he no longer felt afraid of him or even uneasy in his presence. Perhaps he was feeling tired, weary of it all and, as had been his wont, was taking the easy way out. All he had wanted to do was eat a little, drink a little, sleep a lot, and rest. Perhaps in a house like this. Funny about that. He looked about him. There was a strange atmosphere here. It was as if, were he to put his arm along the back of the couch, his mother would be standing there and she would be stroking his hair, bringing the parting to one side or the other, saying, 'Don't have your parting in the middle, James,' and he would say to her, 'I've told you, Mother, it grows like that.'

'What's the matter?' Emanuel broke into his reverie.

'Nothing, Father.'

'You've . . . you've lost your colour, you've gone pale.'

'I'm . . . I'm a bit tired.'

'And upset I suppose. It's understandable. I'm sorry that I've had to speak like this.'

'Oh, don't worry, Father. Have it your own way.' He was about to add, You always have, but checked himself, remembering that this man had been most generous to him and his family for the best part of a lifetime. If only Veronica had been a different . . . But then he remembered he had once loved her, although he was certain now that she had never really loved him. Tolerated him, yes; but only for a short time. He had been a means to an end. It was from then on he had found solace in eating and drinking; he hadn't always had a pot belly, but had once been as slim as Pat was now.

It was as if thinking about his wife caused him to say suddenly, 'I didn't tell you, Father, that some months ago I wrote to the boys; or at least to David, who passes the letters on to John. As you know, John was never a hand with the pen. Anyway, David had asked me why I did not go out there, some time, for a holiday. I told him I couldn't get away.' He paused and laughed before he added, 'I couldn't bear the thought of being seasick during that long journey; and so I suggested that perhaps he should write to his mother and invite her. Well, two days ago, I had a reply, and she had a letter, too. David told me he had asked her to go over, but so far she hasn't mentioned it to me.'

'Well, it would be a good thing for you if she did go. It would give you a chance to pick up your old friend again. Do you still see—?'

Before James could reply the door opened and Pat entered, saying, 'Oh, hello, Father,' then added, 'By! it's cold out there; enough to freeze you.' He walked past his grandfather's chair and straight to the fire and held his

271

hands out to the flame before turning to the old man and saying, 'I met Don McAlister on my walk and invited him along for a meal; d'you mind?'

'Mind? Not at all. As I've told you, that man's welcome at any time of the day or night in my house.' He now leaned towards James and said, 'I don't suppose you've met Don McAlister, have you, James?'

James shook his head: 'No, not that I can recall,' he said.

'Well, I doubt if you'd ever forget him if you had. That's his name, but he's known hereabouts as The Branded Man or some such, because he has a scarred face and has it covered up.'

'Oh. The man who found Marie Anne in London; the monk?'

'No, no;' and Pat laughed now; 'he's no monk. He was brought up by the Brothers in a priory, and he tells some very interesting stories of the life these Brothers lead.' Pat laughed now, saying, 'Apparently, when he didn't want to become a priest, not even a Brother, they sent him off to Rome for a time. Oh, I think you would find him very interesting, Father. What about you staying to dinner?'

'Oh no,' James answered; 'they'll be expecting me back.'

'Well' – it was Emanuel speaking now – 'why not send someone down and tell them you're having dinner in your father's house for once.'

'Yes, do that.' Pat nodded at his father. 'I'll send Mike down.' Then putting out a restraining hand towards his father, he said, 'Don't say no; it isn't often we three get together.'

At this, James nodded in agreement, saying, 'No; you're right there, Pat, it isn't often we get together. Well, thank you; yes, I would like that.'

'Good. I'll go and see Mike.'

'Where've you left McAlister?'

272

Pat grinned at his grandfather, saying, 'In the sitting-room. Marie Anne's with him there, and also your housekeeper, so I should imagine the exchanges will be lively, because Miss Foggerty seems to know a lot about Mr McAlister and he, in turn, knows equally as much about her. Anyway, shall I bring him along here?'

'No.' His grandfather lifted his hand. 'No, don't do that, Pat; but you come back for a few minutes, I want a word with you. Then we'll go along to the sitting-room together.' . . .

At that moment, in the sitting-room, there was definitely an exchange going on between Don McAlister and Miss Sarah Foggerty for, on entering the room, she had remarked on the fact that instead of donning his big soft felt hat he was wearing a close-fitting peaked cap. She was saying, 'Did you make it yourself?'

'Yes, Sarah, I made it myself.'

'It looks as if it's leather.'

'It *is* soft leather.'

When Marie Anne put in on a reprimanding note, 'Sarah, please!' Sarah turned to her, saying, 'Oh, I'm just remarking on the fact that it's an improvement,' and turning towards Don again, she added, 'Why didn't you think about it before?'

'It never crossed my mind, Sarah, until I was invited into a family atmosphere, and I've always understood it is bad manners to wear a hat in the presence of ladies.'

'Well, we've done that much for you anyway.'

'You've done more than you'll ever know for me, Sarah, as has Miss Marie Anne, too.'

'You know, when I was young,' said Sarah, 'we had a Jewish friend. He was kind to our lot with oddments of clothes and things. He lived only three doors away. He always wore a hat that shape.'

'Did he? Well then, that's something in my favour; I feel nearer the Lord now.'

'Nearer the Lord?'

'Yes, of course, Sarah. You're a Catholic, aren't you? so you're bound to know that our Lord was a Jew.'

'Oh yes; but I feel it would be hard to get a priest, like Father Broadside, say, to admit it.'

'It would that,' said Don.

'You know' – Sarah was looking at Marie Anne now – 'we three knew each other back in the East End, didn't we? even if it was only for a very short time, but since we've come here we all seem changed. Have you noticed that?'

Marie Anne was sitting back in her chair enjoying the exchanges between these two she now thought of as dear friends, when Sarah turned to her, saying, 'Well, what d'you make of it, Marie Anne.'

'I don't know, Sarah,' she said; 'I haven't given it thought. I leave all the deep thinking to you.'

'Now, don't take the mickey. Anyway' – Sarah turned back to Don again – 'talking about religion creates wars. Would you like a cup of tea?'

'I would, Sarah, I would,' said Don, smiling widely.

'Well, you'll have it in a minute.' As she went to turn away Sarah gave him one last look and, as always having to have the last word, she said, 'It is an improvement.'

'I'm sorry, Don,' said Marie Anne; 'she doesn't mean to be rude.'

'Oh, please! Please, don't apologise for Sarah. I think I've told you before, she's like a breath of fresh air; someone who speaks her mind. And, you know, she's right in her observation about us all being changed, because you no longer are the girl who lived at the top of Ramsay Court, and Sarah's no longer your guardian and watchdog, because here she is carrying out a task in a post which gives her a feeling of independence. Nevertheless I expect she'll keep on her job of watchdog.'

'Oh yes, I'm sure of that, and at the same time I'm glad

of it, because, you know, it is a good feeling to have someone to watch over you with kindness and love, for it's something I had never experienced before.' There was no smile on her face now. 'For all the days of my life I shall be grateful to her. She was the first woman to show me any affection. Now you, Don, what about you?' she asked softly. 'How do you think you've changed?'

He did not immediately answer, but leaned forward, elbows on knees, his hands joined between them, and the mask side of his face towards her so that she couldn't see the expression in his eyes, before he said, 'The change in me would be very difficult for me to explain and for you to understand. When, eight years ago, I left the precincts of the Brothers' house and came to live in Rill Cottage, I imagined life had opened its doors wide for me; but I was mistaken. Back in the House most of the Brothers were my friends, but once I was settled here I experienced enmity and hate, and it was painful until it was eased a little by Farmer Harding and his wife and the river warden, Bob Talbot. People are afraid of the unusual, or of anything they don't understand. Old wives' tales flourish today almost as much as they did at the beginning of the last century. So, except when I made my twice-yearly visit to the Brothers, I experienced loneliness and isolation. Very often, although I wanted my freedom, I almost made up my mind to go back and join the Brothers, and they all seemed to be waiting for me to do just that. Yet, although there was warm companionship among most of that group of men, each had his own private aloneness to contend with. Aloneness, you know is different from loneliness, being made up of need, despair, and in many cases, rejection. I think there is in each of us a part that I can only describe as aloneness. In the case of the Brothers, I am sure they are helped by giving themselves over entirely to the spirit of God. Probably, for the ordinary man this feeling takes him into marriage, and not

275

only for procreation but for friendship and comfort. He is, of course, lucky if it is crowned by love.' Suddenly straightening up and putting his hand to his brow, he said, 'Oh, dear Lord!' and turning to her, he said, 'Oh! Miss Marie Anne, I lost myself; I forgot who I was talking to.'

Her eyes were wide, her mouth slightly open, and as she swiftly put out a hand and laid it on his, she said softly, 'I hope this is the first time of many that you will forget yourself. I am no longer a very young girl, Don; my experiences in London piled the years on me, so much so that I cannot believe that I am nearly seventeen, for to Grandpa I am still a child and, to Pat, a very young girl. Only to Sarah and now to you am I a young woman, and as a young woman I recognise that I'm bringing into the world an illegitimate child and that later it will be shown contempt; even now, as soon as I move out of the precincts of this house and grounds the finger of shame will be pointed at me. I have committed a great sin, the greatest a young person of my class could commit, and there's no hope that it'll be even condoned by any friend of the family.'

When there was the rattle of the tea trolley again outside the door Marie Anne quickly withdrew her hand, at which he said, 'You must not think that way; we must talk more some time, my dear.'

As the door was being pushed open Sarah's voice came to them, saying, 'I don't know why I'm putting it on a trolley; a tray would've done. Anyway, here it is.'

Don had risen to his feet and now said, 'You shouldn't have gone to all this trouble, Sarah. There was no need for it.'

'Take what's being offered and thank God for it.' Sarah grinned at him, and he came back with, 'I will, Sister Sarah; I'll offer a novena, specially for this tray.'

'Now, don't you start scoffing me, Mr McAlister, else I'll have nobody on my side;' and after nodding at him she turned to Marie Anne, saying, 'I know what you're thinking: you're thinking I'm not suitable for this post, and perhaps you're right.'

'Yes; yes, I think you are right, Miss Foggerty; I'll see you tomorrow morning in my office.'

'Do that, ma'am. Do that. I have me bag packed already.' And with an exaggerated swish of her skirt, she turned about and flounced from the room.

They were laughing quietly together when Marie Anne said, 'Seriously, Don, I'll have to have a talk with her; but I don't know if it will do much good. Anyway, she uses such chit-chat only with you and me. She really does try to play the matronly housekeeper, and up to a point she has succeeded. The girls like her, even Katie in the kitchen, and that hasn't pleased Maggie Makepeace. And the men in the yard, they are very respectful to her. As for Grandpa, I'm sure he looks to her for amusement.'

'Well, don't expect me to make excuses for her, Miss Marie Anne, because I think she is a fine woman with a very warm heart.'

Ignoring this, Marie Anne said, 'Pour yourself a cup of tea and eat that toast while it's hot.'

As he helped himself to the tea and toast she said, 'Are you comfortable in your cottage?'

'Yes; yes, I'm very comfortable. You could say it suits me. But I think you would find it very shabby. The carpet has known no pile for years, and all the covers are well patched and the curtains very faded. But having said that, it has a fine open fireplace, which gives it a homely feeling; and the main thing is, it's mine.'

'Was your aunt your mother's sister or your father's.'

'I don't know; I knew nothing at all of my parents or their families; I know only that, as a baby, I was discarded.'

'Oh, I'm sorry; I wasn't meaning to pry.'

'I know that, I know that. When the weather changes

perhaps you and Sarah might care to walk along and see my abode. But then, it's a good mile from here, and that's taking the shortest way along the back, and then through the wood. Going by the road you would have to go through Harding's farmyard and across a couple of fields.'

On the sound of voices coming from somewhere in the hall he said quietly, 'Let me say one thing more: the fact that I've been welcomed into your grandfather's home has meant and is meaning more to me than any words I could use . . . could express.'

As the door was opening and her family entered, Marie Anne was able to mutter only, 'Well, we are more than pleased to see you, I in particular.'

3

It was the end of February and an unusually calm day, with the sun shining. In the night there had been a smattering of snow, but this had thawed in the morning sun; and now it was two o'clock in the afternoon and the air was quite warm, so much so that Marie Anne opened the neck of her green coat and took off her fur-lined gloves as she bent over to stroke Mr Harding's prize sheepdog.

At one side of her stood Mrs Harding, and a short distance away her husband was talking to Nathaniel Napier.

Marie Anne had met Mr Napier on the other two occasions she had visited the farm. He was new to the district, having bought a small farm adjoining Mr Harding's, and the farmer had taken him under his wing for, as he said, the fellow was a bit of a greenhorn where farming was concerned.

Both the farmer and Mr Napier were now laughing at the tussle taking place between Don and his newly acquired friend, who was showing strong objection to having been introduced to a lead.

Marie Anne and Mrs Harding had joined in the laughter, when there came into view over the low stone wall a woman rider walking by her horse, which appeared to be lame. But when she was about to pass the opening to the farmyard Mr Harding hurried forward, saying, 'Good afternoon, Miss Evelyn. Having trouble?'

'Oh, good afternoon, Mr Harding. It's his left hind hoof.'

'Oh! Well, now, we can likely see to this,' and he turned to call to his new neighbour, saying, 'Having been a bit of a vet at one time, this should be right up your street.'

With the exception of Marie Anne, the others had moved towards the road. Mr Napier, now smiling at Evelyn, said, 'I can but look;' then gently picking up the horse's hind leg he turned it to expose the shoe, and his fingers moving gently within it he seemed to shake his head when he said, 'Oh. Oh, here's the culprit. Poor fellow. Poor fellow!' then looking up at Farmer Harding, he said, 'Have you a pair of pincers handy?'

At this the farmer darted back into the yard and to his tack room, and within a minute he was handing Mr Napier one of two pairs of pincers.

'Would these suit?'

'I'd rather have the smaller.'

Having taken these, he now turned his head to one side and addressed Evelyn: 'Hold his head, will you? Talk to him.'

He paused a moment, examining the upturned hoof; then muttered, 'It looks to me like a nail, and I don't know how far it's in, so would you mind, Mr Harding, helping the young lady to hold him steady.'

He gave a sudden twist, then almost fell on his back as the horse reared.

'There now. There now. It's all over.' He patted the haunch. 'It's all over.' And he held out the pincers gripping the nail, saying, 'That must have given him gyp.'

'Well, I never!' Farmer Harding said. 'Look at that!'

Evelyn looked at it; then she looked at Nathaniel Napier and she said, 'Thank you. Thank you very much indeed. It's a very ugly nail, and rusty.'

'Yes, it is rusty. And it had gone through the side of the hoof and into the flesh. I think you had better tell one of your men to get a bucket of hot water and carbolic and then ease his foot into it, as hot as he can bear it. He won't like it at first, but the hotter the better; and to make sure, I think you should call in his vet. You'd better take this with you and show him what caused the damage.'

When he put the nail into her gloved hand, she looked at it for a long moment before she again raised her eyes to his, saying, 'Thank you; I'm very much obliged.'

She did not immediately urge the horse forward but turned to where Marie Anne was now standing nearby, and they looked hard at each other; and it was Evelyn who spoke first. In a very low voice she said, 'How are you?'

'I'm all right, Evelyn, thank you. I'm . . . I'm on my way back, so may I walk with you?'

Evelyn shrugged her shoulders for a moment, then muttered, 'It's a public road.' Then, as if she were sorry for her reply, she added, 'Yes, if you wish.'

Marie Anne turned to say goodbye to Mr Harding and Mr Napier, then in a louder voice she called into the farm-yard, 'Goodbye, Mrs Harding. And thank you for the drink.'

'You're welcome, miss, very welcome any time.'

And to Don, who was still struggling to control the puppy, she called, 'Goodbye, Mr McAlister,' and he, lifting the puppy up into his arms, called, 'Goodbye, Miss Lawson.'

They had walked some distance along the road when Evelyn surprised Marie Anne by saying, 'When . . . when is your baby due?'

'Oh.' It seemed that Marie Anne would have to think before she could answer, 'April, perhaps a little into May. According to Mrs Makepeace it could be up to a fortnight early or a fortnight late.' Her embarrassment showing in her rising colour, they walked on in silence for the next few minutes until again it was Evelyn who spoke, 'Are you afraid?'

'Afraid of what?'

'Well, of having a baby. What else would you be afraid of?'

Marie Anne walked on without answering for a few seconds, and then she said, 'I suppose I am, in a way, if I let myself think about it.' This time she did not add Mrs Makepeace's prediction that a first birth can be very painful but that you forget about it immediately afterwards. Sarah had had some strong words to say about Maggie's country chatter.

Then when Marie Anne suddenly stopped walking and turned and faced her sister, Evelyn had no other option but to pull the horse to a standstill. And now she stared at this young woman so unlike the Marie Anne she remembered, who was speaking vehemently to her. 'I am not a bit sorry for what has happened to Mother or anyone else in the house, except yes, for Father. I *am* sorry for him, and I am both ashamed and sorry that I ever struck you and said those awful things. The only thing I can say in my defence is, I did not understand about love or feelings or anything else at that period. But I have made up for my ignorance during the past year and in a very painful way, so, Evelyn, all I ask of you now is, please, forgive me.'

Evelyn looked at her younger sister, she who had been an irritant to her through all her own young days. She had been born when she herself was ten years old and she had looked upon her as an intruder, as someone who had usurped her position as favourite among the four men in the house. Yet, even before Marie Anne came on the scene, she had had little or no attention from her father, her grandfather had never made a great fuss of her, and she had fought with her brothers. Nevertheless, at that time she had been the only daughter, and she had found great satisfaction when she realised that her mother disliked her new child and left her to a series of nannies whose tenures became shorter as the years went by, because they found the child to be unmanageable.

When she saw tears in her sister's eyes she muttered, 'Well, it's all past and done with, so please don't upset yourself. It was my own foolishness in the first place that brought it about.'

'No, no' – Marie Anne shook her head – 'not foolishness. We are driven towards doing things by feelings we never know we possess; at least, I was, and I'm sure it was the same with you.'

On the sound of a galloping horse, they both turned to see Vincent coming towards them.

The sight of him caused Marie Anne to step back on to the green verge, and when he brought his horse to a skidding stop, almost flank to flank with her own mount, Evelyn cried at him, 'Look what you're doing, man! He's in a fretful mood already; he's got a bad foot.'

She was hanging on to her horse's head now, stroking his muzzle and saying, 'There now. There now. It's all right. It's all right.' Then glaring at her brother again, she said, 'Why on earth couldn't you just ride on.'

'What! and miss the opportunity of having a word with my young sister, the young whore from London? Never!'

'Vincent!' It was almost a scream from Evelyn. 'Stop it! and get yourself away.'

'What d'you say? Get myself away, and leave you to be inveigled like all the others into her camp? She's got Grandfather, she's got Pat, and she's put her man-mad claws out around Father, 'cos he's never away from her blasted place. And now you to stand there talking to her. Perhaps it has slipped your mind, sister, that she's responsible for reducing our staff, both in and out. The next thing, she'll be in Newcastle – oh yes, definitely that – cutting down the firm.'

Suddenly he backed his horse until it was in line with Evelyn's and he even nudged her mount forward so that he could get a closer view of Marie Anne; but apparently not close enough for, with a nudge from his knees, his horse side-stepped almost on to the grass verge, and he urged it forward to within an arm's length of Marie Anne, who was standing with her back against the low stone wall; and now brandishing his whip, he cried at her, 'For two pins I'd bring this across your scheming face and your dirty filthy belly, you little whore, you!'

'You dare touch me and it'll be the last thing you'll ever do, I promise you!'

The old wildness that she thought was dead in her was urging her to spring forward and drag him from the saddle, and at this moment she knew that she had always wanted to strike out at him for the times that he had handled her, and in no brotherly fashion. And he dared to call her filthy! With this in her mind she cried, 'You dare to call anybody filthy, you who handled me like no brother should when I was a child and a girl! You lay a finger on me again ever and I'll . . .'

As his whip was lifted high above his head, Evelyn sprang around his horse's head and brought her crop across his thigh with such a force the impact made him jerk in the saddle and his horse to rear, and now she was crying at him, 'Back! back! and get yourself home! D'you hear?'

Gradually he eased his horse to the right of her mount, then with one last fierce look at Marie Anne he spurred the animal into a gallop.

Marie Anne was still leaning back against the wall, one arm around the top of her stomach, the other holding her bent head.

As for Evelyn, she was leaning against her horse's flank, with one arm across the saddle as if for support. Then turning, she moved towards Marie Anne as far as the horse's reins would allow, and she said quietly, 'Come along; you'd better get yourself indoors.'

Marie Anne made no response for some time, for she

was aiming to regain control of herself; she knew that had he brought his whip down on her she would have dragged him from that saddle and, even in her present condition, she would have fought him, endeavouring to claw at the face that had so many times hung over hers while his hands pinched and groped at her body.

Evelyn pulled her horse a little towards the verge so that her hand could go out to Marie Anne, and gently now she drew her from the wall, saying, 'Come along; you'd better get yourself home and . . . and rest.'

When Marie Anne stepped on to the road again she felt that her legs were going to give way beneath her, and she swayed a little; and at this Evelyn took hold of her arm and, jerking the reins of her mount, they moved slowly on down to the gate that opened on to the drive of The Little Manor, where she said, 'Can you manage now?'

And Marie Anne, speaking for the first time, murmured, 'Yes; yes. And thank you, Evelyn. Thank you.'

'Keep out of his way,' Evelyn said now. 'He's dangerous. If you want to visit the farm, keep off the main road. You can get there by going the back way through the wood, can't you?'

Marie Anne nodded at her sister, then said, 'Yes. Yes, I can, thank you. Thank you, Evelyn,' and turned and walked unsteadily away.

Evelyn watched her for a few moments before leading her horse further down the road and through the main gates . . .

When Marie Anne almost collapsed as she entered the house, it brought instant consternation among the staff and demands from her grandfather to know why she had been allowed to go out on her own. The question was directed to Sarah, who replied indignantly that Miss Marie Anne had insisted upon taking walks alone; that again and again she herself had protested, only to be plainly told that she needed to be on her own some of the time.

A few minutes later, Marie Anne was lying on the couch, Emanuel sitting beside her and demanding to know why she was so upset.

Marie Anne looked at him. Were she to say, Vincent threatened me with his whip, and would have used it had it not been for Evelyn, she knew that the house which she had already inadvertently turned upside down would be destroyed. However, she felt that she would have to tell someone, because now her fear of her brother was deeper than ever it had been. His obvious hate of her was such that he really *was* capable of killing her. He had once said to her, 'I could put my hands round your throat and throttle you. I could do it just like this,' and he had actually squeezed her throat; and so she considered that, more than ever now, she had a right to fear him. She could not tell Sarah, for she wouldn't keep it to herself and would want to do something about it. And so she would wait until Pat came home and ask him to tell her father, and let him see to him. All Emanuel got out of her was that she had walked too far . . .

She was in bed when Pat came in to see her, but she had to wait to say anything until Sarah had left the room. After he had listened to her account, he said quietly, 'Leave it to me, I'll see that you're never troubled like that again. Would you like me to call in Dr Ridley?' and she exclaimed, 'Oh no, no! I'll be all right; I just need to rest. It . . . it was the shock and the way I felt towards him as much as what he said to me, because within another minute I think I would've tried to drag him from that horse. It was an awful feeling, frightening.'

His face was straight and his voice very quiet as he said, 'Leave it to me, Marie Anne. Leave it to me.' And as he bent to kiss her, he added, 'I'll be back very shortly. Now you rest . . .'

He made his way to the library, where his grandfather was sitting reading, and he said to him, 'I'm off down to the House for a minute or so. I want a couple of books,' and to this the old man looked up and asked, 'How did you find her?'

Pat hesitated for a moment before answering, 'She's over-tired. She forgets what she's carrying, I think,' then turned and left the room.

The night was dark and the grass was already stiff with frost; the warmth of the afternoon was as if it had never been.

When Pat entered the house his father was crossing the hall and for a moment he looked surprised to see him. 'Anything wrong?' he said.

'Yes, Father, you could say there's something wrong. May I have a word with you?'

'Of course. Of course. Come up into the study.'

In the study, James said, 'Sit down,' and Pat replied, 'No, I'm not going to stay; I just want to tell you that Vincent attacked Marie Anne today.'

Pat watched his father's face screw up in disbelief whilst saying, 'Vincent did what?'

'He attacked her.'

'Never!'

'Yes, Father,' and he went on to tell James all that had happened; then added, 'Grandfather doesn't know anything about it, and she doesn't want him to know. She came in all distressed and she practically passed out, so I understand, but she blamed it on walking too far. Nor has she told anyone else about it, and she's asked me to speak to you, because if he attempts to molest her again, then with or without help she'll do him an injury. So strong is her feeling against him, it almost matches his own, and I've given you word for word the names he called her. It's no wonder that she wanted to claw at his face.'

'Dear God! what next.'

'Yes, Father, what next. She knows she's been the cause of the break-up in this house, but she admits she's not a bit sorry that it has affected Mother and him, only that it has hurt you and me, and yes, even Evelyn, because as she said to me, she's felt very guilty about what she said and did to Evelyn, even though at the time she felt she had cause.'

For a moment James stood with his head bowed, and then he asked, 'Is she all right?'

'She seems to be, but one doesn't know if there'll be repercussions; you see, she's well on in her time. I'm not sure, but I think the child is due in April, some time in April, or thereabouts. I didn't like to probe about that. Anyway, would you like me to . . . well, to deal with this?'

'No; no!' The words were emphatic. 'Oh no! I'll deal with it. Yes, indeed, I'll deal with it. And you say your grandfather doesn't know?'

'No; she didn't want him upset.'

'Well, it will be better if you keep out of it, too. There were no servants about when you came in?'

'No.'

When they reached the hall Green was standing near the door, which he opened as Pat bade his father a quiet good-night; then after he had closed it, James turned to the man who had valeted him for a number of years and under his breath he said, 'Nobody has called, and you haven't seen Mr Patrick.'

'Yes, sir, I understand.'

'Where are the family?'

'The mistress is in the drawing-room with Mr Vincent, and Miss Evelyn, I think, is up in her room.'

'Well, get one of the girls to go and tell her that I would like to see her immediately in the drawing-room.'

'Very good, sir.'

As he entered the drawing-room, James saw that his wife and son were both sitting on the couch and had definitely been in close conversation.

He moved slowly up the room, and when he was

within a couple of yards of them he stopped and, looking at his son, he spoke in a tone that neither Vincent nor his mother had ever before heard him use, 'Get to your feet!'

'What?'

'You heard what I said, and I don't intend to repeat it.'

Vincent cast a sidelong glance at his mother; but she was staring in astonishment at her husband.

Slowly, Vincent pulled himself to the front of the couch, then as if it were an effort, he stood up, and with almost a leer on his face, he said, 'What now, Father?'

'You'll know soon enough.'

His wife, too, now rose from the couch, saying, 'Oh, if it's about this afternoon, I'm aware of it. Evelyn should not have been walking with her and then it wouldn't have happened.'

'Well, it's a damn good job Evelyn was walking with her, because if my brave son here had brought his whip down on her, I can tell you for nothing he wouldn't be standing there with his pampered face as it is now. Even in the state she's in she—'

The opening of the door and Evelyn entering the room stopped his tirade, but Veronica's voice was loud as she immediately addressed her daughter, crying, 'If you had shunned her as you should have done, as I told you before, this incident wouldn't have taken place.'

'And as I've told *you*, Mother, if I had not been there to stop him striking her with his whip and calling her all the vicious and horrible names he could think of, he would have struck her. It was only because I struck *him* that he stayed his hand. From what I know now she hasn't mentioned it to Grandfather, or Vincent wouldn't be standing in this house at this moment, I can tell you that. He'd have been out on his neck.'

Evelyn turned now to her father, saying, 'She hasn't told Grandfather, has she?'

'No, Evelyn; she hasn't told your grandfather because

289

had she done so this noble individual here, whom I hate to call son, would definitely, as you put it, be out on his neck. And I am going to say this to you, Vincent. I am still master of this house; depleted as it is of unnecessary staff, I remain its master, and I'm warning you, if you go near my daughter again – and no matter what she has done, she is still my daughter – if you go near her or molest her in any way, then I shall take it into my own hands to see that you leave this house, and for good. I shall also go further and cut you out of the business, even if I have to go to court to do so. And it isn't just today or yesterday I've harboured such thoughts.' He now turned quickly towards his wife and, his finger stabbing at her, he cried, 'And don't you butt in with your opinion because to me it doesn't matter any more. But you're going to hear mine, and it's just this: I intend to visit my father and my daughter whenever I feel so inclined, and if you don't like it, madam, then I can arrange for a separation, when you can leave with the only one of your brood who has taken after you; and you are well matched, for there's a cruel streak runs through you both. You'll be surprised that I know you have been invited over to see the boys, and if I were you I would avail myself of the opportunity. It would ease the tension all round.' He turned now to Evelyn, who was staring wide-eyed at him, and his voice didn't change as he said, 'I understand that your sister apologised for her past manner towards you. Whether or not you accepted the apology, I don't know, but that you continued to walk with her, I think augured that you had. You also struck out in her defence, and for this I thank you.' Then turning to his wife again, he said, 'Well, I've had my say. It's been over-long in coming, but I advise you, and you too' – he cast his gaze towards Vincent – 'to consider my words very carefully.' Then he turned and walked smartly from the room.

The door had hardly closed on him when Vincent

almost jumped towards Evelyn as she too was about to leave and, gripping her arm, he pulled her round to him, and his words came grinding through his teeth: 'Whose side d'you think you're on? You who hated her guts sucking up—'

'Leave go of me!'

'When I'm ready. And now listen to me. You go down there just once . . .'

When she brought her hand hard across the side of his face, it was his mother's cry, 'Girl! What's come over you?' that drowned his surprised exclamation, and she went on, 'Oh this house, this house. I think I'll go mad. And it's all through her; again and again she's brought disaster upon us.'

'By God! I'll get even with you.' Vincent growled at his sister, the while holding his cheek. 'You of all people to side with them.'

'I wasn't siding with them. I was walking my horse because it had injured a foot, and a farmer friend of the Hardings extracted a nail from it. She was there talking to the Hardings, and when she went to walk along the road, what was I to do? Pull my horse and walk behind her? or tell her to get out of the way? Of course, Vincent, if you had been in my place, you would've run her down, wouldn't you? Well, strangely, and this is for you, too, Mother, I don't feel like that towards her any longer. When she went for me that time she had a reason of which you know nothing. Now you can chew on that. And as for you, dear brother, think twice before you try to handle me again because I am not the young Marie Anne,' and on this she marched from the room, banging the door behind her.

Slowly, Veronica Lawson let herself down on to the couch, and there, holding her head between her hands, she rocked herself from side to side as she said, 'That girl will not rest, that strumpet of a girl will not rest until . . .

until she has finished us and this house. You'll see, she'll be the death of us both.'

At this Vincent went swiftly towards her and, sitting down beside her, he put his arms around her and drew her close, saying, 'By God! she'll not, not as long as I'm alive. You leave her to me, Mother; I'll see to her. One way or another I'll see to her.'

4

Between the time of the attack and the never-to-be-forgotten day the child was born there were to occur a number of incidents which would have a further bearing on the future of those in The Manor.

It was towards the end of March. Marie Anne was sitting at her drawing-board in the small room at the end of the house that she had turned into a studio. Sarah too was there, sitting by the fire and knitting laboriously because, as she said, she was no hand with needles of any kind.

Sarah glanced towards the window. The sun was shining brightly, and there was little wind today, and she sighed as she bemoaned, 'This is another nice day gone. We'll be in April next and it'll be raining cats and dogs and you won't be able to get out before you're ready for bed. Look, dear, why don't we just dander down as far as the gates?'

Marie Anne put down her pencil and sat back in her chair, and wriggling from one side to the other for a moment as if to find a comfortable position. She was carrying the child high and her whole body seemed weighed down with it. She too sighed before she said, 'Oh Sarah, I'm tired of telling you, I . . . I don't want to go out. I'm quite happy where I am.'

'You're as pale as lint, girl.'

'Yes, I may be, but I do wish you would realise that I am quite all right; I mean, without taking walks.'

'As I understand it, you were the one who at one time didn't only walk but you galloped. And don't forget what

293

you said before that last business happened: you said, Sarah let me walk and on my own. That upset me, you know: I felt unwanted; but then I understood, for we all want to be alone with ourselves at some time or other. And don't forget, going by your dates, you have nearly another month to go. That's if the witch-doctor in the kitchen isn't right, when you could have it either two weeks before or two weeks after. Huh! And of course if it's twins, you'll have to go eighteen months!'

At this Marie Anne put her hands on her stomach as she said, 'Oh Sarah, please don't make me laugh, it's painful.'

'Well, it's something if I can make you laugh again, because you haven't done much of that lately, have you?'

Marie Anne made no reply, but she slowly rose from the chair and made her way to the small settee opposite the fire and within an arm's length of Sarah, who put her knitting aside, then took Marie Anne's hand softly, saying, 'What is it, love? Is there something on your mind? Is it . . . is it still him?'

'I . . . I don't know, Sarah' – Marie Anne's voice was breaking – 'I only know I feel a great dread on me.' She now looked into Sarah's eyes. 'I feel as if I'm going to die, as if I'm being willed to die. I don't think I'll ever see the child.'

'Oh my dear! My dear!' Sarah was sitting beside her now, holding her. 'You'll see your child and you'll live to enjoy it, whatever it be. All this feeling is because of that rotten swine. But I can tell you he wouldn't dare come near you now, because I wouldn't put it past your grandpa to go and shoot him if you had any more trouble with him. You know what happened when it leaked out why you were in that state; he went over there and raised hell. Come on now, love, and cheer up, cheer up and believe what the oracle tells you.' She pointed to herself, 'Don't take any notice of the witch-doctor or anybody else, only me.' She thrust her face towards Marie Anne, then smiling, she said, 'Oh I must tell you this bit of news. Things that I hear when I'm not supposed to! Miss Brooks, our Katie, you know, in the kitchen, is supposedly being courted by one Bobby Talbot, the river man. Well, this Bobby notices things and he relates them to Katie; and Katie, who loves delivering news of all kinds, good, bad and indifferent, tells Fanny and Carrie the latest, and it concerns your sister Evelyn.'

'Evelyn?'

'That's who I said, your sister Evelyn, who has taken to riding that way at least twice a week. She might have passed more often, he said, but at least twice a week he saw her, and because that was unusual Mr Bobby was interested, and apparently he had only to walk to a certain rise to see which road the rider took, and he found, what d'you think?'

'I don't know and I can't think, but go on, Sarah.'

'Well, it was towards that new farmer's place. It turns out that Miss Evelyn Lawson visits Mr Nathaniel Napier, and that is the sole object of her riding that way. And it would appear that her visits have grown longer with time. So what d'you think of that?'

Marie Anne did not answer for some moments for she was recalling to mind Mr Nathaniel Napier. He was well spoken, quite gentlemanly, a nice man, she would consider him, and it would be wonderful, she thought, if Evelyn's apparent attraction to him were reciprocated; oh yes, because the guilt she still felt with regard to her sister would then be lifted. But dear! dear! if he were just a poor farmer, her mother would go mad, for she'd had great expectations of at least one daughter making a fine match. Oh, indeed, when their mother got wind of this, as Sarah would put it, there would be hell to pay.

Those were the very words that Vincent was addressing to his sister at that moment: 'Do you realise that when

Mother gets wind of this there'll be hell to pay? And talk about letting yourself down! My God! a farmhand. I can't believe it.'

They were astride their horses, the animals practically flank to flank, with Vincent's mount within an arm's-length of a stone wall, on the other side of which was high shrubbery.

Pointing to a five-bar gate further along the road, Vincent said, 'Well, I can put a stop to this, and by God I will! You go in there and you'll see what'll happen.'

For answer Evelyn swung round in her saddle until she was square with him and in a low tone she said, 'You do! You go inside that gate and say one word and I can tell you this much: I'll be at the registry office as soon as ever it's possible to sign my name to a marriage certificate, and then I'll marry a farm labourer, as you call him. D'you hear? And another thing I'll tell you, brother: you're on very delicate ground here. You've been trailing me, I know you have, but what will happen when I decide to trail you; or at least, to pay someone to trail you? Oh, Grandpa would supply the money just to know what you do with your weekly visits to Newcastle. Overnight visits at times, weekend visits at others, you've never said, not to the women of the family, no. And I think the men imagine you are disporting yourself in some brothel, being a man, but remembering your hatred of females – I remember it from when I was small, but you didn't get your own way with me as you did with Marie Anne – if you had the power, you would torture women, would-n't you? Well now, brother, you be careful. You enter that gate down there and before God I swear to you that I'll go into your past or your present or whatever it is you are enjoying in Newcastle. It couldn't be a mistress, oh no; I couldn't imagine any woman ever taking to you. So, what other entertainment could a man of your physique and temperament be enjoying, eh?'

She paused and then said, 'Oh, brother, you are losing your colour. One minute it was scarlet, now you look like a field lily. Have I made myself plain?'

She watched him grinding his teeth; then she added, 'You would like to do for Marie Anne, wouldn't you? because you won't recognise that *she's* not the real cause of the break-up, it is Mother. Well, let me warn you: if you were to do anything to her you wouldn't live for very long either for, as I understand it, she's got a champion who would see to you.'

She now settled back into the saddle, pulled the horse to the side and saying, 'Get up there!' she walked it slowly towards the five-bar gate, bent over sidewards and lifted the latch, then passed through, turning her horse so as to close the gate. And Vincent remained where he was, his jaw working and his face still pale. Then, with an almost vicious kick at his mount, he turned it about and went back the way he had come.

In the small farmyard Evelyn dismounted, tied her horse to a post, then glanced into the barn, only to find it empty. She looked towards the house. The kitchen door was open.

He usually came out as soon as he heard her enter the yard. She now turned and looked about her, and when her eyes were drawn to the hedge that bordered the stone wall she saw him. He was standing looking towards her, a bucket in his hand, and to his side a partly built wall. She knew what he was doing; he was building a set of piggeries, and he must have been there for some time and within earshot of all that had been said. She bowed her head as she thought, Oh my God, another mistake. Another mistake.

She now turned her back on him, so that she did not see his approach; although she heard him washing his hands at the pump. Then she knew he was just behind her when she heard his voice. 'Come indoors, my dear.'

Like a biddable child she walked towards the farm-house and into a very pleasant, low-timbered room. It was a typical farmhouse kitchen but with the added comfort of a deep easy chair and a long padded settle. In the middle of the room was the customary large working table, with a chair at each side of it. Pulling one from under the table, Nathaniel Napier pointed to it, saying quietly, 'Sit down.'

She sat down, her head still bowed, until a finger lifted her chin and he looked down into her face, and said, 'Would you go to a registry office with me tomorrow?'

'Oh. Oh, I'm sorry, but I . . . I was so angry.'

'Yes, I can understand that, my dear, but I ask you again. Although we have only known each other a matter of three to four weeks, I'm putting the same question to you: would you go to a registry office with me tomorrow?'

Now she looked up into his face and she said, 'Yes; yes, I would.'

'That's all I want to know.' And with that, he pulled the other chair from under the table and brought it towards her; and when he sat down they were knee to knee and he asked the question, 'Have you given this any thought before?'

She considered for a moment before answering, 'Yes; yes, I have, but I couldn't see any way out.'

'But what I mean, Evelyn, is, have you thought what marriage to me would mean?' He now stretched out his arm and flapped his hand backwards and forwards as he said, 'This kitchen-cum-dining-room, a parlour, three decent bedrooms and a box room and the open attic running the length of the house, and we mustn't forget the wash-house. It's a very good wash-house, with its own boiler. There would be no servants, no being waited on, except what we did for each other. I have just enough money left to buy a small amount of stock. Since he's been

298

allowed to lease more land from your grandfather, Mr Harding has let me have a couple of fields to run a horse. Without Mr Harding's help I wouldn't have been just a failed horse doctor, but I'd have been a failed farmer too. You might ask why I bought this place; why, if I was a veterinary surgeon, which I was at one time, I didn't keep it up, and so I will explain. But first, I must tell you what I know of you. I seem to know all about you, but it has been through second and third opinions, none of which seem to tally with the person I have found you to be. Well, having said that, you know nothing about me, so here goes. I had just gone into business. I was twenty-four. I had bought this old veterinary establishment after the owner's retirement. It was situated in a small town and there were just enough people and animals there to give me a living, and it *was* just a living. However, I was extremely happy, because I had married the owner's grand-daughter, a beautiful girl of twenty. We had been married three years when she and the baby died in child-birth.' He was still looking at her and she at him, but she saw no quiver on his face at the recollection of such a tragedy; and then he went on, 'I did my best to carry on, but it was no good, I went to pieces. Apparently, I am not a very strong character; another man might have ridden that period, but I couldn't. There was this healthy, lovely young woman and a beautiful baby both dead through the negligence of a midwife, with either dirty hands or dirty instruments. Of course, no blame was directed towards the doctor who didn't come when he should, because he was suffering from a late-night drinking bout. I sold the business and lost on it. I left my friends. My parents were dead, but I had a very kind sister and her husband. However, they were no solace to me, and so I started to wander from one job to another just to eat. I went to sea for two years. That taught me a lesson as to what extent a human being can suffer physical pain, especially when one's hands become glued to the ship's railings with ice. Back on shore, my wanderings started again. Then my sister, dear soul that she was, died. She left me enough money to set up another business, hoping, I think, I would likely go back into veterinary work. However, I knew I couldn't tackle that again, yet I still wanted to deal with animals. To cut the rest of the story short, I went on a walking tour, and I heard this little farm was available. The owner had apparently died and his widow wanted to leave and go and live with her daughter. She was very generous in the deal, leaving me all the furniture, some of it very old but all good solid stuff. Apparently this is the remnants of a much larger farm that the old lady's grandparents had. Anyway, I think I was very fortunate to get it, and also that it should be situated next to people like Farmer Harding and his wife, because they're so kind and helpful.

'Well, it should happen that one day, while seeking his advice once more, a lady comes along the road walking a lame horse, and from the moment I saw her there stirred in me something that had been dead for years, although I felt there was no hope of making her acquaintance. Mr Harding told me something of her circumstances and the turmoil her home was in at the moment. Also, on that day, I had already made the acquaintance of the person supposedly the cause of all the trouble, a young, pregnant girl, and when I saw the two sisters walk off together I imagined that would be the last I would see of either of them. And then' – he held out his hand now and took hers – 'a few days later you came into the yard there and thanked me for saving your horse. My response was an invitation asking you to call on me again, even though I knew I was piling up trouble for myself. And each day since I have looked forward to your coming; and I knew I was falling in love with you.'

Evelyn now put her other hand on top of his as she said

softly, 'You could be telling my own story. You see, you are trying to tell me you have nothing to give to me but yourself and this small farmhouse; well, I, too, have nothing to bring to you, only myself and a small dress allowance that wouldn't keep a donkey in hay.'

Her voice dropped and there was a definite break in it as she said, 'I've been up for sale for a long time now, Nathaniel.'

'Oh! Evelyn, don't say that, because you're such a beautiful young woman; I'm really amazed that you're not married already.'

She smiled at him now, saying, 'Oh as a result of the last campaign, I could easily have been, but you see he was forty-eight, had five children, one nearly as old as myself, and his stomach was already protruding.'

As his laugh rang out he got quickly to his feet, and pulling her up, he put his arms about her and, holding her close and with his lips almost touching hers, he said, 'Tell me honestly, dear one, would you really marry me and come and live in this house and be prepared to do the chores it demands; and not only inside, because a farmer's wife is expected to work outside too. Would you be prepared to do all that?'

Slowly she lifted her hand and ran her fingers through his unruly fair hair, and softly she said, 'Yes, Nathaniel. If you are willing to take on someone who can neither cook, nor clean nor wash clothes, then I say I'd be happy to marry you. Oh yes, happy and willing.'

When his lips fell hard on hers, her arms went about him and they swayed until they fell against the edge of the table. Then they parted, flushed and laughing.

He now held her face tightly between his hands and, looking into her eyes, he said, 'I'm happy as I never thought to be in my life again; and to the very best of my ability, my dear Evelyn, I will aim to make you as happy as myself.'

'Oh, Nathaniel.'

'Not Nathaniel any more; that's too much of a mouthful, at least for a wife. It's Nick from now on. And look, as it's Saturday afternoon and even the would-be farmer has to have a break some time, let's go to the Hardings and see Sally, because I'm sure she will become your teacher. Would you like that?'

'Anything you say . . . Nick.'

'Well then, madam, I'm going to spruce up. I'll do it in the wash-house; there's more room in there. In the meantime, I'll leave you to go over the house and judge for yourself if this is where you'd be content to spend the rest of your life.'

Their hands touched before they parted, then she went out of the kitchen and into the small hall, and from there to the plainly furnished and not very comfortable sitting-room. Upstairs she found the three square bedrooms plainly furnished. Then the large box-room. She did not climb the ladder into the attic, but she stood on the landing and looked out of the long window, then said to herself, I'll make it into a home, a loving home; that is, after I have won the battle with Mother, for a battle there will surely be.

5

'You shall *not*, girl; I will *not* be humiliated any further. A farm labourer indeed!'

'He is not a farm labourer, Mother; he is a farmer. A small farmer, yes, but he is a farmer.'

'How can he be, girl, when Vincent says his land is no bigger than our kitchen garden? Anyway, you are not marrying a farmer, I shall see you dead first. Oh, how can you, knowing what I have suffered. Imagine how you've been brought up, how you live now . . . yes, even with a depleted staff, still waited on hand and foot. Do you think you can spend the rest of your life in a little farm-house on what's no bigger than a workman's stint, so I understand?'

Evelyn's voice was low and steady when she replied, 'I'm picking up your words, Mother. How I live now . . . how we live now; like hermits. Do we ever go out visiting? Of course, you couldn't possibly go out visiting, could you? in the small carriage, oh no. And do we ever have any of our old friends dropping in on us? Two of your old cronies, Lola and Bertha, two wizened old maids who spend their lives going from one house to the other carrying gossip, they love to come here and pour on your head all that's being said about you, but done so expertly that you can't get back at them. Every word you say goes back to The Hall, The Mount, the Bluetts, the lot of them. Well now, even if I am going to be just a farm labourer's wife, I'll have some variety.'

'Variety, girl?' Veronica Lawson was screaming now,

her self-control seeming to have left her entirely. 'Do you know what you'll have to do? Do you, girl, you who've been pampered since the cradle?'

It seemed that Evelyn's voice was as loud as her mother's as she screamed back at her, 'Yes! Yes, I do know. I shall have to cook and clean and wash clothes. Yes, wash clothes. I'll have to muck out stables. Now I know how to do that, I've seen it done many times; and add to this, piggeries and hen crees. Mrs Harding does it, and she's an expert teacher. She knows the whole lot, and so shall I, in a very short time.'

Veronica Lawson just stood gaping at her daughter. Then she turned from her and marched to the mantel-piece. There, gripping the edge of the marble slab, it was as if she were about to wrench it from its fixture; but then, suddenly swinging round, she cried, 'We'll let your father deal with this. Surely he'll have enough pride left to put his foot down on this last piece of degradation I'm being asked to suffer. One daughter a whore about to give birth to a bastard, and now you, the proud Miss Evelyn Lawson lowering herself to the dregs of society.'

'I will contradict you on those two points, Mother. Marie Anne is no whore. She slipped up, as I once nearly did, and she actually witnessed the event, which had no result such as hers. It was what she saw that disgusted her and made her hate me. Yes; stretch your face, Mother, stretch your face. And I'll tell you something further: the incident took place with Lady Mabel's cousin, he who got the maid into trouble. Remember? Now, if you wish me to leave this house before I am ready, I'll do so, and I'll go along to my grandfather's; or, rather, I'll go along to Marie Anne's, where I know I'll be welcome. Isn't that funny, Mother? Marie Anne will welcome me. I'll pack some of my things in readiness. You can give me your answer later on as to whether I am to stay or go, but go I will, and to a registry office.'

It wasn't Evelyn who now left the room, but her mother. She did not so much leave it, but staggered blindly from it, and silently.

As Pat emerged from the woodland into the patch of open ground before Don's cottage, he called, 'Hello there!' and when he received no answer he knocked on the cottage door.

On getting no welcoming call, he pushed the door open. The fire was burning brightly, but there was no sign of Don. But as he turned and looked through the open doorway towards the river, he heard the dog bark, and up over the green sward came the bouncing pup.

As the sheep-cum-Labrador dog, now all legs and hair, bounded towards him he saw Don emerging from the far end of the woodland that ran down to the river bank, and, almost simultaneously, they hailed each other.

'I looked into the house,' said Pat; 'I thought maybe you had got drunk and were sleeping it off.'

'What d'you want at this time of the day? How are the ships leaving the quay without you?'

'Oh, I've ordered them to wait. I wanted a word in private with you.'

'Yes? In private?' Then on a laugh Don said, 'That'll cost you; I only hear confessions by the hour.'

At this Pat laughed. 'I've often given thought to you Catholics and confessions,' he said. 'Do you really spill the beans?'

'Yes, boy, every one of them, 'cos if you don't, you know what's going to happen to you.' He nodded his head solemnly now. 'You keep anything back and you're for hell. Oh yes, boy, hell. And you have to take your own driftwood with you.'

At this Pat laughed outright and said, 'Well, Father, I'll keep nothing back, I promise you.'

With Nippy prancing around them, they went into the

305

cottage, and inside Don said, 'Would you like a cup of tea?'

'No, thanks, Don,' Pat replied; 'I really have work to see to. The fact is, I want to be married.'

'What?'

'I said, I want to be married.'

'Yes, I heard you, but what's so important about that to bring you from your work? And to me.'

'Well, it's like this: I want to marry a Catholic, and I should like to be clear on what this might entail. You see, we've never discussed religion, and her people are strong Catholics, with their only son a priest. They're a lovely couple. And there's another snag. Knowing how Mother's courted the county all these years has caused me to keep my affairs quiet. You see, Anita's father is the manager of a pit; it's a very good position, but Mother would never see it that way, especially now that Evelyn has broken the last straw, because she is determined to marry her farmer. But to get back to religion. Quite candidly, I don't want to become a Catholic, but I know that Anita would want her brother to marry us. Nothing has actually been said, but where would I stand? Would they marry us if I still remained a Protestant?'

Don gave a short sardonic laugh as he said, 'Yes; but only after your head was bloody and bowed with the pressure of why you refuse to turn. One thing would be demanded of you: that you agree to your offspring being brought up as Catholics. Even if you do this, from the day you are married, your wife will be under pressure to get you into the Catholic Church. You see, they will still consider you to be living in sin, especially her; the penalty for failure on her part will be high in the hereafter.'

There was silence between them now until Pat uttered one word. 'Really!' he said.

'Haven't you discussed it at all with the family?'

'No; not even about becoming engaged. It's odd, now

I come to think of it, but on my last two visits to Anita's home for tea, there was a priest present, a Father Nixon. He had little to say to me, but I knew he was weighing me up. Afterwards, too, her father made a joke about him, which I thought was rather significant: 'It was said of him that if he could get the devil into a room for an hour he'd bring him out a Jesuit, he said.'

'Oh-ho!' Don nodded. 'I've heard that one before. It's the oldest in the Brothers' joke box. Why had you to go and pick a Catholic to fall in love with?'

'I didn't; it just happened. It was about two years ago. I had just come up from the stokehold with the engineer. I remember rubbing my hands on a bit of tow when we were both startled by girlish laughter coming from the quay; and there were two young women chatting with what I assumed were two officers from the French boat moored next to us. They were still laughing when they moved away, and as they passed our ship I don't know what made me do it, but I raised my hand and gave them a sort of salute; then one of them returned the salute on a laugh. It was a gay, youthful sound. She stayed on my mind for a day or two, but there was no way of getting to know who she was. And so a whole year passed. Then Henry Morton, one of our clerks, who was about to leave us after thirty years of good service, brought some relatives to the farewell do we were giving him, a Mr and Mrs Brown and their daughter Anita. It was strange but we recognised each other immediately, yet previously we had seen each other only for a matter of seconds . . . Well, that's how it started. She is twenty-four years old; she teaches French at a private school; and I doubt if you would consider her beautiful, but to me she is the loveliest and gayest creature alive. And I mean to marry her, whether she be Catholic or Protestant or whatever.'

Don laughed, saying, 'Well, you have been forewarned, and my advice to you is, gird your loins for a fight, for fight there will be if you are determined not to join the fold. Are you?'

'Yes, I am. I know very little about it; but what I've heard so far, and you've added to it, it's not for me. Do you know, Don? something's just struck me. We . . . I mean our family, hasn't one Catholic friend; the whole lot of them are Church of England. You are the first Catholic to have become a friend of the family.'

'Well, I'm honoured, Pat, indeed I am; but what about Sarah? She might not be much of an openly practising Catholic, but you scratch the surface and you'll find whose side she's on. And doesn't it seem strange to you that it should be she who befriended and saved Marie Anne? I seem to have been given the credit for bringing Marie Anne home, but that's misplaced, I couldn't have done anything without Sarah.'

'Yes, you're right,' Pat said, rising to his feet. 'And apart from religion, it's very odd, but she's brought a different atmosphere into the house. By the way, you'll likely soon get a visit from her if you're not careful. You've been only once to the house for nearly a fortnight. They're all wondering what you're up to.'

His tone now changing to one of enquiry, Pat said softly, 'Do you ever get lonely here?'

Don did not answer, but turned his half-masked face away from Pat: Lord; Lord; what a question to be asked, Do you get lonely? He couldn't say, I get more lonely here now than I did before I started to visit your home. And what if he should add, and for women's company? What he did say was, 'Yes, Pat, naturally I do get lonely; but this last week or so I've been working hard on a piece of sculpture, and I suppose I've been too tired towards the end of the day to spruce up to make a visit. You know' – he now pointed down to the settee – 'that's a comfortable old couch; and if the logs are burning brightly and I have a little drop of the stuff that warms the heart, I drop off to sleep . . . But tell them I'll be along shortly. Please convey my excuses to them.'

Looking closely at Don, the thought passed through Pat's mind: Yes, there were excuses. But what reasons he could give for thinking so, he could not tell. He said, 'Well, I'll be off, Don. And thanks for your help. And you have been a help, believe me you have, because I'm going to that pit village, at least to a house beyond it, on Saturday to open my mouth wide. And you know something, Don? I hate going through that village, because the pit-head is at the end of the street. Have you ever been down a mine, Don?'

'No; never.'

'Well, if you're ever given the opportunity, refuse it, for you'll never look upon human nature in the same way again. I've always thought it dreadful the way some shipping companies treat their crews, especially the stokers. That was until Mr Brown took me down his mine, when I actually saw men crawling like ants on their bellies, and young lads – they must have been fourteen, because of what is called the Children's Act – pulling and pushing bogies; and my eyes wouldn't believe that men were crawling and digging along passages not eighteen inches high. You know something, Don? I realised that day that I had never before really experienced fear; but I wanted to turn and run from that hell-hole and get into the animal cage and up to earth. I was so ashamed, but I was almost sick when I breathed in fresh air again. Yet, that very night I went to a concert in the village, and there were some of those same men singing their hearts out in harmony and under a real conductor.'

Don nodded. 'Yes,' he said, 'I have heard that down there is the nearest place to Hades. Yet families, generation after generation, follow each other down. There should be some other way to earn a living.'

There seemed no answer to this, and they both moved

towards the door, where once again Pat gave Don thanks for his help, and extracted from him a promise that he would be along to dinner that evening.

In the bedroom of the cottage Don drew the Nottingham lace curtains across the window but left the heavy, faded, tapestry side ones hanging. He now went to the low chest of drawers, on which was the small double-door cabinet and knelt down before it; then opening the doors, he stared at the crucifix. There was still enough light in the room to enable him to see the words written in beautiful script on parchment attached to the inner side of one door, and although the contradiction of the words written there was engraved in his mind, he nevertheless read them aloud to himself:

I BELIEVE, HELP THOU MY UNBELIEF.

Now crossing himself, he looked at the face of the crucified Christ whose lifeless eyes seemed to be staring back at him, as they had done in the chapel.

For perhaps two minutes his mind seemed utterly blank; it was asking no questions, and so was receiving no answers. That was until, taking in one long slow deep breath, he said aloud, 'I did what you suggested, so what now?'

He waited, and the answer came: Remember, I said, if you cannot stand the ache, don't expose yourself to it; so apparently you, who always ask for help then go your own way, must have decided you couldn't bear the ache, so you curtailed your visits.

'The whole situation is hopeless, isn't it?'

If you say so and you decide it is hopeless, then it is hopeless.

'Well, it is, for what woman, never mind a young girl, could stand this?' and the flat of his hand came on to his cheek with almost the force of a blow. The answer came back to him immediately: Someone who had got to know you without your unveiling yourself.

'Yes, but when I am unveiled, what then?'

Well, if she loved you enough, then her feelings for you should be strengthened.

There followed a pause before he said, 'She's not yet seventeen; merely a girl.'

When the voice came again it rapped out the words, She's about to have a child. There are no longer immaculate conceptions, remember, so if she's about to have a child she has been with a man. Had you forgotten?

Don's voice, too, was sharp as he replied, 'No. No; I haven't, and I see that picture every time I look at her sweet innocent face. So, are you suggesting that because that happened she'll be prepared to take second best?'

The voice that answered this was more calm, saying, I'm not suggesting anything; you are, and never forget that. You are the master of your mind, you are the conductor of your thought; I am but a sounding block, the echo of which, you hope, will make you see more clearly the road you are to follow.

He now stared at the inanimate body on the cross; then slowly he closed one of the gates; the other, he glanced at. There was a sheet of parchment attached to this one, too, and he had no need to read it, for the words were indented on his mind:

YOUR BEGGING HAS BEEN REWARDED.

YOUR BEGGING BOWL IS FULL.

GO, SHARE IT.

The doors closed, he rose from his knees, then sat on the edge of the bed, one hand across his eyes, and he asked himself why he continued to do this. When had it begun? He couldn't recall when he had first imagined that the figure on the cross in the chapel spoke to him, or when the realisation came that he was simply talking to himself, that it was what was now being called his subconscious mind that was answering him. All he had was the knowledge that he had been rejected from birth. Of this he had become aware, not through the Brothers but through the nuns and their chastising of him: he was a naughty boy; God didn't love him; that was why his mother had given him away. It was fortunate that the Brothers had appeared in his life at this point. Yet it was from them that he learned the reason he was with them at all; it was because of his face; he had overheard an elderly Brother relating the story of his birth to a newcomer. Perhaps it was from then that he had started talking to the cross.

He rose from the bed and went to the small dressing-table with its swing mirror. After gazing into it, he took off the cloth mask from its frame and replaced it with a clean one; then, before he put on the leather cap which he always wore whenever he went to The Little Manor, and which gave him the excuse to remove the slouch hat, he took a comb and ran it through his thick fair hair. If it grew any thicker or longer he would be unable to keep the little cap in place.

He continued to stare at his reflection, then quickly parted his hair so that where it came across his brow it covered the top of the scar. Then bending forward again, he said aloud, 'Why not? Why not let it grow back and front. Some men do, artists and so forth; and he himself was an artist of sorts. Wouldn't it be wonderful if he never again had to change this piece of cloth.

Of a sudden he swung round, and his thoughts again giving voice, he almost yelled, 'Forget it! Forget it!' before stalking out.

6

When Pat pushed open the door of The Little Manor and entered the hall, he was surprised to see Marie Anne standing fully dressed in cloak and scarf and withdrawing a hatpin, and he exclaimed loudly, 'Well! You've been out?'

'No, Pat, I haven't; I was just about to go, but Sarah says there's a wind and that this hat is not suitable, so she's gone to get that silly woollen thing that ties under my chin like a bonnet and makes me look ridiculous.'

His voice low now, he said, 'Have you been out before?' And when she shook her head he added, 'It's getting near your time, isn't it?'

'No. There's some time to go yet.'

'Well, I wouldn't go very far.'

'I'm going as far as the wood where the tree-stump seat is.'

'That's plenty far enough, I would say. Why?'

'Well, I'm wondering, and I'm not alone, for Sarah is too; we're both wondering why Don hasn't visited again. If I get as far as the tree-stump, I can sit there while she goes through the wood to the cottage to have a word with him. Are you aware of anything that's the matter with him?'

'No; but some time ago he said that he had quite a bit of work to get through for the Brothers.' Pat now put his hands to her neck and drew the ends of her scarf together, saying, 'I wouldn't go as far as the stump seat if I were you.'

313

She said quietly, 'Pat, Don is a very lonely man. His affliction makes him so, and I feel that I owe him so much. If he hadn't brought me back, and, knowing how I've felt these past months, I don't think, no matter what brave face I put upon it, that I would have been able to stand those stairs to that garret in this condition. Another thing, he seemed to come alive and be so different during the first weeks I was back. You remember, he dined with us three times in one week and kept us all laughing with his tales about the Brothers and Father Broadside and his parishioners. So I feel, well, something must have stopped him coming, and when I see him – if I see him – I'll ask him outright.'

To this Pat nodded and said, 'Well, you do just that. By the way, is Father here?'

'No, that's another thing. He didn't call in yesterday either. What's the matter with everybody?'

'Oh' – Pat closed his eyes for a moment – 'to use Sarah's expression, there's been the devil's fagarties on along there. I wanted Mother to meet Anita, and she raised the roof. It was bad enough, she said – and she didn't just say it, she practically screamed it – that her daughter was going to marry a farm labourer, but that I was going to lower myself so much that I had to go into a pit village to find a wife, and the daughter of a pitman, et cetera, et cetera. I had hoped to bring Anita over today – I took the trap. Barney's just stabled it – but Anita's mother's in bed with influenza and she felt she couldn't leave her, and although I was sorry for the poor woman, because she's a very nice person, I was glad in a way, because I would have brought her straight here, as Grandfather had said he'd be pleased to meet her, but she would have wondered why she wasn't meeting Mother. I haven't told her about the set-up here, but I feel I must do so soon. Anyway, I'll slip down now and find out what's happened to Father.'

'Hello! Mr Pat.' It was Sarah.

'Hello! Sarah' – he turned to her – 'Don't let her go any further than the beginning of the wood.'

'Not even that far, if I can stop her. If you want my opinion, she's mad to go out on a day like this. There have been other days, nice days when I've tried to get her out, but she would have none of it. And now she picks on today.'

'Only because, Sarah, you said you would go along there yourself and use your Irish diplomacy to get him here. Well, if I know anything about your Irish diplomacy, that would as likely send him flying back to the Brothers.'

'Oh you!' Sarah flapped her hand at Marie Anne; then quickly thrusting the woollen bonnet on Marie Anne's head she pulled the sides well down over her ears, saying, 'Come on! Let's get out. The quicker we get away, the quicker we get back.'

Pat asked now, 'By the way, where's Grandfather?'

It was Sarah who answered him, saying, 'He's in the library, Mr Pat. He was snoring gently the last time I looked in.'

'Does he know you're going out?' Pat asked Marie Anne; and she, shaking her head, said, 'No. It was a last-minute decision, and I didn't disturb him because, as our friend here would say,' and she thumbed towards Sarah, 'I'll be back before I've gone, if I go at all.'

Pat laughed as he opened the door for them, saying, 'Come on now! get yourselves away before there's a war on. In the meantime, I'll go down and see how Father's faring.'

He was still smiling to himself as he walked towards The Manor. I'll be back before I've gone, if I go at all. That Sarah is a caution . . .

Before reaching the house, Pat could see his father walking into the stable yard; but when he reached it he was brought to a halt by the sound of his father talking to

Vincent in a loud voice, saying, 'I've warned you, mind; I've warned you,' and Vincent seeing Pat, turned and made for one of the horse boxes where a groom was about to rub down a sweating animal. And James, catching sight of Pat, said, 'Hello, Pat! Anything the matter?'

Pat, knowing to what his father was referring, answered, 'No, no; nothing yet. I've . . . I've just left her; she's gone for a stroll with Miss Foggerty. It's the first time she's been out in weeks, apparently. They tell me they're just going as far as the wood, but I doubt if they'll get that far in this wind. Everything all right this end?'

'Did you ever know anything ever to be right at this end?'

This attitude of his father was new to Pat, for here was a dominant man speaking, and surprising him more every day now, and so, without answering his father directly, he said, 'Will you be over today?'

For answer, James said, 'Were you going inside?'

'Not necessarily.'

'Well, I'll walk back with you. I need some fresh air.'

They had walked some way before James said, 'Things are coming to a head shortly. Before she goes across to the boys I am going to apply for a separation.'

'Oh my! Oh my! I can't see her standing for that, Father. There's no other woman, is there?'

'No. But I've been denied her bed for twelve years or more. That should be sufficient . . . What am I talking about, twelve years? Seventeen, more like it. After the night Marie Anne was conceived, I never got near her again. And that event followed an unbelievable shindy.'

Marie Anne. Always Marie Anne. Conceived in battle, and her life one long battle since. And here she was, ensconced in The Little Manor after breaking up the family. Of that there was no doubt. Yet it would never have happened if she'd had a different mother.

316

*   *   *

Marie Anne and Sarah had left the shelter of the gardens
and the boundary of the estate and had for some little time
been walking along an unrutted path from where they
could see Farmer Harding ploughing one of his fields.

Sarah, taking Marie Anne's arm, said gently, 'You've
had enough, haven't you, dear? What about turning
back?'

'I'd have to sit down first, Sarah. My legs are like jelly.'

'Of course they are; you're walking on hard ground. I
told you before we came out, didn't I, when you said you
weren't on crutches, that you'd find it more difficult to
walk over rough ground than treading on carpets all day.'

'Oh yes, you did, wise woman. Oh yes, you did.' Marie
Anne smiled and pushed Sarah gently from her as she
pointed, saying, 'Look! we're nearly to the wood, and
from here the old tree-stump appears to me like an
armchair.'

It was some minutes later when Marie Anne sank down
on the tree-stump and smiled up at Sarah, saying, 'Oh,
that's lovely. And we're sheltered back and front.' Then
pointing into the wood, she said, 'Look over there at the
clearing, that beautiful patch of bluebells.'

'My! yes. Now that is bonny. And the sun hitting them.
You know something? I've always wanted to pick bluebells. When I was little I could see my arms full of
bluebells and I don't remember ever picking one,
because there was no woodland round where we lived,
but I must have seen a picture of a child in a book with
arms full of bluebells because that feeling remained with
me for a long time.'

'Well, now's your chance,' said Marie Anne, 'because,'
and now her voice sank, 'I don't think I can stay out long
enough for you to fetch Don.'

'Oh my!' Sarah's voice and attitude showed her anxiety
as she said, 'You've got a pain or something?'

317

'No, no, woman, I haven't got a pain.' She laughed. 'And stop looking like that. But I do know that by the time you manage to find Don and bring him back here I would just have time to say hello and goodbye. And, Miss Sarah Foggerty, I admit that I am feeling slightly fatigued.'

'Oh' – Sarah shook her head impatiently – 'I'll tell you what I really think, and—'

'And you'll walk out. Yes, yes, I know. You've said it before. But now listen to what I'm going to say. Go over there and fulfil your life's dream: pick a small bunch of bluebells, and then we'll make for home. Go on now. Go on, because I'm not going to move until you fulfil that dream. Go on, the quicker you do it the quicker we start back for home.'

Sarah drew in a long breath, then turned and almost on a tripping run made for the patch of bluebells, the while Marie Anne asked herself, as she had done repeatedly over the past months, what she would have done without the companionship of this woman. Of course, it would have been wonderful to be home and cared for, but if Sarah had stayed in London as she had first intended, life here, following on her London experience, would have been very dull.

The sun was warm on her. Behind her and to the left was a screen of tangled scrub that was acting as a wind-break, and as Marie Anne loosened the strings of the bonnet, then unbuttoned her cloak, she thought, if only this tree-stump had a back to it, everything would be perfect.

She was putting up both arms to stop the cloak slipping from her shoulders when there was a rustle in the under-growth behind her, and she half-turned her head to look at what she expected to see, a rabbit scurrying away.

The hand came across her face so quickly she had no time to scream. She only knew that she was falling the short distance to the earth; but when her eyes saw the arm uplifted and the piece of wood in the hand, both her arms went up to shield her face. One sleeve of her dress had fallen back to the elbow, the other was held at the wrist by the handkerchiefs pressed into the cuff.

Her first scream was muffled, for she felt she was choking, but when the second blow struck her bent arms her scream rent the wood; but this was nothing compared with the piercing screech she let out when the piece of wood was brought across her high belly. She could hardly have been conscious of the last blow, which was to her head, or of Sarah's screaming as she cradled her head and shoulders, at the same time as she glanced towards the thicket from where she could hear the crashing noise of the attacker's retreat.

When Sarah looked up into the faces of Don on one side of her and Mr Harding on the other, she whimpered, 'I was just gathering bluebells; she made me go and gather them.'

'Did you see who it was?' Mr Harding was asking the question, in answer to which Sarah shook her head, then said, 'But . . . but . . .'

She did not go on, for Don was pressing her aside as he took Marie Anne from her arms, and looking up at Mr Harding and his voice trembling, he said, 'We can't leave her here until help comes, and it's too far to carry her back to the house, so help me to take her to the cottage.'

Getting on to his haunches now, Don looked down into the blood-smeared face and, his voice almost a whisper, he said quietly, 'Marie Anne, I'm going to lift you up. You'll be all right. You'll be all right.'

Marie Anne made no sound at all, not even a moan, when Don put his arms under her shoulders and Mr Harding thrust his under the back of her knees and her lower back. Then they inched themselves on to the rough path.

They were walking crabwise along when Don

suddenly said to Sarah, 'Go back to the house, Sarah, and tell them to send for a doctor. If Mr Pat is there, tell him to come, but not to tell her grandfather anything yet. If Mr Pat or his father are not there, bring two of the men back with you. But first, make sure they fetch a doctor.'

When Sarah made no move to obey him, his voice rose to a shout and the words were delivered as a command:

'SARAH! Do as I tell you; and now!'

As if emerging from a daze, Sarah turned, picked up her skirts and ran, the way they had come, back to the house . . .

After thrusting open the door of the cottage with his back, Don shuffled inside, then humped Marie Anne further up into his arms before looking towards the couch.

'We can't leave her there,' he said. 'We'll put her in the bedroom.'

It was with some relief that they laid her on the plank bed that was covered merely with a biscuit pallet.

'God help her,' Fred Harding said. 'Why has she had to suffer this, and so near her time?' and he glanced at Don as if for confirmation, but all Don did was to shake his head.

'Is she conscious?'

Tenderly Don raised one of Marie Anne's eyelids, then said softly, 'Yes, I should say she is.'

'They'll . . . they'll never get her back in this condition.'

'We'll have to see what the doctor says.'

'Well, God knows when he'll land,' said Fred. 'I hope they have the sense to tell him to come by the main road and through our place. Look; I think the best plan is for me to go and fetch Sally. You see, she was a midwife. Admittedly, it was years ago, but she knows about these things, and we've had three of our own. She'll come like a shot. I'll be there and back in five minutes. Will you be all right?'

320

'Yes; yes, of course.'

Lifting his eyes from the blood-stained face to the bowl of water standing on the wash-hand stand, Don immediately went to it and took from the small top drawer a handkerchief that had been folded into a square but not ironed. This he dipped into the bowl of clean water, picked up a towel that was hanging over a rail attached to the wash-hand stand, and went back to the bed, where he gently sponged the blood from her face, muttering, 'My dear. My dear.'

He could now see that the blood was still oozing from a jagged cut between the top of her ear and her brow; and the arm lying across the mound of her belly looked in a bad state. It was covered with blood, like the rest of her; even her stockings showed red.

When he lifted his eyes to her face he was amazed to see the tears running from beneath her lashes, and as his deep inner voice was crying, Oh, my dear one, my lovely, the words he actually spoke sounded cool: 'Now Marie Anne, you're going to be all right. Can you hear me? Yes, yes, I know you can. Now listen: the doctor'll be here shortly.' But his voice trailed away when through her blurred gaze she said, 'I'm going to die, Don.'

'What! Don't be silly. Now listen!'

But again she spoke: 'Don, I knew it was coming. His hate has been with me all the time. I knew he would kill me in the end. I was drawn out of the house today for that purpose.'

'Marie Anne, now listen to me: you are talking nonsense. You are not going to die. You are bruised, you are bleeding, you are shocked, but you're not going to die. You are going to live and give birth to your baby.'

Even as he spoke his eyes flickered to the cabinet on top of the low chest of drawers, and his mind took him down the ages. He could hear St Aloysius saying quietly,

'I know on which day I am going to die,' and die he did on that day.

Oh God, get that out of his head; she can't die, she can't. I couldn't suffer that. The voice was still with him, distant yet clear: There you go again. You couldn't suffer the ache of her; you couldn't suffer the sight of her because she created an ache in you; now you can't suffer her dying. It's how you feel, isn't it? Always you, always the I, I, I.

He was feeling the urge to scream abuse at the inner voice when Marie Anne spoke again. Not only did she speak, but she lifted her uninjured arm and caught at his hand, and her voice was low but firm as she said, 'Don't . . . don't worry, Don. I . . . I've known for some time what would happen. I didn't know how he would do it, I only knew he would, because he wanted to do it even when I was a child.'

'Oh, Marie Anne.'

'Listen. Listen, Don. I . . . I waited for you to come. When you didn't, I felt I must see you once more. I . . . I don't know why, but I just felt like that. I really wanted to talk about this.' She now took her hand from his and laid it on the mask, but now her voice began to fade and her eyelids half closed as she muttered, 'You know what I would want to say, but it doesn't matter any longer.'

He still had hold of her hand when the door opened, but now blindly he turned from the bed as Sally Harding took his place, saying, 'Good gracious me! girl. But don't worry, doctor will be here soon. In the meantime I'll cover you up and keep you warm.' Then turning to glance at Don, she said, 'Now if you'll just leave us, I'll get on with it.'

When the door had closed on him, Sally Harding, bending down to Marie Anne, asked softly, 'Are you paining anywhere, dear?'

When Marie Anne did not answer, Sally said, 'Listen;

you must tell me: have you got a pain anywhere?'

With a slow movement Marie Anne put her hand across the mound of her belly, and Sally said, 'You've got a pain there? Oh well; now we know where we are, or we think we do.' . . .

Standing in the living-room, Farmer Harding said, 'Has she any idea who it was?'

'She's got more than an idea, Fred; she knows who it was, as I do.'

'You do?'

'Yes. It was her brother.'

'The older one? Vincent? I heard a rumour that he had gone for her before.'

'You heard right.'

'Is he mad?'

'I wouldn't say he's mad, but just bad; full of hate and evil.'

'But she's just a lass and he's . . . well, he's kicking thirty.'

At this moment the door was thrust open and Pat came in, gasping as he said, 'What's he done to her now? Where is she?'

'It's all right. It's all right,' said Don, putting a hand out towards him.

'Sarah . . . Sarah said he battered her . . . her head, every-where.'

'She's all right. Well, what I mean is, we'll know what damage is done when the doctor comes. Have you sent for him?'

'Yes; Barney's gone post-haste. Took the trap. I told him to bring it to your place, Mr Harding.'

'And rightly, sir. Yes, you did right; he'll get here in half the time.'

'Who's with her?'

'My wife, sir. She knows about such things; she was a midwife once. She'll . . . well, she'll know soon if there's

323

any damage been done; I mean, to the child.' Turning now to Don, Pat said, 'Sarah said it was Vincent. And of course it would be; who else? yet it's hard to believe that he would go this far.'

'Where is Sarah?' asked Don now.

'She's with Father; they're coming along. She herself nearly collapsed when she got inside; we couldn't get any sense out of her. She was yelling so much that we had to push her into the kitchen quarters in case Grandfather heard her, for we didn't want to upset him until we knew exactly what had happened.'

They all now turned towards the bedroom door as Mrs Harding came into the room, saying in a low voice, 'You've brought the doctor?'

'No, no. We've just sent for him,' said Pat.

'Well the quicker he gets here the better.' And now addressing her husband, she said, 'There's a cut in the back of her head an' all. Her hair's all matted.'

'Is she conscious? May I see her?'

'Yes, Mr Pat. I suppose so, but I wouldn't let her talk much.'

When he stood by the bedside, almost as a child would, Pat's hand went sideways to his mouth and his teeth bit into the soft flesh of his index finger as he looked down on his young sister.

Marie Anne's eyes were closed. The cut and grazed skin on her brow were still oozing blood, her eye and cheek were swollen and slowly discolouring, and there was blood soaking into the towel on which the arm was resting. The pillow behind her head, too, was showing blood.

After a moment he bent over her and his voice was thick and breaking as he spoke her name, 'Oh, Marie Anne. Marie Anne.'

Slowly she opened her eyes and her voice stammered his name, 'P–at.'

'Yes, dear, it's Pat.'

'Pat.'

'Yes, dear.'

'He meant to kill me some . . . time. But not the baby. Save the baby, Pat.'

'Be quiet, dear; don't talk. You'll be all right. You'll be all right; and the baby too. The doctor will be here soon. And here's Sarah and Father.' He turned with relief as the door opened, and his lids were blinking rapidly as he looked at his father, and all he could find to say as he pointed to the bed, was, 'She's . . . she's very tired,' and straightaway pushed past Sarah and went from the room.

Now it was James Lawson who stood looking down on his daughter, and the only words his mind offered him were those used by all men of whatever class when confronted with emotions they could not express: 'My God! My God!'

When her eyes opened and she slowly lifted her good hand to his, he took it and held it between his own for a moment, but found it impossible even to speak her name; it was she who spoke to him: 'Don't worry, Father,' she said.

James had to close his eyes for a moment before he could look at her again, and when she added, 'Please don't tell Grandpa . . . not yet.'

For the life of him he could not speak, not even her name, but what he did was to bring her thin fingers up to his lips and kiss them; and when her hand dropped from his he turned blindly to look at Sarah, but she spoke no word either . . .

It was nearly an hour later when Doctor Ridley arrived at the Hardings' farm. Mr Harding had just finished milking and he gave him a rough idea of what he would find at the cottage. Being a naturally jovial man, he had also to narrate how, when he heard the screams, he had left his ploughing, only to find, on his return, that the horse had eaten so much grass from the side verges of the field, he wouldn't get any more work out of him that day. Then he had gone on to say that his wife had taken charge of the matter up in Mr McAlister's cottage and was awaiting his arrival.

That Doctor Ridley was surprised at the situation he found in the cottage was not evident in either his speech or his manner, as he was shown into the bedroom and to the young girl bruised and bleeding from several parts of her body and lying, as he saw immediately, on a plank bed.

He stood looking down on the heaving bedclothes that covered the mound of her belly while he slowly took off his coat; then handing it to Mrs Harding, who was standing at the foot of the bed, he said, 'Hello, Mrs Harding,' and she answered, 'Good afternoon, doctor.'

Then looking at the person who seemed to be impeding him, because she had hold of the limp hand of the patient, he said, 'Would you mind?'

Sarah could always recognise sarcasm; on this occasion, however, she did not rise to it, but said under her breath, 'I'm not holding her hand, doctor, she's gripping mine.'

'Oh. Oh, I see. Well, then' – his voice was as low as hers – 'would you mind trying to disengage your hand? It would be a help, so that I could begin my examination.' And these words were now accompanied by a smile, but she did not respond to it. What she did was to take her other hand and, one by one, lift Marie Anne's fingers and embedded nails from her flesh.

When at last her hand was free and she went to move it from the bed, the doctor picked it up and examined it. There was a row of small blood spots on the hand where the nails had pierced the flesh and, his tone changing completely, he said, 'I see. I see. I'm sorry.'

'That's all right with me.'

Her Irish brogue and the way she had delivered the last words caused him to turn and look to where she was now moving towards the window. Then he found that Mrs Harding was standing close to him and, her voice scarcely a whisper, she was saying, 'They're great friends, Doctor.'

'Oh. Oh.'

This news surprised him further, for the Irish woman was certainly no lady, whereas the girl lying on the bed there, he recalled seeing some years ago when she had a broken ankle.

Gently now, he began his examination . . .

It was twenty minutes later when he went into the other room, and without any preamble said to the three men waiting for him, 'I shall need quite a lot of linen. Sheets, pillowcases, proper blankets, bed covers, towels and such;' then he turned and looked at Don, and there might have been a quirk to his lips as he said, 'and soap. You don't go in for refinements, Mr McAlister, do you?'

'I have never found the need, Doctor.'

'No, no; of course not. Well, now, that is the beginning.'

'What d'you mean, sir' – it was James speaking – 'the beginning?'

'Just what I say, Mr Lawson. There will be lots of things, many more, required if your daughter is to stay here for any length of time.'

'But she can't stay here!' James's voice expressed his indignation. 'How can she stay here? We must find something to get her across to Mr Harding's farm, and I'll have the carriage there. One thing is certain, though, she can't remain here.'

The young doctor stared at the portly figure before him. He had never heard any good about this man, yet he had never heard any bad either. He seemed to be an indifferent figure, not worthy to be included in any of the gossip that went round about that house.

Sensing the feeling of antagonism between his father and this very good doctor, Pat said in a placating tone, 'You see, doctor, my father's very worried about my sister, and as she is soon to have . . . a baby . . .'

'Yes, yes; I understand that,' said the young doctor impatiently. 'So I would advise you to advise your father to go ahead, as long as he has an undertaker and a hearse waiting at the house; in her present condition she could not survive the journey.' He now turned back to James as he added, 'She has not only been beaten severely, arms and stomach, yes, and stomach,' he emphasised, 'she is expecting the baby soon, as your son says, and let me tell you it might be sooner than you think. I understand from Mrs Harding that she has twice shown signs of labour pains, and I myself have just witnessed another, yet she is in so much shock and so weak that I doubt but there is to be a long battle for her, and for us too, I might add, before she can thrust her child into the world, whether alive or dead.'

This last statement seemed to stun the three men, and the doctor remained silent in order to allow the import of his words to sink in. When he went on it was to address Don: 'Your sleeping arrangements are crude, to say the least, Mr McAlister,' he said, 'but your board bed might come in handy after all if I have to use it. But we'll wait and see; another twenty-four hours should give us the answer; in the meantime I'm sure one of you' – he now looked from father to son – 'will want to stay the night and you'll need a place to sleep, because that' – he pointed to the couch – 'doesn't offer much comfort.'

'It is sufficient for what I need,' put in Don stiffly, and the doctor replied, 'No doubt. No doubt.' But then, his voice softening and even taking on a jocular tone, he said, 'We're not all as strong and hardy as you. Anyway, here's one that isn't, and if I need a rest between times, I should like a mattress to lie on. So, would it be possible—' he was now addressing James as he went on, 'to let us have three single mattresses? Two for out here and one inside the bedroom, because your housekeeper seems determined to live in there as long as your daughter is there. She says she can keep going for twenty-four hours or more. Maybe she can, but if her will is to give way to her body I would like to think she'll have somewhere to place it.'

'You'll have everything you need, doctor,' said James. 'And now I'm going to ask you one straight question, and I would like a straight answer: What is the exact condition of my daughter?'

Doctor Ridley stared at the man. Then, in an unusually quiet voice, he said, 'This is one time, sir, when I must tell you I find it impossible to give a straight answer. I can only say that at the present moment she is in shock; her temperature is rising; she must be in a great deal of pain, which I could alleviate. But this would only sap her energy, all of which she will need if she intends to bring the child naturally. That's all I can tell you at the present.'

'But what, sir, do you mean by naturally?'

This was Pat asking the question, and the doctor turned to him and said, 'Well, to put it bluntly, if she won't give birth to the child in the ordinary way it will have to be taken from her.'

'Even if it is alive?'

'Yes, yes, of course if it is alive. But let us all hope for the best. She is young and, as I recall, has a strong spirit, both good assets at a time like this. And now down to very mundane and practical matters: food. For the moment she will need only drinks. But having said that, there is the rank and file to be thought of. I don't suppose' – he was looking at Don now – 'you have a supply of tea, sugar, butter, bread, milk and such like to meet the occasion that has arisen?'

'No, sir; I'm sorry I haven't, but I can always see it is provided.'

'Oh, that is good and kind of you. Well, now,' – again he was looking at James – 'if I could ask you, sir, to see to the requirements we will be needing to get us over tonight and tomorrow. We will talk again about what will be needed during the further weeks.'

'Further weeks?' James's face was screwed up as if in enquiry, and the doctor answered, 'Yes, of course; further weeks. After she has had the baby she will be in need of a fortnight's rest at the least in her state.'

'But, sir . . .'

'Yes, Mr Lawson?'

James could find nothing more to say to this man. He wasn't used to dealing with doctors, at least not of this ilk. At the house, whenever there had been need of one, they had been attended by Dr Angus Sutton-Moore . . . but of course, he recalled that this young man – and, to him, he still seemed very young – was the one who had attended Marie Anne when she broke her foot and who laid down certain rules as to how she was to be treated. Well! He suddenly turned away and, picking up his hat and without speaking, he went to the door.

Looking from the doctor to Don, Pat said, 'No-one has asked your opinion about using your house; we've taken everything for granted.'

'Well, go on doing just that. Please.'

After a long pause and an exchange of glances, Pat said, 'Thank you, Don;' then he turned and followed his father.

As they hurried towards The Little Manor, Pat thought that he had never heard his father talk as he was doing now. Granted he had given him some surprises over the past few weeks, the main one being his frequent visits, not only to see his own father but to spend hours at the house, which Pat knew would have inflamed his mother's anger still further, but now here he was saying that he was going to take all that was necessary for the doctor's needs and the comfort of others from The Manor. He also said it was a night some people would not forget in a hurry.

Before they parted at The Little Manor, he said to Pat, 'Father will likely have got wind of something now because I understand Foggerty usually takes him a cup of tea in the middle of the afternoon. You must impress upon him that he cannot go along there tonight because there's no place for him to sit, never mind sleep, but tell him you'll take him first thing in the morning.' And with this his father had left him at The Little Manor and continued to march on to the house, for marching he was.

On arrival, he went straight to the yard, and definitely startled the men by standing in the middle of the yard and calling, 'Young! Young!'

When the coachman hurried out of the harness room, James demanded, 'Where are the others?'

'Well, sir, Bill Winters is . . . is in the barn seeing to the hay; I mean, the feed.'

'And Crouch?'

'Well, sir, he's seeing to Mr Vincent's horse. It's been sweating a lot again.'

'Get them here!'

Young hurried as he hadn't done for some time, calling his subordinates into the yard, although both men were already aware that the master was there and in an unusual hurry.

On their appearance James, pointing to them, said, 'You two, come with me. You, Young, get one of the others from the garden to give you a hand with the dray cart.'

'The dray cart?'

The man had hardly finished stammering the last word when James almost bawled at him, 'Yes! you heard, the dray cart. But first get someone to go to the laundry and bring me as many empty wash-baskets as they can find.'

For a moment the three men stood perfectly still, the same thought running through their minds: he's flipped his nut at last. But he wanted wash-baskets and the dray cart, and so they actually scattered to fulfil his command, only to be halted again by James yelling, 'You, Young, bring the dray to the front door, and see that those two bring the baskets into the hall.' And with this he went round the side of the house and into the hall.

There, he also startled Green by shouting, 'Get me Mrs Piggott!'

As if by magic Mrs Piggott appeared from a side passage at that moment, saying, 'Yes, sir? I . . . I'm here.'

'Well then, Mrs Piggott, two of the yard men will be here shortly with a number of wash-baskets, but first, I want you to go upstairs and show them where they can pick up four single mattresses.'

'Four m-m-mattresses?'

'You heard me, Mrs Piggott,' and he stressed each word. 'I said four single mattresses, and have them brought down here into the hall ready to be loaded onto the dray cart, which should be at the door very soon.'

Mrs Piggott dared to take her eyes from her master to glance enquiringly at Green, but he did not meet her gaze, for he was looking out of the tall window to where two of the yard men were carrying wash-baskets and making for the front door.

'And when they have done that I want you to accompany me to the linen room. Are you taking in what I am saying, Mrs Piggott?'

'Oh yes, sir. Yes, sir.'

'Well, stop gaping; and for your information, and you can pass this on, I have not gone mad; not yet, anyway.'

Robert Green was now opening the front door to the two evidently embarrassed and very puzzled yard men, and their bewilderment was not lessened when they were ordered to go with the housekeeper, who would show them where to get four single mattresses, which were to be brought down and placed on the dray cart. And the maids were to bring down the bedding for them.

At the top of the stairs the slightly distraught housekeeper was met by her mistress, who looked at the two men carrying wash-baskets, of all things.

'What on earth are you doing, Mrs Piggott?'

Mrs Piggott, swallowing deeply, faced her mistress and said, 'I am carrying out the master's orders, ma'am.'

At this Veronica Lawson leaned over the balustrade to see her husband looking up at her and she yelled at him, 'What does this mean?'

'If you will come down, my dear, I will tell you exactly what it means.' And he turned as if to walk into the drawing-room, but stopped and, addressing Green again, he said, 'When the dray cart comes to the door see that the bottom is entirely clean. If it isn't, put dust sheets on it. You understand?'

'Yes, sir. Yes, sir.'

Mr Lawson was standing in the middle of the drawing-room when his wife entered. She, of course, had to speak first, and she made a statement: 'You have gone mad.'

To this he answered, 'Not quite yet, my dear. I likely shall before this night is out; and you too, if you have any conscience left in you, you too may be feeling mad. Anyway, for your information I am at present directing that a quantity of bedding and linen et cetera should be taken to the cottage of Mr McAlister. You have heard of Mr McAlister, haven't you? He is the gentleman, and I repeat, *gentleman*, who was the instigator of your daughter's returning home. Well, she is at present lying in his cottage and is near death's door, and I am not exaggerating when I say this, because that statement has been confirmed by Dr Ridley.'

'Huh!' It was almost a laugh from Veronica now as she

said, 'Because she's having a premature baby she's lying near death's door? Poor soul!'

'No! woman. It isn't because she's having a premature baby that she is lying near death's door, but because your son battered her almost to death.' The words had come out on a whispered hiss, and she staggered back from them.

'What? What did you say?'

'You heard what I said. He has battered her almost to death. Head, face, stomach and all.'

'Nonsense! Nonsense! Why would Vincent want to . . . well, as you say, almost batter her to death?'

'Because of you. It appears he has inherited traits from you and he's hated her since she was little. It's been pointed out to you before, woman, that you knew of his feeling against her, because it was as strong as your own, and you could have put a stop to it. But no; you let it go on until now, and – wait for it – if she dies, and I repeat this, my dear Veronica, if she dies I shall see to it that your son also dies.'

When her hand went out to grip the back of a chair he knew that for once he had got through to her, and now he added, 'She was found just a few hours ago, and I can follow every step he took to carry out this' – he shook his head now, searching for words – 'diabolical attack. But even if I couldn't, she has named him, and there are other witnesses. But I shall deal with him as soon as I have seen to what is needed at Mr McAlister's cottage for, being a lone man's abode, it is ill-prepared for an occasion such as this. So, madam, inform your son I want him in this room, ready and waiting for me, no matter how long I may be in returning.'

She uttered no word. Her eyes were wide, her whole body was trembling, and to herself she was repeating the words, 'That girl! That girl again!' . . .

Fifteen minutes later the linen room was depleted by

six pairs of the best sheets, matching pillowcases, and a dozen towels of various sizes. The blanket room, too, gave up three of its best blankets.

The wash-baskets, full to overflowing, followed the mattresses down into the hall; but apparently the master was not yet finished. After ordering his housekeeper to have two large hampers taken to her store-room, he then made her heart ache because, not satisfied with sweeping two shelves almost bare of their daily necessities, he went to the so-called delicacy cupboard, where he picked out tins of pâté, pressed tongues, salmon, and fruits, saying, 'These won't go very far with four or more people so, Mrs Piggott, will you kindly go to your meat store and pick out a ham and a small side of bacon, as well as a loin of lamb from which chops could be cut.'

The housekeeper made no reply to this; she was past talking; her face was colourless and her mouth dry; she felt she had come to the end of her world . . .

It was a full half-hour later when the piled-high covered dray cart was driven out of the yard by an indignant coachman accompanied by the two yard men. Harold Young had his orders to drive the cart into Mr Harding's farmyard. Once there the three of them would unload the articles and carry them across the two fields to Mr McAlister's cottage.

The floor of the hall, empty now of its miscellaneous baggage, was being cleaned by two scurrying, nervous maids who, now that the master had clearly gone out of his mind, could see themselves without a job in the near future, because things were definitely going from bad to worse in this house. In the drawing-room the mistress was now shouting at Mr Vincent, and he was shouting back at her.

May Dalton, the first chambermaid, gave a discreet cough and Susan Fowler, her assistant, recognising the signal, doubled her efforts with the polishing mop, for the master was coming from the direction of the kitchen, followed by the footman carrying a wine basket in which there were four bottles, and he was saying, 'What would you like me to do with these, sir?'

'Oh yes. Well, I can't take them out like that, can I? Wrap them up individually and get someone to take them along to The Little Manor. They're for the cottage, but I'll pick them up there. Do it right away.'

'Yes, sir.'

Robert Green waited until the drawing-room door had closed on his master, before he turned quickly to the maids, saying, 'Get yourselves out of here!'

'We've got to . . .'

'Do what I say. And look, take this.' He handed the wine basket to May Dalton, saying, 'Wrap them up, as he said, individually, then put them into a hessian bag and bring it back here.'

May Dalton looked at him hard, and had she dared she would have said, And leave you here so you can listen in? But both girls did as they were bid, leaving Green with the hall to himself.

He was standing in the middle distance between the drawing-room door and the front door. At one time, when he'd had less to do, this would have been the position he would take up; besides affording him a view of the approaching visitors, it was also a good listening post.

James had closed the drawing-room door slowly behind him. For a moment, he stood with his back to it and surveyed his son, who was standing by the head of the couch, and his wife, who was seated at a small table on which she was drumming her fingers. But on the sight of him standing there making no move forward, she rose sharply to her feet, saying, 'Barking up the wrong tree, as usual. How dare you say such things about your own son!'

James walked slowly forward towards the middle of the room, taking no heed of his wife but concentrating

336

his gaze on Vincent as he said to him, 'How have you managed to convince her that you're in the right again?'

'I don't know what on earth you're getting at, Father. And it's a serious accusation you're making.'

'It is indeed.'

James took no notice of his wife's interrupting, strident voice, but continued to stare at his son, and slowly he said to him, 'You were in the yard when I asked Pat if anything was wrong. He knew I was referring to Marie Anne and he answered "no", but that she was going for a walk as far as the wood. To me that meant Sarah Foggerty would be with her. But you weren't to know that, so you made it your business also to take a walk to the wood by the top road. Likely you were disappointed when you saw she had company; but then, what did her company do but leave her sitting on the old tree-stump before going picking bluebells. It was then you saw your chance, and you took it. There must have been plenty of broken branches for you to choose from, and you picked on a heavy one. You started on the side of her head, and proceeded systematically to beat her. It was only Sarah's yelling and approach that stayed your hand, for Marie Anne, by then, must have been past screaming.'

Vincent was now looking at his mother and shaking his head wildly as he said, 'He's mad! He's mad! I told you. Shortly after you left the yard I came indoors and I spoke to Mother here. Didn't I? Didn't I?'

'Yes, you did' – Veronica was yelling again – 'and he never left the house.'

James looked from one to the other. She was lying for him; but she was doing so with such emphasis it was hard to disbelieve her.

'Would you swear on that, my dear?'

He watched her glance towards Vincent, then swallow deeply as she said, 'Yes. Yes, I would.'

'And following on that, I suppose you would say you

337

had witnesses to support your statement?'

'Yes, I would, that too. And . . . and I can fetch one. Just you wait! Just you wait!'

She almost ran from the drawing-room, and she hadn't far to go to find her footman.

'Green!'

'Yes, ma'am?'

'Today about three o'clock, you . . . you let Mr Vincent in through the front door.'

'I . . . I don't remember, ma'am.'

'Listen to me, Green! Today, at about three o'clock, you're not sure of the time but you are sure that you let Mr Vincent in through that door.' She pointed now to the door itself, and he turned to look at it, then back towards her. And now her voice low, she said, 'You have been promoted, Green, you have a good position here, you could go further, you understand? or you' – she drew herself up – 'could be without a post, do you understand?'

'Yes, I understand you, ma'am.'

'Then come along and answer my questions in front of my husband.'

She entered the room, followed by Green, and the man stood back near the door almost as his master had just a few minutes earlier. That is until she demanded, 'Come forward, Green. Come forward.'

After the man had walked slowly forward she faced him, saying, 'You tell the master whom you let in the front door this afternoon between half-past two and half-past three.'

For answer the man, looking straight back at her, said, 'I'm off duty between half-past two and half-past three, ma'am. Since you altered the times, I have been allowed an hour free because of my extra work and curtailed leave.'

For a moment all was quiet in the room; then Veronica Lawson turned and glanced at her son before looking back at the footman and saying, 'But you said you let Mr Vincent in the front way at around that time.'

Again there was silence before the man answered, 'No ma'am, I didn't say that; you said it.'

'Green!' Her voice was almost at screaming pitch now. 'Don't you stand there and lie. You said . . .'

She got no further because James, his voice matching hers, yelled, 'Shut up! woman. You cannot make the man lie for you.' Then turning to the footman he said, 'That's all, Green,' only to check his step immediately by saying, 'Just a minute. I'll tell you what you can do for me, and for Mr Vincent' – he almost spat out his son's name – 'You can go up to his room and start packing his cases or anything that you find belonging—'

'By God in heaven! you don't . . . he doesn't! You dare go near my room!' Vincent had left the support of the couch head and had moved towards the footman, when he was checked, not only by his father's voice but by an arm thrust out and pushing him backwards with such force that he almost overbalanced; but he continued to shout at his father, 'You won't do this to me! You've gone mad . . . mad.'

'Not quite. But by the time I have finished with you that might be the case.' James turned again to Green, saying, 'Do as I say. Everything you can find belonging to my son, pack it, and have it brought down into the hall.'

After the door had closed on Green, Vincent stepped towards his father and growled at him, 'You won't do this to me! You can't do this to me! This is my home and I intend to stay here.'

'From this day onwards, this is not your home and if you don't leave it quietly I shall call the police and have you charged with assault and battery; yes, maybe murder. Do you hear? you lecherous, dirty, filthy coward of a man. You're not a man. No, you're not a man, you're an evil beast. Ever since you were a youth you tried in most ways to interfere with your sister; I know that now. Playful horseplay *she* would call it,' he said, thrusting out his arm to point to his wife. 'It was only Marie Anne's temper that kept you at bay. She was glad to get away to London and out of your clutches, as well as away from her mother's hate. And the very thought that some man had been where you wanted to be has driven you mad, hasn't it? So what d'you do? You try to finish her off good and proper; and her child. Well, let me tell you, there's just a chance that you have succeeded and that they both could die within the next twenty-four hours. If that happens I shall see that justice is done.'

Vincent moved a step back and his hands began to flail the air, the while tossing his head, as he appealed to his mother, saying, 'He's crazy. I tell you he's crazy, Mother. Talking about justice. I've done nothing, nothing, and he can't prove anything.'

For once Veronica Lawson did not come back with comforting words that would have substantiated his statement, but she groped backwards at the chair she was standing by; and she almost fell into it as she listened to her husband, this strange man, this man she had never known, say, 'You will go to your friend's house. It is at twenty-three Bingham Close. Oh yes; I know it, and all about him too.'

It was almost on a high scream now that Vincent cried, 'He is not my friend in that way; you're barking up the wrong tree, old man. He has a—'

He glanced at his mother, and she stared back at him, her eyes now wide with other questions, which her husband answered for her, saying, 'Well, yes, he has a sister, a lady of high standing. Married. If I'm correct, her husband is an explorer. Well, well. But what does it matter whether your friend is male or female, you visit his house and stay there for long weekends. Well, this time you will stay until you are ordered to leave, which will

340

depend upon what happens to Marie Anne. If I cannot contact you at that address then I shall immediately put the matter into the hands of the police. Do you understand me? because I mean to make you pay and to the full – and I repeat *to the full* – for destroying my daughter's life. One more thing before you leave here. You are finished in my business. I shall leave orders that you are not allowed back into the office. I shall give you double their value for the shares you hold. Once you start to quibble, I shall withdraw the offer.'

'You'll not get away with this, you'll not. I'll see you damned first. You're not going to shame me. I refuse to leave this house.'

'Oh well; I told you what would happen if you didn't leave on your own, so you have chosen.' And with this, James took three quick strides to the bell-pull at the side of the fireplace, an action which was enough to make Vincent clutch his father's wrist and wrench it away from the cord.

What happened next brought Veronica Lawson springing from her seat, for her husband's fist had flashed out and caught her son full in the face, knocking him sideways. At this moment, too, the door opened, apparently in answer to the short ring of the bell, and Green, looking amazed to see his master, his podgy, flabby-bellied master, taking up a fighting pose and waiting for his son to come back at him. And the mistress was standing over her son, where he had fallen on to the edge of the couch, and she was pleading with him, 'Come, come along, dear, come along. I'll go upstairs with you, and you will come back. I'll see to it. You *will* come back, for this is your home. But come now, come. Your . . . your father' – and she turned a glaring look on her husband – 'will regret this. Oh yes, he'll regret this to the end of his days.'

When Vincent went to push her away, she clung tightly onto him saying, 'Let it be. Let it be. Come along.' And she actually edged him as far away from James as she possibly could; and now seeing Green standing to the side of the open door, she cried at him, 'Get out of my way, you!'

But the man did not move because he wasn't in her way. Green now walked to his master, whose fighting pose had slumped and who was now gripping the back of a high chair as if for support, and quietly he said, 'I have brought three of Mr Vincent's cases down, sir; and I've had the travelling trunk brought from the attic. He will need this to take his suits.'

The only response James showed to this information was to lift his head, and then, after a moment, to say to Green, 'The others won't be back from the cottage for some time. Go and tell Pinner to get the buggy out and that he is to take Mr Vincent and his luggage to the station.'

'Yes sir; I'll do that.'

After Green had gone, James stood for a moment looking about the room. Had he really said and done all he had said and done in the last ten minutes? Had he hit Vincent? Oh yes, he certainly had. He looked down on his portly belly. It must indeed have been a lucky punch. Oh, he didn't know so much about luck; there had been strength in it, the strength of anger. How odd that the first blow he had ever struck against anyone had to be against his own son.

He again surveyed the room and realised that he had never liked it. It was too much like his one-time bedroom; a battle arena.

As he walked across the hall towards the study he glanced to where the cases lay by the front door, then the stairs down which Green and the boot-boys were laboriously edging a large travelling trunk.

Once in the study, he sank into a deep leather chair, lay back and closed his eyes, and for a moment it seemed as if his mind had gone blank. He could think of nothing; he could recall nothing. The only desire in him at this moment was to fall asleep.

When his thinking slowly took over again, he heard a distant voice say, 'Sir.'

Then again, 'Sir.'

He opened his eyes to see Green holding towards him a tray on which stood a glass of port, and at the sight of it he slowly eased himself up in the chair, saying, 'Thank you, Green. That is very thoughtful of you. It is exactly what I need at this moment.'

'I thought you might, sir.'

As Green stared down at the florid face of this man he had served for years, he recalled hearing the phrase, and believing it to be true, that no man could be a hero to his servant. Yet in his eyes at this moment this man, whom he had seen for years as a self-indulgent, hen-pecked, gutless individual, definitely stood out as a hero, for he had put his wife in her place. More so, he had given that big, swaggering, cowardly upstart a blow that, unless he was vastly mistaken, would be evident tomorrow as a beautiful shiner. And he had been ready to deliver another given the chance.

'Would you like me to get a hot bath ready for you, sir, before dinner?'

'No, thank you, Green; I must get back to Mr McAlister's cottage.'

'Is . . . is Miss Marie Anne very badly hurt, sir?'

'I'm afraid so, Green, very badly; and what is more, she's likely to lose her child.'

'I am indeed sorry, sir; and I can tell you that the rest of the staff will be also.'

'Thank you, Green. Thank you.'

At the quiet opening of the door they both turned to see Evelyn, who said, 'Oh! there you are, Father.'

'Hello, my dear.'

343

'Good evening, Green.'

'Good evening, miss.'

As Green went out he thought, there's another one changed for the better; it evens things out a bit.

Pulling a chair up to her father's side, Evelyn sat down, saying, 'I can't believe what I've heard. Is it true that he beat her up? I mean, is . . . is she really bad?'

'She's not only bad, my dear, but it's doubtful whether she will recover. Even if the baby survives.'

'I can't believe it. I . . . I met Pat on the road – he was in the trap with Grandpa. He just gave me a rough idea.'

'Oh no. This'll finish Father off as well. He'll have to walk across that field and it's rough going. Why couldn't Pat . . . ? What am I talking about? nobody can stop Father when he wants to do anything. But I must get along there and see that he gets back home, or we'll have him lying on a mattress on the floor.'

Quickly now, he finished his port and pulled himself to his feet, and with this Evelyn rose too, saying, 'And you've actually thrown Vincent out, Father?'

'Yes, yes,' he nodded. 'I've actually thrown him out. And it's a good job I'm not a man of bigger stature or else he mightn't have lived to walk out.'

'I . . . I saw him leaving the yard; he's like someone gone mad.'

'There's one thing I can tell you, Evelyn: if anything happens to Marie Anne he'll wish he *had* gone mad.'

'And all this happened this afternoon since I went out.' She shook her head.

'No, no, my dear. It started years ago, even before you were born. Anyway, you say he's gone from the yard?'

'Yes, and Mother was standing at the top of the drive. She was almost wailing, and she spoke to me for the first time in days; but in the form of a threat, of course, that if I continue on the road I'm on, she'll do something desperate, because she cannot stand any more.'

'That sounds familiar, my dear.'

'Is there anything I could do to help, Father? I mean that seriously: I'm no longer the mean, pampered individual I was, because Mrs Harding doesn't make one's path smooth; she always starts at the hard end of a lesson, and she's always much more pleasant when you've achieved something. Have you ever mucked out a pigsty, Father?'

James bowed his head as he shook it, then his hand covered his eyes for a moment. 'Don't make me laugh, Evelyn,' he said, 'because there is no space for laughter in anything that's happened this day, but' – he took his hand away from his eyes to look at her – 'don't tell me she had you cleaning out a pigsty.'

'Oh, that's nothing, Father, nothing. Did you also know there's a correct way to swill a cowshed without splashing the cows' udders?'

He now put his arm around her shoulders and walked her towards the door, saying, 'Don't tell me any more, my dear, but keep your stories for another evening when, pray God, we can laugh about them. In the meantime you asked if you could help. You really could, by dropping in on your grandfather during this bad period and also during the week when Pat or I are at work, for one of us must be there. And you could also be a great help by finding out what they'll likely need from day to day.'

'I'll do that, Father, yes, I'll do that. Where are you off to now?'

'I'm going back to the cottage. You've just told me Father's there, and my task will be to get him back home tonight. Speaking in the kindest way about Don's, Mr McAlister's habitation, it's a very comfortless place.'

'Is it dirty?'

'Oh no, no! not in the least, not dirty. The only way I can describe it is to say it's worn, everything is worn. It's shabby.

'Anyway my dear, I'm going now, but I would ask you

one more thing. Don't cross your mother any further than you can help tonight; bite your tongue if you have to, because she's had a number of shocks during the last few hours, and there's only so much any individual can stand, even her.'

7

When James reached the cottage it was to find his father sitting on the couch with a cup of tea in his hand and to be greeted with, 'Hello, James.'

James did not answer him immediately, but looked at Pat, who was standing behind the couch. But he said nothing, only spread out his hands, which was significant enough.

Dropping down onto the other end of the couch, James said tartly, 'You shouldn't have done this, Father. There's enough to worry about as it is.'

'What're you talking about?' the old man snapped back; 'I'm not going to cause any worry, except perhaps to myself. If I were back there on my own, I'd go mad not knowing how things were going with the poor child. And look,' his voice dropped now and he leant towards James, 'I am not in my box yet, and at this moment there's much more life in me than there looks to be in you. What happened back there?'

'I'll tell you later.'

'Well, I'll tell you now' – the old man's voice was a hiss – 'he'll do time for this if nothing else, do you understand?'

'Yes, I understand, Father, and he does too. He's not there any more.'

'What d'you mean? He's skipped it?'

'No; but I saw to it that he left, bag and baggage.'

The old man drew back from his son and put his head

to one side as if he were surveying him anew, and he said, 'You did? You threw him out?'

'Yes. Yes, I threw him out. And don't look so surprised. Like you said about yourself, I too am not dead yet.'

When a faint cry came to them from the other room the old man murmured, 'That poor child. That poor child.' And James, leaning towards his father, put his hand on his knee and said softly, 'Father, there's going to be a lot of coming and going and there's no place here where you can sleep. You'd be much more comfortable at home.'

At this the old man demanded, 'What did you have the mattresses brought for?'

'Not for *you* to sleep on, Father.' James now looked at Don, who had appeared from the kitchen, and he said, 'Apart from those,' and he pointed to the mattresses where they lay on the floor in the far corner, 'where have you managed to stack everything?'

'Oh, that was easy,' said Don, with a touch of impatience just managing to cover up his real feelings. 'There happens to be a little room in which I store all my bits and pieces for the studio. It has shelves and a cupboard; we've crammed all the linen in there. As for the food' – he thumbed back towards the kitchen door – 'the larder, I would say, has never held so much food since it was built.'

Looking up at Don, Emanuel said, 'Good. Good. But will I be any great trouble to you if I were to stay here tonight?'

'Not to me, sir; no, none at all; but there's no other bed of any sort.'

'I don't need a bed. You've got mattresses over there, haven't you? and it won't be the first time I've laid on a shakedown, so will you inform my son, Mr McAlister, that I won't be in anybody's way.'

Don replied, 'I'll do that, sir,' at the same time thinking, These people! They seem more concerned about

348

mattresses, food, and the old man than about her; and as if in a prayer he added, Please God, keep me from expressing my real feelings. And, oh yes, yes; keep her with us; rid her of the idea of dying.

He now beckoned Pat into the kitchen, and there said tersely, 'It's a matter of bread.'

'Bread?'

'Yes; yes. Your father thought of everything; butter, cheese, ham, everything, but no bread.' He smiled wanly; and again he wondered how he could be standing here talking about the need for bread when his whole body and mind were in the room next door holding her, soothing her, begging her to give birth to the child before it was too late. Yet, here he was, supposedly concerned with bedding people and feeding them. Some part of him would like to thrust the lot of them out of the door, leaving only the doctor, Sarah, and his beloved Marie Anne. Why should she have been almost battered to death within yards of this cottage and she about to give birth to her child? The feeling that had been in him since Sarah had suggested that the conception had not resulted from rape but through a certain fondness for the older man had now, on top of everything else, become almost unbearable.

Pat was saying, 'I'll see to it, Don.'

They heard the bedroom door open; then the doctor's voice calling softly, 'Mr Lawson,' brought them both from the kitchen. 'I suppose all the baby linen is ready back at the house?' asked John Ridley.

'Yes; yes, I'm sure it is, doctor,' said Pat.

'Well, I think you'd better get some of it over here as soon as possible.'

Flustered, Pat said, 'Well, yes; I was going for bread. I'll have the linen brought back.'

Ignoring the old man on the couch, who had remained silent throughout this exchange, John Ridley returned to the bedroom, thinking, What a lot! That fellow, talking about bread and his sister dying, for dying she certainly was. He had worked in some queer set-ups but none to beat this. A lovely girl, pregnant, battered almost to death, about to give birth to a child in this mean habitation, where a scarred man lived the life of a hermit, and the three male members of the family ready to doss down on the floor, and that Irish woman forever sitting like a stook, never opening her mouth except to mutter something to the patient!

The cottage was quiet; the mattresses were occupied; even Sarah had been forced to lie down. But in the bedroom, the doctor was saying, 'We can't wait any longer, Mrs Harding; I'm going to take it away. Let's get on with it. I'll give her a whiff of chloroform. If she is to have a chance, it's either forceps or a Caesarean; and there's really no fitting place here for a Caesarean.'

After washing his hands, he took from his bag a small bottle and a pad of cotton wool, a pair of forceps and what looked like a long pair of scissors. These he arranged on a towel on the dressing table; then looking at Mrs Harding, he said, 'Here we go! and may God go with us.'

He dabbed the pad of cotton wool with the chloroform and placed it gently over Marie Anne's nose and mouth, and after she had drawn two quick breaths he dropped it to the side, picked up the scissors-like instrument and snipped at each side of the vagina; then gently inserting his hand, he felt for the position of the child.

A few minutes later, he started to speak as if to the child, saying, 'That's it . . . that's it,' and after a moment, he grabbed at the forceps and after inserting them in the womb, he began to pull gently, saying, 'Come on now! Come on! Let us have you . . .'

When his forearm jerked, he grunted; then slowly, very slowly, he drew forth the baby; and it lay on his hands for a moment before he cut the cord and almost threw the live bundle into Mrs Harding's waiting arms, then immediately concentrated his attention on Marie Anne.

When the child opened its mouth and gave a cry, Mrs Harding exclaimed, almost gleefully, 'A girl! Lovely. Lovely,' and, whipping up a towel, she wrapped it around the infant.

When she managed to open the door, only Don stood there. He was so close to it, it was as if he had been about to enter the room, and she said, 'It's all right, she's fine. It's a girl. Bring the kitchen bowl and warm water and put it on that table there.'

When he did not move, she said, 'What's the matter with you, man? Well . . . Look here! hold her, and I'll see to what I want.'

And so he held Marie Anne's child; and he looked down on its little face, each side somewhat reddened, and the thought came to him that he could have been its father and she could have inherited his brand.

8

It was more than forty-eight hours later and close on ten o'clock at night. The cottage was quiet. In the main room Sarah lay on a mattress near the wall and to her side was a very ornate crib holding the child.

To the right of the fireplace, James was lying on another mattress, and it was evident he was in a deep sleep. Only a few hours earlier, Pat had taken his grandfather home. This was after much persuasion and on the grounds that he could do no good for himself or anyone else, sitting as he was doing, propped up on the couch both day and night.

Mrs Harding had gone back to the farm for a much needed night's rest, and at seven o'clock that evening the doctor had left after his second visit of the day, and his last words to Don had been, 'None of us can do any more. She's very weak, and there's a great tiredness in her. That's only to be expected; she's lost a quantity of blood, and this coming on top of everything else will likely prove to be too much. Only time will tell.'

He had bent over Marie Anne and gently moved a strand of her hair away from her bandaged brow. Then he had turned to Don, who was by his side, and remarked, 'You're up to sitting with her? I mean, you're not all done in? Apparently you haven't closed your eyes for the past forty-eight hours.'

'I'm all right; I'm used to vigils.'

As if he were addressing a monk, John Ridley nodded – the word vigil had conjured up long penances such as monks endured. Then he said, 'Well, I'll leave you with her now. If you think there's any change for the worse, do as has been arranged and call her father.'

'I'll do that.'

'I'll be around first thing in the morning.'

'Thank you, doctor.'

Left alone, Don turned down the wick of the lamp that was standing on the chest of drawers. His eyes slid to the little cabinet that had been pushed back against the wall, and although he knew he wouldn't be disturbed he had no desire to open it and talk. He was past talking to Him and praying. He returned to the head of the bed and took his seat. He stared at the discoloured and unrecognisable face on the pillow and repeated to himself the doctor's words: 'One way or the other.'

The little clock on the mantelshelf showed twenty minutes past ten. There was a long night before him, and it might be her last night.

He gently picked up her good hand lying limp on top of the coverlet, and he stroked the fingers for a moment before whispering her name: 'Marie Anne. Marie Anne.'

There was no answer to the plea in his voice.

He stared down into the flushed face. Like St Aloysius she had willed herself to die and like him she *would* die, but why? Just through fear of that vile beast of a man.

He tapped the back of her hand gently now as he said, 'Marie Anne. Marie Anne, can you hear me? If you can, listen. Listen to what I am saying: You need fear him no longer, for he has gone; his father has banished him. He'll never trouble you again.' He knew that these last words were just wishful thinking; the man might be banished from the house, but he was still in her life and he would always remain there, until the one or other of them went, and she knew it. Should he himself ever come face to face with him, he knew he would not only want to do so, but would endeavour to carry out that wish.

He said again, 'Marie Anne, listen to me. You are not going to die; you mustn't die. You are not going to die; you mustn't die. You are being selfish, do you understand that? You are. Think of your grandfather; how is he going to feel? And your father, who is in great distress. Then there is Pat, and Evelyn. Evelyn has already put off her wedding. But above everyone, everyone, there is your Sarah, your dear Sarah, who no longer talks, does not even mutter a word. If you should leave us she will go back to London. Even caring for your child won't make her stay here. Are you listening, Marie Anne? Make some movement to tell me that you can hear me.'

He looked at her hand; he looked at her face; she had made no movement whatsoever; and now his voice scarcely a whisper he said, 'There is someone else who will miss you, Marie Anne. His heart is aching now, and has ached for a long time. That's why he stopped paying visits to your home, because he couldn't bear to see you. There was no future in it. You were too young; he was a disfigured man. But if you should go, his heart will not only ache, it will break. And hearts do break, Marie Anne. Oh yes; hearts do break. It is not just a silly saying, but hearts break and a heart like his, one that knows it can only love you, and love you, and love you, without any hope of affection in return, will become so unbearable that he will likely take the path you are considering. However, in his case with much more reason, for he would be unable to bear living, knowing that the only beautiful thing that had come into his marred life was no longer on this earth.

'A little over three days ago you were going to tell me something, Marie Anne, but you were interrupted and you never did. I knew then what you were going to say; that you were my friend and that you didn't mind my face. That is what you were going to say, wasn't it, Marie

Anne? But, my dear, you have never seen my face and I hope you never will.'

He became silent now, just stroking her hand. Then his voice still a whisper, he said, 'Stay with us, Marie Anne. Stay with us.' And in a despairing plea, he added, 'Oh Marie Anne, stay for me. Please! Please! stay for me.'

There was still no movement from her face or her hand. He glanced at the clock again. He could hardly believe it, it showed something to twelve. He hadn't been talking to her all that time, had he? No, no. Then he must have just been silent in between times.

He released his hold on her hand, then drew himself quietly to his feet, stretched his arms well above his head, then jerked his shoulders as if to relax the muscles before he walked to the window, and there, pulling the curtains apart, he looked up into the sky.

It was a perfectly clear sky, a deep, midnight blue, and there was a moon shining. He could not actually see it but it was lighting up the little rill to the far side of the back garden. It had turned the water to silver where it was dropping from the stones and running into the gutter that it had carved for itself over the years and then emptied into the river.

He looked up into the sky again. There was a great expanse of it. It was a beautiful night; it was a beautiful world; only living was ugly. He closed the curtains and walked softly back to the bed, and there, sitting down, he again took hold of her good hand, and he spoke to her as if she really was listening to him: 'It's a lovely night. I often walk by the river on nights like this and I let the wind blow on my face . . . my *face*, Marie Anne, without its cover. It's wonderful to feel the wind on your face, all your face; and there was a time, you know, when I used to talk to it, my face, I mean, that part. I used to say such things as, That feels better, doesn't it? I'm sorry you can't always feel it. But these were dangerous mutterings, and

355

I had to stop them, for I knew where they would lead in the end. You know, Marie Anne, I don't think of my face as a whole, I am two people, one who talks to God, and the other who denies His existence. There is a big cross in the Brothers' chapel, and even as a boy I argued with the hanging figure. The Brothers tried to stop me. They managed for a time, but I took it up again when I came here. I made a miniature – it's in the cabinet over there – then one day I realised, well, I'd realised it for some time, but wouldn't admit to it, I was just talking to myself and giving myself answers. Yet since, I've thought that if God is anywhere, He's guiding from afar through the still small voice of conscience. I suppose you've heard that phrase, haven't you, Marie Anne, the still small voice? There was one period when I knew I was near madness. I must have been between sixteen and seventeen. I was growing very tall and broad with it and one part of my face told me that while I could have been quite pleasant to look upon, the other, that I was so hideous that I had the desire to smash everything within reach. One day I did; I wrecked a whole bench of dear Brother Percival's work and like a distraught infant I lay on the floor kicking and screaming; well, actually fighting two hefty Brothers. The Brothers were very kind; they called it a breakdown. That's one of the reasons why I feel I must always go on working for them. I could have repaid them, you know, Marie Anne, by becoming a Brother, or better still I could have repaid them with interest by becoming a priest. That's when they sent me to Rome. But, inside, I knew that, in spite of everything, I was too much of a worldly man, wanting something, but not knowing what, until I met you.'

Suddenly he felt tired. The feeling was overtaking his body and he had no power to resist it, and so he let it have its sway . . .

There was a crick in his neck. His whole body was in cramp. He became aware that his brow was resting on his forearm and that this was along the edge of the plank bed. He tried to open his eyes, but the lids seemed gummed, until a voice sprang them wide: 'Had a nice sleep?'

The pain of raising his head was agonising, but what met his gaze was amazing, for there, at the other side of the bed, stood Sarah, one arm supporting Marie Anne, the other holding a cup to her lips.

He dragged his cramped body to his feet, and when Sarah said, 'You could do with a cup of tea?' his throaty answer was, 'I . . . I must have fallen asleep. I'm sorry.'

'Yes, you did; and for a long time. Do you know the time?' She looked towards the clock. 'A quarter to seven.'

'I'm sorry,' he said again, to which Sarah came back quickly, 'Oh man! don't be sorry. Can't you see she's turned the corner?'

He looked at Marie Anne. Her blurred gaze was on him, and he had the strange feeling that a long time had passed since he had last seen her, as if he had been away somewhere, to a refreshing place. It must have been a good sleep. But there she was, she was back.

Quite suddenly he felt elated and exclaimed loudly, 'I'll go and have a dip in the river first;' and as he hurried through the room and through the kitchen, Sarah's laugh followed him.

9

For three weeks Marie Anne lay on the plank bed, refusing to have it changed for a mattress. When she did get up, she would sit by the window, the baby in its cot by her side, and all the while there were comings and goings and bustle about her.

She'd had two special visitors. One, Evelyn, she had been very pleased to see. She had come in the other day and sat opposite her by the window, and just as Marie Anne knew that Evelyn would be seeing a great change in herself, she was also seeing a great change in her sister. Gone was the arrogant, haughty woman. In fact, Marie Anne could not imagine that the young woman sitting before her was the same one who had shown such a dislike of her.

There she had sat, laughingly describing how she was being trained to be a farmer's wife and byre assistant. She had also given her some information that none of the others had mentioned: their mother had gone to Canada for a holiday and Vincent had accompanied her. Could Marie Anne remember David and John? she asked.

Oh yes, yes, she had replied; she could remember them both. One was very tall and the other, in comparison, seemed to be short.

At this, Evelyn had explained that the short, quiet one was David, but that John was more boisterous and, if she remembered rightly, was always fighting with Vincent; so she imagined that Vincent's surprise visit might not be welcomed by John. However, she understood David had a house of his own and it would be there that their mother and Vincent would stay. John had married the daughter of a rancher who, like himself, was a horse breeder, and so had taken up his abode there. Evelyn had also said, rather shyly, that her own delayed marriage was to take place in a fortnight's time, but that it would be so quiet, she had ended on a laugh, that the registrar himself would hardly notice it.

The other surprising visitor was Pat's young lady. Marie Anne had expected to meet someone tall and slim and, being of Pat's choice, rather beautiful, but Miss Anita Brown turned out to be almost the opposite. She was small and dark and, she guessed, very vivacious. She was a teacher of French. She wasn't beautiful, nor yet plain; perhaps her profession had made her petite. This, together with an infectious laugh, had made her very attractive. She hadn't mentioned when Pat and she were to be married; nor had she herself asked. Also the fact that Sarah took to her right away seemed to add to her prestige.

Her grandfather, weather permitting, visited her most days; that was after he had had duckboards laid across the two fields from Mr Harding's farmhouse. Mr Harding had, of course, willingly acceded to this . . .

The five weeks she had spent in the bedroom had seemed like another lifetime; but this morning, standing in the stripped room of the cottage, facing Don, she was well aware that this was the only time since her recovery that they had been alone together.

Looking up at him, she said, 'How on earth have you put up with us all this time! There must have been days when you longed for the peace and quiet among the Brothers back in London.'

He threw back his head and laughed as he said, 'Peace and quiet among the Brothers! My dear, if you want a taste of bedlam you should be with them during what is termed the leisure hour, especially if the meeting happens to be in the kitchen or when Brother John is taking the opportunity to practise his mouth organ. Or when Brother Jacko is determined to pin me down to German for an hour.' Then the smile going from his face, he looked deep into her eyes as he said, 'I can say to you, Marie Anne, that these have been the happiest five weeks of my life, that is after the baby was born and you decided to stay among us.'

Marie Anne turned away from his penetrating gaze and walked towards the fireplace, saying quietly, 'I would have gone but for you.'

He remained staring at her back, willing himself not to move towards her, and when she turned to face him again she said, 'You won't neglect us as you did before, will you? You'll come over as often as possible, won't you? And if I may, I shall come here and see you.'

He still did not move: what could he say to that? Don't come here; you'll get yourself talked about, or, That would be dangerous in a way you're not aware of. He could see himself being drawn to The Little Manor frequently; but the danger was minimised there, for there were people about; but here, when they would be alone together, that would be a danger.

He now heard himself saying, 'You will be welcome at any time, you know that; but don't forget that I am a working man.'

When she made no answer to this, but just continued to look at him, he said, 'You'll soon be seventeen; the second of August, isn't it?'

'Yes, the second of August. When were *you* born?'

'Oh, me? Well, quite close to you; the thirty-first of July, and I'll be thirty-three, almost twice your age, old enough to be your—'

'Don't say it!' Although her voice was harsh, it had a break in it, and there was no smile on her face; in fact, she looked angry as she said, 'That is a trite remark, and you know it. As for me being seventeen, that is the age of a young girl and I am no longer a young girl, if I have ever been one.'

'All right, all right.' He had put his hand out towards her and his voice was soft as he said, 'You are no longer a young girl and I am sorry for my trite remark, but please don't disturb yourself, I was merely trying to point out—'

'I know what you were trying to point out, Don; what you're always trying to point out.' She stopped and looked towards the door; then her voice changing, she said, 'Here's Father. I'm . . . I'm sorry if I've disturbed you in any way.'

The door opened and James greeted her with, 'All ready for the road, my dear?'

'Yes, Father; but I was just telling Don it will be some time before he is able to put his house in order, after all the wear and tear.'

'Yes, yes,' James put in, nodding towards the floor. 'There's been some tramping done on this over the past weeks, Don.'

'There was a lot of tramping done on it before; you've been very kind not to notice the holes. Anyway, I was thinking about getting a carpet and altering the whole set-up, because I've never done anything by way of renovation since I first came here, so please don't worry about the carpet or anything else. There is one thing, though, I can tell you: I'm going to miss you all. This place will feel like a morgue until I can get used to the silence again.'

'Well, you know what we all think, Don: we'll never be able to repay you.'

'Oh, don't you worry, I'll see that you do in meals, wine and music,' and he nodded towards Marie Anne, adding, 'You must get in more practice to make up for lost time,' only to close his eyes tightly and say, 'Oh, that was a dubious compliment, if ever there was one, for I don't consider you need further practice.'

'Nor do I,' said her father. 'But come on now. Let us away. And we've got to get across the fields and to the farm, and bid goodbye to Mr and Mrs Harding, those very good people who have certainly helped us through this ordeal.'

And so Marie Anne left the cottage where her child had been born and she herself had lived through a revealing lifetime, for now she knew what love was all about.

It was early afternoon when Don returned to the cottage. He had walked by the woodland path and he was very surprised, on coming in sight of the cottage, to see Dr Ridley standing at the door, and to be greeted by him calling, 'No wonder I couldn't get an answer.'

'They've all gone; I'm on my own,' said Don.

'Yes, yes, I know that, that's why I'm here; I want a word with you in private.'

In the sitting-room John Ridley exclaimed, 'Good gracious! it does look empty. Are you glad to have the place to yourself again?'

'No, not at all.'

'I thought you mightn't. May I sit down?'

'Of course. Of course. Can I get you a drink?'

'Not for a moment. I've got something to say and I don't know how to begin, so will you sit down, please? You look overbearing standing there.'

Don laughed as he sat down, saying, 'Well, that's the first time the word overbearing has been applied to me!'

John Ridley folded his arms and lay back in the chair; then looking straight at Don, he said, 'I'm not much older than you, am I?'

'I don't know,' said Don; 'forty, I would say.'

'You're near the mark, thirty-nine. And you?'

'Thirty-three, shortly.'

'Yes; yes, I thought that. I'm going to call you Don since everybody else does, and I think we've got to know each other over the past weeks, don't you?'

'Yes; yes, I would agree with you there.'

'At least on the surface.'

There was a pause before Don said, 'Now what d'you mean by that, Doctor?'

'Well, that's what I've come to talk about; what goes on under the surface. But believe me, I am not speaking or asking questions out of idle curiosity. Do believe me on that, won't you, Don?'

Evasively Don now said, 'That remains to be seen. Am I right in surmising that this,' and he pointed to the mask, 'is what you want to know about?' and John Ridley, blushing slightly, said, 'Yes; yes, you're right. But, as I said, not just out of curiosity. You see, I did my training in London and spent my last two years in a hospital that specialised in skin complaints, ranging through the gamut of them. Quite a number, children and adults, attended the clinic for port wine or strawberry skin stains, as some people call them. Not uncommon, although in a way just as prevalent, was a stain of a different kind; in fact, it was horrifying to see a young girl with half her body or more covered with a black or dark brown scar. This stain or scar never appeared smooth like the port wine stain, but was made up of nodules and ridges, varying in shades of a dark hue. It had a name—'

He stopped, and Don, the unmarked part of his face deadly white now, said, 'Yes, it is known as congenital melanocytic nevis.'

John Ridley's colour too had changed, but it had gone to a deep pink; and now he muttered, 'I'm . . . I'm very sorry; you've been into this, then, but my intention is not to deal with the skin, but with your disguise. I thought it might be other than a stain because of this ugly apparatus you wear. I can't see any reason why you cannot wear

363

something less noticeable. I happened to surprise you the other day with your cap off. Did the hospital supply it?'

Don's voice was flat now as he said, 'I have never attended a hospital; it was made by a kindly Brother so that I could face the world.'

'Yes; yes, I see. Again I say I'm sorry, but' – he now put out his hand and gripped Don's knee – 'I would like to be of some help to you. Do you mind if I ask you some questions?'

'Not at all. No; not at all.'

John Ridley wetted his lips now and said, 'Does it cover other parts of your body?'

'No.'

'No?'

'That's what I said, no. That is the irony of it; it's marred only a very small portion of my skin, from my hair-line to my breast-bone.' And when Don almost sprang to his feet and tore at his headpiece, John Ridley remained quiet as he looked at the ugly seared skin that marred this young man's face. And it *was* ugly, being made so, not just by its colour, but by its roughness. It resembled warts on a pig's back.

It was a long moment before he could say, 'Sit down, Don . . . Now look, there is nothing I can think of at the moment which will give you any hope that that cursed stain can be dealt with, but I do know that in Germany attempts are being made to lighten the colour. However, what can be done and right away is to fit you with a proper mask. It should make all the difference in the world . . . Now it's like this.' John Ridley rose quickly from his chair and sat on the couch beside Don, and his voice was eager as he said, 'Let me explain. There's this young fellow. He's a patient of mine. He hasn't any legs, but he has a pair of hands that can work miracles; at least, I think so; but that's when you can get him interested. He works with papier mâché, not just for fancy trays and such, but he can shape figures and masks, and all so lifelike. He doesn't take to everybody, mind – he has an unusual temperament. I know he had an offer to do masks for the theatre group, but wouldn't take it on. He's of a very caring family. His father is a painter in the shipyard, and two of his brothers are apprenticed there – one a riveter, the other a carpenter – and so they live comfortably and, strange to say, happily, for they have another invalid in the house. Unfortunately, their twenty-one-year-old daughter won't be with them much longer, I fear, for she has been consumptive since a child. They live in a terraced house, and the usual front room has been turned over to Joe, a bedroom-cum-studio-cum-meeting place. It's a very interesting family. I'm sure you would agree if you met them and had a natter with Joe. I've told him about you and for once got him interested in someone. So, what about it?'

'Why are you doing this . . . taking this trouble?'

'I ask myself that many times; it's because, I suppose, I'm an interfering busybody. My real reason, which I apply to most things is that I hate to see good stuff going to waste.'

When Don exclaimed loudly, 'Huh!' John Ridley echoed it, and Don went on, 'I don't consider I am going to waste.'

'It all depends upon what you mean by that. It's possible that you could be made to spread your wings, and live a different life away from this little hut' – he flung one arm aside, indicating the room – 'in which you mainly hide yourself . . . All right! All right!' – his voice was loud now as Don again bounced up from the couch – 'Don't take up a boxing stance with me, because what I said is true. Anyway, I am asking you to do this, because I think you owe me something.'

'Owe you something! How? Why?'

'Well, you *are* more than fond of Marie Anne, aren't

you? Yes, you can look like that, and so I'll not say, "more than", but you're fond of her, and you've likely thanked your God for saving her. Well, let me tell you, He couldn't have done much without my help in the first place.'

At this, Don drew in a long breath, then turned, and walking to the fireplace, he gripped the rough oak mantelshelf.

Some part of him wanted to laugh; but only a part of him, for he was considering this man a little too prying, and far too knowledgeable.

He did not turn about when John Ridley's voice came to him quietly now, saying, 'I'm off. You needn't show me out; I know the way. But think over what I've said. You just need to write "Pick me up" on a sheet of paper and post it, and I'll arrange to fetch you. And instead of standing there like an angry bull, you should be thanking me.'

It was minutes after the door had banged that Don straightened up and again took in a deep breath.

Talk about revelation; he had been given the whole book this morning, and he didn't like it, not any part of it.

10

There was a family gathering in the sitting-room of The
Little Manor. Present were Emanuel and James and
Patrick and Evelyn and Marie Anne. Also present were
Patrick's future wife and Evelyn's husband; and, of
course, there was Sarah. At this moment, she was pouring
tea.

As Pat lifted two cups of tea from the tray Sarah pointed
to one saying, 'That's the master's, with two sugars, and
that one's Mr James's, no sugar; and be careful, don't spill
them in the saucer.'

He turned his head to the side and laughingly said, 'No
ma'am; no ma'am. I'll be careful I will, I will that, I will.'

'Go on with you and your mockery, Mr Pat!'

When Pat reached the couch and handed his grandfather and his father their cups, Emanuel said, 'Why has
he gone off to Dr Ridley's again today? That's the second
time within a week. Farmer Harding says he was there last
week too. Anything wrong with him physically, d'you
think?'

'I shouldn't think so, Grandfather. To me, he looks as
fit as a fiddle.'

'I suppose nobody thought of asking him, but perhaps
Marie Anne's got an inkling. Marie Anne!' he called above
the chatter of the women.

Marie Anne, who was sitting with Anita and Evelyn,
called back, 'Yes, Grandpa?'

'Do you know why our good friend Don has been taken
up by Dr Ridley?'

'No, I don't, Grandpa. Nor do I intend to probe.'

'Well, somebody should. I'll ask him myself next time we meet up.'

'Huh! huh!' This sound came from the tea table and all eyes were turned in Sarah's direction, and the old man now called to her, 'Did I hear you make a remark, Miss Foggerty?'

And Sarah, in the act of passing the last cup of tea to Nathaniel Napier, replied, 'It was no remark, sir, just a sort of expression.'

'A sort of expression?'

The old man now exchanged a quick glance with James, after which James bent his head and bit on his lip and waited, as did the rest of the company, for the exchange they knew would follow.

'May I ask what the expression was supposed to convey?'

Sarah was back at the tea-table dabbing at some spilt tea with a napkin, and when she did not answer the voice came again, now in the form of a demand, 'May I have your attention for a moment, Miss Foggerty!'

Sarah turned and walked towards the couch and stood dutifully and, what would appear, docilely before her master, and after he had repeated, 'I asked what your expression was supposed to convey,' she said, 'Well, sir, were I to translate it you might consider it out of place, like.'

'Well, you can leave me to be the judge of that, Miss Foggerty, so I would thank you if you would kindly translate the meaning of "Huh!"'

There was an absolute silence in the room, then Sarah broke it by saying briefly, 'Some hope.'

The choked ripple that went through the others was quickly silenced by a look cast on them by the old man who again demanded of Sarah, 'What did you say?'

'I translated as you wanted, sir, the meaning of Huh! It meant some hope.'

Again there was a strangled titter.

James's head drooped further. There were actually tortured expressions on the faces of the others.

Emanuel Lawson kept his face perfectly straight as he said to her, 'So you don't think that I would have any success if I questioned Mr McAlister as to the reason why the doctor collects him?'

'Well, going on what he said to me, sir, I should say you don't.'

'Oh! You asked him?'

'Yes, sir.'

'You mean, you asked him why he was going to Dr Ridley's?'

'Just that, sir.'

There was an expectant hush around the room now. James had raised his head and was staring at this Irish woman whom, as he put it to himself, demanded to be liked, and so he requested of her, 'And may we ask what his reply to you was?'

'You may, sir.'

'Well, go on.'

'Well, sir, I could put it briefly and say he refused to tell me, or I could give you his answer in full.'

'Oh. Oh. By all means, Miss Foggerty, let us hear his answer in full.'

Sarah looked towards Marie Anne and she gave an almost imperceptible shrug of her shoulders as if to say, Well he's asked for it, so don't blame me. Then turning to Emanuel, she said, 'Well, it went like this, sir: after I'd put the question to him, he said, "Well, you know what you are, Sarah Foggerty? You are a Nosey Parker, and were I to tell you, you would go strutting round this house throwing off hints to all concerned that you knew something that they didn't, while knowing that they were

369

breaking their necks to find out. Oh, you'd make your knowledge pay all right, but this, I think, would touch on the sin of pride; and so your ignorance will save you from that temptation."'

'Well, I never!'

'Did he really say that?'

Sarah turned and faced them, saying, 'Yes, he did that. I've got a good memory for insults, no matter in what shape they come.'

Leaning back, his hand across his mouth and his eyes sparkling, Emanuel cut off further remarks by saying to James, 'We should get down to business. Are you sure he's going in the morning?'

It was Pat who answered, 'Yes, definitely; his bag, full of pieces, is there and waiting by the door; and there was another case that was full of objects still to be painted and glazed. By! he had some stuff in that studio. At the moment he's working on a piece of stone, but he wouldn't tell me what it was to be. Anyway, the carpet men have been given a good idea of what they'll need. And we all agreed that the couch and chairs would be more suitable for him in hide or leather, and so Anita, here, picked out what she called a military tan. The old sideboard will have to be stored with most of the bedroom furniture, but the refectory dining-table and chairs are lovely; they will stay as they are. What will take time is the painting and decorating.' And now turning to Marie Anne, he asked, 'Did he give you any idea of when he'll be back?'

'He said, in a week or more; it all depended.'

'On what?' asked her father.

'I don't know.' But as she said this, a surprisingly niggling thought came into her head. Why not ask Sarah? He talks to her more than he does to me. And that was true. She often saw them chatting together. He rarely chatted with her, and knowing the feelings he stored in his heart towards her, she had to question herself if, in

370

fact, she had dreamed it all. And so she answered her father, 'It'll be over a week; for two days will be taken up with travelling.'

'Well, once Mike has dropped him at the station tomorrow, we can start counting from then,' said Pat.

Back in the sitting-room, Emanuel had stopped his son rising from the couch when the others were preparing to leave the room by saying, 'Stay awhile; I want a word with you.'

So now he said, 'You received a letter by the late post. Was it from her?'

'Yes.'

'Well, go on. What's transpired?'

'She's willing to accede to my suggestion; but she's asking a price; it'll take practically every spare penny I have, but it would be worth it to be rid of her.'

'But you're not thinking of giving her what she's asking, are you?'

'No, no; of course not, because don't forget he's out there with her, and if he's got this idea of setting up a horse farm he'll want much more money than was allotted to him. David says that if Vincent's going to stay on he would prefer him to get settled a good few hundred miles away. As for John and his Kate, neither of them can stand him.'

There was silence between them for a moment; then Emanuel said, 'With Evelyn gone, you're going to find it very lonely down there, unless when Pat marries they make it their home.'

'There's no chance of that, Father. I hinted at it, but Pat came back flatly, saying that in no way would he want to start his married life there. But don't worry about me, Father; I'll be glad of a little peace and to know that it's going to be permanent. You've got no idea what relief that brings.'

Again there was a short silence, before Emanuel startled James by saying, 'Why did you stop seeing your woman those years back?'

'What d'you mean, Father?'

'Just what I say, James, just what I say. I told you before that I knew about it. Why did you stop seeing her? Oh, don't look like that; I knew what was going on, have done from the beginning. Likely the same way as you found out about Vincent; just keeping my ears open and putting two and two together.'

With James rising to his feet, Emanuel said, 'Now don't get on your high horse, 'cos I can tell you I was glad you had some diversion from that mistake you made; and she was a mistake; I always said so.'

'Well, Father,' James had moved towards the fire now and stood staring into the low embers as he said quietly, 'she wasn't a diversion, and she wasn't what you call my woman. She was in no way a person of such character. She'd had no male contact since her husband died, until we met up; and when I found I loved her, really loved her, I was humbled by the fact that she loved me, because she was a highly intelligent woman and had seen quite a bit of the world in her travels with her husband. And what was more, she was pretty well off; she bought the Thornton estate.'

'Yes, yes, I know, and that's a nice place; but I ask you, what broke it up?'

'Well, as she said, she wasn't made to be a mistress; she wanted to be a wife again and in a settled place with her dogs and sick animals. That was her main interest, sick animals. She wanted me to divorce Veronica. Well, I knew I hadn't a hope in hell in that direction for, had I even broached it with Veronica, she would have ferreted out who was behind it, and I don't think Elizabeth could have taken the exposure. So, well, it petered out, and my consolation became food and wine.'

'You never see her at all now?'

'Oh yes; yes, now and again, but always outside; I mean, at a dinner party or an afternoon meeting for a cup of tea or something like that. I never go to the house.'

'How long is it since you were last at the house?'

'Ten years or so.'

'And she has never married?'

'No, no; she's never married.'

'How old is she?'

'Oh, about sixty now; she's older than me by a few years.'

'Bloody fool!'

James turned and looked sharply at his father, and the old man repeated, 'That's what I said and that's what you are. Why the hell, man, didn't you come out in the open and face that vixen, for I doubt if she would have made any scandal; that wasn't her line. She would have fought like hell to keep you, yes. You held the upper hand had you but known it; you could have had your cake and eaten it. But that's a point: what cake did you ever get from her without lowering yourself to battle for it? Well, there's nothing to stop you from renewing your acquaintance with your Elizabeth now, is there?'

'Oh no, Father, no; she wasn't the kind of person to be dropped, as it were, then picked up again. Unlike everyone else at that time I think she did not consider me gutless, yet I was. And don't worry about me, I'm all right; or I shall be once I get the Canadian business settled. Another thing: it'll be a relief for Marie Anne knowing she will never again see Vincent.'

The door opened abruptly and Sarah, about to enter, said, 'Oh, I'm sorry sir. I thought . . . I thought you had all gone. The girls were about to come in and clear the things.'

As Emanuel pulled himself up from his chair, Sarah put

in quickly, 'Don't you trouble yourself, sir.' And with this she closed the door.

Emanuel looked at his son and laughed as he said, 'Oh! that woman. Imagine her at The Manor! How long do you think she would have reigned?'

'Not for a split second, Father, not for a split second.'

At this, Emanuel laughed and said, 'Yes, a split second. But you know, I think it seems for once that God knew what he was doing when he made Sarah Foggerty a maid to that mean skunk of a woman up there in London. It would seem that He directed her life so that one day she would take under her wing a young and hapless girl, because where on earth would my Mary Anne have been without her? I just dare not think. No, I just dare not think.' . . .

There were only three for dinner that evening, Emanuel, James and Marie Anne. As usual, they were waited upon by Sarah and the maid in much the same way as would have a butler and footman.

Following the meal, the new routine in The Little Manor was that Sarah should share her mealtimes with the new nanny, because, of course, you couldn't expect a nanny to eat in the kitchen with the rest of the staff; it wasn't done. So it was during the hour following the evening meal that Marie Anne could have her daughter to herself and gaze as though upon her reflection. Except, that is, for the deep brown eyes which, at times, brought a little tremor into her heart, when she would say to herself, he was nice. Yes, he was, and she would wonder where he might be now, and if he thought of her; or, if he realised that by now he was the father of a child.

Alone with her child, she could hug her; she could talk to her and tell her she wasn't sorry she had been born, and that she loved her, and always would.

She had not heard the front door-bell ring and when

the tap came on the sitting-room door and Carrie, pushing it open, said, 'Mr McAlister to see you, ma'am,' she was reminded she had become ma'am to the staff since the baby was born. As he entered the room, she hitched herself on to the edge of the couch, saying, 'Is anything wrong?'

'No; what could be wrong?' He walked slowly towards her; then stood looking down on the baby as he said, 'This is the first time I've seen you nursing her since you came home.'

'It's because I don't get a chance. There's a new routine in the house, which I don't think is going to last; in fact, I'm sure it's not. Do sit down.'

He drew up a chair to the side of the couch, then said, 'I promised Sarah to pick up a package to take to Annie on my next trip up to town. I feel sure, in this case, it's only a means to an end, because it'll be some money I have to carry, and she could send it, as she usually does, by postal order; but I think she wants news of how the family is faring, especially, to put it in her own words, how the young-uns are rigged out.'

'Well,' Marie Anne put in now, 'if I know anything about Annie, after food she'll have spent whatever she gets on the children.'

'She must send most of her wages back there, I think.'

'No, not all; she sends half. The rest goes into her bank.'

'May I hold her?'

'Yes, yes; of course.'

He lifted the child from her lap and laid it in the crook of his arm, and after a moment he said, 'Have you finally decided on a name?'

'That was a foregone conclusion. We've tried everything, but we've decided it's just going to be my name reversed, Anne Marie.' She smiled at him now, saying, 'It sounds better than Marie Anne anyway, don't you think, or even Mary Ann?'

'I'm not going to answer that question; she might feel hurt.'

They laughed together; and then he said, 'It's your birthday next week and I'll be away.'

'Yes; yes, it's my birthday next week. If I remember rightly we've been into birthdays before, haven't we, Don?'

'Yes, we have.'

'And it still remains the same. I'll be seventeen and no younger and you'll be thirty-three and no older. But the same difference remains.'

'As you say, madam, as you say. But why I mentioned your birthday again was because I have a present for you, but it's in the making and you'll not get it for some time.'

'It's a piece of your work?' she asked softly.

'Yes, it's a piece of my work.'

'That's kind of you.'

'Oh, yes' – his head moved widely – 'very kind of me, so kind of me.' Then, his tone changing, he said, 'Don't give me replies like that; it's the type of answer you would have given had it been a box of chocolates.'

Now her face was straight as she said, 'You are taking what I said the wrong way. I've noticed lately you've been doing that, putting a different meaning to the things I say.'

'Have I?'

'Yes, you have, Mr McAlister, and I don't like it.'

'Oh well, then, I must pull myself together, and you must tell me how I must address you in the future.'

'There you go again. What is wrong with you? You've been seeing Dr Ridley; is it something physical?'

His head went up and he laughed as he replied, 'No, my dear, it's nothing physical. But how do you know I'm seeing Dr Ridley? As regards my physical health, I'm perfectly fit.'

'People talk; and when a doctor's gig comes to take you for a ride, there must be a purpose behind it.'

His lips went into a quizzical smile: 'You're right there, . madam,' he said; 'there is a purpose behind it and all will be revealed in good time. Until then . . . we'll change the subject.' And he looked down at the child and remarked, 'Just look at her. She says she's very happy to know that I'm to be her godfather.'

When he looked up, they stared at each other, no smile on their faces; but Marie Annie's was asking herself, why, when she felt as she did about him, should she at times, such as this, have the urge to lash out at him with her tongue? while he was thinking, I can't stand much more of this. While I'm in London I'll just have to sort myself out; her nearness is getting too much for me; I'll break through one day and scare her to death. Anyway, what is going to be the final outcome? the new face is still but a mask and there remains the hideousness beneath. And another thing: if any one of them knew what was in my mind concerning her, I'd be shown the door. I know that.

Suddenly he almost thrust the baby into her arms, saying, 'I must be going.'

When Marie Anne went to rise he did not put out a hand to help her, and so she pushed herself up with one hand while cradling the child with her other forearm.

'I hope you enjoy your stay,' she said.

He turned and looked at her; then answered quietly, 'Yes; I'll enjoy it in a way, for I always like seeing the Brothers.'

At the door now, he turned fully around and said softly, 'The point is, I won't be able to stay away too long.'

Marie Anne stood staring at the closed door; then, her head bent over the child, she muttered, 'He'll never speak out, never! And I can't, for I'm half afraid he might return to the Brothers. In any case, were I to come into the open, imagine the effect on Grandpa, on Father, and Pat, and Sarah . . . oh yes, Sarah.'

11

Don had been away for nine days. His train had been due in Durham at about three o'clock in the afternoon; but here it was seven o'clock, and he had not yet put in an appearance. Emanuel's annoyance was definitely evident when he banged his spoon into his empty soup plate, saying, 'Well, damn him! We did it for the best. It was the only way we could think of thanking him.'

After gathering up the soup plates from the rest of the family, Sarah was heard to mutter, 'He could be overcome.'

'What's that, Foggerty, you're muttering?'

'I was just thinkin' to meself, sir.' She now uncovered a large meat dish holding a shoulder of lamb and, carrying it to the table, she placed it before the old man, who then demanded, 'Well, what were you thinking to yourself, woman?'

'I said, sir, he might be overcome.'

'Overcome?' He screwed up his face at her.

'Yes sir; it isn't everybody who can say "thank you" easily. They know what they want to say but they find it difficult bringing it out.'

The old man stared at this Irish woman, this card of an Irish woman. He'd never had much time for the Irish, although he found them to be good workers when they were well directed, but put some money in their pocket and you mightn't see them for days.

As she passed behind his chair his head turned and his gaze followed her to the sideboard, only to be checked by his son saying jokingly, 'Father, I like my lamb hot.'

'Oh. Oh do you? Well, why didn't you start cutting it?'

'Well, if I'd done that, I know what would have happened; I would certainly have been put in my place as regards your fitness to go on carving.'

Marie Anne, Evelyn and Pat laughed and the old man was about to come back with some retort when, instead, he held up his hand and said, 'Shush! a minute, the lot of you. Quiet! That was the door-bell.'

As they waited Sarah slipped towards the door and opened it, and now they all could hear the distant voice saying, 'I'll wait in the sitting-room, thank you.'

'You'll do no such thing! You'll come in here this minute!' and the old man's roar rattled the glasses on the table. When Don appeared in the doorway saying, 'I'm . . . I'm sorry, but I'll . . .' Emanuel continued to bellow, 'Shut up! Come in and sit yourself down.' He pointed to a seat at the bottom of the table, next to Nathaniel; then addressed Sarah, saying, 'Set another place, and be sharp about it.'

After Don had sat down he looked from one to the other, then drew in a long breath before he said, 'I . . . I was held up. Oh, dear me!' He put his elbows on the table and drooped his head into his hands, and so tight was he pressing on his cheek that he seemed to push the mask further onto his face rather than away from it towards his ear, and very quietly, he said, 'The little I did for you . . . and were I to go on doing it for the rest of my life it would never . . . never be worth all that, all that kindness. All the effort it must have taken to transform that cottage into a beautiful home. I . . . I may receive other surprises in my life, but never one greater than . . . than when I approached that once familiar place. I could see it was different, but why? how?' He took his hands from his face now, but continued to look down on the empty plate; then he went on, 'I saw what had been done outside, to the outbuildings too, and . . . and when I opened the door I . . . I couldn't enter; I stood leaning against the doorpost like . . . like someone drunk. To put my feet on that carpet seemed a sin.

'The sitting-room and the kitchen are so transformed I can't believe how it was possible to do it; and with such taste and in so short a time. But . . . but, oh! the bedroom.' He now looked directly at Marie Anne and his smile widened as he said, 'The Brothers would have me on my knees for a week in penance if I had even dared to think of anything like it.' Then turning back to the old man, he said, 'And the bed. Oh the bed! I don't expect to sleep tonight because I've slept on boards ever since I can remember, and Marie Anne has had a taste of them.'

Again he was holding his head, but only his brow now, and his voice trembled as he said, 'What *can* I say to you good people, because *never, never* in my life have I received such a gift and such kindness. The Brothers were kind in their way, but there is kindness . . . and kindness and yours is overwhelming.'

'Nonsense! nonsense!' This was Emanuel speaking again. 'Well, anyway, you've said your piece, so would you mind if we eat?' and straight away said to Sarah, 'Bestir yourself and send those vegetables to the table.'

Sarah made no immediate reply, but motioned to the girls; then she herself took up the gravy boat and moved around the table with it. But when, lastly, she came to Don, she said politely, 'Good evening, Mr McAlister,' and Don replied with equal politeness but with a twinkle in his eye, 'Good evening, Miss Foggerty;' then in a very soft tone Sarah said, 'I'm so glad you like your house, but you wouldn't have enjoyed it in its present state for long if I hadn't pointed out to them all the cracked tiles round the chimney pot, and they'll swear . . .' only to be interrupted by the sound of someone spluttering, and the head of the table coughing as if he were about to choke; but above it all, Marie Anne's voice was heard in the form of a polite request, one which could have been taken for a command, as she said, 'Would you see to the dessert, Sarah, please, and in the meantime we'll see to ourselves.'

And ushering the girls before her, Sarah left the room.

Rubbing his face with his napkin, Emanuel muttered, 'Something'll have to be done with that woman; you'll have to see to it, Marie Anne.'

'I'll do nothing of the sort, Grandpa. If she has to be checked then you'll have to do it yourself, because you've encouraged her right from the beginning, and you ask for everything she hits you with.'

'I didn't ask for that about the roof.'

'No,' put in Pat now as he wiped his wet lids; 'but the funny thing about it is she's nearly always right in what she says' – and he now nodded to Don – 'and she was then. Nobody had thought about the tiles, and as you know, they were in a bad way.'

'Oh yes, I know that.'

'Well, she's right. In no time you would have had the water in.'

'I can't believe it, you know.'

Emanuel turned to his son saying, 'What can't you believe, James?'

'Well, for instance, I can't believe in the atmosphere here compared with that at the dinner-table at The Manor.'

It was at this point that Evelyn turned to Don, saying, 'I suppose you've heard from the Hardings that I confiscated nearly all your old furniture?' But before Don could answer, Nat put in, 'Not quite confiscated, Don; we put it in the stable until you could decide which pieces you would like to keep.'

'Take what you want,' said Don. 'Any additions of any kind to those rooms would now be an intrusion. You know, the Hardings were waiting for my reaction, too;

Sally had a big tea all lined up. That was why I was late; they, too, have been so kind. She had made a large cake for me with "Welcome Home" iced on it.'

'Did you like it?' asked Evelyn.

'Yes; it was very nice.'

'Just very nice?' – there was a note of indignation in Evelyn's voice – '*I* had a hand in that cake.'

'Oh well, then,' said Don with mock heartiness, 'I must say it was simply delicious; I've never tasted anything like it before.'

Amid the ensuing laughter, Marie Anne asked in some sincere surprise, 'You helped to make the cake, Evelyn?'

'Yes, I did. Let me tell you, miss, I've graduated from mucking out cow byres, cleaning pig sties, and feeding swill. I've now moved on to the culinary arts.'

'I don't believe you've ever been closer to a pig than to hear its grunts.'

'You don't? Well, you come over with me tomorrow and I'll give you the pleasure of partnering me in my chores.'

When, of a sudden, her grandfather laid his hand on Evelyn's, she became silent as did the others, because the action showed commendation that no words could have conveyed.

It was Don who cut through the air of slight embarrassment by saying, 'Farmer Harding tells me you never succeed with a pig unless you can get it to stand still while talking to it, by which time you've likely mesmerised yourself.'

As fresh laughter ensued, Marie Anne thought, That was such a nice gesture of Grandpa's; it so touched her she could have wept: recently, there had been a number of occasions when she herself had felt the urge to make a similar gesture.

Don now caught her attention by asking, 'Did you have a good birthday party?' and she answered, 'Well, I wouldn't say it was a party; more a family tea, and we spent most of the time talking and arranging the christening.'

'Oh; you've set a date, then?'

'It'll be in a fortnight's time.'

'Oh! A fortnight. As soon as that?'

There had been a surprised note in Don's voice and which was reflected in his expression and caused Pat to put in quickly, 'You're going away again, then?'

'No. No; I'll be here for the christening. Yes; yes, indeed.' And when he laughed he had all their attention, but his next words left them more puzzled when he said with some emphasis, 'Oh, I wouldn't miss the christening for anything.'

12

It was a week before the christening was to take place. James had alighted from the carriage to greet his father.

'It's a beautiful day, Father, isn't it?' he said.

'Yes. One of the rare ones, soft and warm. I can really breathe in this air; and it's lovely to walk outside without having to be happed up against wind and weather.'

'You're not as happed up at times as you should be, with that chest of yours.'

'Never mind my chest; anything new?'

'Not about business, no. But I am intrigued by one of two letters I received today.' And he withdrew from his pocket a square envelope which he handed to his father with the words, 'See how it's addressed: Miss Marie Anne Lawson, c/o The Manager, Lawson Shipping Company, Newcastle, England.'

Emanuel glanced at him, saying, 'It's a Spanish stamp.'

'Yes; that's what intrigued me. Where is she now?'

'She went out for a walk with Sarah; the baby was sleeping.'

'There's some other news, too. They've bought the ranch, out there in Canada. David says, that'll put some distance between them; three hundred miles, I think. But by what he says it can't be nearly enough; it seems that Vincent has become impossible to live with. He says Veronica is a changed woman from what he remembers of her; he doesn't know how she puts up with Vincent. She has much more patience than he remembers when he was at home. Anyway, our letters have likely crossed;

I had told her my solicitor says I can get a divorce in three years' time by doing nothing, because she left me, I didn't leave her.'

'Well, that's a blessing, and in no disguise,' said his father; 'and you can now plan your life ahead whether it be sooner or later. Ah! Here they are, returning now,' and he turned towards the approaching figures.

When Marie Anne and Sarah came abreast of them, Marie Anne said, 'Isn't it a glorious day, Father?' and he answered, 'We've just been discussing that. By the way,' James now handed her the letter he still held in his hand, saying, 'that came to the office for you, my dear.'

Marie Anne seemed to hesitate before she took the proffered envelope from him. For a moment, she stared down at it before raising her gaze to the two men, then turned to look fully at Sarah.

She appeared to be about to speak; but when she did it was as if she were ignoring the letter: 'We could do with a cool drink,' she said. 'I'll be glad to get my hat and dust-coat off. Why one must always wear a hat in the open air I shall never be able to understand.' And turning abruptly, she left the two men and went into the house, followed by Sarah . . .

Five minutes later they were seated in Marie Anne's work-room: she had avoided the sitting-room and made for this seemingly more private apartment.

'Well! It won't open itself; you'll have to open it some-time.'

'I know that! I know that!' Marie Anne almost snapped the words at Sarah.

When Sarah's head drooped and she looked away, Marie Anne said, 'I'm sorry. I'm sorry. But what if he's now coming back and wants to see not only me but also the child.'

'In that case,' Sarah said flatly, 'I don't see how you could stop him seeing his child, as a court would give him that much leave. They're always for the man's side of it, good, bad, or indifferent. Anyway, what are we yammering on about? Open the thing.' She reached out and picked up a paper knife from the writing-desk and handed it to Marie Anne.

Marie Anne unfolded the four-square piece of paper and looked at the small squiggly writing. Then she began to read:

Marie Anne, my dear,
    When you receive this letter I shall no longer be on this earth . . .'

At this point, her head jerked upwards and she stared wide-eyed and with open mouth at Sarah; but she said nothing, and her gaze dropped to the letter again:

and I fear to die without saying to you that I am sorry, and deeply, to have brought disgrace on you, and sorrow.
    Your child . . . my child, will have been born by now, and daily I think of it . . . of you both, oh yes, indeed of you both – and it was an intention in my mind some day to see you. This was to be when I had got my letters to enable me to teach without hiding. And it was coming about, for my dear and old friend . . . with whose family I have lived since I came back to Madrid, had got me a half-time position at The Academy, whereon I could use the rest of the time to practise for the valued letters.
    But it was destined not to be, for after two attacks to my heart, I am in a seizure, which has taken part of my body, evident in my handwriting, you will see. I know that my time, as you might say, is running out; and so I write this letter with the promise from my friend that he will post it to you after I am gone.

386

Put your mind at rest: he knows nothing about you other than that you are a friend.

Lastly, I will say, my dear Infanta, that what happened between us was out of pure love, for there had never been anyone to come to my life like you.

I go to God, or whatever, with thoughts of you still deep in my heart.

Think of me kindly, my Infanta.

Carlos.

Marie Anne now lay back and pressed the letter to her chest; then she added, 'He's dead.'

'Dead?'

'Yes, dead. That's what I said; he's dead.'

'God help him! God rest his soul,' Sarah said.

The words had been muttered, but now she added aloud, 'You seem pleased; not a bit sorry,' which brought Marie Anne to sit up straight and say, 'Don't say that! I am not pleased, but I suppose I am relieved, for, at first, I thought he might be aiming to come. And that would have been dreadful.'

'Why so dreadful? He could have been doing what he thought was the honourable thing and offering you marriage.'

'Sarah!' There was a shocked note in Marie Anne's voice.

'Yes, Marie Anne . . . Miss. At one time, you liked him, more than liked him; and he wasn't a bad fellow. No, he wasn't; quite a gentleman, in a way.'

There was silence between them now while they stared at each other; then, in a much softer voice, Sarah said, 'What did he die of? And who told you he is dead?'

Marie Anne slowly handed Sarah the letter; then watched her expression change as her eyes travelled down the page.

After Sarah had finished reading it, she did not hand the letter back to Marie Anne but laid it on her knee, and looking down on it, she murmured, 'Poor devil! You can say only one good thing; he lived with kind friends, and died among them, too.' Then raising her eyes again to Marie Anne, she said, 'You'll have to write and thank him . . . the man.'

'Write and thank him! I shall do no such thing. What are you saying? Start up a connection there? You would have them over here then; and they are supposed to know nothing about the child. That's how it should be, and that's how it's going to be. She is mine, and mine alone now. Anyway, there's neither the man's name, nor the address.'

'You could write to The Academy he mentions.'

Slowly, Sarah rose to her feet and, looking down on Marie Anne, she asked quietly, 'How long do you think she'll be yours alone? Come the day, she'll ask questions.'

'She won't ask questions; she need never know.'

'Don't be silly! Anyway, what if you should marry?'

Marie Anne, too, was now on her feet, and vehemently she said, 'I won't marry! I'll never marry.'

Again they were staring at each other in silence. Then drawing in a long slow breath, Sarah now uttered words that held both bitterness and sadness: 'Don't be a hypocrite! You'd be married tomorrow, given the chance. You know it, and I know it.' And on this, she turned and strode from the room, and the door banged behind her.

Marie Anne stood, part of the letter crumpled in one hand, the other part across her mouth.

Sarah! Sarah! What could she mean? surely she hadn't given herself away. Yet those words had been plain enough.

For a moment she wished she had never insisted on bringing her back here; yet she knew she couldn't go on without her, for she needed her in so many and different ways. But she saw too much.

What now? . . . Yes, what now?

13

It was the day of the christening. Emanuel, James, and
Marie Anne were in the sitting-room dressed and waiting
for the others to arrive. Emanuel, who was sitting in the
big chair, leaned forward and took hold of Marie Anne's
hand, saying, 'You are satisfied that her name is to be
Anne Marie?'

'Yes, Grandpa; quite satisfied.' Then on the sound of
voices coming from the hall, she said, 'Here are the
others.'

When the door opened, Pat and Anita came in ahead of
Evelyn and Nick, followed by Dr Ridley. The latter
surprised her, for she had expected him to go straight to
the church.

Amid the chatter, she watched him cross the room to
greet her grandfather: 'How d'you do, sir? I hope I see you
well?'

'Yes; yes, I'm well enough, Doctor. And I am glad to
have a word with you and ask you a question, one that is
troubling us all, and it's just this. Is there anything wrong
with McAlister?'

'No, sir; much the reverse.'

'Well, from what I understand, people don't visit
doctors when they're well; in fact, if they're wise they'll
keep out of their way. However, I must speak as I find
about you.'

'That's very civil of you, sir, very civil. It is this very
point I have come a little early to explain about Don and

his visiting, which really wasn't to me at all. I was just the go-between.'

He turned and glanced at the company and saw he had all their attention now. Then, addressing Emanuel again, he said, 'It was like this. As a doctor, I couldn't help but see that that contraption he wore must be hiding something pretty bad to need a mask. This set my mind working, until I felt obliged to present him with a plan. This would bring in a legless young man named Joe, who, I am sure, has been given the power to perform little miracles. It was like this.'

John Ridley proceeded to tell them about Joe's artistic bent, finishing by saying, 'He has created a mould of the finest papier mâché, tinted to appear like flesh, Don's flesh, and kept in place by a cap-like crown of doeskin. And you'll never believe where the doeskin came from. His mother had picked up a pair of ladies' long evening gloves from a church bazaar. They were of a pale fawn colour, merging into a light tan. And although I say this, and with some pride, the whole has made a new man of our Mr McAlister, one entirely acceptable to himself. I can also say that it was no easy job to get him to Joe's; nor was it easy to get Joe to take on what, at first, seemed an impossible task. But now they are firm friends; I can even say Don has found a new family.

'I don't know what your reactions to him would have been had I not put you in the picture. Likely, he would have been overwhelmed by questions, and not a little embarrassed. So how you receive him, I leave to you all.'

'Ah! Here he is now.'

Pat was about to hurry to the door when his father said, 'Take it slowly.'

'Oh yes; yes, of course.' . . .

Fanny Carter had opened the door to Don and her reaction was, 'Eeh! Mr McAlister,' and Don, forcing himself to reply lightly, bent towards her over the bulky object he was carrying in his arms and said, 'Eeh! Miss Fanny Carter,' which brought a high giggle from her. Then he jerked off his soft hat as the sitting-room door opened, and Pat stood there. But it was some seconds before Pat spoke; moving slowly forward, he said, 'Well I never! What a transformation, Don; it's marvellous.'

'Thanks, Pat.'

Pat stood aside to let Don enter the room. He did not look towards the group of people all staring at him, but went straight to a chair and gently laid on it the bulky, cloth-wrapped article he was carrying. When he straightened up they swarmed towards him, their voices and opinions mingling like spray about him.

'Why! Don.'

'Oh, you look marvellous.'

'Really! Don. Your hair looks lovely.'

Even Emanuel had risen to his feet.

When Don stood in their midst it was as much as he could do to stem the rush of hot tears.

Marie Anne had moved forward with the rest but now remained somewhat apart and voiced no opinion, until he looked her fully in the face, when she said softly, 'It's so lifelike; I mean, it's almost the colour of your skin. And the way it's moulded to your face . . . it's amazing.' She shook her head almost in disbelief at what she was seeing.

Don did not respond to this, but said, 'I have your birthday present here.' At this, he moved from among them and went to the chair and unwrapped the object lying there.

When he straightened and held towards her the piece of sculpted marble, there was a concerted gasp.

Together, Marie Anne and Emanuel walked towards him, and it was Emanuel who emitted the soft words, 'Dear Lord!' as Marie Anne took from Don the pair of hands on which, partly swathed in a rough garment, lay a new-born child, whose facial structure depicted the features of Anne Marie. It *was* the child. The mouth was slightly open as if it were gasping for its first breath of air. Even the hair on the head was there. And the hands that were holding it were live hands, his hands, each finger long, the knuckles over-large, the flesh seeming to have been scraped on the bones between the joints. They were live hands.

She heard him saying, 'It's a kind of two-way gift, a much belated birthday present and the reminder to my god-daughter-to-be that, after the doctor and Sally, I was the first to hold her.' Then his voice very soft, he entreated her, 'Oh, please! please, don't cry.'

When there came a slight pause in the adulation of the work, during which Marie Anne had handed the sculpted child back to Don, her grandfather, standing to Don's side, now put out his hand and stroked the folds of the garment that covered the child, murmuring, 'Such work. Such work.'

When Don took his work of love to stand it on a nearby table, James said, 'I think we had better be going. Surely that child is dressed by now,' and at this there was a concerted movement into the hall, there to see the nurse descending the stairs, carrying the child in its christening robes, and followed at a distance by Sarah, whose sudden cry of 'Don! Don!' startled everybody, and more so when she jumped from the second stair and almost straight into Don's arms, crying, 'It's wonderful! Wonderful! Wonderful! You look splendid.' And then, as if unaware of the company or where she was or even her position in the household, she lifted her arms and pulled down Don's head towards her and kissed him on the mouth. It seemed to have all happened within a second.

The ensuing laughter was slightly forced, but Don, putting his hands on each side of her cheeks, bent towards her and, softly but for all to hear, he said, 'Sarah, that to my knowledge is the first time in my life I've been kissed by a woman; and it couldn't have been by a finer one,' and with this he returned the kiss, gently but firmly.

If it hadn't been the day it was, the day on which the child was to be christened; if it hadn't also been the day when they saw this man appear in a different light; if it hadn't been the day he had brought into the house a beautiful piece of sculpture, then perhaps the verdict on that last scene would have been, 'Too theatrical for words' or 'She's been made too much of; she doesn't know her place'. Instead, the embarrassing situation was made laughable by Anita, of all people, approaching Don and saying, 'Now why didn't you give me a hint; I'd have obliged at any time,' only to be pulled away quite roughly by Pat, saying, 'That's enough of that! Behave yourself.'

'Are we going to a christening or not?' demanded Emanuel, as he made for the door and the waiting carriages.

However, it seemed that Marie Anne had purposely lingered, as, too, had Sarah. They exchanged looks that were deep with feeling, which on the one side could have expressed hate . . .

Everyone said it had been a wonderful day. So many odd things had happened and there had been so much laughter and bantering among them all; but now the house was quiet and at rest; at least, some of its occupants were at rest.

In Marie Anne's room the lamp was burning low. She herself was sitting propped up by pillows. Her hands lay on top of the counterpane, the right fingernails picking at the left ones, a sure sign of her inward irritation.

She was telling herself that she had never felt so unhappy in her life. Until today she had thought that never again would she be consumed by blind anger; she could foresee no need for it. But after witnessing the kissing scene in the hall she'd had to make the greatest effort to control her rage; she had experienced a great desire to slap Sarah's face, as she had done Evelyn's some years ago; that she should have made a spectacle of herself and her feelings like that . . . And him. That was something she couldn't understand, her anger against him too. For him to openly state, 'This is the first time I have been kissed by a woman;' how could he say such a thing? and in public; to admit such a thing in front of other men, not to mention all the staff grouped at the end of the hall. She had told herself that it wasn't likely he would have been kissed by a woman, because of how he looked, only for her mind to come pelting back at her, throwing the truth at her until she was stunned by it: 'You are mad because time and time again he has thrown away the opportunity to kiss you, and if he really loved you he would have risked it, wouldn't he? *Wouldn't he?*'

When the denial came, 'No; not him,' she had screamed back, 'Don't make excuses for him. If his feelings for me are as he has implied in so many ways, they would have been strong enough for him to take advantage of one kiss in private. But what does he do? He waits until there's an audience. And with *her* of all people!'

Never before in their association had she ever thought of Sarah as *her*.

Her grandpa had been right the other evening. He had said in a joke that she must put her foot down and put *her* in her place. Well, now she would do it; yes, she would. But how? How? Perhaps tomorrow things would look clearer, when she would know what to do, what to say.

No, she wouldn't. She flung herself round in the bed. Tomorrow things would be worse, because whatever she said would bring emotions into the open and expose her own feelings. She couldn't say that she didn't want her to leave. Then what did she want her to do?. . .

Sarah was in her own sitting-room. She was fully

dressed. She would have liked to go up to her now and deliver her decision; but she would wait until tomorrow and do it in a way that would make her absence acceptable, at least for a time.

As she rose from her chair to go to her bedroom she told herself two simple truths: all good things came to an end, and hearts did break . . .

In the bedroom next to his grandfather's, Pat lay on his back with his hands behind his head. It had been an odd day; he couldn't think of a stranger one. So many things had happened. And then there was that business in the hall. Anita hadn't spoken about it until he was taking her home, when she had surprised him by saying, 'You were annoyed, weren't you, at what you thought of as my silly remarks to Don? Well, I want to tell you that it was in response to the knowledge that I was witnessing a man baring his soul, but in the wrong place, and that it would be causing embarrassment to your sister. There was that telling pause. It was in the hope that a little frivolity would lessen the drama of the moment and give her time to recover herself, that I said what I did. And when Pat had asked her, 'What are you talking about?' she had answered, 'Are you blind? Marie Anne is in love with that man. What she witnessed caused her to drop her smiling mask for a moment. I happened to be looking her way and was amazed to see that she looked so furious, and I'm sure it wasn't only with him but also with her beloved friend, who, I understand, is never out of her sight. You once told me that she wasn't the serene individual I imagined, but that she had the devil of a temper and that she had once actually slapped Evelyn's face. Well, today she looked as if again she could have slapped someone's face; perhaps both their faces. I was trying to prevent another slapping session, this one likely just verbal. So, Mr Lawson,' she had ended, 'remember that there's more ways of killing a cat than drowning it, and that my frivolous remarks were of good intention and were not the self-exposure of my so far hidden flirtatious character.'

He brought his hands from behind his head and punched the pillows into a comfortable position, then turned on his side and prepared for sleep, thinking that he was glad he had met Anita: so sensible, so kind and so loving, and definitely understanding. Nevertheless the kissing business had annoyed him, and now, according to Anita, Marie Anne was in love with the fellow. He liked the fellow all right; yes, he did; but for Marie Anne to think of marrying him . . . for, new mask, or no new mask, there was still his face, and always would be.

Sarah brought in Marie Anne's early morning cup of tea. She pulled back the heavy curtains and opened the window just the slightest, saying, 'It's a real September morning, with a slight frost on the grass.'

When she returned to the bed she did not look directly at Marie Anne but straightened the frill attached to the top cover, and as she did so, she said, 'After breakfast, could I have a word with you?'

Marie Annie's voice was soft as she replied, 'Have a word with me, Sarah? Do you ever need to ask to have a word with me?'

'No; but this is a special word.'

'Special word?'

'Yes, yes. Now drink your tea while it's hot; I'll get about my duties.'

Marie Anne's hands shook as she lifted the cup from the side-table. A special word, she had said. She knew what that meant: Sarah was going to bring the matter into the open, and she wouldn't be able to bear the embarrassment.

Last night's thinking had been diluted into the new approach she was determined to take on the whole matter. Her reason had finally dictated that if she were to ignore the whole business and act as normally as possible, then Sarah would do nothing about it; and with regards to him, well, it would have been impossible, in any case, to broach the subject of his open confession.

The matter resolved in her mind, she had waited for the appearance of Sarah, and had been relieved by the ordinariness of her approach. It had been as usual: at least, she had imagined so until she had asked for that private word, which indicated without any doubt that she had made up her mind about something. Oh, she told herself, she knew her Sarah. Then the question came, Did she? Had she known that Sarah loved Don? and love him she did. But what about him? 'You are the first woman who has ever kissed me.' There had been a depth of feeling in his voice. Did he care for her in some way? No; he couldn't, after all he had intimated towards herself. It might have been unspoken love, but it *had* been love, of that she was certain. Well, there was one thing still sure in her mind: she could overlook Sarah's part in yesterday's little play, but never his, no, never his, and she would make that clear to him in the future. Oh yes, she would. Yes, she would.

Marie Anne was in her sitting-room, the baby lying on the couch to her side. It was kicking its legs in the air and gurgling, but for once Marie Anne did not take any joy in witnessing these antics: she was looking at Sarah who was standing a little way in front of her and saying, 'Well, reading between the lines, I think Annie is not well at all; but she's not sayin' much about it, so, if you don't mind and if I'm due for a holiday, I would like to take it now.'

'Don't say things like that, Sarah. What do you mean, if you're due for a holiday! You know you can take a holiday any time you like. And when did you get the letter?'

Sarah seemed to think for a moment; then she said, 'The day before yesterday.'

'Well, why didn't you mention it to me then?'

'For the simple reason' – Sarah's voice had risen – 'I didn't realise what was written between the lines, so to speak, until . . .'

'Yesterday?'

'No; not yesterday. There were other things to think about yesterday, if you remember; but I thought about it, well, more fully early this morning, and I thought it wouldn't do me any harm to have a break; that is, if it was agreeable to the household.'

'Oh, be quiet! Sarah.'

'Very well, I'll be quiet. The only thing I'm asking is, is it all right for me to leave tomorrow?'

'Tomorrow?' Marie Anne's voice was high; then she shook her head for a moment before going on, 'Well, yes, I suppose if you're anxious about Annie, the sooner you are there the better and the sooner you get back. How . . . how long do you think you'll stay?'

'Oh; how long does one usually have for a holiday?'

Again Marie Anne looked away; and now she bit on her lip before she said, 'Would a fortnight be all right? Would a fortnight suit you?'

'Yes; yes, that would suit me fine. Everything will be straightened out within a fortnight.'

'What d'you mean, straightened out?'

'Just what I said; straightened out.' Then her tone changing, and nodding down to the baby, she added, 'You needn't worry about her. I haven't much time for Nurse Clark, as you know but, give her her due, she knows her business. And then there's the girls; they're good backers-up, not forgetting Maggie Makepeace; she knows the routine of the house better than I do.'

These words should have been conveyed with a smile, but they weren't.

'Oh, Sarah!' It was almost a piteous cry from Marie Anne now, but Sarah did not respond to it as might have been expected. Instead, what she said was, 'Don't you worry; everything will turn out all right. Now, if you'll excuse me, I must get on.'

After the door had closed on her, Marie Anne lay back on the couch and covered her face with her hands. The tears were almost choking her. The rift between them, for rift it was, was so wide she couldn't see it ever closing. Not even if she went to her now and said, 'I never meant to look at you like that, Sarah. I'm a stupid individual, and I'm so sorry;' it would make not the slightest difference. And anyway, she couldn't put herself over as a silly individual who hadn't meant to look as she did, so furious, and her expression must have been furious if it had expressed the ferocity of her feelings at that moment. She had never before imagined Sarah doing anything that could arouse in her a harsh word.

Now she was so full of remorse that she felt she could die.

By afternoon the staff knew that Miss Foggerty was going away for a fortnight. The decision seemed to have been very quickly decided on, but then, apparently her sister wasn't well and obviously, she hadn't wanted to bring this up before the christening. And it had been a lovely day, yesterday, hadn't it? Oh, it had been a lovely day . . . lovely, lovely. And then there had been that lovely scene between her and Mr McAlister. It was like something you would see on the cinematograph. Carrie agreed with Fanny that she had wanted to cry, and wasn't he a lovely man. Oh, and had they ever seen such a change in anybody as that mask had made in him? Oh, he looked lovely, handsome, real handsome . . . lovely. And his hair, too, hanging over his brow. It was a lovely colour.

Finally, they all agreed it would be a rather quiet house until Miss Foggerty returned. They didn't exactly know how or why; it wasn't just her quaint Irish sayings and how she put them over; it was just something about her. You couldn't put a finger on it, you only knew you missed it when it wasn't there . . .

As Fanny let Miss Foggerty out of the front door Sarah said to her, 'I'm just going for a stroll and to get the air, Fanny. If anybody should need me, tell them I won't be long.'

'I'll do that, miss. I'll do that. Be lovely walking the day, with the sun shining and the air so crisp. Enjoy your dander.'

'Thanks, Fanny. I will.' And they exchanged smiles and parted.

Once clear of the house, Sarah hurried along the well-known path towards the wood, and her step did not slow as she entered it, but she did cast her eyes towards the tree-stump where she had left Marie Anne sitting that day while she herself picked bluebells.

When she emerged from the wood and came in sight of the cottage there was no sign of its occupier, and even when she tapped on the door no-one came to open it. Slowly she turned the handle and went in to what was now a beautiful room, and she looked around her appreciatively before she called softly, 'Don. Don.'

She was wondering if he was down at the farm when she heard the muted sound of hammering. Straight away she made for the studio and there, knocking on the door, she called, 'It's me, Don . . . Sarah.'

'Oh my goodness!' Don stood before her in a knee-length grey smock. 'Where've you sprung from? Have you been here long?'

'No, no; I've just come.'

'Well, I meant, have you been down to the farm?'

'No; I came straight along the top. I was just out for a walk. I . . . I thought I'd look you up. Where's the dog?'

'Oh, she's out scrounging, looking for a rabbit. Just a minute while I take this off; and stand back, and don't

401

come in here else you'll be all dust.'

In the living-room, he said, 'Look; it's just like me, I've let the fire go down. I'll make it up presently; you'd like a cup of tea now, wouldn't you?'

'Yes; yes, I would, Don; and I'll see to the fire.'

She saw to the fire, and he saw to the making of the tea, and when they were sitting together on the couch with a small table in front of them holding the tea things, he said, 'This is a nice surprise. I never thought to see anyone for days and I was going to get down to some work, real work.'

When she didn't make one of her Irish responses he looked hard at her, then asked quietly, 'What's the matter, Sarah?'

'Nothing much, Don, nothing much, only I'm going on . . . well a holiday, in the morning.'

'A holiday! Where? Why? This is sudden, isn't it? Where're you going?'

'Well, where would I go? Now ask yourself. I'm going to Annie's. She's not too well.'

'Is she in trouble?'

'Oh, I don't know about trouble, not that kind of trouble, only that she hasn't seen me for some time. Anyway, I'm due for a break, I think. I put it to . . .' she paused, then repeated, 'I put it to Marie Anne, and she agreed that I could have a fortnight.'

'That was kind of her.'

Now she did give a slight laugh, as she said, 'Yes; yes, it was.'

'Well now, Sarah Foggerty, that's your official version; but what's the true one? Yesterday, there was no talk of you going on holiday, nor when I left you last night.'

'No; it was . . . it was a quick decision.'

'People don't make quick decisions unless there are reasons, valid ones. Now, out with it. What's the matter?'

'Nothing, Don; nothing untoward, just that I'm in need

402

of . . . well, say a break in order to bring myself down to earth. I've been living in the upper layer of clouds for a long time now, and you don't see life as it really is from that height. I've had it too good of late.'

'Don't talk silly, woman. You've never had it too good in your life. You've never had your due, and no matter how kind they are to you down there, it's no repayment for what you have done for them, and what you go on doing for them daily, from the old man downwards. And he certainly appreciates your presence in that house. It's an awful fact that nobody of your type, the selfless type, ever gets a fair deal or their due because, no matter how you feel, you put on an act. Rising to the occasion, the Brothers would call it, and they have to do a lot of it. You see, I know, you, Sarah; I know you like I know myself. See here.' He reached out for her hand, which was near her cup, only for her to exclaim, 'Look out! will you. Just look at the tray cloth; that's a mess for you.'

'Damn the tray cloth!' He lifted the whole table to one side; then hitching himself nearer to her, he gripped her hand, saying, 'Come on; we're friends, you and I, Sarah, two of a kind, very special friends. You know it and I know it, and we're joined together by the affection that we hold for one person, isn't that so?'

She looked into his face, but did not give him any answer, and so he remained silent for almost a minute; and then he asked softly, 'Something, perhaps, has happened between you and her?'

'No, no, no! nothing, nothing.'

'I don't believe you. What is it?'

He let go of her hands, sat back from her, turned his head to the side as if thinking, and then said, 'No, no; not that! She couldn't take umbrage at that.'

'Don, listen to me. I don't want to talk about yesterday, or anything else, I just want to get away for a time and be

403

quiet, or be among the noisy rough gang on the third floor of Ramsay Court, where I know I shall be able to pull myself together. You see, Don, I'm all at sea in a leaky sculler, you could say.'

'That's daft talk, and you know it. Look at me.'

'I'm looking at you, and you're quite nice to look at. Oh yes, you're quite nice to look at.'

'None of your soft soap. I'm going to ask you a question. Is all this swift change due to our spontaneous piece of operatic acting yesterday?'

She actually laughed now as she repeated, 'Operatic acting! Was that how it looked? When I come to think about it, it must have, at least to most of them, especially so when Miss Brown pushed forward to say her piece. I liked her for that.'

'I'm right, then. I even guessed it yesterday, when she never opened her mouth to me, nor to you either, I noticed. But I should be glad, I should really be over the moon, because it proves something to me which I would rather have proved in a different way, because I wouldn't have you hurt for the world, Sarah' – he again had hold of her hand – 'you're such a fine woman. And let me tell you, I'm not at all sorry that I voiced my gratitude to you yesterday as I did. I knew that behind the laughter there was likely the overall thought "how embarrassing; fancy him voicing a thing like that." But that didn't matter to me . . . Sarah Foggerty, if you cry I shall cry too and that will make me appear more unmanly still.'

Sarah sniffed loudly, then blew her nose, saying, 'You! unmanly? You're more man than anyone I know of.'

Don laughed, saying, 'There you go again. You're asking for a repeat of yesterday, Miss Foggerty. Look! let's have some fresh tea.'

'No more tea for me, Don' – Sarah had risen to her feet – 'I've got to get back. I said I was just going out for a short

404

walk, but I thought I would like to tell you myself what's going to happen.'

He was now standing over her, saying, 'What d'you mean, what's going to happen? You're going for only a fortnight, aren't you?'

'We'll see. We'll see.'

'Sarah. Sarah. Now . . . oh please, don't desert her; she'd never get over it. She loves you above everyone else; I know she loves you, and her gratitude to you is so deep there are no words to explain it. I know that from the way she has talked to me about you.'

'We'll see. We'll see, Don.'

'You're not going on that, we'll see; now promise me you'll come back in a fortnight.'

'I can't, Don, I can't promise; not the way I'm feeling now.' She gave a wry smile as she added, 'I feel like me Aunt Harriet must have done when, after forty-seven years, me Uncle Patrick walked out on her. Everybody in the family and for miles around knew how he adored her. They were married when she was sixteen and he eighteen. He was forever praising her to the skies. Nothing on this earth would separate them but death, he'd say. Then one day, when he was sixty-five years old, he ups and tells her he's leaving her. I understand that his last words to her were, "All good things must come to an end". The woman he went off with was just on forty, and when the family commiserated with Aunt Harriet, all she could say to them was "All good things must come to an end". There is a tie between the two incidents if you think about it, Don, although mine lasted only two years, not forty-seven.'

He said nothing but when he bent forward to kiss her, she turned her cheek to him and he kissed it; then in a thick voice, she said, 'Goodbye, Don,' and she had opened the door and was on the step before he answered, 'Goodbye, Sarah.'

She was some yards along the path before he went to the door; but he didn't follow her; he just watched until she was lost to his sight, when he went back in and closed the door. He stood with his back to it, his teeth grinding together, and through them he brought out the words, 'Damn her!' then couldn't believe he had uttered them.

PART FOUR

1

'The house hasn't been the same since she left.'

'No, Grandpa.'

'Do you miss her?'

'Yes; yes, of course I miss her, Grandpa; of course I do.'

'Well, you've been very quiet of late; you've hardly spoken about her. You know, Mary Anne, I never thought I would say this about a servant, but I felt she was an asset to this place, that she did something for us all. She made me laugh and want to laugh and I've never before experienced anything like that in my life from either my equals or my superiors, and certainly not from a servant. But then she was a different kind of servant; she was your friend. She was the woman who gave you back to me; and she herself should've been back here yesterday; her fortnight's leave was up then, wasn't it? And I want her back to get rid of this nurse you've planted on me. Who needs a nurse for a cold?'

'You haven't a cold, Grandpa, you have severe bronchitis, and arthritis, too; and if you would do what you're told, it would help everyone all round.'

'The woman's a fool. And so the quicker you get Foggerty back here, the better. What's keeping her, anyway?'

'It's Annie, Grandpa, her sister; she's not well.'

'Yes I know' – with a bellow the old man interrupted Marie Anne – 'yes, I know Annie's her sister. I know all about the family, from Shane the clever one to the last one in the basket. She would talk to me about them on the quiet.'

'She did?'

'Yes, she did; and about other things too. At bottom she is a very wise woman. She isn't the Irish idiot she at times makes herself out to be for our amusement. That's all it is; to keep others happy. Anyway, when did you last write to her?'

'The day before yesterday.'

'Did you tell her you were expecting her back?'

'Of course. Of course I did.'

'I don't know, I don't know what to believe. I think there's something fishy going on. McAlister's only been here three times in the last fortnight. He tells me he's working on something quite big. That might be so, but he's changed too. It couldn't be that he's missing Sarah, could it?'

'I don't know, Grandpa.' Her tone was high, her voice stiff, and when he added, 'Could there be anything between them, do you think? You know what I mean?' she actually shouted, 'Yes; yes, I know what you mean, Grandpa, and I still say I . . . I don't know.'

When the break came in her voice he looked directly at her but said nothing. Then he watched her turn from him and hurry to the door, mumbling, 'I'm . . . I'm going up to the nursery.'

The old man twisted around in the bed, which movement brought on a spasm of coughing. This over, he lay looking towards the fire. So that was it, was it? He recalled to mind the little dramatic scene on the day of the christening, when that good fellow owned up to never having been kissed by a woman. He himself had been greatly touched by that and the courage of the man who could openly confess to such an omission, if that's what it was. And he had kissed Miss Foggerty as if he meant it. Oh yes; yes, he had. And if his memory was recalling aright the

410

expression on her face, that woman had enjoyed it too.

Now if such was the case, what about his dear Mary Anne? Where did she stand in this? Apparently on the outside. That would come as another blow in her life. First, being cast out by her mother and into the dubious care of that woman in London; then being raped; and rape it must have been, because he couldn't imagine the child willingly acceding to such a thing. And then the trauma of that period of poverty, only to be brought back to suffer the murderous attack by her brother. Surely she could never have come through without Sarah Foggerty. And now where was that woman? Supposedly looking after her sister. There must be something behind all this . . . He moved uneasily in the bed as he thought, Here comes that blasted nurse. I can always tell; she has flat feet.

He sighed deeply.

Two days later the final letter came. It began:

Dear Marie Anne,

You know what I'm going to say, don't you? I won't be returning to the house. I knew I wouldn't when I left, because by then all my thinking on the matter had been done, and I know I've chosen the wisest course.

But there's one thing you can be sure of, Marie Anne; I shall always love you. For a period you were my child, my daughter, and my friend. But that period is finished, and from now on you can start a new life, and if you are wise you will not hide your feelings. I'm sure you know what I mean.

Please don't worry about me. I'm all right; and I'm with my family again. Also I have got part-time employment. Having said all this, it is not to say that I won't miss you so very much, and, too, all those kind people

411

*in your house, especially your grandfather. If you
should get talking to him some time, give him my love,
because I found him a very lovable man.*

Good night, my dear, and God bless you always.

Your Sarah.

Marie Anne crushed the letter against her chest and her
mind cried, No! No! Oh Sarah! Sarah! What am I to do?
What am I to do?

She began to pace about the room like someone
demented: she couldn't tell her grandfather that Sarah
wasn't coming back, nor could she tell her father, for her
father would be looking for more reasons than would her
grandfather. She could talk about this to Pat; but Pat was
in Newcastle working, as was her father. She could go to
Evelyn; but then again, although Evelyn was much
changed, she was bound to think as their mother had
done, that she courted disaster, that her very presence
caused discord. Hadn't it been apparent since she was a
child?

She stopped in her tramping. There was Don.

Oh, how could she go to him? She'd have to tell him
the truth, that is if he didn't already guess it, for the few
times in the last fortnight he had called at the house, there
had been little warmth in his greeting of her. Oh, he had
been polite, yes studiously so, but it was only he who
knew Sarah and who might have some influence on her
. . .

Don had just finished a cold meal when the knock
came; and he was wiping his mouth with his handkerchief as he opened the door; then the surprise showed
in his voice: 'Marie Anne!' he said 'Oh, come in. Come in.
I'm . . . I'm sorry' – he motioned towards the table – 'I
was still eating.'

'I've interrupted your meal?'

'Not at all. Not at all. It was just a cold snack; and I was

412

about to make a cup of tea. Would you like one?'

'No thanks; not now.'

For a moment he looked closely at her, then said, 'Sit down, please,' and he motioned to the couch that was already pulled up at an angle towards the fire in which logs were blazing merrily. He moved to one side the little table on which lay his dinner tray; then he drew up a chair and sat facing her.

'Is anything wrong?' he asked.

She drooped her head as she murmured, 'Yes, Don; yes, something's very wrong. I've . . . I've had a letter from Sarah: she says she's not coming back.' She swallowed deeply here before looking up at him and adding, 'Apparently she has known she wasn't coming back from the day she left and' – again she swallowed – 'and I'm to blame.'

He did not say, Oh, I wouldn't say that, or, Why d'you blame yourself? but just waited; and after another session of gulping she went on, 'I've been deluding myself, telling myself I'm a sensible person who wouldn't take umbrage at silly things. Well, I know now that I'm not a sensible person and that I do take umbrage at silly things. At times I am petty in my attitude to people, mostly those that I love, and I love Sarah. I still love Sarah, and always will, and yet I could act as I did to her. You see, I know why she left.'

Her eyes wide and bright, her lips trembling, she waited for him to say, Do you? But when he spoke he didn't ask a question, he made a statement.

'I do too,' he said.

She now felt the colour seeping over her face, but she couldn't take her eyes from him as he went on, 'She impetuously kissed me and I returned it, and with fervour and gratitude. Yes, and meaningfully and gratefully because she *was* the only woman who had ever kissed me. The whole incident might have appeared stagey to

413

all those present, but I didn't think about that at the time, and it wouldn't have mattered if I had because, through my confession, I knew I was returning a little happiness to a woman who has spent her life unselfishly giving happiness to others. She is such a good woman, and at that moment I loved her, and I still do. There's all kinds of love, and I repeat, I still do. From when I first met her I realised that her life was made up partly, or mainly, of an act: she was out to please, to make others happy, to create laughter. I knew that, and I thought there was someone else who did too, and that someone else I imagined was you.'

The tears were now running unbidden down her cheeks. His words were tearing her apart, but she didn't ask herself why she was sitting here suffering them, in spite of being aware that whatever chance she had had of him ever kissing her, of ever owning up to his love for her, she had killed. And his next words seemed to put a stamp on it, for he said, 'I thought *you* would understand, knowing her so well, and knowing me' – he paused – 'not a little. But whatever you conveyed to her in your look must have shaken her very deeply for her to take the steps she did, because I think she assumed you knew that she would never do anything in this world to hurt you, that you would always come first with her, no matter what her own feelings were. Then, by your look or your manner, or whatever you did – and here I must tell you I'm just putting my own interpretation on it – I think she must have felt that she was no longer the close, wonderful friend of this young woman, but was merely her servant who had stepped out of line and who was making a fool of herself in front of guests. Moreover she was taking advantage of her association with me. But as for that, I must say that nothing could be further from the truth, for if I were to claim a deep friendship with anyone in your household, or back during our short acquaintance in

London, say, it would have been with her, for ever since we first met in Ernie's Eating House she has looked me straight in the face. She looked at me then as if the mask and the slouch hat didn't exist. To her I was a man. It is rarely that I have had that response when a woman has peered under the felt hat, before turning her gaze swiftly away.'

Marie Annie's face was awash with tears. Her head bowed, she sprang up from the couch, crying quite loudly, 'Stop it! Stop it! You are being cruel. All the time you are being cruel. I came here to ask . . . to ask for your help. I knew I had done wrong and I felt low enough in my own estimation, but now you have left me with not even any self-' – she choked and gasped before she could bring out the word – 'respect; and let me tell you,' her head was up now and she licked the tears from her lips before nodding at him as she said, 'I can do without your advice because, like Sarah, I knew before I came here what I should do, and I'll do it, and I'll tell you— ' She was gulping again as she searched in the deep pockets of her overcoat for her handkerchief. Then dabbing her face with it, she repeated, 'And I'll tell you this. As I listened to you pontificating, I thought it was a pity that you *hadn't* become a priest or a monk or a Brother or some such, so that you could find a real outlet for your domination. And finally, and this is my last word to you, why, I ask you, did you bring me back from the grave with the talk of needing me, your only real friend?' Her mouth was now agape; her eyes were wide and unblinking as she stared into his face; then her mouth clamping shut and her eyes screwing tight, she swung about and ran blindly towards the door.

But he was there before her, and his arms about her shoulders and his voice soft, he said, 'Marie Anne. Marie Anne.'

She was actually wailing now, her crying unrestrained.

415

Gently, he led her back to the couch. When she dropped on to it, she laid her forearms on the arm and drooped her head on to them; and thus he let her stay for a minute or so.

When he pulled her round to him and cradled her head on his shoulder, holding her with one arm, he took the pin from her hat, which had gone askew on the back of her head, and threw them aside. Then, his arms about her, he held her close, saying soothingly, 'There now. There now. It's all right. It's much better out . . . That's what I would like to do at times, too. Crying is a wonderful cleanser, so why is a man considered weak if he indulges in it? There now. There now.' Gently he brought her face upwards and with a clean handkerchief he wiped it, talking softly the while: 'I'm so glad you came. I was lonely for the sight of you, but mad at you for losing Sarah; yet all the time understanding why you lost your temper; and it was temper, wasn't it? I've been told that you have a real devil of a temper.' He was smiling gently at her; but she didn't respond, for she was still full of pain; and so he went on, 'And why Sarah went off as she did. Then I have been so cruel to you when you came asking me for advice. Well, only I know why I reacted so, and now is not the time to tell you, not yet anyway. You are the mother of a baby, but you are also just seventeen; you imagine childbirth made you into a complete woman; but you must know that your grandpa, your father, and even Pat, all still consider you a very young girl, even still a child not yet touched by life. Now, what do you think would happen if I were to go to them and open my mind about you? What! a man of my age, and appearing as I do – for God knows what they imagine lies under the mask – and asking for the hand of their fledgling? I would be shown the door.'

She made no response whatsoever, other than to stare into his eyes.

He leaned forward and touched her red lids with his fingertips, saying, 'You'll have to wash your face in cold water before you go home or the questions will be flying at you, especially from your grandfather. And another thing, my dear, I could kiss you now and you would be the second woman I have kissed, but I would kiss you as you've never been kissed before. Yet you don't want me to, because you'd hardly be out of the door than you'd be telling yourself it was only because I was sorry for you; or that it was a way of apologising for being so harsh, or it was an aftermath of all that has happened. When I do kiss you, Marie Anne, it's not going to leave any such thoughts in your head, I assure you.' He now smiled at her before continuing, 'I don't know if this is the priest, the monk or the Brother speaking, but I only know it's taken a lot of their willpower to make me talk and act as I'm doing at this moment, when all I desire to do is something entirely different. But it is not the time.'

He now brought her hands together and held them to his chest as he asked her, 'Tell me what you intend to do.'

She drew in a long breath before she said quietly, 'Go up to London and try to bring her back.'

'Yes; I thought you might do something like that, and I think it's the only way you *will* get her back; and you know in your heart that things will never be the same unless she returns.'

Still holding her hands, he pulled her up from the couch, saying briskly, 'Go and wash your face; and while you're doing that I'll write a short letter to Sarah.'

She made no response to this, but went into the kitchen, and he, going up the room to the writing desk, sat down, pulled a piece of paper towards him and wrote simply:

Sarah, dear,

Your sacrifice has backfired, because I know she won't have anything to do with me unless you return. And let me tell you, you are much missed in that house. The old man is lost; he is very unwell with bronchitis and seems to be giving everyone hell. As for me, I am lonely, for there is a space in me which only you can fill. Come back, my dear.

Come back.

Yours,

Don.

After he had sealed it, he rose to his feet, to see Marie Anne standing by the couch pinning on her hat. He went to her and, handing her the letter, he said, 'It's just a note. Will you give it to her?'

'Yes, of course.'

'When will you be going?'

'Tomorrow morning.'

'Are you letting her know you are coming?'

'No.'

'That's the best way.' He now made an impulsive movement towards her and, putting his hands on her shoulders, he said softly, 'Marie Anne . . . Marie Anne, I wouldn't have you hurt for all the world. Believe me. When you come back, things . . . things will be different, you'll see. You'll be happy again. I promise you. In the meantime I shall look forward to your eighteenth birthday, all the while gathering the courage to present my credentials. You understand?'

He now let loose of her, saying, 'Wait a minute; I'll get my coat, I'll walk to the house with you. I won't come in.'

'No! no!' she protested, and with her hands raised as if warding him off. 'I . . . I want to think. And there's much arranging to be done before tomorrow.'

He opened the door for her; and just as he had watched

Sarah walk away, now he watched Marie Anne. But on his closing the door, his reactions were different: he did not stand with his back to the door and damn her, but after walking towards the fire and staring down into it, he began to stroke the side of his mask, the while thinking, it'll all depend. She'll have to see this first and what she'd have to live with.

2

Marie Anne arrived in London at three o'clock the following afternoon. Less than half an hour later a cab deposited her at the opening to Ramsay Court, and as the ever-pervading smell of the yard struck her, that smell that was re-created daily by hot cinders meeting wet rubbish, she experienced the strangest feeling: she had come home. Gone were the years before her short sojourn in this yard and the time since she had left it, for it seemed to her that she had had no life other than that which she had spent here, because every minute of it passed through her mind in a series of bright episodes.

There was no-one in the yard, not even children scampering about; lavatory doors were all ajar; there were no poss tubs outside the wash-houses or the sound of mangles grinding.

When she entered the hallway she stood still for a moment looking up the stairs, for here she was being enveloped in a different smell, that of cooking, cabbage water, and the odour of bodies in close proximity.

On the second landing she stood opposite Annie's door. She was panting slightly with the unusual exertion and she was also shivering inside as if fearful of her reception. Her knocking on the door was more in the nature of a tap, yet it was quickly opened, and there stood Annie, looking aghast but exclaiming, 'Dear God in heaven! Where've you sprung from?' Then, 'Well I never! Come in. Come on in.'

Except for the youngest child the room was empty.

There was no sight or sound of Sarah.

'Sit down, won't you? Well, I never! Of all the shocks to get. Last night we sat talking about you until the small hours. He's away on a job and the children were in bed. Eeh!' – she put a hand to her brow – 'I can't believe it. D'you want a cup of tea?'

'Yes, I could do with a cup of tea, Annie, thank you.'

'Just a second while I put the kettle on.'

During the time it took Annie to fill the kettle and put it on the fire, Marie Anne looked about the room. It was so familiar. Everything was in the same place as she had last seen it, and that was almost a year ago, but the youngest child was no longer in the wash-basket, but standing in the far corner holding on to a small chair which she was aiming to push towards her, until her mother cried, 'Stop that! Rose. Sit down! Be a good lass.'

The child sat down, but still held on to the chair, and Annie explained, 'She's learnt herself to walk by pushing that thing. Himself says he's going to buy her one of those scooter things, as she's always wanting to use her legs . . . There you are, then! we'll let it brew for a minute,' and she patted the teapot on the hob, before sitting down opposite Marie Anne and saying, 'Eeh! girl. . . miss. I can't get over it.'

'Where's Sarah?' Marie Anne asked quietly.

'Up above. Where else? She hasn't been gone up there more than ten minutes since. She works from eleven to three.'

'Where?'

'At Ernie's; you know, pulling pints.'

Marie Anne bowed her head: Sarah pulling pints. Oh no! Yet she must prefer doing that to staying with her.

'It's all right, it's all right, miss.' Annie's hand came across the table and patted Marie Anne's. 'She's fine; although I've said to her, in the name of God! woman, have you gone out of your mind comin' back here, for

421

what's here for anybody? Although, mind, we've been a lot better off since she's been with you. But to come back to this shanty! I haven't really been able to get to the bottom of it. All you can really get out of her is, all good things must come to an end, and that you're wise if you recognise the end and don't press your luck. Did you ever hear such a thing! What happened? Did you have an up-an'-downer? I mean, a big row?'

Marie Anne raised her head as she said, 'No, no; not a big row. It was my fault entirely. Really, Annie, I was to blame. You see, I have a number of faults, but the biggest one is that I have a temper that flashes out and doesn't wait to be reasoned with.'

'Oh well, you're not the only one, believe me. Now she . . . well, I can tell you, I wish she had a temper that flashed out. You would know how to deal with her then. But no. She's a funny one, is our Sarah. As me ma used to say, if you knew her two days in the week you were lucky, 'cos she would do things at the drop of a hat, and with no explanation; and not until she had done what she wanted to might she then tell you why. She actually walked out of mass one day, and it was during a mission – you know, when different priests would come and rattle you up if you were slackin' in your duties. She was just on fourteen at the time. Oh, there was a how-d'you-do about it, because this particular priest was all for hell-fire and brim-stone, and he rammed it home in no small voice that there were gridirons down there on which people were made to sit starkers. There was nothing symbolic about his particular hell; it was the actual thing, and you could feel your backside frizzling. Well, that was too much for our Sarah and, as I've said, she was only fourteen and was still sittin' on the children's side of the church, so when she gets up my mother, thinking she's going to be bad or sick or somethin', hurriedly goes after her. And in the porch there are the three Brothers, you know like the ones in

422

the priory here. They always stood at the door on a Sunday morning with plates for this foreign mission or that foreign mission. And what d'you think she was sayin' to them? That she didn't believe a word that priest said, and that he was only out to scare the wits of children. And apparently she didn't lower her voice. You talk about temper. Well, I'll never forget that Sunday, because when me da heard about it he took the belt to her. Aye, he did, for disgracing him and the family and darin' to speak against the holy church, and her but an ignorant little slut of a thing. Eeh! there was real hell to pay in the house that day. What d'you think she did then? She walked out. She went to me granda's, that was me ma's da, if you get what I mean, because she knew he thought like her. Me Granny was church-goin', but he wouldn't go near it, although he was a Catholic. So, me dear, I wouldn't worry about losin' your temper because you can't hold a candle to her. Her trouble now is that she doesn't shout about what she's goin' to do, she just does it, and it's like knockin' your head against a brick wall and tryin' to make her see other than what she's determined to see herself, if you see what I mean. Oh' – she shook her head – 'I'm no good at explainin' things, but all I can say, an' I said to himself when he was on about her bein' a bloody fool an' such and walkin' out of your fine house, with the position she had, there must have been a reason for it and that it was to your benefit, because she wouldn't do anything in this world to upset you, miss, not really. But, as I said, she must have upset you by walking out, as she did me, by using me as an excuse, because I haven't been bad; I've never felt better for years than I do now.'

Suddenly there came two taps on the ceiling, and Annie said, 'That's her. She wants me up there for some reason or other. Look, will you go up first? But what about your cup of tea? I'll tell you what: go and get it over, whatever it is, and I'll bring you up a cup, both of yous.'

'Thank you, Annie.' Marie Anne rose to her feet, and putting her hand out towards the unkempt-looking woman, she said, 'It's lovely to see you again. It is really. And Sarah's lucky she has you and your family.'

'Well' – Annie's head was wagging now – 'God knows why, but nevertheless thank you very much. Go on now. Go on.'

Marie Anne mounted the last flight of stairs. She did not knock on the door but opened it gently, to hear Sarah's voice coming from the bedroom. 'Come in here a minute and see these springs. I told you what they were like, but you wouldn't believe me. Those two must have bounced on them half the night to make them sag like this.'

Marie Anne didn't move towards the bedroom but stood looking about her. This room too was just as she had left it. Perhaps the furniture hadn't been polished so much, but everything was clean and tidy, and the fire was burning brightly in the grate. The feeling of being home was even stronger here. She had been happy in these rooms. She had lived for each day, not looking to the future. This she had left to Sarah.

Sarah's voice came again, louder now, saying, 'Look! Come and see this a minute. I've put up with them for weeks. They're for downstairs again.'

There being no response, Sarah appeared at the bedroom door and, her hand going to her mouth, she held it there for a moment while she closed her eyes and muttered, 'Dear God! no.'

She was walking slowly towards Marie Anne who was now holding on to the back of the high chair as if for support, and when she was an arm's length from her she stopped and said, 'Why! in the name of God, what's brought you?'

For answer Marie Anne smiled and said, 'If that question was being put to you, you would likely reply, the train and a cab from the station.'

This brought a long drawn out, 'Aw!' from Sarah, before she flung about and went to the fireplace and there, gripping the wooden mantelpiece with both hands, she knocked her head twice against it. But she did not speak, and Marie Anne, walking towards her, said, 'I had to come, Sarah, if it was only to say how sorry I am, and ungrateful and . . . and ashamed.'

'Oh, don't pile it on, please.' Sarah had turned from the mantelpiece and, bobbing her head now, she said, 'It is all over and done with. You should have accepted it and got on with your life.'

'How could I when the support of my life had left me?'

'Well, it's about time then you learned to stand on your own two feet. And I was never the support of your life; you were strong enough to speak your mind when the occasion warranted.'

There came not a tap on the door, but the sound of a foot kicking it, at which Sarah moved quickly to open it and let in Annie with a tray of tea, and saying, 'Now drink it straight up, else with the time it's taken me to get up those stairs balancing it, it'll only be ready for the sink.'

As she put the tray on the table, Sarah addressed her, saying, 'What d'you think of this?'

'Of what?'

'Don't act thick-skulled, our Annie. She's not an apparition, is she?'

'Huh!' said Annie. 'Well, I thought she was at first. Anyway, there's your tea, so get on with it. I'm not goin' to stand here listenin' to your kind of reason; I've listened to it all me life. And I've got to get back anyway, or that one down there will already have pushed her chair down the two flights, and begod! she will one of these days, and soon. Be seein' you, Marie Anne.'

'Yes, Annie, yes; and thank you for the tea.'

'Huh! but isn't it nice to be thanked for a cup of tea. Isn't it, sister Sarah? You can serve cups of tea to the

425

militia in our house and never get a thank you.'

'Get yourself away.'

Laughing, Annie got herself away, and Sarah handed a cup to Marie Anne, who received it without thanks. When they were seated facing each other, Marie Anne said, 'I . . . I have a letter here.' She opened her bag. 'It's from Don.'

It seemed for a moment that Sarah wasn't going to take the letter from her hand. When she did, she used the handle of the spoon to open the envelope. After she had read the few lines she lifted her eyes and looked at Marie Anne, before reading the letter again. Then slowly, she folded it and returned it to the envelope, saying, 'Well, well!'

What Marie Anne said was, 'Grandpa sent you a special message.'

'Yes?'

'He said, if you come back for no-one else, will you please return for him, because he is missing you so much. And the house—' She started to gulp in her throat and made the greatest effort to check back the tears that were ready to spurt from her eyes, before adding, 'The house is not the same since you left, and if your sister needs convalescence you must bring her here and arrange for someone to take over the family there for a time.'

Sarah screwed round in her seat until her back was almost to the fire. Her head was bowed and her hand was covering her face; then almost bouncing round again, she cried, 'It isn't fair! I did what you wanted me to do. You wanted me out of the house at that time, as far away from him as possible. Yes, you did. Yes, you did.'

'Oh no, Sarah; no!' They were both on their feet now. 'No, it wasn't like that. I . . . I was jealous for a moment, yes. Yes, I admit it, I was dreadfully jealous for a moment. Not that you kissed him; and yet, yes, it was because you had done what I had wanted to do for a long time and

426

daren't. But you were yourself, you could be yourself and you kissed him. But that wasn't the end of it; it was just the beginning, and it was when he kissed you back so fervently and told you you were the first woman he had ever kissed. I'm telling you now, Sarah, that was the moment I was hurt to the core, because he had given me to understand that he loved me. I know, when I was very ill that time, that he brought me back to life by telling me of his feelings when he thought that I was unable to hear, and so that scene cut me to the bone. Can you understand that? If only I'd been courageous enough to kiss him even with that dreadful old mask on – I know you would have done that – or he'd been strong enough to kiss me and tell me that I was the first woman he had ever kissed. Can't you understand how I felt in that moment, because honestly I wasn't aware of your feelings for him, nor of his for you. He does love you, and not only in a certain way. He made that plain yesterday.'

Sarah's eyes widened: 'What do you mean, he made that plain?' she said. 'This letter doesn't say that. What happened yesterday?'

'Well, you could say we fought.'

'You fought?'

'Yes, verbally. I considered he was cruel in the things he was saying to me, pointing out my defects and that I'd hurt you.'

'He would never hurt you, that man would never hurt you, Marie Anne.'

'But he did. He knew exactly what my reactions had been to that scene, and he threw them all back at me, and so I told him what I thought about him. And then he changed his tune, but I couldn't accept it.'

'Oh, dear God! There's a pair of you; there is, there's a pair of you. Look, Marie Anne; let me put things absolutely straight and in plain language. That man loves you. He's loved you since the first time he clapped eyes on you. I knew that from the look on his face then, and it's only intensified with time. He would do anything in this world for you. But he is marked. You might capture him through love and pity, but there is your family. They have befriended him because they owe him a debt, and he is well aware of this. He is also well aware of his own position compared with theirs. He cannot claim any station in life other than that of a sculptor. What you call his love for me is a sympathetic reaction to his recognition of our similar concerns for you. He also knows that his disfigurement means nothing to me. I took to him from the first minute I saw him. Do I love him? I suppose I do; but it's in a different way altogether from the way he loves you and the way I love you. You came first with me then, and you still do, no matter where either of us might be. He knows that. We talked about it during your illness, and we have become quite close.'

'Well now, Sarah, are you coming back?'

'Oh my dear, my dear; I've been away over three weeks now; I can't see myself somehow falling back in the routine. More than that, I can't see myself being accepted again. They'll ask why I stayed away so long.'

'Oh, that's easily explained: your sister has been so ill; that's why I have come to see if I can be of any help.' Though her eyes were full of tears Marie Anne was smiling. 'Grandpa set the picture yesterday, and Father really believes your sister is ill. As for Pat, he knows there is something amiss, but he fell in with Grandpa's orders to Mrs Makepeace to have a guest room made ready, because Miss Foggerty's invalid sister might be coming for a short stay.'

'He said that?'

There was the first touch of laughter in Sarah's voice, and in her eyes too; and then musingly she added, 'He's a lovely old man. Yet why do I call him old? he's so young in his thinking; and when he laughs it's like that of a boy.'

Marie Anne's hands now went out and caught Sarah's and she entreated her softly, 'You'll come back then, will you? You'll come home with me, for good?'

Sarah bowed her head; then when Marie Anne's arms went about her they clung together, their tears mingling and Marie Anne crying, 'Oh! Sarah. Sarah. Never leave me again. Please! please! no matter what I do or what I say, promise me you'll never leave me again.'

Pulling herself away from Marie Anne's embrace, Sarah said, 'I'm making no promises; I could be dead next week. Now, now; stop it. Stop that crying.'

'Well, you stop it too. If you're not crying that must be beer spilling from your eyes. Fancy pulling pints again!'

Once more they were leaning against each other, laughing now while endeavouring to dry their faces.

After a moment or so Marie Anne sat down and quietly said, 'It's wonderful, wonderful; I never thought to feel happy again ever. We'll get the twelve o'clock train back tomorrow. And I tell you what I'd like to do, Sarah, now I'm here; I'd like to call at the *Daily Reporter* and see Mr Stokes or Mr Mulberry. I had such a nice letter from Mr Mulberry, the assistant, a little while ago. You remember they had ideas about developing a series of the funny cartoons, the ones about the children. Well, with one thing and another, I didn't answer, but I would like to go and have a word with them.'

'Don't see why not; and on our way we'll have to call in at Ernie's to give my notice in. They won't like it, but they'll be so pleased to see you. Perhaps you would give them a tinkle on the piano for five minutes; that would please them. Yes, we'll do that.'

Sarah now seemed like her old self, so much so that she said, 'Let's go down and tell Annie. That poor soul, I can tell you, has been as worried as any of us, and I've even got to like her man during the last few weeks. One night he came up here and talked as I never imagined he could.

429

Mind, there was a lot of bloodys and buggers inter-
spersing his commonsense remarks but nevertheless,
what he said was right and to the point. And what d'you
think? He also thanked me for helping the family. It's odd
how you can change your opinions of people; but I know
that what transpired between us pleased Annie because
she's always said he wasn't so black as he was painted.
And now I can understand why she's always found an
excuse for him, and why she has stayed and given him
that tribe. But mind, although I say it meself, they're good
kids, all of them. So come on, let's go down to her.' Then
laughing, she added, 'I think she's got a mutton stew on.
That was your first meal here, wasn't it?'

'No; it was the first meal I saw the children eat. And if
they're eating again, I'll likely get the idea for another
cartoon.'

Marie Anne rose from the chair, and for a moment they
stood silent, looking at each other. Then putting out her
hand and taking Marie Anne's, Sarah said, 'Come on away
home.' And like this, hand in hand, they went downstairs.

3

Sarah's welcome home started at the station, where she and Marie Anne were met by Mike and the carriage; and they had hardly stepped down from it when the door of The Little Manor opened; and there were Fanny and Carrie exclaiming, 'Welcome home! miss. Glad to see you back. How's your sister?'

To the last Sarah answered, 'She's much better. Much better.'

In the hall, they were joined by Maggie Makepeace and Katie who, in her usual tactless way, said, 'Glad to see you back, miss, although the place has been nice and quiet since you left,' which brought her a push from Maggie, who said, 'She always says the right things in the wrong way, miss; but for me meself, I'm glad you're back. Maybe you'll be able to persuade the master to eat his meals.'

There was further laughter when Katie added, 'And to stop yelling so much at the poor nurse.'

One or another of them had taken Marie Anne's and Sarah's outdoor things; and Marie Anne, addressing Maggie Makepeace, said, 'Is my father in, Maggie?'

'No, ma'am,' Maggie answered; 'nor Mr Pat; but we're expecting them at any minute.'

A yell penetrating the house caused them all to look up the stairs, and Fanny, laughing, said, 'He must have got wind of you, ma'am.'

'You go on up, Sarah,' Marie Anne said; 'I'm going to the nursery first.'

Sarah's tap on Emanuel's door brought no verbal response, but the door was opened by a weary-faced woman who stared at Sarah for a moment, then was about to turn towards her patient when he yelled, 'Get by! and let her in, woman,' and at this the flustered nurse stood aside.

Taking in the situation, Sarah smiled at the woman and said, 'Good evening, Nurse Gallacher.'

'Good evening, miss. I *am* glad to see you,' the nurse replied fervently.

'Well, you're not the only one,' Emanuel called; 'so leave us, please, will you?'

The nurse needed no second bidding; and then Sarah was standing close to the bedside looking at the hand outstretched towards her. She took it, saying, 'How do you do, sir?'

The answer came to her in no small voice: 'Don't ask me how I do, woman . . . walking out on me like that! It was supposed to be for a fortnight; but then you've got to be fetched back. There's something fishy here, and I'll get to the bottom of it. I'm halfway there as it is.' And Emanuel heaved a long sigh and added, 'Oh, I am glad to see you back, woman. Now things will return to normal; and the first thing you can do for me is to get rid of that nurse.'

'Pardon me, sir, but I'll do no such thing, for, from Marie Anne, I understand she has got you over a bad bout.'

'Time gets me over these bouts, not nurses. I'm speaking from experience. Anyway, she has flat feet.'

Sarah laughed, and said, 'Poor soul. Fancy holding that against her.'

'No matter. What she does for me you can take on.'

'I couldn't and I wouldn't, sir; I'm no nurse, not that kind, anyway. Now, if you'll excuse me, I'll go and have a wash and brush-up; it was a very dusty journey.'

'Yes; yes, of course. I'm sorry. But I mean it about that nurse; if you don't budge her, I will.'

As Sarah turned towards the door, she laughingly said, 'You do that, sir, you do. Take it into your own hands; but don't expect me to come to your aid after she's gone; I'll have my own duties to see to.'

'Duties, be damned!'

'Yes, just as you say, sir, duties be damned!' and she went out, still laughing.

She was only halfway along the landing when James and Pat appeared; and they both greeted her with, 'Oh, hello! You're back then,' to which James added, 'And you didn't bring your sister with you?'

'No, sir; she's much better, and she's got the children to see to.'

Pat, nodding back towards his grandfather's bedroom, asked softly, 'How did you find him?'

'As usual, in a sparring mood, sir. My first order is to get rid of the nurse.'

'And what did you say to that?' James asked, smiling now.

'Certainly not! sir,' said Sarah, turning away.

'Good for you,' called Pat gently after her. 'Ten to one he's out of that bed in the next few days.'. . .

Taking a side passage, Sarah reached her sitting-room without meeting anyone else and there she lay back in an easy chair and looked about her.

She had never expected to see this room again. Was she glad to be back? Yes; yes, in one way so glad; yet, in another, part of her could wish to be miles away.

Her mind now dwelling on this matter, she rose from the chair and entered her bedroom. First, she turned the key in the door; then going to the dressing-table, she picked up a three-inch crucifix carved from a piece of bog oak, and, going to the bedside, she knelt. The crucifix held in her joined hands, she stretched her arms across the eiderdown and laid her head between them.

She did not pray in the ordinary way, but what she said now was: 'Lord, if you won't ease this pain in my heart, help me to bear the sight of him, and to think of him only as a friend.'

4

The events leading up to Christmas were, in general, uneventful; in fact, as it was said, the house was running on oiled wheels. However, in November, much excitement was generated by the proposal that the staff of the two houses should plan together for a servants' ball. And this had the blessing of James Lawson.

There had also been a conversation between Don and Sarah which had troubled them both.

It took place shortly after her return. Don had remarked to her, 'I have just heard from Pat that the man . . . the father of the child, has died . . . Did you know?'

'Yes; I knew before I left.'

'I understand that the letter was from the man himself and that he knew he was dying.'

'Yes; that's right. And it was a beautiful letter.'

'She let you read it?'

'Yes, she did.'

'Well, apparently that's more than she did to Pat and her father. Pat said she wouldn't discuss it. But the man must have had good friends, because one of them sent it on. However, from what Pat says, she is not prepared to acknowledge his kindness. What did you make of it?'

'What I made of it, Don, nearly caused us to quarrel: I felt she should acknowledge it to the sender. But she didn't see it that way. Of course, she has a point: it would create a link with his friends in Spain. You see, she looks upon the child as entirely hers. As yet, she can't visualise her growing up and asking questions. But there'll likely come that day, and I hope I'm not here when it happens.'

When she next said, 'I suppose it's a good thing for all concerned that he's gone,' Don silently agreed with her, for, in a strange way and to all intents and purposes, the child might have been his, a feeling he had experienced since she first lay across his hands.

Surprisingly, he said to her now, 'What kind of a fellow was he, really? You must know more about him than anyone?'

She had paused a moment before answering, 'I really got to like him, and more so after I read that letter.'

'Then you don't really think he raped her?'

'Rape her? No; no. Face it or not, she had been in love with him for a time.'

Don had shaken his head as he said, 'You would never convince either the old man or her father that she wasn't raped. I sometimes wish they could see her as she really is.'

Sarah, putting out her hand, patted his arm, saying softly, 'As long as *you* do, Don, that's all that matters.'

5

It was on 2 January that a disturbing letter came to James from David.

First, it detailed what had happened at the new ranch Vincent and his mother had bought. Then, it had been thought that Vincent had suffered a heart attack. However, the diagnosis by the doctor was that he showed no sign of heart trouble; and the blunt man had stated further that the attack was one of pseudo-angina, brought about by strain and a bout of nerves. It was suggested that a change of occupation and a long rest were needed.

This had infuriated Vincent, even though his mother had pointed out that the ranch would be well managed by the foreman, Serge Nordquist, a Swede, who had managed the place for fifteen years, ten of them for the widow of the previous owner, a man in his late forties, a fine horseman and an affable fellow.

And so, she was trying to persuade Vincent to take a trip to the United States.

The tone of the letter seemed to suggest to him that his mother was now more willing to settle down. However, this did not prevent her from producing the usual tirade against Marie Anne, and the injustice meted out to Vincent, David said.

As he folded up the letter, James thought: There is always something to worry about. Life had gone on so smoothly during the past months: his father was up and about again, and his temperament much more affable; that is, since Foggerty had returned.

Funny about that woman, and the changes she had made in this house. He couldn't put a finger on it. She was nothing special to look at; and it wasn't only her Irish chatter that amused one; there was just something about her.

And look at that Christmas do. Had The Manor House ever seen such an event as a servants' ball? Even his father, muffled to the eyes, had come down to join the rest of them, and had applauded the jigging of the two fiddles and the pipe, and watched them waltzing and dancing the polka, accompanied by Marie Anne at the piano. But the highlight of the evening had been when Foggerty, tucking up her skirts, had danced the most intricate Irish jig, the first she had done, she said, since she was a young girl.

Another memory of that night was that no-one could get McAlister to dance, not even Marie Anne and her pleading.

Now there was their relationship to be thought about, too. Pat had suggested there was something between them, a view which Evelyn had endorsed. Well, he couldn't see it coming to anything. Oh no! Apart from his disfigurement, the man was twice her age. And just imagine if this facial trouble could be passed on. No; he must put his foot down there.

But to get back to the letter, he would let Pat see it, but he wouldn't mention it to his father. What he would do straightaway this very night, was write to David, asking him to keep him in touch with Vincent's further movements, because he wouldn't put it past his son, in the state of mind he seemed to be in, to come back some time and make his presence felt again.

6

Don could not tell himself he was any happier now than before Sarah had returned with Marie Anne, even though the feelings he and Marie Anne had for each other were evident, if not expressed.

One thing he did know was that it seemed he could never get a word with her in private, and he asked himself if it was his imagination that her father monopolised her during the three evenings in the week he was invited to dinner.

The Queen was dead and the country was supposed to be in mourning, but in many quarters the black represented only the relief that the old girl had at last gone and that a man was now on the throne. And so, stemming from this, the after-dinner discussions were generally of a political nature. Also, the winter months having again taken their toll on the old man's chest, it had been decided he move his quarters to the annexe, and Marie Anne would then take over the main part of the house. This would save much running up and down the stairs, not only for the servants but more so for Sarah, whose time seemed to be taken up with answering the old man's beck and call, as he still refused the services of a nurse. Altogether, there were twenty-seven rooms in The Little Manor, not counting the butler's pantry and such storerooms. Seven of these rooms made up the annexe. These now supplied a bedroom, a dressing-room and a sitting-room for Emanuel, and a bedroom and sitting-room for Sarah, leaving two rooms, one for a nurse, should her services be necessary, the other for a bathroom.

After much thinking and talking to the figure within the folded doors, Don had made up his mind that the day Marie Anne was eighteen, he would present his case to the three men. Strangely, he imagined that only the old man would show little surprise and would put forward no dissent. Apart from him, he also felt he might have Evelyn's blessing.

However, circumstances so arranged his life that he did not have to wait until she was eighteen to be given their consent. In fact, it transpired that he did not need anyone's consent.

It was the second week in June. There had been five marvellous days of full sunshine; in fact, everyone was now beginning to grumble about the heat.

Don had packed the last bag of sculpted pieces ready for his journey to the Brothers, but this night was his evening for dining at The Little Manor.

The front door was open, as were all the windows on the front of the house. He had just entered the hall when he saw James beckoning to him from the end of a short passage.

When he reached him, James said, 'Come in here a minute,' and he pushed open the door of the little study.

To Don's surprise he saw that Sarah and Evelyn were already there; and after nodding from one to the other, he greeted them: 'Good evening. How are you standing this heat?'

Neither of them answered, because James put in quickly, 'Let's sit down a minute. There's not much time; Marie Anne will be downstairs shortly, and she mustn't know about this; oh no, she mustn't.' He now tapped his breast pocket as he added, 'You know that my wife and son have bought a ranch out in Canada, and you have heard us talk about Vincent's supposed heart attack

440

which turned out just to be a form of nerves; well, I have learned over the past months that he went to the United States for a restful holiday, but that he did not like it there. Well, some weeks ago he had another bad turn and the doctor ordered him away for a complete change. In the letter prior to this one,' and he again tapped his breast, 'my son David told me that Vincent had gone to France to stay with friends; but then a letter sent to him by his mother was returned, saying, "Gone away". Now the worrying part is, not so much that we don't know where he is, but that it is only a step across the water to England and a train journey to Newcastle. And the state of mind he's in, he could be making for here and Marie Anne.'

It was Sarah who now said, 'Whatever happens, she mustn't get wind of this; it would frighten her to death. And then there's the child.'

'Well, we can't keep her locked up, so what is to be done?' Evelyn turned to Don. 'As I've just said to Father, she could come to us, but we're right on the open road; he could be in and out within minutes.'

'He could be in and out of *here* within minutes,' her father put in. 'And if I were to warn the yard-men to work close to the house, she would soon want to know why.'

Now addressing Don directly, Sarah said, 'Yours is about the only safe place. It's bordered by the river and Farmer Harding's fields; the only way in would be through the wood.'

Don did not answer for a moment: but he looked from one to the other, then directly at James, to whom he said, 'I'm not with you in this; I mean, about keeping her in the dark. I think she should be told, and right away, to put her on her guard. And yes, my place is comparatively safe, but it could be approached from the back. I do agree, though, that she mustn't be left alone.'

They looked at him in silence, as if waiting for him to go on; and so, hesitantly, he said, 'I had already decided

441

not to go to London tomorrow; I hate travelling in this sort of heat. And so I could be with her tomorrow, while you, sir, try to fathom out a way of telling her without causing her alarm.

'Tomorrow, we could arrange a picnic, couldn't we, Sarah? We could do some paddling. The beach by my place is really good; I had a dip first thing this morning when the sun was just coming up. It was wonderful. I could bring up the suggestion casually over dinner, sir.' He was again addressing James, and he, after a long moment, nodded and said, 'Well, yes, it would give us a little breathing space. But I can tell you, Don, I dread telling her that he's about. She'll go all to pieces again.'

'No, Father, she won't; she's tougher than you think.'

'Nonsense! Evelyn,' James almost snapped at her. 'She's not tough, she's still a mere girl.'

At these words, Don bit on his lower lip, turned about and gazed out through the open window into the garden. There it was again; she was a girl, and would always remain one in these men's eyes.

Sensing Don's feelings, Sarah put in, 'I think the paddling and the picnic is a good idea. It'll get us through another day, anyway . . . oh! there goes the master's bell. Away to your duties, Sarah Foggerty,' she said as she got up to leave the room.

And James, turning to Evelyn, said, 'Will you excuse me; I must go and clean up for dinner,' and to Don, he added, 'I'll be seeing you, Don.'

Alone with Don, Evelyn said, 'I'm worried, Don. I'm more worried than I can say. He's mad, you know, quite insane where she's concerned; and if he gets at her this time, he really will kill her. You're right about her being told. It would put her on her guard and prepare her for a fight of some kind. They still think of her as a little girl, the three of them, but you don't, do you, Don?'

'No, I don't, Evelyn. But nevertheless, she would have

442

little chance against that maniac. And, to tell you the truth, I'm frightened, too. You see, we're in a cleft stick: we can't go out to find him, but he will come to find her, and he'll pick his moment. Still, we'll see how tomorrow goes.'

'Yes, Don. But it's funny, you know, for tonight I came over to give the family a piece of news at dinner, but now I don't think tonight is the right time, not with Father in that state; but I can tell you. Funny that; yes, it is, that I can tell you I'm going to have a baby. Nick hasn't come down from the clouds yet. He was with the pigs when I told him. You wouldn't believe the mess we were both in.'

She was chuckling as Don took both her hands, and, pressing them between his own, he said, 'How wonderful for you! Let it be the first of many.'

Evelyn laughed outright now. 'It'll have to be a boy, because Nick says he wants help with the cattle. The second one he'll want for a pig farm. The third he'll make into an accountant so that he can count the money we'll never make.'

As their laughter mingled, Evelyn again thought how strange it was that she could talk like this to a maimed man and, stranger still, how everyone in the house used him in one way or another.

7

The next morning, the three of them, Marie Anne, Sarah and Don stood in a group in the hall. Sarah was saying: 'I can't go, even for the morning, and leave him. This heat's getting him down. And Anne Marie has the summer sniffles and Nurse won't let her out of the nursery. That leaves just the two of you. So don't spoil a good day like this; it's so heavy, it could be the last before the storm. Have a paddle and a picnic. And as you said last night, Don, you don't need our picnic baskets; you have everything in your cool larder to make a beach meal.'

Marie Anne looked at Don, and he back at her, and when he asked quietly, 'Well, what about it? Am I to waste my day-off alone?' she turned to Sarah, saying, 'You'll be all right?' And Sarah, lifting her eyes towards the ceiling, appealed, 'Lord in Heaven, listen to her. How does she imagine I manage for the other six days in the week.' Then bringing her gaze down to Marie Anne, she said on a laugh, 'Get yourself away, woman! You're wasting time. And I don't want to see you till this afternoon; there's nothing harming here, and you know it. And there is no need to change. That's a light frock you have on; you only need your big straw hat, and off you go.'

When, after shaking her head, Marie Anne ran up the stairs to fetch her hat, Don said, 'Thank you, Sarah; you managed that beautifully,' and, unsmiling now, Sarah answered, 'You can never do too much for a friend.'

* * *

Marie Anne was lying in the shade of the old willow tree, roots of which strayed from the land into the water. Its boughs, following suit from a pollarded trunk, showed its age.

A glass of spring water, with pieces of lemon bobbing on its surface, stood on a small tray to her side. Beyond, lay Don, his back supported by the bank.

Speaking softly, Marie Anne said, 'This morning, when I woke up, I never dreamed I would later be picnicking here. It's lovely, so peaceful. You are lucky to be so close to the river, you know.'

Don broke in, saying, 'See there!' and he pointed up the river; 'two more swimmers are coming down;' then he sat bolt upright when Fred Harding's voice came from across the water; 'Hello, there! Taking it easy, are you?'

Don got to his feet and from the edge of the water called back to the farmer, 'What are you doing across there?'

'Well, did you hear those screams a little while back? They may have been of delight, but it could have been otherwise: six bairns from the village had got themselves on to one of the little islands, and not one of them could swim. They were out for a picnic, the twelve-year-old told me; bottles of water and bread and dripping, you know the kind. I got them off and took them back to the farm and Sally gave them a feed. I've now set them back on their way home because there's a mother of a storm coming up fast. You see' – he pointed – 'it's black over Durham, and I'm not the only one who'll be glad when it comes. This weather makes the animals uneasy . . . Nice to see you, miss. How are you keeping?'

Marie Anne had not risen, but now she got on to her knees on the sand, and called back, 'Fine, Mr Harding. Fine.'

'And the baby?'

'Oh; she's in fine fettle, too. But it's too hot to bring her out.'

'Hi-ho! Listen to that!' Fred Harding pointed into the distance, saying, 'That's nearer.' Then his voice dropping into a loud whisper, he added, 'Have you seen this one that's coming down? He's been in the water on each of the last four days. He's a strong swimmer, but why, in a slow river like this, he's wearing automobile goggles, I don't know.'

Don made no reply, but stood with Marie Anne beside him, waiting for the swimmer to come into view.

The swimmer appeared, moving steadily, his head well out of the water. His hair looked long and dark, and was held down at the back by the strap of the goggles. He seemed to have a small beard. When he was opposite the beach, he turned his head and looked towards them, then continued steadily on.

Not until the swimmer had disappeared round a bend in the river beyond the woodland did Mr Harding speak again. 'I wonder where he's left his automobile? I know where he's left his clothes. They're on a little island below the dam. It's a good job those bairns didn't come across them. Oh! there we go again. And look; the sun's hazing over, so I'd better be off. Bye-bye, miss . . . Look in some time.'

'Goodbye, Mr Harding. And yes, I will.'

'Are you afraid of storms?' Don asked Marie Anne now; and she answered, 'It's odd; no, I'm not. Strangely, I rather enjoy them. When I used to run, I always stayed outside in a storm. I would gallop like some wild animal through the wind and the rain.'

'In that case,' Don said, 'I'll slip up and make us something quick to eat, and we can have it out here before that storm actually reaches us . . . You'd like that, wouldn't you?'

'Oh yes; yes. And just to lie back here. It's so peaceful.'. . .

How long she lay with her eyes closed, dreaming of

446

what might happen before he took her back to the house, she never afterwards remembered, only that it seemed a long time, during which there were further rumbles of thunder and the sun disappeared altogether. What she was to remember was the moment the hand came over her mouth; she knew she had felt it before, and the scream inside her swelled her body against it and the pain of her hair being pulled from its roots as she was dragged to and through the water.

She had glimpsed the goggles before her assailant thrust her face downwards in the water, but the rage that was now filling her body gave strength to her limbs, and blindly she clutched and clawed at his loins, which caused the hand to be lifted from her mouth and allowed her head to come up, enabling her to let out a most piercing scream.

When her head was again pulled under the water, her arms groped upwards and her hands clutched at the face, bringing the goggles down on to the man's throat, which she gripped so hard that her thumb broke through one of the goggle glasses.

Then she became aware of there now being other arms about her, dragging her from the man, and as she was thrown aside she realised Don was locked in combat with the man and that they were moving further out into the river; and she could see blood seeping from the man's throat.

When they disappeared beneath the water, she dragged herself up to grip one of the overhanging branches of the old willow, and gradually pulled herself along to its end. The water was now up to her oxters and she dare not go any further.

She tried to call Don's name but found this impossible. Then almost, as though in a mirage, two bodies rose from the river. They were locked together.

And now she did cry out, 'Don! Don!' and her heart

447

gave a great jerk of relief when Don began to swim towards her, using one arm, the other dragging the man with him.

Now Don was standing beside her, struggling to draw in deep breaths, and there, on the surface of the water, not a foot from her, lay her brother, Vincent Lawson.

'He's dead! He's dead!' she cried. 'You've killed him, Don. Oh! you've killed him, Don.'

Don looked at her, and all his mind could say was, Dear God! Dear God! He now looked at the gash in the man's throat made by the broken glass.

A flash of lightning lit up the darkened sky, and with the crash of thunder he shuddered; then, in a mass of stinging pellets, the rain came, and he mouthed to her, 'Go back! . . . inside,' and as he thrust her away, he pushed the body towards the middle of the river, and remained treading water until the stream took hold of it, and with the rain now blinding him he was unable to see how far downstream it drifted.

So dark was it now that it was almost impossible to see beyond the bank; and when he found Marie Anne lying there, her face buried in her hands, he yelled above the torrent of rain, 'Come on! Get up! Get up out of that,' and roughly hauled her to her feet and up the bank. From here, and blindly, he half carried her to the cottage.

The door was still open, but this he closed with a backward kick before dragging her to the mat lying before the dead fire; then dropped down beside her and lay inert.

His body was aching; he had a great desire for sleep. For a moment he imagined he was in the river again, thrashing at the body as they both dropped into deeper water. He had known he must have air or be finished, and when his feet hit a shelf of rock they were sent bouncing upwards. When his head broke the surface he had gasped, spluttered, then drawn in air, the while realising

448

that the man's arms were still around his shoulders, but hanging limp, as though he were unconscious.

When it came to him that the man was dead, he recalled the blood rushing from the man's neck before, locked together, they had sunk to the bottom. The neck was now washed clean of blood, although a piece of glass remained partly embedded.

It was at this point he had heard Marie Anne screaming his name; then her voice saying with relief, 'You've killed him, Don. Oh! you've killed him, Don,' and his mind answering, 'My God! She thinks I killed him.'

'Don. Don; are you all right?' Marie Anne's voice was now a low tremble. She had turned her head towards him, and he, as if coming up out of sleep, muttered, 'Yes, yes.' Then his hands went up to his head to straighten his mask, to find it wasn't there but was hanging over his shoulder. Immediately, his hand covered his cheek.

They were sitting up now, staring at each other through the dim light. Instinctively, he was about to grope for the mask and to slip it on when his mind yelled at him. 'No! No; there'll never be another moment like this. Let her be repulsed. That will determine the way for us both.'

Slowly his wet hand dropped from his cheek, and there it was, the long ugly scar, at this moment looking worse, if that were possible, for the ridges were still glistening wet, and small pieces of river debris were clinging to the distorted skin.

He watched her eyes travel from his brow down to his chin and on to his bare chest, where the black merged into grey before taking on its natural skin colour.

His heart was racing, even more so than when he had been combatting the river and the man. He watched her eyes close for a moment before her mouth opened as if she were about to speak. However, no words came; instead, she lifted her hands and cupped his face, and when her lips fell on the scarred cheek, he uttered a deep cry.

Then his arms were about her and he was kissing her, her eyes, her cheek, her mouth, her neck, and with a fierceness that sent them down onto the mat again, gasping with exhaustion, even more so than when they had come up out of the river.

Marie Anne began to speak, her words coming in stilted phrases: 'I love you, Don. I love you. When did I start loving you? I don't know. All my life. You've been a necessity to me for so long, like the wind and the rain and the sun. The feeling I have for you supersedes all others, even that for Anne Marie.'

His face alight, Don lay listening to her; and now he said quietly, 'Will you marry me?'

Marie Anne gave him a push, saying, 'What have I just been saying to you?'

'Yes; I know, my dear, but I should have added "in spite of", not because of my face – that you have accepted, thanks be to God – but in spite of the three men who now rule your life. What do you think they're going to say when I, a man almost twice your age and looking as I do, and with no great prospects, say to them "I am going to marry this beautiful young girl of yours"? Your grandfather will likely yell the house down and say, "The hell you are!" Your father will look at me with that cold stare he assumes at times, and Pat will likely react with, "Oh, I like you, Don, but this is not on." That surely is what will happen, isn't it?'

'Well, if that is so, you know what I shall say? "You, Father, can stop me marrying until I am twenty-one, in which case I propose to take Anne Marie and live with him . . . in sin in the cottage, until such time as we can marry . . . Scandal, Father? I'm not afraid of scandal; I have served an apprenticeship in that, haven't I?" '

'Oh, my love, my love' – their wet bodies were

entwined again – 'You would do that?'

'Yes, Don; I would. I would do that, and more, for you.'

When he squeezed her hand, she gave a little cry of pain, and he said, 'What's the matter?'

'I don't know, only something in my finger hurt me.'

After peering at her hand, he said, 'I can't see anything in this dimness; I must light the lamp.'

When he returned with the lamp, he held up her hand to the glass globe; and as he rubbed along the inside of her third finger, she winced again, and he said, 'Oh my! there's something here,' and then exclaimed, 'Yes, I can see it. It's a tiny sliver of glass sticking out from the skin. Don't touch it; I'll get some tweezers.'

She did not touch it, but she started to shiver. There was the feeling again of her thumb pressing on the glass of the goggles; then the blood, so much blood, and the way it disappeared in the river as Don grappled with her.

'Stop shivering. It's only a tiny piece; it'll be out in a minute.'

It was out in a minute, but it was followed by a narrow streak of blood and the sight of it made her want to vomit.

As he pulled her to her feet, he said again, 'Stop shivering. Are you cold?'

'Yes,' she replied; 'yes, in a way. I think we must get back, so that I can get out of these wet clothes; and you, too.'

He glanced towards the window and said, 'It's coming down in sheets; but we can't get much wetter than we are. Can you still run?'

'Yes,' she said. 'Not so fast as I used to, but I can still run.'

'Come on then, darling; we'll make a run for it.'

'Oh! Don, Don.' Her arms were around his neck. 'That's the first time you have called me darling.'

Before they were again enfolded, he said, 'It was a mistake, madam; I apologise.'

451

As her hand touched his cheek he exclaimed, 'Oh my! I had better not go out without my camouflage, had I?' and straight away pulled the mask from his shoulder and on to his face. Then, as he was about to pull her towards the door, she stammered, 'When he's f-f-found found, what will happen, Don?'

He replied quietly, 'I don't know, dear; that's to be seen. Only one thing is sure; he was out to murder you.'

'Oh, Don! Don!'

'Please, dearest, don't cry. Don't cry. Come on!' At the door, he said, 'Now for it! Keep your head down, dear.'

Then, hand in hand, they were running blindly through the woodland; and neither of them exchanged a word; it would have been impossible to shout above the torrent.

When they burst into the lamp-lit hall, Sarah, who was descending the stairs, exclaimed, 'God in heaven! Why did you come out in this? You should have stayed put in the cottage.'

'Sarah. Sarah.' Don was gasping. 'Let's go and talk for a minute or so, and then Marie Anne must get out of these wet things, and to bed; she's had a shock.'

'Shock? What kind of a shock? You're shivering. Oh, dear God! He hasn't . . . ? You haven't . . . ?'

'He has, and she has, Sarah. And look, the best thing is to get Fanny to help her off with her clothes, and into bed. Look; go on, dear.' He pressed Marie Anne towards the stairs. 'I'll explain to Sarah, but you say nothing, d'you hear? nothing to anyone.' He said this in a low whisper. 'I'll see to it, dear; just leave it to me.'

Marie Anne just looked at him lovingly for a moment, then went up the stairs slowly, as if she were dragging her feet.

Sarah drew Don into the morning-room, saying, 'What happened?'

'Well, he came, but not as we had expected; he was in disguise: dyed hair, beard, goggles, the lot. Farmer

Harding had seen the man swimming the river on previous days. It was he who pointed him out to us swimming downstream. Anyway, I left Marie Anne on the beach while I went up to the cottage to make the lunch. The first thing I heard was her screaming. He had come upon her from behind the old willow, then he dragged her in and tried to drown her.' He paused, then looked down as he said, 'We fought and drifted to the middle of the river, into deep water. We both went down, and when we came up I found he was dead.'

'Oh, my God! Don. But don't worry, it would have been either you or him, or her and him. Is he still in the river?'

'He must be; he was carried down by the storm. But see to her, Sarah, will you? She's bound to have a reaction to this.'

'Yes, I'm sure she will; she'll have a reaction to this, all right.'

'But one last thing, Sarah: she's going to marry me. She's seen my face and it doesn't matter.'

'Oh, Don.' Although her voice sounded joyous, nevertheless the sound was wrenched through pain. But when she took his hands and held them, between hers, pressed to her breasts, she was smiling; and when he kissed her she closed her eyes tightly, savouring it.

'As you can imagine, Sarah, there'll be combined opposition from the men were I to ask for their permission. But I am not going to ask; I shall merely tell them what we intend to do.' This brought a laugh from Sarah, who said, 'Good for you, Don. I should like to be there when you're doing it, I would, that. But what you must do now is get back and into some dry things.'

It was somewhat later in the evening when he decided to take a walk along the river bank. Earlier in the day he had returned to The Little Manor to find out how Marie Anne was. Sarah had told him she was sound asleep. Apparently

Dr Sutton-Moore had been paying his weekly visit to Emanuel, who had asked him to look in on Marie Anne, whom he thought might be heading for a chill after being drenched in the storm. The doctor's diagnosis was that, like many others, she was suffering from slight sunstroke, and he had given her a draught.

He had left a message for Marie Anne with Sarah to the effect that he was off to London first thing tomorrow morning, but hoped to be back on Tuesday.

His mind was in a turmoil, as he wondered what would happen if the hotel-keeper, or whoever Vincent would have been staying with, were to notify the police of his absence and they found his name . . . his real name among his possessions. Having tried to disguise himself, it wasn't likely he had registered as Vincent Lawson.

He cut through the wood, and found that, in places, the water had come over the bank.

Nearing the river bend he could see Mr Harding in the distance examining one of his fields that was partly flooded. With him he had three dogs. One was Gyp, whom Fred always took care of whenever he himself was absent from the cottage.

Not feeling inclined, at this moment, to talk to anyone, he did not hail him, but stepped back and around a large clump of bushes, the end of which bordered an inlet, and seeing what was lying there brought him to an abrupt stop.

What might have been a small hen cree had been caught up in the overhanging branch of a willow, and with it a bale of hay and some sacks attached to a long plank of wood. Lying with his head half on the sacks as if resting, was Vincent.

A split to the waist up one leg of the bathing suit showed starkly the whiteness of the skin; the broken goggles still hung from his neck; but the face was streaked with black, which was probably dye from his hair.

Don felt his stomach heave. He looked about him: no-one could see the body from the opposite bank; there was too much debris caught up in the inlet. The river, already running fast, would continue to rise and very likely take this lot with it before morning. What should he do? Go back to the house for Pat and his father and bring them back here? Or should he let the river have its own way, and that would be that?

But it wouldn't be that: the worry would still be there and they would still be waiting for his coming. And on this thought he hurried back to The Little Manor.

As he approached it, he could see Mr Lawson apparently taking leave of Pat, and he called softly, 'Hello, there! Wait a minute.'

James immediately stepped back into the doorway, out of the rain, awaiting Don's coming; and he was surprised when Don, seeming to ignore him, said to Pat, 'Put on a mackintosh and come with me; there's something I want you both to see.' And when he took James's arm to pull him on to the drive, James said, 'What's the matter, Don? What's the matter?'

'You'll see soon enough, sir.'

It was the same question Pat asked as he caught up with them: 'What's the matter, Don? What's up?'

'In a minute, Pat. In a minute.'

The minute had turned to ten before they reached the inlet and Don pointed to the figure bobbing on the rising water.

It could have been a prayer coming from James's lips as he said, 'Oh! Almighty God.'

Pat said nothing: he was staring wide-eyed and open-mouthed at his brother, for in spite of the camouflage, his brother he was.

Softly now, James said, 'How did it come about?'

'I left Marie Anne lying on the beach while I went to make some lunch. I heard her scream, just the once. He was aiming to drown her. When I grappled with him we both went down into deep water, and he was dead when we surfaced again. I was almost in the same condition myself. What she's suffering from is not sunstroke but shock, and it might take some days for her to get over it.'

Sounding almost like a child, Pat spoke for the first time, saying, 'What are we going to do with him?' and Don almost barked in answer, 'Nothing, only pray to God the river soon moves him from there and he goes out with the debris into the North Sea. If he comes up in the dock or anywhere else there'll be an enquiry. And if he's here under his real name, I leave you to guess what that'll lead to. Thankfully there could have been no witnesses to the affair.'

When James swayed slightly, Pat put an arm about him and gently urged him: 'Come away from here. What Don says is for the best.'. . .

It was half-past five the next morning when Don waded through a foot of water towards the inlet, there to see it clear of all debris, including the body.

He could only hope that the storm, which had continued into the early hours, had carried it all out to sea. But this remained to be seen.

8

As it had done for the previous two nights the screaming seemed to hit Pat and brought him upright in bed, his hands over his ears.

As he got out of bed he groped dazedly for his dressing-gown, muttering, 'What's the matter with her anyway?'

He did not knock on Marie Anne's bedroom door but thrust it open, there to see Sarah endeavouring to hold down Marie Anne's flailing arms as she cried, 'He drowned, Don, didn't he, Don? he drowned. After, there was no blood, was there? I didn't stick it in, did I, Don? My hair's all wet. And they were his eyes.'

'There now; there. Be quiet. It's all over. You're all right: you didn't do anything wrong; you didn't. That's it; lie down and go to sleep. There now. There now.'

Sarah had been leaning half over the bed. As she straightened up, she pulled together the opened neck of her nightdress; and when she shivered, Pat said, 'Put your dressing-gown on, woman.'

After one more glance at the sleeping figure in the bed, Sarah went to the dressing-room, Pat following her and whispering, 'In Heaven's name! what's all this about? I have my own ideas, but I just can't believe them.'

In the room, Sarah picked up her dressing-gown from a chair, the while saying, 'Well, if you have your own ideas, that's all right, isn't it? Stick to them.'

'Sarah!' Pat's voice was harsh. 'Don't be so close. You know what all this is about; come out with it.'

'I know no more than what you've heard yourself, Mr Pat.'

'Well, Sarah, what I've heard myself over the last three nights makes me put two and two together and voice what I'm sure you already know; that Vincent wasn't drowned by Don; she killed him in some way.'

'Well, as I've just intimated, Mr Pat, if you've come to that conclusion, I can't alter your mind.'

Pat straightened up, and they stared at each other in the lamp-light, until Pat said softly, 'And he's carrying the can for her.'

When she made no response, he said, 'The things that fellow does for this house, and with no reward.' Sarah came back quickly, 'Oh, he'll have his reward this time: he's going to marry her.'

'What! He's certainly not.'

'He is. Hell or high water, they're going to be married. She's just been waiting for him to speak;' and she added, 'I'm not giving anything away here. As soon as he comes back he's going to confront The Blessed Trinity' – here she gave a small laugh – 'the three of you.'

Pat, too, chuckled, then said, 'Well, I'm not all that surprised, but I can't speak for the other two.'

'Well, I can tell you, whether they are vexed or pleased, that if they try to put a spoke in his wheel it will make no difference to either of them; they know what they're going to do. I only hope I'll be around when he has his say.'

He smiled as he touched her shoulder, saying, 'Knowing you, Miss Sarah Foggerty, I have not the slightest doubt you will indeed be near at hand.'

At the foot of page two of the Tuesday edition of the local newspaper, was a brief announcement concerning a missing man.

The manager of the Waverley Hotel, Durham, has reported to the police his fears concerning one of his guests. On the day of the great storm, Mr Henry Culmill had reportedly gone swimming, and he has not been seen since. The police are investigating.

As he had promised, Don returned on the Tuesday. He didn't get in until five o'clock, but after a wash and a change of clothes, he was at the house by six.

The trap in the yard told him that Pat was home, and he hoped that his father might also be here.

This was confirmed by Fanny Carter when she opened the door to him and said, 'Hello, Mr McAlister. The gentlemen are in the master's room; but Miss Marie Anne . . . I mean ma'am, is in the sitting-room.'

'Thank you, Fanny.'

When he opened the sitting-room door Marie Anne sprang up from the couch and ran towards him. They embraced and he held her tightly for a moment before he kissed her.

'Oh! my dear, dear. You haven't been out of my mind for a moment since I last saw you. You look peaky; has anything more happened?'

They walked towards the couch, but not until they were seated did she burst out, 'Oh! Don; I've been so frightened: I've had the most terrible nightmares. I've been over and over every moment of it since it's happened. I . . . I didn't do it, Don, did I?. . . I mean—' But before she could finish, he put in, 'No! No, of course you didn't. You know what happened: he must have drowned as we went down fighting; as I've told you, I almost did myself. Now stop worrying, it's all behind us.' . . .

It was odd, but at that moment, at the other end of the house, James was saying, 'Well, he drowned, Don said he did.'

459

'He was lying,' said Pat. 'She said he did; she was ter-rified at what she had done. It's this that is causing the nightmares. And let me tell you, Father, there are not many men who would take that on their shoulders for the rest of their days; and there you are, getting on your high horse because I tell you they are going to be married, and you saying, it's too much; that you will put a stop to it; that you have control over her until she's twenty-one. Well, let me tell you, Father, if you do put your foot down, they'll put *their* feet down and walk along to that cottage and live in sin, or what you like, until they can marry.'

'He said that?'

'Not to me; but I got it straight from the Foggerty's mouth.'

There was now a movement from the basket-chair as Emanuel hitched himself upwards; and his body shook as he said, 'I can see them doing just that.'

'You are for it, then, Father? Have you thought that that business of his – I mean his face – might be hereditary?'

'No; I haven't got that far. But what if it is? as long as they inherit his character as well as the brand.'

'Has she seen it, do you think?' It was James now asking the question of Pat.

'I don't know. Likely she has. But I don't suppose it'll matter a bit, or anything at all, come to that, what it looks like; it's him she wants.'

'And so you're for it, too?'

'Yes; because I like the fellow. And don't you think it's about time Marie Anne herself has a little real happiness?'

Happiness and Marie Anne. Looking back, she had caused havoc in the house since she was born. But that hadn't been her fault; she hadn't been wanted by anyone . . . Happiness, and she returns from London pregnant by some man, about whom they knew nothing other than that he was a Spaniard and was now dead . . . Happiness, and look at the great reshuffle his father had then made on her return and which had altered all their lives. It had driven away his wife; not that he hadn't welcomed that, but it had deepened into madness the evil in his son. And now she had killed him. He had likely intended to kill her, but she had killed him first. And where was he now? At the bottom of the dock or in the middle of the North Sea.

With this thought, a wave of pity welled up in him. After all, he had been his son, and conceived during a happier period of his marriage.

With the knock on the door he blinked his eyes and raised his head towards it.

When Pat opened the door and saw it was Don, he exclaimed, 'Talk of the devil!' And to this Don answered, 'You've never been more right, I would say, and particularly on this occasion.'

'Hello, Don,' Emanuel greeted him. 'You're back then?'

'Yes, sir,' said Don briefly.

'Sit down, then. Sit down.'

For answer, Don said, 'I have something particular to say, sir; and I would rather stand. It's just this—' he now addressed James: 'As you, sir, are Marie Anne's father, the right thing to do on an occasion such as this is to ask for the hand of your daughter. Well, sir, I am not asking for the hand of your daughter, nor for the approval of her beloved grand-father,' who was now sitting bolt upright on the lounge chair, 'nor you' – he now half turned about to look at Pat – 'her beloved brother, because I know you each will have your own reason why this should not come about, such as, the man is disfigured; that he is old enough to be her father; and thirdly, what has he to offer her? a cottage to live in, and a mere subsistence from an unusual business.'

The three of them were staring at him now with different expressions on their faces. They watched Don

461

wetting his lips twice before he added, 'Whatever happens we are going to be married. I have already spoken to Father Prior, and he says he will be delighted to perform the ceremony in the chapel there.'

It seemed that James bounced in his seat as he said, 'But you're a Roman Catholic and she is Protestant.'

'I know that, and he knows that.'

'Didn't he make any fuss about bringing her into the faith?'

'No; he's a very wise man.'

'Oh, I only wish I'd had him to deal with.' Pat had turned to look at his grandfather, who seemed to be shaking with silent laughter, and he said, 'I hadn't expected to drop my news today to you, Grandfather, or to you, Father. After what has happened this past week, I thought it could keep. But after Don's bombshell I can tell you now that Anita and I have arranged our wedding for early in October. And wonder of wonders, it too will be celebrated in a Catholic Church.'

'Oh no!' All the laughter had disappeared from Emanuel's face. 'You said you would never turn.'

'And I haven't, Grandfather. No; no, I haven't. I've stuck out against priest, bishop, the lot.'

'The bishop?' The old man's eyes were wide with surprise.

'Yes; that dyed-in-the-wool priest dragged me to the bishop. Oh, and there was a diplomat if I ever heard one. They say "as smooth-tongued as a Jesuit," and they are right. He had a halo and the crown of Heaven on his knees ready to hand to me. Anyway, when we parted we shook hands, for he had been tactful enough not to bring up what you had told me about, Don, concerning the signing of a paper stating that any children would be brought up in the Catholic faith. But when later, I actually barked a final "No!" to the old bigot of a parish priest and said I wasn't signing my children's minds away, I

462

thought he would collapse where he stood. If he could then have stopped Anita's brother taking the service, he would have done, but he had been given a warning by the bishop about that.'

Pat looked down at his father, now sitting hunched up in his seat, and he said, 'Well, Father, what have you got to say about it?'

There was a sad note in James's voice as he replied, 'What can I say? It's all cut and dried. I can't see there's much we can do about it.' He turned to look at the old man. 'Your grandson is to be married in a pit village, and in a Catholic church, and your grand-daughter is to be married in London and, of all places, in a monks' house—'

'A Brothers' house, sir,' Don put in quietly. 'And the chapel is beautiful.'

'Well, whatever! We'll be called upon to do very little in either case.'

The cane chair was creaking vigorously now, drawing their attention to Emanuel, who now said, 'Who said we would be having nothing to do with it. Tell me, Mr Donald McAlister, the date you have decided upon to marry my grand-daughter.'

Don hesitated before he replied, 'I haven't suggested a date yet, sir.'

'Then would it be too much to ask you to wait until October when, perhaps, you could make it a double event and celebrate it here, not in your London Brothers' priory or whatever, but side by side with Pat? I'm sure your priest or your bishop wouldn't put any spokes in that when the bridegroom's not, what shall we say? far removed from a priest, monk or Brother.'

Amid the laughter Don protested, 'I never aspire to any of those titles, sir.'

'I don't know so much about that,' said Emanuel, 'because some of the atmosphere has stuck to you.'

Don now turned to Pat and asked quietly, 'How do you feel about this?'

'First rate. First rate.'

The three of them were startled now by Emanuel yelling at the top of his voice, 'Come out of there! Foggerty. You've heard it all; now go and fetch Miss Marie Anne.'

The dressing-room door slowly opened and Sarah came into the room. She did not look at her master, nor did she answer his bawled order in any way, but she went to Pat and, holding out a hand, she said, 'Congratulations, sir! And may you never need a hot-water bottle for your feet.'

'Oh, Foggerty!' In characteristic fashion Pat pushed her on the shoulder, and amid the laughter she turned towards Don. She did not now hold out her hand, but she looked into his face, and he back into hers, and what she said was, 'May all good things never end for you.'

It was a second or so before, unsmiling, he answered her: 'Thank you, Sarah,' and with this she went smartly from the room.

When she opened the sitting-room door, Marie Anne was standing in the middle of the room. Her 'Oh; Sarah,' showed that she had expected to see Don.

'Off you go!' Sarah had extended her hand. 'They're waiting for you along there.'

'No, no! Wait a minute. What happened? Did he ask Father?'

'No. He didn't ask your father, or your grandfather, or your brother; he just told them what he intended to do. But I'm telling you no more, except that you have another surprise coming to you.'

'No, no! don't pull me, Sarah. It's very odd, but I'm nervous, frightened.'

'What are you frightened of?'

'I don't know. Oh! Sarah. I feel that now we're in the

open, life is bound to change, and . . . and I'm asking myself if I'll be able to cope. There's one thing, Sarah, I want to make sure you know,' and she now almost threw herself on Sarah and put her arms about her. 'I love you. You are mother, sister, friend, everything to me. Promise me you'll never leave me.'

'O . . . oh! Now! Now! Now!' Then Sarah swallowed deeply before she added, 'As long as I'm needed I'll stay. But you will find you won't need me all that much. You'll have a husband. Yes, yes; you'll have a husband; and he's an unusual man, one in a thousand – ' here she paused before she went on, 'and being so, let me say, dear, there'll be times when you may find him hard to understand.'

'Never! never! Because I love him so much.'

'Love, let me tell you, Marie Anne, has nothing to do with understanding. And he is a man who was brought up in a kind of monastery, and as your grandfather said' – she jerked her head towards the wall – 'a bit of the priests, monks and Brothers has rubbed off on him. And he's right. I know he has fought it so as to be like an ordinary man, but it's there, deep within him, just as the Catholic Church is. He may not go to mass very often, but deep inside he's a dyed-in-the-wool Roman Catholic.'

'Why are you saying all this, Sarah?'

After a long sigh, Sarah said, 'Because love isn't everything.'

'No? You think it isn't?'

'I know it isn't. But no more; I'm not going to talk any more. For the last few minutes I've been speaking as a mother, but as the housekeeper I am under orders from the Major-General in the basket chair to fetch his granddaughter, and I would like to bet you a shilling that within a minute or so that damn bell of his will be ringing. Lord! . . . the prophecies I make. There it goes! I hate the

465

sound of that bell; the only way I could stop it is to go and live with him in that room.'

Swiftly putting out her arms, Marie Anne drew Sarah to her and kissed her; then giving her no time either to speak or to respond in any other way, she took Sarah's hand and ran with her from the room.

9

When, towards the end of June, there had been no public mention of a body having been found either in the river or in the dock, those concerned could hopefully presume that Vincent had been swept out to sea at the height of the storm.

Although relief was felt all round, nevertheless James was disturbed by the two letters he had recently received from David. The first was to the effect that his mother felt she must write to the office of the Governor-General for help in tracing the whereabouts of her son, who had gone to France for a rest cure following a nervous breakdown. The second letter stated that, following the receipt of a negative and terse reply, she felt she must return home, for she was sure he would be in England and would make for the house. It was all the fault of that girl, she had stated, and that she couldn't care less what he would do to her; however, she was worried for him, in the state she knew him to be.

James's mind was in a quandary. He had not shown the letter, nor discussed it, with either his father or Pat, although his father had questioned him as to what Veronica might do when she eventually accepted that Vincent was not going to return to the ranch. Did he think it would bring her back home?

Although knowing the answer to this, James had feigned ignorance.

And so, sitting alone in his study now, he asked himself what he should do. The two houses were agog with

467

preparations for the double wedding and were he to hint to either Pat or Marie Anne of the probability that their mother might put in an appearance, he dared not think of their reactions; and not taking into account those, too, of his father and Don. If only she didn't come until after the wedding. He must write to David straight away and ask him to try to arrange her passage so that she wouldn't arrive until late October . . .

However, his letter must have crossed with one from David telling him that Veronica had for some time been troubled with stomach pains and diarrhoea and had made arrangements to see a woman's specialist; and that she was determined, while in Winnipeg, to book her passage to England.

It was five weeks later that he received another letter from David. The early post had been late, and so he did not open it until he was in his office. After reading the first short paragraph, he dropped the letter onto the table, and placing his hands flat upon it, he fell back into his chair and closed his eyes, seeing the words again:

Father, no matter what ill-feeling there was between you, I am sure you will be shocked to know that we buried Mother yesterday.

Slowly, he pulled himself forward and, picking up the letter, he read on:

You remember that in my last letter I told you she had an appointment about the pains in her stomach, and the diarrhoea, et cetera. Well, I took her to Winnipeg, and when she came out of the specialist's room she looked so shaken she had to sit down and drink a glass of water. I left her with the nurse and went in to the doctor to enquire what the matter was. His opinion was she had cancer of the stomach and must

468

go into hospital for an operation.

She had not booked her passage home, nor did she speak until I suggested she stay here for a time with me. But she would have none of it; she wanted to go straight back to the ranch.

Three days later I was woken up at five in the morning by Nordquist, who was in a dreadful state. The house woman had found her lying on the floor: she had taken all the painkillers the doctor had given her and had drunk a half bottle of whisky.

I am feeling terrible, Father. I feel I should have done more for her; yet what could I have done? It wasn't my company she wanted, it was Vincent's.

I hadn't told John the whole story of Vincent's devilry towards Marie Anne, because, as you know, John didn't like him to start with, but he could hardly believe it; nor that Mother could have backed Vincent all through this trouble. I am surprised he hasn't turned up at your end.

Don't let it upset you too much, Father. I shall always remember that when we were young you did your best for us.

My love to you.
David.

James folded up the letter and returned it to his pocket. She was dead. The last worry of his life was gone. Pat's mother was dead; Evelyn's mother was dead; Marie Anne's mother was dead; his father's daughter-in-law was dead; and not one of them would sorrow for her, as no-one sorrowed for Vincent; yet were he to tell them, her going would surely cast a shadow on the weddings.

Two old sayings came into his mind: Let sleeping dogs lie; Let the dead bury the dead.

So be it.

10

It was half-past two in the morning. The last carriage had
rolled down the drive. The last three brakes had rolled
down the drive. The last two waggonettes had rolled
down the drive, to be followed by four traps. The lights
in the two houses were still blazing, but the outside
hanging lanterns were fast being extinguished.

In Emanuel's bedroom the fire was blazing brightly and
he was sitting on the cushioned wicker bed-chair in his
long nightshirt and dressing gown; and sitting to his side
was Sarah. She was still in her day clothes; or, at least, her
wedding finery; a soft pink woollen dress with rose-
coloured collar and cuffs and distinguished by the broad
pink suede belt, which showed off her small waist and an
altogether attractive figure which had for years been
hidden by a uniform.

'Peace, perfect peace.'

'As you say, sir,' she nodded towards Emanuel, 'Peace,
perfect peace. I've told them downstairs to leave everything until the morning and Mr James is giving the same
order along at The Manor, because you know, sir, a band
of Egyptian slaves couldn't have worked harder than the
staff have done these past weeks, and with such a
magnificent result, don't you think so, sir?'

'I do, Sarah. I do. I never thought to see such a display
in my houses. Never; never. One hundred and seventy-
five guests. Where did they all come from?'

'That's what Mr Pat said, but he had added, laughing,
"What am I talking about? she's bringing half the pit

470

village with her." But her people are nice, don't you think so, sir, Anita's people?'

'Very pleasant. Very pleasant indeed. Her father's a very intelligent man. He's promised to call and put me in the picture as to how a mine is run. That will be interesting, and I told him that if he did, I would then tell him how we get an iron ship to float on water.'

Sarah laughed as she said, 'Her mother was funny: she said she was so happy she cried all last night.'

Emanuel now lay well back in the chair and stared towards the fire for a moment or so before he said, 'I have never before experienced the feeling, and I never shall again, as that when I saw my little wild bird come down those altar steps on the arm of Don, and I thought it strange that all her life, from when she was born, in fact, she has not looked like other people. She was always beautiful, but in a strange way, and everything that has happened to her has been unusual in its hate and its love; and even now she has married the strangest of men, because Don is no ordinary man. He is, I have found, a deep spiritual being and in his own maimed way he appears as odd as she does. He's handsome, and she's beautiful, but both have that odd look about them, his through his scar, hers through her temperament, I think; and oh! didn't he look fine.'

'Yes; yes, sir.' Sarah's voice was low and had a far-away sound to it. 'Yes sir, he did look fine. He's a fine man altogether, a wonderful man.'

'Yes, Sarah, he is indeed a wonderful man; and you know something? Although the girls were dressed beautifully, it was thoughtful of Anita, wasn't it, to refuse any falderals of lace and a train, because she knew that Marie Anne, being already a mother, would not be in white. And my grandson, my dear, dear Patrick, the lovable Patrick, he looked as if he was walking on air. As for Don, I've never seen a man walk so proudly. And do you know

471

something else? half that crowd outside weren't there just to see a double wedding, they were there, so I understand from low quarters, to have a peep at the branded man. And what did they see? A handsome individual with longish fair hair and a not so noticeable mask that matched the colour of his skin. And did you notice Don, as they came down the aisle, put out a hand to the young fellow in the wheelchair, and his best man, the doctor, do likewise when he followed on?'

'Yes; yes, I saw it all, sir. And Marie Anne, when she first told me her wedding dress was to be in French grey, I thought, oh my goodness! What will she look like? But what did she look like? Nobody's seen a gown like that. I never thought grey could be so beautiful; it went creamy in some lights.'

'Yes, I know. She put it on for me last night, or was it the night before?' He laughed now. 'And it was trimmed with that delicate blue. And then that little bonnet of forget-me-nots on the back of her head. Beautiful, beautiful, a picture. And then, there was Evelyn, too. She looked magnificent. She showed no animosity about the pomp she had missed at her own wedding: she is so happy with her man and her coming child. But I was talking about the feeling I had when Marie Anne stepped down from the altar, for as she passed she looked at me, and the look was full of pure love, yes indeed, pure love.' He drew in a deep breath now and his voice rose as he said, 'Not that I didn't love my dear, dear wife. Oh yes, I loved her. But, Sarah, there are so many variations of love, so many grades. You know, I see kindness as a form of love, and I recognised long ago in the little Mary Anne, as she was, the same trait as was in myself for . . . for I've never forgotten a kindness done me, nor indeed a bad turn. And isn't she proving this by spending the first week of their honeymoon in that awful part of London? They visit the Brothers today. That is so, isn't it, Sarah?'

472

Sarah laughed softly now as she said, 'Yes, he's going to show her off to the Brothers and especially to his old tutor, Brother Percival, and they'll have dinner with them all. Then the next day being Saturday, they are taking Annie's lot up the river, and Annie with them. Of course, there won't be so many of them, with the two girls being here and Shane away at the monastery school. I'll never forget the look on the faces of Margaret and Maureen when they entered this house. Maureen was too dumb-founded to speak, but Margaret said, "Eeh! Aunt Sarah, it's like coming into Heaven." The invitation to be brides-maids to Marie Anne had come to them like a gift actually dropped from Heaven. Oh, they've had the time of their lives these last few days. They certainly won't want to go back tomorrow, back to that quarter, that quarter in which Marie Anne insists on spending the first week of her honeymoon. But when they visit Ernie Everton's Eating House, oh I wish I could be there, just to see Mrs Everton's face. And I know she'll get Marie Anne to play the piano. Then she'll load them with sausage and mash, or pie and peas and beer . . . oh yes, and beer. That's where I pulled pints; I told you, sir.'

'You did; you did. But I can't imagine you behind a bar.'

'Oh, there are worse places to work. By! yes, sir, worse places. But wait till she introduces Don to Paddy's Emporium. She's sure he's never been in there, although he knew the district well. Then finally they're going to end up at the *Daily Reporter*. I'd like to be there too. Those fellows'll get a gliff, especially when they see Don, for they'll spot a story there and be at him to talk. But Don's wise. Anyway, she's had the choice of their daily excursions, but he's seen to the evenings: each night he's booked either for a theatre or a variety or concert of some kind.'

'Well, I'm glad about that, for that kind of thing goes more with the Grand Hotel I had booked for them. I

473

wonder what the manager will think about their daily excursions? He'll likely have them deloused before he lets them back in again. And what do you think about them also going to Paris for the second week? It will be strange if they meet up with Pat and Anita.'

'Yes, sir; it will be, but it's a small world. Anyway, wherever they go they're together and that's all they want, just to be together.' As her voice sank he put out his hand and gently laid it on hers, saying, 'Are you hurting inside at all, Sarah?'

'No! no!' her answer came back swiftly; 'no, not at all, sir. He is my friend and always will be, and that is something to value. As for her, she is my daughter. It's very odd, but I never thought I would marry; in fact, I never wanted to; I'd seen enough of it over the water with their big families, besides Annie's tribe. I knew that wasn't for me. But Marie Anne came into my life fully made, needing my care and needing my love, because she had left yours and Mr Pat's behind. Looking back, I know I gave it to her from the beginning. You say, sir, there are many kinds of love; well, in my case, she comes first. The other love follows behind and, as I said, forms a friendship. And that is something to value, because romantic love, you know, no matter how hot, has to cool down and adjust to life, especially if a family comes along. I've got a theory, sir, which may seem weird, but I've watched it work out in the family back home, and in all those round about: when a child is born a man loses just that bit of his wife, consciously or unconsciously she has given it to the child. It might sound daft but that's how I see it.'

When he lay staring at her without speaking she said, 'You're ready for sleep, sir; I'll be away so you can get into bed.'

'I feel very comfortable lying here, Sarah. This is as good as any bed, so if you'll just put the guard round the fire, I'll settle down here. But before you do, I'd like to say something to you. I'll likely mention it again, who knows? but this is a very strange night, a sort of magic night. My young grandson has been married and my younger grand-daughter, too, and I'm sure there has never been a double wedding like it before, and I doubt if there'll ever be one like it again: Anita and Pat were made one, as were Don and Marie Anne, and by that young priest, that young kindly priest, Anita's brother. And there has been happiness on more faces this day than I've ever seen in my life before. And what made me especially glad was the presence of the woman my son proposes to marry as soon as he is free. She was to my liking too: kind, bright, and what you yourself would call homely. And I'm sure she'll turn The Manor into the home that it has never been for years, not since I first took my wife there as a bride. But now this is what I want to say, and to you, Sarah. Whether you are aware of it or not, my dear, there is something about you that touches on all the lives you come in contact with. Intentionally or not you change people. I've tried to pinpoint your particular virtue and I've put many names to it, but I think the simplest and the nearest is that of your innate kindness. You seem to know what people need. You seemed to know from the first that I wanted a little brightness, a little fun, say, even joy, in my last dreary years, because it wasn't forthcoming in my surroundings or in those around me. You see, the light that Marie Anne radiated went out when she left for London; and I doubt, yes, I really doubt whether it would have shone again if she had come back alone; but she brought you with her. At least she blackmailed me into taking you on; and thank God she did, because . . . well, here I come to the point of what I want to say to you. If, my dear, you had come onto my horizon ten years ago when I had still some vitality left in me, I would, and believe this' – he now took her hand and held it between his own – 'I would have asked you to marry me. Yes; yes, I would, and have said be damned to convention and all its faults and tangents, because I consider you a woman in a thousand, Sarah. You might never have loved me as you did Don, but we would have been the closest of companions, and loving companions. Yes, yes. Oh my dear, my dear, don't . . . please don't cry.'

'I'm not c-c-crying sir, it's hay fever. I always get it in winter.'

He began to chuckle. 'There you are; that's one of the reasons I've always wanted you near me; you can make me laugh. It isn't everybody that has that power, but . . . but you believe what I say, Sarah, don't you?'

It was some time before she could reply, when she said softly, 'Yes sir; I believe you, and if you had asked me, I would have accepted.' She now smiled through her tears. 'That is, after I had picked myself up off the floor I would have said, and very simply and sincerely, "Yes, Emanuel, I will marry you; and I will grow to love you." That's what I would have said to you. But now, sir, I can say, and without the offer of marriage, that I do have a love for you. It stands high up among the tangents we have talked about, and because of it and through it I am willing to serve you to the end of your days, or mine.'

'Oh! Sarah. Sarah.' He now put up both hands and drew her face towards him, and gently he kissed her on the mouth; then holding her face away from his, he said, 'That kiss might come from old lips, but it was born in a young and grateful heart. Good night, my dear Foggerty, and thank you. And when, tomorrow, I bully you into making your cheeky retorts, you will respond as always, while we both know we hold a secret known only to us. Good night, my late love.'

Slowly, Sarah withdrew her hands from his and when she rose to her feet she couldn't see him, nor did she see the fire-guard that she placed round the still glowing coals, and when she reached the bedroom door and turned and looked back towards him, still she did not see him, nor his raised hand, for she was so blinded by this love that had taken hold of her heart and obliterated all others.

THE END

JUSTICE IS A WOMAN
by Catherine Cookson

The day Joe Remington brought his new bride to Fell Rise he had already sensed she might not settle easily into the big house just outside the Tyneside town of Fellburn. For Joe this had always been his home, but for Elaine it was virtually another country whose manners and customs she was by no means eager to accept.

Making plain her disapproval of Joe's familiarity with the servants, demanding to see accounts Joe had always trusted to their care, questioning the donation of food to striking miners' families – all these objections and more soon rubbed Joe and the local people up the wrong way, a problem he could easily have done without, for this was 1926, the year of the General Strike, the effects of which would nowhere be felt more acutely than in this heart-land of the North-East.

Then when Elaine became pregnant, she saw it as a disaster and only the willingness of her unmarried sister Betty to come and see her through her confinement made it bearable. But in the long run, would Betty's presence only serve to widen the rift between husband and wife, or would she help to bring about a reconciliation?

0 552 13622 0